# PRAISE FOR ANDREY KURKOV

"A post-Soviet Kafka." —Colin Freeman, *Daily Telegraph*

"A kind of Ukrainian Kurt Vonnegut." —Ian Sansom, *Spectator*

"This time, the Ukrainian author of *Death and the Penguin*, known for his brilliantly dark humor, has written a modern-day odyssey, with a return that is ambiguously hopeful." —India Lewis, *Arts Desk*

"Strange and mesmerizing . . . In spare prose, Ukraine's most famous novelist unsparingly examines the inhuman confusions of our modern times and the longing of the warm-hearted everyman that is Sergeyich for the rationality of the natural world."
—John Thornhill, *Financial Times*

"A warm and surprisingly funny book from Ukraine's greatest living novelist." —Charlie Connelly, *New European*

"Kurkov's poignant tale explores the violent, largely depopulated area between the Ukrainian Army and pro-Russian separatists, where days are slow but dangerous and pleasures are few. Through the eyes of a stranded beekeeper who frets and dodges artillery shells, Kurkov masterfully captures the desperation, longing, humor, and resilience of people trapped in the wrong place at the wrong time."
—David O. Stewart, author of *The New Land*

"Carries top notes of Beckett and Pinter, along with a slug of Kafka."
—*Strong Words*, One of the Top 20 Books of the Year

# GREY BEES

*Andrey Kurkov*

# GREY BEES

*Translated from the Russian by Boris Dralyuk*

DEEP VELLUM PUBLISHING
DALLAS, TEXAS

Deep Vellum Publishing
3000 Commerce St., Dallas, Texas 75226
deepvellum.org · @deepvellum

Deep Vellum is a 501c3 nonprofit literary arts organization
founded in 2013 with the mission to bring
the world into conversation through literature.

Copyright © 2018
First published in the Russian language as *Serye pchely* by Folio, Moscow
English translation copyright © 2020 by Boris Dralyuk
First published in Great Britain in 2020 by MacLehose Press, an imprint
of Quercus Carmelite House

First Deep Vellum Edition, 2022
Fifth Printing

Library of Congress Control Number: 2021949951

ISBN (TPB) 978-1-64605-166-3
ISBN (Ebook) 978-1-64605-167-0

This book is a work of fiction. Names, characters, businesses, organizations,
places, and events are either the product of the author's imagination or
are used fictitiously. Any resemblance to events, locales, or actual persons,
living or dead, is entirely coincidental.

Cover design by Emily Mahon

Interior layout and typesetting by KGT

PRINTED IN THE UNITED STATES OF AMERICA

# Foreword

Seven years ago, in 2013, Vladimir Putin's failed attempt to tear Ukraine away from Europe and fold it into his "family of fraternal peoples" – that is, into his revived version of the Soviet Union – ended in revolution. As a result of the popular uprising that came to be called "Euromaidan", the nation's pro-Russian political élites, led by the then-president Viktor Yanukovych, were forced to flee Kyiv for Moscow. In 2014, as power passed into the hands of pro-European forces, Russia managed to capture the Ukrainian peninsula of Crimea and to send officers, volunteers, and activists to Donetsk, Luhansk, Kharkiv, Odessa and other cities in the east and south of the country, in order to foment anti-Kyiv revolts. Thus began a war that Russia does not wish to end, and which it regularly refuels with military personnel and thousands of tons of equipment and ammunition. Putin's calculation is simple: a Ukraine with a permanent war in its eastern region will never be fully welcomed by Europe or the rest of the world.

And indeed, the world has largely forgotten about Ukraine and its war, as it always forgets about "quiet", unfinished conflicts. The front line between Ukrainian troops and pro-Russian separatists in the breakaway "people's republics" of Donetsk and Luhansk in the east is about 450 kilometres long. And the "grey zone" between these two sides is of the same length, but its width ranges from several hundred metres to several kilometres, depending on the intensity of hostilities and the landscape along any given stretch. Most of the inhabitants of the villages and towns in the grey zone left at the very start of the conflict, abandoning their flats and houses, their orchards and farms. Some fled to Russia, others moved to the peaceful part of Ukraine, and others still joined the separatists. But here and there, a few stubborn residents refused to budge. They stayed where they were, in the midst of a war, listening to the whistle of shells overhead and occasionally sweeping shrapnel from their yards. Some of these holdouts have already been killed, but others have endured in this new, strange and harsh reality, in villages that were once densely populated but are now devoid of life, where all the shops, post offices and police stations have been shuttered. No-one knows exactly how many people remain in the grey zone, inside the war. Their only visitors are Ukrainian soldiers and militant separatists, who enter either in search of the enemy, or simply out of curiosity – to check whether anyone's still alive. And the locals, whose chief aim is to survive, treat both sides with the highest degree of diplomacy and humble bonhomie.

Since the winter of 2015, less than a year after Russia's annexation of Crimea and the start of the conflict, I have taken three journeys through Donbas, the eastern region that contains Donetsk, Luhansk and the grey zone. There I witnessed the population's fear of war and possible death gradually transform into apathy. I saw war becoming the norm, saw people trying to ignore it, learning to live with it as if it were a rowdy, drunken neighbour. This all made such a deep impression on me that I decided to write a novel. It would focus not on military operations and heroic soldiers, but on ordinary people whom the war had failed to force from their homes.

These people have certain things in common. They try to remain inconspicuous, almost faceless, partly in order to remain unnoticed by the war. But they have always been that way in Donbas, a land of coalmines and metallurgical plants. In Soviet times, these people were proud to play an inconspicuous part in the "great industrial whole". The Russians even came up with a special designation for them, "the people of Donbas", as if they were the children of mines and slag heaps, without ethnic roots.

The protagonist of my book, Sergeyich – a disabled pensioner and devoted beekeeper – is one of these "people of Donbas". The winds of fate carry him down to Crimea, where he hopes to arrange a proper

8

holiday for his bees. Sergeyich's southern sojourn, however, proves to be an ordeal. Try as he might, Sergeyich cannot remain entirely neutral as he observes the constant oppression of the Crimean Tatars by the new authorities. His sympathy for these Muslim people arouses the suspicion of the Russian security service – the notorious F.S.B. – and, even more alarmingly, endangers his beloved bees.

My family and I last visited Crimea in January 2014. Even before the annexation, Russian flags fluttered everywhere in Sevastopol. The second half of this novel is, in some ways, my personal farewell to the Crimea that may never exist again.

Nor do I know when I will next return to eastern Ukraine, or when the conflict will end. But I sincerely hope the war leaves the residents of the grey zone alone – that it goes away, and that the honey made by the bees of Donbas loses its bitter aftertaste of gunpowder.

ANDREY KURKOV

*Kyiv, 2020*

# 1

Sergey Sergeyich was roused by the cold air at about three in the morning. The potbelly stove he had cobbled together in imitation of a picture in *Cosy Cottage* magazine, with its little glass door and two burners, had ceased to give off any warmth. The two tin buckets that stood by its side were empty. He lowered his hand into the nearest of them and his fingers found only coal dust.

"Alright," he groaned sleepily, put on his trousers, slid his feet into the slippers he had fashioned out of an old pair of felt boots, pulled on his sheepskin coat, took both buckets and went into the yard.

He stopped behind the shed in front of a pile of coal and his eyes landed on the shovel – it was much brighter out here than inside. Lumps of coal poured down, thumping against the bottoms of the buckets. Soon the echoing thumps died away, and the rest of the lumps fell in silence.

Somewhere far off a cannon sounded. Half a minute later there was another blast, which seemed to come from the opposite direction.

"Fools can't get to sleep," Sergeyich said to himself. "Probably just warming their hands."

Then he returned to the dark interior of the house and lit a candle. Its warm, pleasant, honeyed scent hit his nose, and his ears were soothed by the familiar quiet ticking of the alarm clock on the narrow wooden windowsill.

There was still a hint of heat inside the stove's belly, but not enough to get the frosty coal going without the help of woodchips and paper. Eventually, when the long bluish tongues of flame began to lick at the smoke-stained glass, the master of the house stepped out into the yard again. The sound of distant bombardment, almost inaudible inside the house, now reached Sergeyich's ears from the east. But

*11*

soon another sound drew his attention. He heard a car driving nearby. Then it stopped. There were only two proper streets in the village – one named after Lenin, the other after Taras Shevchenko – and also Ivan Michurin Lane.[1] Sergeyich himself lived on Lenin, in less than proud isolation. This meant that the car had been driving down Shevchenko. There, too, only one person was left – Pashka Khmelenko, who, like Sergeyich, had retired early. The two men were almost exactly the same age and had been enemies from their first days at school. Pashka's garden looked out towards Horlivka, so he was one street closer to Donetsk than Sergeyich. Sergeyich's garden faced in the other direction, towards Sloviansk; it sloped down to a field, which first dipped then rose up towards Zhdanivka. You couldn't actually see Zhdanivka from the garden – it lay hidden behind a hump. But you could sometimes hear the Ukrainian army, which had burrowed dugouts and trenches into that hump. And even when he couldn't hear the army, Sergeyich was always aware of its presence. It sat in its dugouts and trenches, to the left of the forest plantation and the dirt road along which tractors and lorries used to drive.

The army had been there for three years now, while the local lads, together with the Russian military, had been drinking tea and vodka in their dugouts beyond Pashka's street and its gardens, beyond the remnants of the apricot grove that had been planted back in Soviet times, and beyond another field that the war had stripped of its workers, as it had the field that lay between Sergeyich's garden and Zhdanivka.

The village had been quiet for two whole weeks. Not a shot fired. Had they tired themselves out? Were they conserving their shells and bullets? Or maybe they were reluctant to disturb the last two residents of Little Starhorodivka, who were clinging to their homesteads more tenaciously than a dog clings to its favourite bone. Everyone else in Little Starhorodivka had wanted to leave when the fighting began. And so they left – because they feared for their lives more than they feared for their property, and that stronger fear had won out. But the war hadn't made Sergeyich fear for his life. It had only made him confused, and indifferent to everything around him. It was as if he had lost

12

all feeling, all his senses, except for one: his sense of responsibility. And this sense, which could make him worry terribly at any hour of the day, was focused entirely on one object: his bees. But now the bees were wintering. Their hives were lined on the inside with felt and covered with sheets of metal. Although they were in the shed, a dumb stray shell could fly in from either side. Its shrapnel would cut into the metal – but then maybe it wouldn't have the strength to punch through the wooden walls and be the death of the bees?

# 2

Pashka showed up at Sergeyich's at noon. The master of the house had just emptied the second bucket of coal into the stove and put the kettle on. His plan had been to have some tea alone.

Before letting his uninvited guest into the house, Sergeyich placed a broom in front of the "safety" axe by the door. You never know – Pashka might have a pistol or a Kalashnikov for self-defence. He'd see the axe and break out that grin of his, as if to say that Sergeyich was a fool. But the axe was all Sergeyich had to protect himself. Nothing else. He kept it under his bed at night, which is why he sometimes managed to sleep so calmly and deeply. Not always, of course.

Sergeyich opened the door for Pashka and gave a not very friendly grunt. This grunt was spurred by Sergeyich's resentment of his neighbour from Shevchenko Street. It seemed the statute of limitations on his resentment would never run out. The very sight of him reminded Sergeyich of all the mean tricks Pashka used to play, of how he used to fight dirty and tattle to their teachers, of how he never let Sergeyich crib from him during exams. You might think that after forty years Sergeyich would have learned to forgive and forget. Forgive? Maybe. But how could he forget? There were seven girls in their class and only two boys – himself and Pashka – and that meant Sergeyich had never had a friend in school, only an enemy. "Enemy" was too harsh a word, of course. In

Ukrainian one could say "vrazhenyatko" – what you might call a "fren-emy". That was more like it. Pashka was a harmless little enemy, the kind no-one fears.

"How goes it, Greyich?" Pashka greeted Sergeyich, a little tensely. "You know they turned on the electricity last night," he said, casting a glance at the broom to see whether he might use it to brush the snow off his boots.

He picked up the broom, saw the axe, and his lips twisted into that grin of his.

"Liar," Sergeyich said peaceably. "If they had, I would've woken up. I keep all my lights switched on, so I can't miss it."

"You probably slept right through it – hell, you could sleep through a direct hit. And they only turned it on for half an hour. Look," he held out his mobile. "It's fully charged! You wanna call someone?"

"Got no-one to call," Sergeyich said. "Want some tea?"

"Where'd you get tea from?"

"From the Protestants."

"I'll be damned," Pashka said. "Mine's long gone."

They sat down at Sergeyich's little table. Pashka's back was to the stove and its tall metal pipe, which was now radiating warmth. "Why's the tea so weak?" the guest grumbled. And then, in a more affable voice: "Got anything to eat?" Anger showed in Sergeyich's eyes.

"They don't bring me humanitarian aid at night . . ."

"Me neither."

"So what do they bring you, then?"

"Nothing!"

Sergeyich grunted and sipped his tea. "So no-one came to see you last night?"

"You saw . . . ?"

"I did. Went out to get coal."

"Ah. Well, what you saw were our boys," Pashka nodded. "On reconnaissance."

"So what were they reconnoitring for?"

"For dirty Ukes . . ."

"That so?" Sergeyich stared directly into Pashka's shifty eyes. Pashka gave up right away.

"I lied," he confessed. "Just some guys – said they were from Horlivka. Offered me an Audi for three hundred bucks. No papers."

Sergeyich grinned. "D'you buy it?"

"Whaddaya take me for? A moron?" Pashka shook his head. "Think I don't know how this stuff goes down? I turn round to get the money and they stick a knife in my back."

"So why didn't they come to my place?"

"I told them I was the only one left. Besides, you can't drive from Lenin to Shevchenko anymore. There's that big crater where the shell landed."

Sergeyich just stared at Pashka's devious countenance, which would have suited an aged pickpocket – one who had grown fearful and jumpy after countless arrests and beatings. At forty-nine he looked a full ten years older than Sergeyich. Was it his earthy complexion? His ragged cheeks? It was as if he'd been shaving with a dull razor all his life. Sergeyich stared at him and thought that if they hadn't wound up alone in the village he would never have talked to him again. They would have gone on living their parallel lives on their parallel streets and would not have exchanged a word – if it hadn't been for the war.

"Been a long time since I heard any shooting," the guest said with a sigh. "But around Hatne, you know, they used to fire the big guns only at night – well, now they're firing in the daytime too. Listen," Pashka tilted his head forwards a bit, "if our boys ask you to do something – will you do it?"

"Who are 'our boys'?" Sergeyich said irritably.

"Stop playing the fool. Our boys – in Donetsk."

"My boys are in my shed. I don't have any others. You're not exactly 'mine', either."

"Oh, cut it out. What's the matter with you, didn't get enough sleep?" Pashka twisted his lips. "Or did your bees freeze their stingers off, so now you're taking it out on me?"

"You shut your mouth about my bees . . ."

15

"Hey, don't get me wrong, I've got nothing but respect for the little buggers – I'm just worried! I just can't understand how they survive the winter. Don't they get cold in the shed? I'd croak after one night."

"As long as the shed's in one piece, they're fine," Sergeyich said, his tone softening. "I keep an eye on them, check on them every day."

"Tell me, how do they sleep in those hives?" Pashka said. "Like people?"

"Just like people. Each bee in its own little bed."

"But you're not heating the shed, are you?"

"They don't need it. Inside the hives, it's thirty-seven degrees. They keep themselves warm."

Once the conversation shifted in an apian direction, it grew more amicable. Pashka felt he should leave while the going was good. This way, they might even manage to bid each other farewell, unlike last time, when Sergeyich sent him packing with a few choice words. But then Pashka thought of one more question.

"Have you thought at all about your pension?"

"What's there to think about?" Sergeyich shrugged. "When the war ends, the postwoman will bring me three years' worth of cheques. That'll be the life."

Pashka grinned. He wanted to needle his host, but managed to restrain himself.

Before he took his leave, his eyes met Sergeyich's one more time. "Listen, while it's charged . . ." He held out his mobile again. "Maybe you ought to give your Vitalina a call?"

"'My' Vitalina? She hasn't been 'mine' for six years. No."

"What about your daughter?"

"Just go. I told you, I've got no-one to call."

# 3

"What could that be?" Sergeyich wondered aloud.

He was standing on the edge of his garden, facing the white field that sloped down like a smooth, wide tongue and then, just as gradually, rose up towards Zhdanivka. There, on the snowy horizon, lay the hidden fortifications of the Ukrainian troops. Sergeyich could not see them from where he stood. They were far away, and, in any case, his eyesight left much to be desired. To the right of him, sloping gently upwards in the same direction, ran a sometimes-thick, sometimes-sparse windbreak of trees. Actually, the windbreak began to rise only at the turn towards Zhdanivka. Up to that point, the trees were planted in a straight line along the dirt road, which was now blanketed with snow, seeing as no-one had driven down it since the start of the conflict. Before the spring of 2014, you could take that road all the way to Svitle or Kalynivka. It was usually Sergeyich's feet, not his thoughts, that would bring him out to the edge of the garden. He would often wander through the yard, surveying his property. First he would peek into the shed, to check on the bees, then into the ramshackle garage, to check on his old green Lada estate. Then he would walk over to his heap of long-flame coal, which grew smaller every night but still gave him confidence in a heated tomorrow and day after tomorrow. Sometimes his feet might bring him to the orchard, and then he would pause by the hibernating apple and apricot trees. And sometimes, though less often, he would find himself on the very edge of the garden, with the snow's endless crust crunching and crumbling beneath his feet. Here, his boots never sank very deep, because the winter wind always blew the snow down into the field, towards the dip and the turn in the road. There was never much snow left on the higher ground – as here in Sergeyich's garden, for instance.

It was almost noon, high time to head back to the house, but that spot on the field, on the rising slope towards Zhdanivka and the Ukrainian trenches, puzzled Sergeyich and would not let him go. A couple of days earlier, the last time he'd gone out to the edge of the garden, the snow-white field had been spotless. There had been nothing but snow, and if you looked at it long enough, you would begin to hear white noise – a kind of silence that takes hold of your soul with its cold hands and doesn't release it for a long time. The silence around here was of a special sort, of course. Sounds to which you have grown accustomed, to which you no longer pay any attention, are also fused into silence. Like the sound of distant shelling, for example. Even now (Sergeyich forced himself to listen) they were firing somewhere to the right, about fifteen kilometres away – and also to the left, unless that was an echo.

"A person?" Sergeyich asked aloud, peering at the spot on the field.

For a moment it seemed that the air had become more transparent.

Well, what else could it be? he thought. If I only had some binoculars . . . I'd already be making myself warm at home . . . Maybe Pashka has a pair?

And then his feet led him in pursuit of his thoughts – to Pashka's. They carried him around the rim of the crater by the Mitkov place, then down Shevchenko Street, following the trail of the car about which Pashka might have been telling the truth or, just as likely, lying through his teeth; it was all the same to that man.

"Have you got any binoculars?" Sergeyich asked his childhood foe as he opened the door, without so much as offering him a greeting.

"Sure. Whaddaya need them for?" Pashka had also decided to forego greetings: why waste words?

"There's something on my side on the field. Maybe a corpse."

"Wait!" Pashka's eyes lit up with an inquisitive glint. "Hold on!"

Soon they passed the crater at the Mitkov place. Along the way, Sergeyich looked up at the sky. It seemed to him that it was already getting dark, though even the shortest winter days do not end at half past one. Then he glanced at the massive old pair of binoculars, which dangled from a brown leather strap and rested on Pashka's bulging sheepskin-clad chest. Pashka's coat would not have bulged, of course, had he not turned up his collar, which now stood like a fence around his

*18*

thin neck, protecting it from the frosty wind. The rest of the coat was scrunched beneath it.

"Where is it?" Pashka raised the binoculars to his eyes as soon as they reached the edge of the garden.

Sergeyich pointed. "There, straight ahead and a little to the right, on the slope."

"Alright," Pashka said. "Ah, there it is!"

"So what is it?"

"Casualty. But who is he? Can't see his chevrons ... Laid himself out awkwardly."

"Let me have a look," Sergeyich said.

Pashka lowered the binoculars and handed them over. "Here, bee-keeper – maybe your eyes are sharper."

What had looked dark from afar turned out to be green. The dead man was lying on his right side, with his back towards Little Starhorodivka – which meant he was facing the Ukrainian trenches.

"Make anything out?" Pashka said.

"Sure. A dead soldier. But was he one of theirs, one of the others ...?"

"Got it." Pashka nodded, and the movement of his head inside his upturned collar drew a smile from Sergeyich.

"What are you grinning about?" Pashka said suspiciously.

"You look like an upside-down bell in that thing. Your head's too small for such luxuries ..."

"It's the head I was given," Pashka snapped back. "Besides, it's harder to hit a small head with a bullet – but a big dome like yours? Hell, you couldn't miss it from a kilometre away ..."

They trudged together through the garden, orchard and yard to the gate on Lenin Street, silent all the way, never once looking at one another. Sergeyich asked Pashka if he could keep the binoculars for a couple of days. Pashka agreed, then walked off to Michurin Lane without glancing back.

# 4

That night, Sergey Sergeyich awoke not because he himself was cold, but because someone else was, in his dream. More precisely: he had dreamed that he was the dead soldier. Killed and abandoned in the snow. Terrible frost all around. His dead body was growing stiffer and stiffer, but suddenly it turned to stone and itself began to radiate cold. And in his dream Sergeyich lay inside this stone body. He lay and felt this cold horror both within the dream and outside it – in his own body. He bore it as long as the dream had hold of him. But as soon as the dream began to weaken, he rose from his bed. He waited for his fingers to stop trembling from the cold he'd endured in the dream, then poured some "chestnuts"of coal from the bucket into the stove and sat down at his table in the dark.

"Why won't you let me sleep?" he whispered.

He sat still for half an hour, his eyes slowly adjusting to the dark. The air in the room was layered horizontally; his ankles grew cold, while his shoulders and neck grew warm.

Sergeyich sighed, lit a yellow candle, went over to his wardrobe, and opened the left-hand door. He brought the candle closer. There, among the empty hangers, hung his wife's – his ex-wife's – dress. Vitalina had left it on purpose. A transparent hint. One of the reasons for her departure.

In the dim light of the small, quivering flame, the pattern of the dress wasn't easy to read, but Sergeyich didn't need to read it. He knew its inelaborate pattern, its humble plot, by heart: thick, close-set columns of big red ants running up and down the powder-blue fabric – thousands of them, by the looks of it. Just imagine an inventor of clothes coming up with such an idea! Oh no – it can't just be simple and beautiful, like every other dress, with polka dots or daisies or violets . . .

Sergeyich snuffed out the little flame in his usual manner, with the thumb and forefinger of his right hand. The candle's sweet farewell ribbon of smoke drifted up to his nose. He went back to bed. It was warm under the blanket. Such warmth ought to give rise to warm dreams, not ones that pierce you with cold horror.

His eyes seemed to shut of their own accord. And now, with his eyes closed, falling asleep, he saw it again – the dress with the ants. Only it wasn't hanging in the wardrobe. The dress was on Vitalina. It came to below her knees. The red ants seemed to be scurrying up and down the fabric because Vitalina was walking along their street, and the dress was fluttering in the breeze. No, she wasn't walking – she was swimming. Just like the first time she had left their yard. The first time she had "got out", you could say – so as to present herself to the street and the village, as if she were some kind of important document the very sight of which was supposed to make everyone step aside and stare. She hadn't yet unpacked all her bags and suitcases that first day after the move from Vinnytsia, but she had immediately dug out the ant dress, ironed it, put it on, and headed for the church that stood at the end of their street. He'd tried to stop her, had begged her to put on something else, but nothing doing . . . Yes, it was hard to cope with her personality, and her love of "beautiful" things. Impossible, even.

She had thought that Sergey was going to walk along the street with her, but he had stopped at the gate, too embarrassed to accompany his wife and her red ants.

And so she'd set out by herself, stepping boldly, even arrogantly, drawing all the neighbours to their fences, windows and gates. Little Starhorodivka was full of life in those days, almost every yard ringing with children's laughter . . .

Needless to say, for the next few days she was the talk of the village, and not in a good way.

But after all, it wasn't on account of some dress that he fell in love with Vitalina and took her for his wife. She was much better without the damn thing on, and then she was all his . . . A pity that it didn't last as long as he'd hoped.

The dream that now engulfed Sergeyich showed him Vitalina's first promenade through the village differently, not as it had actually happened. In the dream, he was walking beside her, holding her hand.

And he greeted each of his neighbours, nodding, although their eyes stuck to the ant dress like flies stick to those gluey ribbons that are hung over tables in the summer.

They reached the church but did not enter its open gate. Instead, they walked around the house of God to the grounds of the cemetery, where the silent crosses and gravestones stifle any desire to smile or speak loudly. Sergey led Vitalina to the graves of his parents, neither of whom had made it to fifty, then showed her his other relatives: his father's sister and her husband; his cousin with his two sons, all three of whom had died in an accident, driving drunk; and even his niece, although they'd put her at the very edge of the cemetery, above the ravine – all because her father had tangled with the chairman of the village council, who got his revenge the best way he could. You live somewhere long enough, and you'll have more family in the ground there than above it.

Memory reminded the dream-rapt sleeper that they had, in fact, gone to the cemetery on her second or third day in the village, but she had been dressed appropriately – all in black. She looked awfully good in that colour, Sergeyich had thought then.

There was a loud crash outside the window. Sergeyich started, lost the thread of his dream. The cemetery disappeared, Vitalina and the ant dress evaporated, and he himself vanished. It was as if the projector had snapped the film.

But Sergeyich did not open his eyes.

So they blew something up, he thought. Wasn't that close – just a big-calibre gun. If it had been close, it would have thrown me out of bed. And if the shell had hit the house, I'd have stayed in my dream, where it's cosier and warmer than in life. And even the ant dress didn't seem so annoying . . . Kind of got to like it.

# 5

"He's right under their feet!" Pashka did nothing to hide his angry bewilderment. "They should bring his body in."

A cold, sharp wind was blowing from the direction of the bombed-out church. Pashka seemed to be pressing his head into his shoulders, trying to hide from the wind behind the upturned collar of his coat. His indignant profile reminded Sergeyich of the fiery revolutionaries depicted in Soviet textbooks.

They were standing at the edge of the garden again. Pashka had been sulking all morning, from the moment he opened his door to his childhood foe an hour earlier, without inviting him inside. Still, he did agree to accompany Sergeyich and got ready quickly.

"Alright, so he won't let you sleep," Pashka had grumbled on the way. "But what's it to me? Let him lie, for all I care. They'll get him down in the ground soon enough."

"But you're talking about a human being! A human being should either live or lie in a proper grave."

"He'll have his grave," Pashka said dismissively. "We'll all have our graves when the time comes."

"Listen, let's crawl out there – we could at least drag him off towards the trees, get him out of sight."

"I'm not crawling out there! Let the people who sent him go out and fetch him." The harshness of his frenemy's tone told the beekeeper that there was no point in discussing it further.

"Hand me the binoculars," Pashka said.

He looked through them for a moment or two, his lips twisting. He didn't like the sight any more than Sergeyich did, but the thoughts it inspired in him were very different from the beekeeper's.

"If he was crawling away from them, that means he's a Uke," Pashka reasoned aloud, lowering the binoculars. "And if he was crawling towards them, then he's one of ours. Now, if we knew for sure that he was one of ours, we'd just tell the fellas in Karuselino to come and get him at night. But he's laid out sideways! Who knows which way he was walking or crawling? By the way, Greyich – did you hear the blast last night?"

"I did," Sergeyich nodded.

"I think they hit the cemetery."

"Who?"

"Damned if I know. Say, got any spare tea?"

Sergeyich bit his lip. He felt that he could hardly refuse, since he had dragged Pashka out here, but he wished he could have.

"Sure, let's go."

Sergeyich walked ahead of Pashka, wondering what he should put the tea in. If he used a matchbox, Pashka would take offence, but a mayonnaise jar – that's too much.

Both stamped their soles against the concrete threshold, knocking off the snow.

In the end, Sergeyich did use a mayonnaise jar, but he didn't fill it all the way.

"You still want the binoculars, or have you seen enough?" Pashka said, trying to appear grateful.

"Leave them here a while," the beekeeper said. This time they parted on friendly terms.

When Pashka had gone Sergeyich went out to the shed to visit his wintering bees and make sure everything was in order. Then he ducked into the garage to have a look at his estate. He thought of starting the engine, just to check, but decided it might disturb the bees – they were just beyond the wooden wall; the shed and garage were as close as twin brothers, almost under the same roof. The early winter twilight was approaching. Sergeyich had stocked up on coal for the night, poured half a bucket into the stove, closed its glass door, and put a pot full of water on one of the burners. He was planning to have salted buckwheat for dinner, then read a book by candlelight. He had a lot of candles – more than he had books. His books were old, from Soviet times, and lived behind glass, in the sideboard, to the left of the china. They were old, yes, but easy to read; the letters were large and distinct, and everything was clear, because the stories they told were simple. The candles, meanwhile, lay in the corner – two full boxes of them. They lay in tightly packed rows, separated by waxed paper. This waxed paper was itself a thing of great value; you could use it to start a fire in the rain, even in a hurricane. Once it gets going, there's no dousing it. When a shell hit the Leninist church – everyone called it "Leninist" because it stood at the end of Lenin Street – and the church, being wooden, burned to the ground, Sergeyich walked over the next morning and found two boxes of candles in the stone outbuilding, which the explosion had torn wide open. He took them home – first one, then the other. Give and you shall receive – that's what the Bible says. For years and years he had donated his beeswax to the church, precisely so that the priest could make candles. He had given and given, and then received these candles as a gift from the Lord. They came in an hour of need, when the power was cut off. And so they serve him now that light bulbs are useless. This too is holy work, after all – to brighten man's life in dark times.

# 6

After several calm, windless days came an unusually dark evening. It didn't come of its own accord, but was brought about by the agitation of the sky, which was invisible from the wintery gloom below. Up there, heavy clouds pushed aside their lighter neighbours and began to shed fluffy snow. These new flakes fell to the ground, which was plastered with old snow that had grown hard in the dry wind.

Sergeyich, yawning, fed his stove a new portion of long-flame coal, then pinched out a yellow church candle with two fingers. It seemed he had done what had to be done before bedtime. All that remained was to pull the blanket up to his ears and fall asleep until the morning or until the cold woke him. Yet the silence, thanks to the snowfall, felt somehow incomplete. And when silence is incomplete, there arises, willy-nilly, the desire to complete it. But how? Sergeyich had long ago grown used to the sound of distant bombardments, which had become an integral part of silence. But now the snowfall – a much less frequent guest – had blocked out that sound with its rustling.

Silence, of course, is an arbitrary thing, a personal aural phenomenon that people adjust for themselves. In earlier days, Sergeyich's silence was not unlike the silence of others. It easily absorbed the drone of an aeroplane up in the sky or the night-time chirp of a cricket that had hopped in through an open window. All quiet sounds that cause no irritation and don't turn one's head eventually fuse into silence. So it was with Sergeyich's peacetime silence. And so it became with his wartime silence, in which military sounds suppressed and displaced peaceful, natural ones, but, in due course, also nestled under the wings of silence and ceased to draw attention to themselves.

Now Sergeyich lay in bed, seized by a strange anxiety because of the snowfall, which seemed too loud. Instead of drifting off to sleep, he lay there and thought.

And once again his thoughts returned to the dead man in the field. But this time Sergeyich's thoughts hastened to bring him cheer, suggesting that the dead man would soon be hidden from view. After all, snow as heavy as this would cover everything up for a good long time, until the springtime thaw. And in spring all would change: nature would awake, birdsong would drown out the cannon fire – because the birds would be nearby, while the cannons would stay over there, far away. And only occasionally, for some unknown reason – maybe out of drunkenness or drowsiness – would the gunners accidentally drop one or two shells on Little Starhorodivka. Once a month at most. And these shells would fall where nothing living remained: on the cemetery, the churchyard, or the long-deserted and windowless building of the old kolkhoz administration.

And if the war did continue into spring, Sergeyich would leave the village to Pashka and take his bees – all six hives – to where there was no war; where the fields weren't pockmarked by craters but covered in buckwheat or wildflowers; where you could walk without fear through woods, across meadows and along country roads; where there were lots

26

of people and, even if they didn't smile at you, life would still seem easier and warmer, simply because there were so many of them.

The thought of bees eased Sergeyich's mind, and it seemed he was drifting closer to sleep. He recalled the day, dear to his memory and heart, when the former governor, the boss of Donbas – and almost of the entire country – had first paid him a visit.[2] Now that was a man you could understand in all respects, understand and trust, like an old abacus. He had come in a jeep, with two guards. Life was very different back then, quiet. They still had ten years to go, if not more, before the onset of military silence. All the neighbours had come out of the woodwork to watch with envy and curiosity as that mountain of a man passed through Sergeyich's gate and clasped his hand in his own gigantic paw. And maybe some of them had heard the governor ask: "So you're Sergey Sergeyich, eh? And I can take a nap on your bees? You think this up all by yourself?"

"No, someone else thought it up – I saw it in a beekeeping magazine. But I built the bed myself," the beekeeper said proudly. "Well, let's have a look," the guest boomed, offering a stiff but friendly smile.

Sergeyich led him to the orchard, where six hives stood back to back in twos. They were topped with a sheet of wood, on which lay a thin, straw-filled mattress.

"Should I take off my shoes?" the guest said.

The host looked down at the guest's shoes and froze in astonishment. They were sharp-nosed, exquisite in shape, and the colour of mother-of-pearl as iridescent as the film of petrol on a puddle of water in dazzling sunlight, only nobler by far than petrol. Their mother-of-pearl shone so brightly that the air above them seemed to melt, as it does in great heat. Melting and losing its full transparency, the air added volume and extraordinary vibrancy both to the colour and shape of the shoes.

"No, no need," Sergeyich said, shaking his head.

"Like them, eh?" the governor said, smiling. These words forced the host to tear his eyes from the shoes.

"Yes – I've never seen anything so beautiful," Sergeyich confessed.

"What's your size?" the governor asked.

"Forty-two."

The governor nodded and approached one of the beehives in the middle, turning his rear end towards it. There was a wooden step stool at the hive's base. He got up on the stool, carefully lowered himself onto the thin mattress, lay down on his right side, stretched out his legs, then looked at Sergeyich somewhat childishly, like a schoolboy faced with a strict teacher.

"Is it better to lie on my back or my stomach?" he asked.

"Back is better," Sergeyich said. "Maximum connection between the body and the hives."

"Alright, then. You can go and I'll take my nap. They'll call you," said the governor and glanced at his guards, who stood a little way off from the bee-bed. One of them nodded, acknowledging that he had heard.

Sergeyich returned to his house and turned on the television – they still had power then. He tried to distract himself, but he couldn't tear his thoughts from his important, gigantic guest. He was afraid that the legs of the hives might collapse under the man's weight. He drank some tea to calm himself, but he couldn't stop worrying about the fragility of the hives. After all, when he was building them, his only concern had been the comfort of the bees; he hadn't yet learned of the health benefits of sleeping on top of the creatures.

After his nap, as a sign of gratitude, the important guest had given Sergeyich three hundred dollars and a bottle of vodka. From that day on, all those who had never liked the beekeeper or had simply ignored him began to greet him cordially, as if he had been touched by an arch-angel's wing.

A year later, also in early autumn, the governor paid him a second visit. By then, Sergeyich had built a little gazebo around the bee-bed. It was light and foldable; you could assemble and disassemble it in under an hour. And he'd made the mattress even thinner, so that the straw wouldn't block out even the slightest vibration from the hundreds of thousands of bees beneath it.

The governor looked tired. He now had ten guards with him, and there were as many cars parked by the fence along Lenin Street. Sergeyich had no idea who was in those cars or why they wouldn't come out. This time the boss of Donbas slept on the bee-bed, or just lay there, for a full five or six hours. As he left, he not only gave Sergeyich an envelope containing a thousand dollars, but also hugged him with all his might. A proper bear hug. As though he were saying goodbye to a dear friend.

Well, it's over, Sergeyich decided. Luck like that doesn't strike twice. He won't be coming again.

This was a sensible thought, for several reasons. One of which was banal: people were now advertising bee-beds in every district centre. Competition was running wild, while Sergeyich, for his part, didn't advertise at all. True, everyone in the village knew that the governor had come all the way from Kyiv to sleep on top of Sergeyich's bees, and they spread the word to their friends and relatives in other villages and towns; so those wishing to sleep on top of "the governor's bees" turned up at Sergeyich's gate in numbers that other beekeepers could only envy. Still, Sergeyich didn't push up the modest price he usually charged, and he even treated the nicer customers to tea with honey. His customers liked to chat with him about this and that, about life. At home, by that time, there was no-one for Sergeyich to chat with: his wife and daughter had run off while he was out at the wholesale produce market in Horlivka. They had left a wound in his heart. But he persevered. He gathered all his will into a fist and didn't let the tears that had welled up in his eyes roll down his cheeks. He went on living – and life was calm and satisfying. In the summers he enjoyed the buzzing of his bees, and in the winter the peace and quiet, the snowy whiteness of the fields and the total stillness of the grey sky. He could have lived out his days in that way, but something intervened. Something broke in the country, in Kyiv, where nothing had ever been quite right. It broke so badly that painful cracks ran along the country, as if along a sheet of glass, and then blood began to seep through these cracks. That was the start of the war, the sense of which had, for three years now, remained a mystery to Sergeyich.

The first shell hit the church, and the very next morning people began to leave Little Starhorodivka. First, fathers bundled their wives and children off to safety, wherever they had relatives: Russia, Odessa, Mykolayiv. Then the fathers themselves left, some becoming "separatists", others refugees. The last to be taken away were the old men and women. They were dragged off weeping and cursing. The noise was awful. And then, one day, things grew so quiet that Sergeyich stepped out onto Lenin Street and was nearly deafened by the silence. It was heavy, as if cast in iron. Sergeyich was suddenly afraid that he'd been left all alone in the village. He set off cautiously down the street, peering over each fence. After a night of cannon fire, this silence weighed on him, pressing down on his shoulders like a bag full of coal. All the doors were boarded shut. Some of the windows were covered up with plywood. He reached the church, just under a kilometre from his home. Then he crossed over to Shevchenko, the parallel street, and began to make his way back on shaky legs. Suddenly he heard a cough, and it thrilled him. Sergeyich went up to the fence from which the cough had come, and there was Pashka, sitting on a bench, a bottle of vodka in his left hand, a cigarette in his right.

"What are you doing here?" Sergeyich said. They had never, ever exchanged greetings.

"What am I doing here? Am I supposed to give all this up? My cellar's plenty deep. Push comes to shove, I can hole up down there."

That was the first spring of the war. And now they were in its third winter. For almost three years he and Pashka had been keeping the village alive. If every last person took off, no-one would return. This way, people were sure to come back – either when all that nonsense in Kyiv stopped, or when the landmines were gone and the shells stopped falling.

# 7

Two nights and two days had passed since the snowfall. In that time, Sergeyich had only gone outside to get coal. Now his feet sank gently into the fresh white carpet. But something surprised him: he noticed bald patches, with the old crust peeking out. Well, it hadn't been a blizzard, after all – just snow falling freely and easily, then moving, floating this way and that. Or maybe a low wind had blown it off towards some natural barrier, where it could have gathered in snowdrifts. But Sergeyich felt no desire to go looking for them.

The kettle was boiling. You can't just turn off a coal-burning stove as you would a gas range, so the kettle had to sit there, boiling idly, until Sergeyich removed it using an old kitchen towel. He poured some of the water into a Mobile TeleSystems mug, with its distinctive logo, enlivening the boiling liquid with a pinch of tea. Then he took a one-litre jar of honey from the floor.

Maybe I should call Pashka over, he thought, yawning. And then: Better not. I'd have to go all the way to the other end of the village.

He still hadn't finished his first mug when a blast thundered somewhere nearby. The windows rattled so loudly that it hurt his ears.

"Fucking bastards!" Sergeyich cried out bitterly, slamming the mug down on the table and spilling some of his tea. He ran to the nearest window to check if it had cracked. It had not.

The other windows were also intact. He thought he might go out and see where the shell had fallen – maybe it had smashed a neighbour's house.

Ah, to hell with it . . . The main thing is mine's still standing, Sergeyich concluded, returning to the table.

Now, if there had been a second blast, that would have been a different story. He would have made straight for the cellar, as he had done three years ago, when shells began to rain down on Little Starhorodivka out of the blue.

There were still two hours to go before the early February sunset. And this, too, was surprising – the fact that a shell had hit the village in daytime. Had it been dark, you could have chalked it up to a mistake. But in the daytime? Were they drunk or something? Bored by the silence? And which "they" were they, anyway: the ones in Karuselino, or the ones dug in between the village and Zhdanivka?

Sergeyich diluted his bitter thoughts with honey and felt better.

He refilled his mug and grinned at the sight of the logo. His mobile was on M.T.S. too. Otherwise he wouldn't have had the mug, of course. But the mobile, together with its charger, was now simply a dead weight in his sideboard. If power were restored, he could charge it up and check whether there was still service in the area. But even if he had both power and service, another question would arise: who was there to call? Pashka? It would be cheaper to walk over there. And besides, Sergeyich didn't have his number. And if he were to call his ex, Vitalina, he'd need to pick his words very carefully, well ahead of time, maybe even write them down on a piece of paper and read them out to her – otherwise she would probably hang up. At least he could ask how his daughter was doing. And if he and Vitalina got to talking, he could ask her about life in Vinnytsia. How was it that he had never once gone to visit his in-laws – you could even say, that he hadn't gone anywhere in his forty-nine years of life? The only places he had ever visited were Horlivka, Yenakiieve, Donetsk, and three or four dozen other mining towns and villages, where he'd been sent on assignment before he'd acquired his disability. His job had been an important one: safety inspector. He had been down certain mines twenty times or more. He had got such a lungful of their safety that he became a disabled pensioner at forty-two. Silicosis is no joke. But the fact that it's so common among people who work underground makes it something like the flu. Just people coughing, that's all . . .

A fist pounded at his door.

Sergeyich shuddered, but then immediately laughed away his fear: who could it be but Pashka?

He opened the door and saw his childhood enemy's deathly pale, grief-stricken face. They hit Pashka's house, Sergeyich thought with horror.

"Flattened half the Krasyuk place and took out their shed," Pashka reported in a quivering voice.

"Hmm," Sergeyich responded sympathetically, inviting his neighbour inside.

He sat Pashka down at the table, poured him some tea, and gave him a spoon so that he could help himself to honey.

Sergeyich understood his guest's fear. The Krasyuks were two doors down from his place. So if that was where the shell hit, Pashka's windows were gone – no doubt about it.

The guest looked up at his host. "Listen, Greyich, will you let me spend the night over here?"

"Fine with me. Did it hit your place too?"

"Windows." Pashka sighed. "Every last one of them. I was lucky – a shard whizzed right past my face and landed in the sideboard! I was just getting ready to eat, mashing lard into my potatoes."

Pashka fell silent and peered cautiously into Sergeyich's eyes. The host understood the reason behind his guest's sudden silence. Pashka had slipped up. All this time he'd been claiming he was going hungry, but now it looked as though he had plenty of food. Sergeyich smiled in his thoughts, but not with his lips. He still felt sorry for his childhood enemy – a cold house, twelve below outside. If the house remained windowless for twenty-four hours, it would take three days to warm it back up.

"Alright." Sergeyich nodded. "You can spend the night, but we've got to fix those windows or you'll be moving in for good."

"Where am I going to get the glass?"

"Not very bright, are you?" the beekeeper said quietly. "Too lazy to think. When a person's heart fails, they either bury him or look for a donor. Don't you read the papers?"

"What's that have to do with anything?" the guest said. "What sort of donor?"

"Alright, I've got the tools," Sergeyich said, thinking out loud "Whose house is empty but still has all its windows?"

Pasha was delighted – he had caught Sergeyich's drift.

"Klava Zhivotkina! Hell, she died long before the war!" he said, and then the enthusiasm faded from his eyes. "But she lived in an old hut, with tiny windows. We need bigger ones . . . Maybe Arzamyan's?"

"Is he dead?" Sergeyich said, warily.

"That I don't know." Pashka hesitated. "But he's gone, that's for sure. Took off for Rostov, I think. He isn't Russian, you know. And not Ukrainian either. He's Armenian."

"So what? He lived here, and that means he's one of us. How could I look him in the eyes if he comes back? Think harder . . ."

"The Serovs!" Pashka exclaimed joyfully. "That shell took them out! The whole lot of them, even the kids!"

"Yes." Sergeyich nodded, frowned, and heaved a heavy sigh. He remembered how the Serovs had been the first to flee – they didn't even wait for the bombardment to stop. And that's when the shell hit them, on the road right outside the village. Bang in the middle of their Volga saloon. And the Volga was still out there, all torn up on the dirt road.

"Alright." Sergeyich looked up at his guest. "Finish your tea and let's go. I reckon we'll be done before sunset. I've got a good glass cutter."

# 8

Pashka's gratitude for the new windows and for the night spent at Sergeyich's place had its limits. He let the beekeeper hold on to the binoculars a while longer, but he certainly did not offer him any of the lard he had mentioned. And Sergeyich really missed the taste of lard. Not that he was desperate . . . If Pashka had not mentioned the word, Sergeyich wouldn't even have thought of it. But in this wartime winter, with church candles and no electricity, any mention of past pleasures awakens longings. If Pashka had brought up dried, salted roach instead of lard, Sergeyich would have been tortured by thoughts of fish right now. But of course, the absences in Sergeyich's home were nearly endless. You could spend an eternity listing the things he did not have at hand or in his cellar. The things Sergeyich did possess, however, were easy to list: honey, vodka, various tinctures he had made, bee-pollen remedies and other apian delights. He also had a bottle of Crimean brandy, from the October factory, stashed away somewhere, but he couldn't quite remember where. Had Sergeyich been as bad a blabber-mouth as Pashka, he would have had to split all his supplies with his childhood enemy long ago. Although, to tell the truth, he didn't really see Pashka as an enemy anymore. Every time they met, even when they squabbled, Sergeyich felt closer to the fellow. In some ways they had become brothers – though not by blood, thank God . . .

There was a soft knock at the door.

"Well, well, look at that," Sergeyich said to himself with a grin. "You help a person out, and they start acting a little more civilised."

He picked up a burning candle from the table and went to let Pashka in.

But when he unlocked and opened the door, he was met by the evening darkness and a figure with a face that was not Pashka's. It was a younger face, with tense eyes that reflected the church candle's flame.

Sergeyich froze. And as he stood there, he gradually realised that the stranger was wearing camouflage and had an automatic rifle slung over his shoulder, with its short barrel pointed at the ground.

"Forgive me, I know it's late . . . and unexpected," the stranger said with a note of polite embarrassment.

Sergeyich understood that the stranger was unlikely to kill or rob him. Otherwise, why apologise? He sighed and brought the candle in his left hand closer to the uninvited guest, who was very young indeed – maybe twenty-two, twenty-three.

"May I come in?" the stranger said.

"Sure – if you take off your boots and leave the rifle by the door," Sergeyich said in an exaggeratedly stern manner, though he sensed that his voice was on the verge of trembling with fear. He was, after all, ordering a soldier to hand over his weapon.

"I can take off my boots," the young man said. "But I'm not allowed to abandon my weapon."

"Alright, the boots will do," Sergeyich said.

He shut the door, lowering the iron latch and hook, glanced at the pair of tall boots by the wall, then invited the stranger to sit at the table.

"A little vodka?" he said out of politeness, then mentally smacked himself in the mouth for showing such excessive hospitality.

"No, thanks." The young man shook his head. "But I'd take some tea."

Sergeyich nodded. "Tea it is."

It seemed to him that one candle wasn't enough for two people. He took out two more and lit them.

"Tea it is," he repeated, peering into the stranger's face, just to make sure he hadn't missed anything in the light of the single candle. "What's your name?"

"Petro."

"And where're you from?"

"From Khmelnytskyi."

"Ah," Sergeyich said, sounding as if he had grasped something important. "Ukrainian army, then."

The young man nodded.

"Artillery?"

Petro shook his head. "And what's your name?"

"Me? Sergey Sergeyich – you can call me Sergeyich. So it's probably Peter, not Petro."

"No, it's Petro. Says so in my passport."

"Well, my passport says I'm Serhiy Serhiyovych – but I say I'm Sergey Sergeyich. That's the difference."

"You probably don't agree with your passport," Petro said.

"No, I agree with my passport, just not with what it chooses to call me."

"Well, I agree both with my passport and with what it chooses to call me," the guest said with a smile. It was an easy smile, even disarming – although a rifle hung on the back of his chair.

"Maybe you agree because the name in your passport is the same as your name in life," Sergeyich said thoughtfully. "If that were the case with me, I wouldn't quarrel with my passport either. So tell me, Petro – to what do I owe this visit? You want something from me?"

"That's right," the young man said. "I wanted to get acquainted. I've seen you for more than a year now, but didn't know your name."

"Where've you been seeing me?" Sergeyich said, taken aback.

"Through my binoculars," the young man replied, a little hesitantly. "I'm supposed to observe the village. I would have come earlier, but it's dangerous in the daytime. I'm not really allowed to come in the dark, either – but it's less risky."

"What sort of danger do you expect from us in the daytime?"

"From you personally, none. But from the snipers who've got our nerves shot – and would like to do the same for our heads – plenty. Just three days ago they were taking pot shots at us from the church."

"Nobody comes through here," Sergeyich stated with conviction. "I would've seen their tracks – I don't sit at home all day, you know."

"Four killed this year, three wounded," Petro said calmly, scratching behind his ear. Then he awkwardly placed his green balaclava on the tabletop.

Sergeyich made the tea. He poured a cup for his guest and one for himself.

"So how is it there, in Ukraine?" he said. "Enough lard for everyone?"

"Oh, sure." The young man could not help but smile. "I sometimes get a bit too. Volunteers drive it over. As for the country, same as always . . . People getting ripped off, streets and towns renamed. But they say things will improve after the war. We won't need permission to go abroad."

"If you don't get yourself killed, you mean," Sergeyich said, his lips curling. But then he caught himself. That almost made it sound like he was wishing someone dead. He decided to change the subject. "What names are they changing?"

"Haven't you heard?" Petro's eyes opened wide, and a smile revealed strong teeth. "Oh, I forgot – you don't have any power, so no TV."

The host nodded sadly. "Yeah, power's been out for a long time. Maybe they'll come and fix it?"

"I doubt it. Too dangerous now. And it's probably better that you don't watch TV, anyway – save your nerves."

"Don't worry about me – I've got nerves of steel," Sergeyich boasted. "I was a safety inspector in the mines. You have any idea what that requires?"

The young man's eyes showed a spark of admiration.

"And what did you do before all this?" Sergeyich asked.

"Tourism. Hospitality. Wanted to move down to Crimea, build a little hotel."

"A little late for that," Sergeyich lamented, waving his hand. "I've never been to Crimea myself. Always wanted to go, though – take a dip in the sea, lie around on a beach, come back tanned . . . I've got a friend down there. We met at a beekeeping convention. A Tatar – name's Akhtem Mustafayev. Beekeeper like me. Keeps inviting me, but it hasn't worked out . . ."

"Well, someday," the young man said, perhaps in an effort to console Sergeyich.

"Maybe." The beekeeper did not sound convinced. His gaze darkened. "Tell me, why haven't you taken that body off the field? He's right there, close to where you are."

"The one in camouflage?" Petro said tensely.

"Yes, that one. Maybe the snow's covered him up by now. I didn't check yesterday."

"It hasn't." The young man sighed. "The wind swept the snow away. He isn't ours. And it's too dangerous to send people out there. Could be tripwires under the snow. They might've even booby-trapped the body. Let the separs fetch him. He's one of theirs."

"They'll crawl out to fetch him, and you'll mow them down, is that it?" Sergeyich said maliciously.

"If they come unarmed, with a white rag, we'll let them take him."

"Is that so? You know they say he isn't one of theirs," Sergeyich said, and instantly regretted it.

"And when did they tell you that?" Petro said, narrowing his eyes. His gaze turned cold and hostile.

"They didn't tell me – they told Pashka, my neighbour on Shevchenko Street. They came to see him, so he asked."

"Uh-huh," the young man mumbled, as if drawing conclusions. "Well, if he isn't one of theirs and isn't one of ours, then he must have been part of the third force."

"What is this 'third force'?" the beekeeper asked.

"Who knows? We think they're on our side, fighting without insignia. And the others say the opposite – that they're fighting against us. Maybe it's special forces from somewhere else altogether, fighting against both sides. That's why we celebrate when they knock off somebody over there, and they get all excited when someone in our rear fires a grenade at one of our I.F.V.s . . ."

"Do you want to take some honey with you?" Sergeyich said.

"Oh, I'm not leaving yet," Petro said. "And I don't need honey. Well, I might take some now – with my tea."

"Yes, yes, of course."

Silence descended again, and the beekeeper had no wish to break it. But after a minute he grew interested again in the renaming of streets.

"What are they calling them?" he said, almost in a whisper.

"Well, if they were Marx or Lenin, they've been renamed after Bandera or some writer,"[3] the soldier said.

"I'd prefer a writer," Sergeyich said. "By the way, we're on Lenin Street here."

"When the war's over, they'll rename it."

"What if I want to choose the new name myself?"

"No problem. You just have to come to an agreement with everyone else who lives on the street. And then take it to the local council."

"That'll take a while," Sergeyich grumbled. "A long while . . ."

"Well, I suppose I'll get going." Petro removed the rifle from the back of the chair and slung it over his shoulder. Then he picked up his balaclava with his left hand and slipped his right hand into the pocket of his warm camouflage jacket, pulling out an R.G.D.-5 grenade. He set it down next to his teacup.

"For you," he said, looking respectfully at his host. "Doesn't feel right to show up at someone's house empty-handed, without a gift . . ."

"But, uh . . ." Sergeyich mumbled. "What do I need that for?"

"Self-defence. And if you don't use it, after the war's over, you can bury it in your garden. Oh, and if you want I could charge your mobile. We've got a hell of a generator – it can even power a washing machine!"

Sergeyich was taken aback, but only for a moment. He took his mobile and its charger out of the sideboard drawer and held them out to Petro.

The soldier rose and shoved them into his jacket pocket. Then he scooped another spoonful of honey out of the jar and sent it into his mouth, greedily licking the spoon clean.

"If ever you need help, just tie a white rag to a tree branch in your orchard – so that I can see it," the young man told Sergeyich before he went off into the darkness.

"A white rag?" the beekeeper repeated in a whisper.

He locked the door and snuffed out two of the three candles. The unexpected encounter with a military man had improved his mood – and this surprised him. It was as if he had just watched something interesting on television.

Nice guy, he thought, looking at the grenade. I should have asked him more questions.

# 9

The next morning Sergeyich's head hurt something awful. The grimace on his face might have led you to believe that all his internal organs were aching in unison. He had already drunk cold water from the kettle, had already held a spoonful of sugar in his mouth until it melted away. No use. His angry eyes kept returning to the table, where an open bottle of shop-bought vodka and a shot glass had been standing since midnight. Why the hell had he decided to celebrate the arrival of his uninvited military guest? On the other hand, it's a good thing he began celebrating after his guest's departure into the dark night. If the guest had joined in the celebration, he might never have made it back to his dugout . . . Meanwhile, Sergeyich's head kept on pounding. He groaned from the pain. Not only did it hurt, but he was also offended. How much did he have to drink, after all? Five shots at most. And that meant he wasn't to blame for his terrible state. It was the vodka's fault – must be counterfeit.

He had bought it at the local shop before the war. So what could he do now? No doctors around, no medicine – aside from bee remedies. The shop was long since shuttered. Now he couldn't even tell off the saleswoman for peddling poison.

Sergeyich hobbled to the sideboard and took out his box of bee remedies. He unscrewed a little jar stuffed with bee pollen, scooped out a spoonful, and put it in a cup. Then he added water from the kettle and a spoonful of honey. He stirred the liquid until it was well mixed and drank it in slow sips.

It seemed to help. Either the noise in his head grew quieter, or his thoughts levelled out, becoming clearer and more intelligible. And the first clear thought he heard gave him a fright: "Where's the grenade?"

His eyes – now fearful rather than irritated – returned to the table. The soldier's gift was gone.

Sergeyich pulled out the sideboard drawers – not there. He began to stomp around the room nervously, looking under the pillow, searching every corner. He even checked the coal buckets. Then he remembered he'd gone out into the yard at night.

He put on his boots and looked out of the window. It was still light out – half past one. The snow in the yard was trampled. The tracks led to the shed with the wintering bees, to the garage, and even as far as the front gate.

As he followed his own tracks and peeked into the shed and garage, his headache began to subside.

It'll turn up. I couldn't have taken it very far, Sergeyich thought, thereby allowing himself to return to the house.

But in the house he was seized by a fresh anxiety. The binoculars on the windowsill reminded him of the dead man in the field.

Have to get him out of the way, Sergeyich decided, and he felt a surprising surge of courage in his chest.

Grabbing the binoculars, he went to the edge of his garden. Through the eyepieces he saw the dead man lying in the same position as before, with his back turned towards Little Starhorodivka – that is, towards him, Sergeyich.

*41*

The beekeeper returned to his house, sat down at the table, and scribbled a note: *Pashka, I've gone out to deal with the corpse, maybe cover him up a bit. If they kill me, come and get me right away. Bury me next to my parents. Then you can have my house and everything in it. Farewell.*

Ten minutes later Sergeyich was hurrying down the white field, crouching low to the ground. In his right mitten-warmed hand he held a sapper shovel. The further he went down the snowy field to the line beyond which its other half rose up, the more frightened he became. When he made it to the snow-covered ditch (so that was where the fresh snow from his garden had gone) he looked up at the sky. It had sunk so low that you could have mistaken it for the ceiling of a darkened school gymnasium. The evening murk pressed into the white snow, turning it grey. Ever since he was a child, Sergeyich had liked the colour grey. But in this instance it did not please him. He suddenly thought of the fact that his clothes were dark, and in the snow, be it day or morning, he was as visible to snipers as the murdered man had been.

Sergeyich army-crawled the rest of the way, only occasionally propping his knees against the snowy crust to speed his tired body along.

He sat down beside the dead man and caught his breath. Then he looked back at the field he had crossed. Its far end faded off into darkness. The beekeeper couldn't even see the outermost trees of his orchard. He lay on his side, facing the back of the body, took off his mittens, and rummaged through the pockets of the dead man's frozen camouflage. He even checked the inside and trouser pockets. No documents, no mobile. Nothing. Then he bent over the body and noticed a small gold earring in one of its white ears – the one that was turned to the sky. "Glamour boy," Sergeyich said, his eyes already resting on the dead hand gripping the barrel of the rifle. Of course, most of the rifle, save for the barrel, lay beneath the snowy crust. And there seemed to be something else, next to the rifle.

Sergeyich climbed over the corpse, shovelled away the snow, and uncovered the side of a blue, not at all army-like backpack.

He freed the backpack from its snowy captivity. It weighed no less than five or six kilograms. Sergeyich looked inside and found bags of sweets. He immediately recognised the Red Poppy ones by the wrapper – they used to sell them at the local shop. He dug his hand deep into the backpack, all the way to the bottom. Sweets – cold as ice.

He looked at the dead man and imagined him walking or crawling across the field. He had been making his way towards the trees. So he must have been shot somewhere on his left side.

And he was lying left side up. Sergeyich examined the exposed part of the body, but found no fatal wound.

Then the bullet must have come from the right, Sergeyich thought. He looked in the direction of Little Starhorodivka.

Pulling his mittens back onto his cold hands, Sergeyich tried to dig up some snow with his shovel, but the crust was unyielding, and there was hardly any snow beneath it – just frozen earth. The beekeeper realised that it would be impossible to cover the dead man, either with snow or with earth. He used the shovel like a knife, cutting out a square of crust. Then he lifted the square, which turned out to be heavy, and laid it on top of the body. Once he was satisfied with its placement, he continued cutting. What began as a flimsy construction, from which pieces would topple off now and then, gradually became more durable.

"Alright, that'll do," the weary beekeeper decided aloud, assessing and appreciating his handiwork; he had cut out some fifteen square metres of crust. And now that great weight was pressing down on the dead man; it pressed down on him, but also protected him from the gaze of strangers, as well as from hungry ravens, who had so far refrained from pecking out his eyes, perhaps on account of the cold.

Sergeyich crawled back towards the ditch. His trousers were soaked through, his legs heavy and numb from the cold. The homewards journey was harder – shovel in one hand, backpack in the other. He was short of breath, coughing.

When at last he came to his garden, having taken a break in the ditch, a cramp gripped his left leg. He crawled across his own land like a wounded man, and only rose to his feet at the gate between the yard and the orchard.

Sergeyich opened his unlocked door. He had left it unlocked for his frenemy. Otherwise, how could Pashka have read the note, if the master of the house had been killed?

He took off his crunchy, frozen jacket and his trousers, and immediately felt even colder, so he poured half a bucket of coal into the stove; the note for Pashka went in there as well. He put on some dry clothes and set two chairs with their backs to the stove, hanging the wet jacket on one and the trousers on the other. The boots he placed right in front of the stove's glass door.

Should I warm myself up with a drink? he wondered. But he didn't feel like getting out his home-made honey vodka, and the shop-bought booze had already taught him a lesson. From now on, that stuff was for external use only. And maybe, if Pashka gave him any crap, he'd treat him to a shot as punishment . . .

# 10

Sergeyich spent all the next day in bed, attending to himself as if he were his own ailing child. He listened to himself coughing as if he were outside his body, as if he had been split in two: the patient-self and the healer-self. This wasn't the first time such a thing had happened, either. It happens to everyone who lives alone. Loners become both cooks and eaters. They become tidy-uppers and the ones who will appreciate the tidy room.

In order to spend the whole day in bed, he first had to stock up on a day's worth of coal from the yard and water from the well – not easy to do, weakened as he was by the long crawl through the snow towards the Ukrainian army's position.

Yet Sergeyich prepared himself for his day in bed in the manner of a man who has never relied on anyone else. He had to maintain his health not only for his own sake, but also for the sake of the bees. If something should happen to him, they would perish in all their multitude – and he just could not allow himself to become, whether by his own will or otherwise, the annihilator of hundreds of thousands of bee-souls. Such a sin, such a burden would catch up with him in the afterlife, wherever he should find himself after taking his last breath. And it would never let him rest, forcing him to die again and again, once for each bee lost on his account, be it a drone or a queen. Already dead, he would go on dying and dying, until he wound up at such an infernal depth of death that there was no further to fall . . .

Until lunchtime he lay swaddled in heat and doubt. And then the heat conquered the doubt, and his body began to warm up and to replenish the strength it had expended.

Sometimes he dipped into slumber, sometimes he plunged into a deep sleep. He would awake, then close his eyes again. At one point he felt so hot that he dreamed he was under a blanket with Vitalina. He dreamed he was nearly awake, and that her warm body was overheating his, gearing it up for love. And now he was geared up for love, and even turned on his side, to face his wife. He stretched his hand towards her, and woke up. And then – perhaps in the dream, perhaps in reality – tears welled up in his closed eyes. But in his waking life, he saw no reason to feel sorry for himself. Everything was fine, under control. Well, if not everything, then nearly everything.

And later, in the afternoon, after he had had his tea with honey and lain down again, he dreamed that he was sleeping on top of his hives. On top of his six hives, his bee-bed . . .

And it seemed to him that he was not alone with his bees; someone else was nearby. He opened his eyes in the dream, lifted his head, and saw such beauty all around him . . . The trees' green branches playing with the sun, and perfectly ripe Antonovka apples dangling overhead . . . Sergeyich looked in the other direction, and there, on a folding fishing chair, sat the former governor, reading a book. The governor chuckled as he read, as if the book were making him laugh. When he noticed that Sergeyich had opened his eyes, he offered the beekeeper a friendly nod. Then Sergeyich understood that his guest also wanted to lie on the bee-bed. He got up and straightened the thin mattress. The

45

governor's two bodyguards stood off to one side, beneath the apples; they stared silently at their boss's back.

"Oh, I'm sorry," Sergeyich said to his important guest in his dream. "I didn't notice you there."

"Don't you worry." The governor shrugged, and a heavy, heavy smile that seemed to weigh about a kilo appeared on his broad face. "Go ahead and lie a little longer if you want."

"No, no." Sergeyich began to fuss about. "I'll go and get a fresh sheet."

Still sleepy, still hearing the buzzing of bees as if on a recording in his head, Sergeyich ran to the house and came back with a sheet. The governor took off his astonishing shoes and placed them neatly, sharp mother-of-pearl toes first, on the grass next to the step stool. Then he climbed up, sat down carefully on the middle hive and turned, hoisting his legs up onto the bee-bed. He lay on his back. Before closing his eyes, he grinned, having seen that the beekeeper was gazing at his shoes once again.

Maybe it was the fact that this dream was particularly warm and summery, but Sergeyich stayed in it longer than he did in others – longer, even, than he had stayed in the dream in which he had found himself under the blanket next to Vitalina's sultry body. In the evening, when hunger roused him from his bed, Sergeyich felt he had been well oiled and properly reassembled, like an expertly repaired mechanism. He even ate his noodles without butter or any other accompaniments – only salt – with gusto and something like pleasure. It was not so much the taste of the food that pleased him, of course, as the vigour that had returned to his body, and especially the ease with which he chewed. After all, what is the first sign of illness? When people fall ill, they lose the desire to work their jaws. Now, after sleeping all day, Sergeyich desired everything: to eat, to drink tea, and to bring in a couple more bucketfuls of coal for the night. But there were still some lumps left in one of the buckets, and keeping too much coal inside was a bad idea; each lump comes with its own dust, and that dust can do a lot of harm. It was coal dust that had left Sergeyich disabled.

That, at any rate, is what his medical records and pension fund documents said. Those medical records had been filled out by the lady doctor at the mine management department's clinic. He had brought her a three-litre jar of honey as a gift. She had smiled, said "Alright, then," and declared him chronically ill. But was he really that ill? God knows . . . To be sure, sometimes his cough was so bad that it forced tears from his eyes, but sometimes it disappeared for a whole month, maybe two. Now, for instance, the coal dust that rose as he fed the stove did not trouble Sergeyich one bit.

# 11

The next morning, after downing a mug of hot tea, Sergeyich walked briskly to the edge of the garden with Pashka's binoculars. He cast his eyes over the wintery field: all was white, only the whiteness varied in places, and there was a trail running down the slope – his own footprints. But even following his own trail he could detect no trace of the corpse lying beneath the snowy crust. Sergeyich felt calm.

A dull sun shone high above, as if through a thin film of frosty air, through that translucent grey which in winter usually hides the sky's blueness from the human eye.

Sergeyich walked past the garage and the bee-shed. He walked past his house and through the gate to his street: Lenin Street. He looked towards the church and the cemetery. In another time, his gaze would have come to rest on the dome of the church. And then, as he approached, the church would have risen in front of him with its heaven-blue wooden walls. But "another time" was not now . . . The church was no longer there.

He walked in the middle of the road, safe in the knowledge that the only car in this half of the village was sitting in his garage, awaiting better days. When those days came, he would have to keep close to the fences, leaving the well-worn rut of frozen snow to Ladas and

47

Volgas – and to that little yellow mail van with its blue inscription, "Ukrposhta". He remembered how the van, being slightly too wide for the rut, always leaned to the side.

Sergeyich was contentedly listening to the sound of his own footsteps, when suddenly he felt uneasy. He stopped, trying to identify the cause of this disquiet. The silence was entirely, almost unbelievably peaceful this morning; and now, without the interference of his footsteps, Sergeyich again grew convinced that it was free of even the distant sounds of war. A raven flew by, and its wings flapped so close that, for a moment, the beekeeper pulled his head down between his shoulders.

But then, after following the bird with his eyes, Sergeyich smiled and walked on towards the church. He remembered Vitalina's blue winter coat and her brown leather boots, her downy grey Orenburg shawl. He had given her that shawl. His neighbour Vera used to visit her sister in Russia and bring back goods for domestic trade, including Orenburg shawls. Vitalina wore it, but only in Little Starhorodivka. When she went back to Vinnytsia, as she did every winter, she would leave it at home.

Sergeyich glanced at his neighbour Vera's house as he walked past. The windows were intact, and a board was nailed across the door. The board had grown dark with the changing weather, but he could still see the inscription Vera had made, in black paint: the owners are alive.

"God willing, God willing . . ." the beekeeper muttered.

It was strange, but seeing such an affirmative inscription on a boarded-up house never failed to please Sergeyich. This time, it pleased him even more than usual. That was probably because he had just been thinking of Vitalina. But why was it so easy for him to think of his wife, to remember her, while his daughter didn't seem to enter his thoughts and recollections as readily? Probably because she had been so little back then – too little to have really bonded with her father. She was only four when her mother took her away, leaving him all alone. Maybe it was his own fault . . . Maybe he should have smiled more, and not twisted his lips so often at the sight of Vitalina's outfit . . . And maybe he should have talked less altogether, just grinned – even if it would have made him look half-witted. Women, it seems, are more likely to love, or at least to tolerate, the stupid, or those who play the fool. When it comes to family, who knows which is more important: love or tolerance?

Yes, if Sergeyich hadn't exploded after their daughter was born, they would probably still be living together now. All three of them. But where? With Vitalina's parents in Vinnytsia? No, he would not have moved there. And she would not have stayed here – even if they had managed to get along without a hitch before the war started. What happened was bound to happen, no two ways about it.

Now he had only a little way to go before he reached the blown-up church – just four yards on each side of the street: the Krupins, Dalidzes, Petrenkos and Matsipuras on the left, and the Popovs, old man Leftiy, the Korzons and the Urtsynovs on the right.

Suddenly Sergeyich halted, as if the road itself had stopped him. Something puzzled him, casting his attention back at the ground he had just covered with his own footsteps. He turned round and walked about ten metres. Now it was clear. Lost in his thoughts, he had stepped over a set of footprints that ran like dotted lines across the road. He examined them and saw that they had been laid by multiple trips in both directions. They led from the Popovs' to the Krupins'. Sergeyich followed them. He saw that the Krupins' door, with the two boards nailed across it, had been freed from the frame and was now only partly closed. He pulled the handle. The lower board, hanging loose, scraped unpleasantly against the icy concrete threshold. He stepped inside and the abandoned house's cold breath assailed him.

Three open one-litre jars of frozen pickles and preserves stood on the table in the main room; a fork stuck out of one of them – aubergines and tomatoes. Under the table were two empty bottles of vodka – not the usual Nemiroff or Moskovskaya, but some kind called Awesome . . . He had never seen such a vodka in his life. He picked up one of the bottles and peered at the label: made in the rostov region.

Both wardrobe doors were open, and the sideboard drawers were pulled out.

*49*

A stranger, Sergeyich realised.

He went out again, looked round, and saw that the tracks led to the back of the house. They brought him to the very edge of the garden. He stopped in front of a thick bed of straw; bullet casings were scattered on the snowy crust to the right – about twenty of them.

Sergeyich recalled the soldier's words about the sniper taking pot shots from the direction of the church.

He stood above the sniper's lair, sighed, and shrugged. What he saw brought no comprehensible thought to mind. But it did make him feel cold.

If these guys are shooting at the Ukes from over here, then sooner or later the Ukes will respond with artillery, Sergeyich thought.

And he imagined a shell flying from the direction of Zhdanivka, asking itself: Where should I land? Then he saw it veering in its flight, towards his own house.

The beekeeper shuddered at the terrible game his imagination had played.

And what if he should meet this sniper right now, as the guy was heading to his position? What then? What could he say to him, ask of him, order him to do? A man holding a sniper rifle . . .

Sergeyich twisted his lips. He was suddenly afraid that the sniper might really appear at any moment. He would aim his pistol or rifle at the beekeeper. And what did Sergeyich have? A grenade? He couldn't even remember where he had hidden it in his drunkenness . . . No, he didn't have a damned thing to defend himself with.

Distress seized the beekeeper's heart. He ran out of the Krupins' yard and hurried home.

He stopped at the junction with Michurin Lane to catch his breath. And it was here that he felt his loneliness most keenly – because now he had a choice of paths: either keep going straight, towards home, or turn left, towards Shevchenko Street and Pashka's house.

No, Sergeyich decided after a while. Can't show up empty-handed. I'll bring him the binoculars. Don't need them anymore.

Approaching his house, he cast a glance up at the darkened

sky and saw grey clouds, laden with snow, propelled by an inaudible wind.

# 12

At first, there was no response to his fist knocking at the door. Then Sergeyich added three more knocks, louder still.

"Who's there?" The familiar hoarse voice sounded at last.

"Who do you think?" the beekeeper shouted, so that his voice would penetrate the door. "Me!"

"Oh, you!" Pashka said. "Alright, I'm coming!"

Then he seemed to vanish, leaving Sergeyich perplexed on the threshold, in front of the closed door.

When it finally swung open, the home's warm breath, bearing vaporous traces of alcohol, wafted into Sergeyich's face.

"So, Greyich, what's the . . . latest?" Pashka said.

Slurring his words, the beekeeper thought. Instead of answering, he handed his host the binoculars.

"Ah, thanks. Want some tea? Or maybe . . . coffee?"

"You've got coffee?" Sergeyich said, surprised.

"I've got lots of things," Pashka said boastfully.

You're a fool to go around bragging like that, Sergeyich thought, but what he said was: "Sure, I'd love some coffee. Been a long time . . ."

Shuffling along like an old man, Pashka went into the kitchen and closed the door behind him.

This aroused Sergeyich's suspicion – why should Pashka keep him out of the kitchen? But then Sergeyich smiled, squaring the closed door with Pashka's boast about having "lots of things".

His eyes went over to the window beyond the table. On the sill, behind the tulle curtain, stood a half-empty bottle of vodka and two shot glasses. He frowned, examined the table, and saw breadcrumbs on the old linen tablecloth, which was at least ten laundry days overdue.

He laid his broad palm over a cluster of crumbs and pressed down to check if they were fresh or stale. Stale, it seemed. Prickly.

"You've had guests?" Sergeyich said, when the door to the kitchen opened and his host emerged with two steaming mugs.

"Guests? What're you talking about?" Pashka smiled, playing dumb, baring his crooked teeth.

Sergeyich ignored Pashka and turned his attention to the home-made Dutch oven that stood beneath the other window. Interesting. It held twice as much fuel as Sergeyich's stove, but it served only to warm the house; Pashka never used it to cook or heat his food.

Sergeyich looked back at the kitchen door. "Where do you boil your kettle?" he said.

"Whaddaya mean, where? In the kitchen," said his host, already sitting at the table.

Sergeyich sat opposite Pashka and reached for one of the mugs.

"So you've got a stove in there too?" he said, nodding towards the kitchen.

"What's it to you? You got a problem with that?"

"No, no problem." Sergeyich shrugged. "But I've only got one stove to cook my food on and keep the house warm. I'm always scrimping on coal."

"So you've got one and I've got two – what's the difference? You jealous? Anyway, I see you got sick of staring at your corpse," Pashka said, with a nod towards the binoculars, which he had thrown on the sofa.

"I covered him up with snow."

"You mean you crawled all the way out there?" Pashka said, and for a moment his eyes grew as round as coins.

"What was I supposed to do, keep staring at him every day? This way we can both get some peace, he and I."

Pashka shook his head. "I'd never crawl out there, in the line of fire."

Sergeyich gazed sceptically into Pashka's eyes and said nothing. But then he suddenly felt hungry and made a sour face. "Got anything to eat?"

Pashka silently retrieved a jar of honey from the kitchen – the very same jar Sergeyich had given him. He also brought out a loaf of white bread, a spoon and a knife.

Still standing, he cut three pieces from the long loaf and let them fall to the tablecloth.

Sergeyich smeared his honey onto a piece of Pashka's bread, took a bite, and wondered: Where did he get that loaf?

When he returned home, he lit the candle on the table and went out to fetch some coal. Then he opened his fridge. It was empty and dark; on top of the egg rack sat a dried head of garlic.

He tried to divert himself with positive thoughts. He looked through his cabinet and saw three-litre jars of buckwheat, noodles and millet, with plastic lids. Who the hell knows how long that would last him? True, he was never much of a glutton, so he'd be fine for a while. Fine, yes – but mighty dull fare.

Then he was seized with such melancholy that he grew cold inside. He realised it had been months since he had last tasted an egg.

He used to keep chickens at one point. And his nearest neighbours kept not only chickens, but also geese, two goats and a cow. When they first departed, they had left their chickens in his care. He had fed them and taken the eggs for himself. The neighbours had left him plenty of feed – two whole bags. And then there was a lull in the fighting and the man of the house came back. He drove up in a 4×4 with a trailer and poultry cages, put the hens in the cages, and took them away. Didn't even come in to say goodbye.

What I wouldn't give for three fried eggs, Sergeyich thought.

Or maybe hard-boiled . . .

He poured some coal in the stove and set the kettle on top.

Where did Pashka get that loaf? he wondered. Maybe there was someone hiding in his kitchen. Someone who brought him that loaf, and that coffee, and "lots of things" besides. In exchange for what, Sergeyich wondered?

If only the power weren't out, life would be easier, less time to think, less of these useless worries and suspicions. He would watch television before bed. There would be a pot of noodles in the fridge, already cooked. And if he got hungry, he would toss them into a frying pan and crack two eggs . . .

Sergeyich sighed. Damn it. Those eggs wouldn't let him be. He couldn't stop thinking about them – a priceless commodity that seemed within reach.

Svitle was only three kilometres away. It was already dark, but not yet late. There were lots of people he knew there, including old Nastasya, who had a yard full of chickens and other animals. Why not offer her a litre of honey in exchange for some eggs?

The road was smooth and straight, hidden from the Ukrainian positions, and sheltered by a low hill from Karuselino.

Sergeyich was growing excited at the prospect of travelling to the neighbouring village, which he hadn't visited since last autumn.

He got ready to go – two litres of honey in his bag, mittens on his hands, and the dark road ahead.

# 13

Fear is an invisible thing, subtle and variable, like a virus or bacterium. It can be inhaled with a breath of air, or accidentally imbibed with a sip of water or vodka, or come in through your ears – and you can certainly catch it with your eyes, so badly that its image will remain in your pupils even after the fear itself has disappeared.

These thoughts about fear arose in Sergeyich's mind all by themselves, when he had walked half a kilometre down the road to Svitle, which hadn't been touched by feet or wheels in many months. This road lay straight and flat, as if it had been traced by God with some gigantic ruler. To its left was a strip of bare maple, linden and apricot trees. And beyond that was a field, followed by another dirt road, for agricultural machinery, and then another field, only this one sloped upwards towards Zhdanivka. To the right was a gentle rise and, along its ridge, the horizon, which seemed within easy reach. Beyond that were fields stretching for five kilometres right up to a hamlet called Zayachy. The hamlet was in the territory of the Donetsk People's Republic – "Dee-pee-aria". But it seemed to be deserted. There were five, maybe six houses there, no more. Maybe that's why life in Svitle went on exactly as before; there were no separatists around, and no Ukrainian soldiers either. So almost no-one had left. True, a few fellows did join the Donetsk brethren to fight against Ukraine. And two – the district police officer and the school's headmaster – went the other way, signing up for the Ukrainian army; they were probably scared they might be lynched at night, seeing as they were the "local authorities". Now there was nothing resembling any authorities in Svitle, but it was nice and quiet. Of course, it had always been nice and quiet, so the presence or lack of authorities appeared to have nothing to do with it. The important thing was that the people were peaceful and took far more interest in their livelihoods than in politics.

From somewhere far away – in the direction he was travelling, but beyond Svitle – came the thuds of artillery. But they sounded so distant that Sergeyich didn't even slow down; he wasn't walking very fast in any case. He kept his eyes on the ground directly in front of him. They were accustomed to that greyness. Black plus white equals grey – and so the darkness of evening merges with the snow to make the winter road visible.

It was just at that point that the road began to slope upwards. Svitle was still out of sight. It would come into view – up ahead and a little below – when Sergeyich was about fifteen minutes away.

But suddenly the road vanished. It remained under his feet, but he could no longer see it. He squatted down, touched the road with his hands, and realised that it had ceased to be white. His palm felt the rim of a shell crater – a wide one, wider than the road itself.

The beekeeper rose to his feet. He began to make his way around the edge of the crater, but then stumbled and almost fell. He looked round, squatted again, and saw an unexploded shell. His hand reached out of its own accord and, before he even touched it, Sergeyich felt the severe coolness radiating from the explosive object on the crater's rim. He quickly drew back his hand and put it in his pocket, where it was warmer.

Maybe I'd better go back? he thought, but his legs were already moving forwards again. Only now he was watching the road more attentively. The lights of the village appeared up ahead.

Look at that, they've got electricity! Sergeyich thought joyfully.

He was joyful, yes, but also envious.

Turning onto the principal street, he breathed a sigh of relief. Now all he had to do was reach the other end of the village, where old Nastasya lived.

He was happy to hear, as he walked, the sound of barking dogs. Besides him and Pashka, there wasn't a single living soul in Little Starhorodivka. The dogs were gone, and even the cats had disappeared. There were probably mice and rats hiding somewhere, but they were different, like a part of nature; they would survive with or without humans. Dogs and cats, on the other hand, would have a hard time without humans. And goats, pigs and chickens would never make it . . .

Sergeyich stopped on the threshold and knocked three times.

"Hold on, hold on," a familiar voice responded.

"Oh, Sergey, dear boy!" the old woman exclaimed when she opened the door. "You're alive! Well, come in, come in."

Old Nastasya had not changed a bit since last autumn. She was just over five feet tall, had a round little face, and was dressed in such a way that you couldn't tell whether she was a man or a woman: a pair of warm trousers, a short green jumper dress and a blue jacket with large buttons.

Sergeyich removed his boots and stepped into the main room. "I brought you some honey," he said, setting the two jars on her dresser. "And I was thinking I'd pick up some eggs from you. We haven't got much of anything back home . . ."

"You sit down now, take a rest, and I'll warm up some food." Sergeyich sank into a chair with varnished wooden armrests.

He still had his jacket on, feeling it was too early to take it off. And as soon as he sat down, he drifted off on a wave of fatigue that had some-how failed to overtake him on the road.

Already dozing, he felt his cheeks thawing, growing warmer, felt his fingertips aching as if they had been stung by bees – and all because his blood, encouraged by the warmth, was now coursing with renewed vigour through his veins and vessels, restoring his body's central heat-ing system, which had been crippled by the cold. As soon as he slipped from drowsiness into a light, quivering dream, he heard Vitalina's voice. "Dinner's ready," she called out from the kitchen. The kitchen was a cosier place to eat, especially in spring or summer. The window there looked out on the orchard, not on the brown, coal-stained ground of the courtyard.

In his dream, he came into his kitchen – exactly as he had come into it so many times before at Vitalina's summons, when they had lived together. The air was filled with the strong, juicy smell of borscht.

"Well, give it a taste," Vitalina suggested, nodding towards the table, where he saw a bowl of red borscht, and on its surface (as he had demanded and requested several times, but had never before received – but now here they were!) five golden-brown dumplings. They had been boiled, then pan-fried in sunflower oil until they were crisp, and finally plopped into the borscht.

In his dream, he sat down at the table as lightly and complacently as he had done in life. He looked with approval at Vitalina's pregnant belly; about a month and a half remained until his daughter's birth. His eyes returned to the dumplings. He ate them one by one, then started on the borscht itself.

"So, have you thought about it? Do you agree?" he said with a full mouth.

"No. I do not. I want to call her Angelica," she said firmly. "I don't like your Svetas and Mashas – they're boring. I don't want her to be some tram conductor."

"We don't have any trams around here, so she can't be a conduc-tor!" Sergeyich began to lose his temper in his dream, as he had done in life. "Maybe you only give normal names to simpletons in Vinnytsia, but here it's different. If you call her Angelica, she'll be a laughing stock! Is that what you want?"

"If they laugh at her, we'll pack up and leave!" Vitalina snapped, and she carried her belly out into the main room, with its sofa, bed and large table.

He finished his borscht without enthusiasm. It's alright, he thought, she can't get her registered without me—

And suddenly, when his dream-bowl was empty, the bright aroma of borscht materialised once more near his nose. He opened his eyes and saw old Nastasya carrying a full pot to the table.

Her aged, sweet voice rang out. "Come and sit down – your bowl is waiting."

Sergeyich shook off his dream and rose to his feet. He threw off his jacket and left it on the armchair. At the table, he found a bowl of thick borscht. Only no dumplings – but he had not expected any. That was only a whim of his, a desire to link the past with the present; he had loved dumplings ever since he was a little boy, but he had only developed a taste for borscht after his wedding. But now everything lay in the past, in memory and in photographs. Memory withers away, goes to pieces, but the photographs remain. They stay in their albums: school, military, wedding. And the albums sit in his sideboard, meekly and obediently.

Sergeyich's greedy gaze rose from the borscht up to the ceiling. Up to the light bulb. He licked his lips. The old woman assumed he did so on account of the borscht, but the guest himself did not really know why . . . He scooped up a spoonful. The borscht was hot. Tears came to his eyes.

"What's the matter?" Nastasya said, sounding worried. "Something happen to your wife?"

"No." Sergeyich shook his head, wiped the tears away with the back of his hand, and sent a second spoonful into his mouth. "You've got a good life here. Our power's been out for three years now."

"You mean they never came and fixed it?" The old woman threw up her little hands.

"They said it wasn't worth the bother, since there were only two of us left. And we live on different streets. If a dozen or so had come home, that would be different . . ."

"That's because you're so close to the guns. We're eight kilometres from the Russians, five kilometres from the Ukrainians – right in the middle. Near Gnutivka, where our grey land narrows again, the two sides are nose to nose. Over there it's bang-bang-bang – all day long!"

"But we're not that close to any guns," Sergeyich told her. "In three years, all they managed to hit was the church. Well, a couple of yards too – and the kolkhoz administration. But almost all the houses are still standing. The Baptists come and bring aid every once in a while. Too bad they can't bring my pension, too . . . Haven't got any money . . . But then, what would I do with it? Who the hell knows. Do you get your pensions here?"

"I surely do." Nastasya nodded. "Styopa, the postwoman's son – you know, the one with the short leg – he's got a good friend in Toretsk. So Styopa picks up our little cards, with those 'pencodes', and sends them to his friend. That fellow withdraws our pensions from the A.T.M.s in Toretsk, then sends the money and cards back in sealed envelopes. Well, not all the money, of course . . . He gets a little something for his trouble."

Sergeyich perked up. "Maybe he could get mine too?"

"Have you gone to get re-registered?"

"Gone where?"

"To Ukraine – to let them know you've decided to stay in the grey zone?"

"No, I haven't."

"Well, you ought to. Or they won't give it to you."

"Well, it'll keep," Sergeyich said at last, quietly, to reassure himself.

Then he looked up at his hostess, remembering the purpose of his visit.

"If you could give me some eggs—" Sergeyich began, but his request was cut off by a knock at the door.

The old woman went to open it.

"Ask who it is first!" her guest shouted at her back.

But the hostess just opened the door – and as soon as she did, the warm air of the house was invaded by children's voices.

"Grandma Nastasya, is it Santa Claus?" a boy asked.

"Santa Claus? Oh, heavens no!" the hostess said. "It's the middle of February."

"But he'd promised to come at New Year's – and then he didn't," a girl said.

"Well, that may be, but this isn't Santa Claus," Nastasya told them. "Come and see for yourselves."

Two boys and a girl, all under ten, entered the room with Nastasya.

"See?" She pointed to Sergeyich.

"You're right," one of the boys declared. "Santa Claus was younger."

"You mean I'm older than Santa Claus?" Sergeyich grinned. "Where did you all see this young Santa?"

"He came back in December," the girl said. She wore a pink jacket two sizes too large. "He brought us toys and promised us sweets for New Year's."

"Yes, he was young," a dark-eyed boy in a black coat and ski hat said. "He had a rifle, and an earring."

"Santa had a rifle?" Sergeyich smiled. "Did he happen to be wearing a uniform?"

"Oh, yes!" the girl said. "There's a war, so everyone has to wear uniforms and carry guns. He said he had two kids of his own, but he'd still bring us lots of sweets – a present, from him and his kids."

Sergeyich suddenly felt unwell. He remembered the backpack full of sweets, remembered the dead man and the gold earring.

"Don't worry, he might still bring them," he said, looking at the children with a new, softer gaze. "Maybe they stopped him at a checkpoint. Who knows?"

The children plodded glumly out of the room, then left the house.

"I'll give you some eggs," Nastasya said, gazing compassionately at her guest. "Want anything else?"

"What do you have?"

"The volunteers brought stewed pork. I can certainly spare a can or two . . . And I've pickled some cucumbers. But won't that be too much to carry?"

"Oh, I'll manage," Sergeyich assured her. "I've already made the journey, so going back will be easier. Always easier, walking home . . ."

# 14

If I eat an egg every other day, then these twenty will last me almost a month and a half, Sergeyich thought, watching his noodles warm up in the frying pan on his stove.

The noodles began to hiss. Sergeyich took one egg, gingerly, cracked it open with a knife, and poured the contents into the pan. Then he stirred the yolk and white into the noodles with a wooden spoon.

Five minutes later, in the trembling light of a church candle, the hot and tasty eggy noodles were melting on his tongue. And the kettle had taken the frying pan's place on the stove. It was dark outside, and the alarm clock ticked soothingly in Sergeyich's ears. That was the ticking of time. Soon March would come, pushing winter back. Puddles of melted snow would sparkle in the sun.

And the first bees would set out on reconnaissance, though the vegetation was just beginning to hatch and braid itself over the black earth, so as to warm and decorate it as it awoke from the cold. The bees would not fly far – just long enough to limber up and to refresh their sense of the land. But the hives would already be standing out in the sun, growing warmer, shedding the winter dampness.

The air will be filled with a sweet and pleasing, close and peaceful buzzing – a buzzing that makes every bee-lover's world feel smaller, cosier, more homelike. And then the distant shots and explosions will not seem so important; after all, a person can get used to anything. The important thing will be spring, and the fact that nature is filling up with life – with its sounds and its smells, its wings and winglets.

And towards the end of March, when the bees have finally shaken off the winter altogether, and the hives begin to tremble with a constant tremor, he'll set up his bee-bed: two hives wide, three hives long, topped with a sheet of wood and the thin mattress. He'll dress warmly (nights are still cold at the end of March) and sleep out there for a week straight. Better than any medicine! Better than vitamins! It's like charging up with special human electricity – not the kind that powers light bulbs, but the kind that powers human vision, allowing a person to see further than usual. As he drank his tea, Sergeyich's thoughts returned to what he had seen earlier that evening, in Svitle. The children who had burst into old Nastasya's home to check whether Santa Claus, who had promised to visit them, had not come to her by mistake.

Santa Claus, with his earring and his sweets . . .

Sergeyich pulled a handful of sweets out of the backpack that was resting in the corner and scattered them over the table. He unwrapped a Red Poppy, placed it in his mouth and washed it down with tea. Some things never changed, and that was good to know. The taste of this sweet, for instance, had stayed the same throughout his life. And so had the wrapper. He wanted to eat another one, but then he remembered the children – two boys and a girl. So it turns out I'm eating their sweets, the beekeeper thought. And then he grew frightened: the dead man with the earring now lay beneath the snow and no longer kept Sergeyich awake at night, but his backpack was right here in the corner. It was now clear to Sergeyich that the sweets had been intended for someone. The murdered man had been on his way to deliver them, but he hadn't made it. And now Sergeyich had appropriated them.

He had taken them from the children, and now he was enjoying them, like a child.

He paced nervously about the room, then stopped in front of the stove. To make sure that the heat would last through the night, he poured another half-bucket of coal into it. Then he sighed, sensing that the dead man beneath the snow would not let him sleep.

Then a strange trembling swept over him, and with it came a sense of stubborn resolve. He understood that he was about to set off for Svitle again.

He put on his boots, and pulled on his cap, tying its earflaps under his chin. Then he snuffed out the church candle on the table with his fingers – why should it burn in vain?

He found it easy to walk along the path, following his own recent footprints. It was as if he were carrying his troubles further and further away from home. And the closer he came to Svitle – although he still couldn't see the village with its lit windows – the lighter and quieter his heart felt. It seemed to him that he was walking down the aisle of an enormous church, towards a distant altar. In a church, everyone must speak in a reverent whisper, or remain silent; the priest alone has the right to speak loudly. And so Sergeyich thought in a low voice as he walked; his imagination worked quietly. Churches were always full of marvellous smells. That was intentional, of course. They were built in such a way that everything born inside them – the fragrance of holy oil, the prayerful whispers, and the sense of contact with eternity, which awaits everyone after the end of earthly life – should remain within their thick walls, beneath their high domes, and behind their iron gates. This ensured that people would keep coming back, seeking that experience.

The lights of Svitle appeared up ahead. Sergeyich stopped for a moment and suddenly felt the full weight of the backpack. He rubbed his cheeks with his mittens, wiping away the frost that had stuck to them along the way, then continued on his way.

"What's the matter?" old Nastasya said, surprised, as she opened the door. A familiar noise reached Sergeyich's ears from behind her back. "You forget something?"

"Forgot to give it to them," Sergeyich said, looking at the woman as if he expected her to understand what he meant straightaway. "The kids that came to see you when I was here – they're your neighbours, right?"

"Yes, they're Valya's kids."

"Where do they live? I've brought them presents."

"What a fool," old Nastasya said, spreading her arms. "You couldn't wait till tomorrow? Why'd you decide to come back here in the dark?"

"Well, I . . ." Sergeyich began to explain, but got tangled up in his thoughts. "I don't know. It's nice out here – lights in the windows."

"You miss it, don't you? Poor thing." The old woman shook her head sadly. It even seemed to Sergeyich that tears of sympathy glinted in her eyes. "You haven't had TV for three years, have you? Must be horrible, horrible . . . Well, don't just stand there, come in," she urged him.

"No, let me give the kids their sweets first," he said softly, "then I'll come back."

"It's the second house on the right. There's a wooden star nailed to the fence, next to the gate – their grandfather died in the war, fighting the fascists. The star used to be red, but now it's grey, like the fence."

Sergeyich walked down the right side of the street until he saw the wooden star. Then he entered the yard and knocked on the door.

"Who's there?" a woman's voice sounded.

"Sergeyich, from Little Starhorodivka. I brought a gift for the kids."

The woman named Valya let him in. He was about to take off his boots by the door, but she stopped him and led him directly into the main room. Here, too, the television was on, and it showed people yelling and screaming at each other; their voices jangled almost joyfully.

Sergeyich froze, his eyes fixed on the screen. He held the backpack in his hands, while the two boys, both wearing warm flannel pyjamas, and the girl, wearing blue tights and a green cardigan, stared at him wide-eyed from the sofa. They found him more interesting than the television.

"What's that all about?" Sergeyich finally asked, nodding at the screen.

"Moscow. Arguing about Ukraine," the lady of the house said calmly. "So, what have you got for the kids?"

"Oh." Sergeyich came to his senses. "Here you are, from Santa Claus! A little late, but . . ."

He handed Valya the backpack. She took it over to a table, which was covered with a white lace tablecloth, and pulled out the first bags of sweets. The kids ran up to see what he had brought them.

"Are they from Santa Claus? With the earring?" the girl said.

Sergeyich nodded. "Santa's sorry he couldn't come himself. He's under the weather."

"Better late than never," Valya said.

She handed the empty backpack to her guest.

"Keep it. Might come in handy."

"Well, what do we say?" Valya looked back at the kids.

"Thank you! Thank you! And thank Santa for us!" the kids chorused excitedly.

"I'll thank him when I see him," Sergeyich replied. "Well, I'd best be off."

"You're walking all the way back to Little Starhorodivka?" The hostess's voice betrayed concern. "I don't know how you manage to live there. No shop, no post office . . . Hold on, wait here!"

She ran out into the yard with the backpack in her hands and returned a minute later. The backpack was now full, and she handed it to her guest.

"Be careful," she warned him. "It's a three-litre jar of lard."

Sergeyich smiled in amazement. He had not expected such kindness from a stranger.

He walked back to Nastasya's.

They settled down in front of the television. On the screen, three men wearing ties were seated around a table.

"So why hasn't it fallen apart at the seams?" one of the tele-men asked the other two.

"Because America and Europe are holding it together. They take money from their own poor citizens and send it to the Ukrainians!" one of his fellows replied. "And when these poor Americans and Europeans finally catch on, they'll start their own Maidans!"

"I'm afraid I disagree," the third tele-man weighed in. "When it comes to America and Europe, things are never that simple. For them,

Ukraine is only an instrument – an instrument with which they hope to wipe Russia from the political map."

"Do you understand any of this?" Sergeyich shifted his gaze to old Nastasya.

"Well, not all of it, but enough. It's Russian, after all – not like that stuff from Kyiv."

"And do you get that around here too?"

"It was gone for two years, but now it's back," his hostess responded. She picked up the remote and changed the channel.

A woman appeared on the screen. Her face had been doused with green dye.

"I'm going to sue!" she declared to a journalist who was holding out a microphone, which had also been partially anointed with green. "I am a People's Deputy of the Verkhovna Rada, and I am entitled to my opinion!"

"But that's . . ." Sergeyich recognised the green-faced lady. "She's from around here! What's her name? Bondarenko!"[4]

"See what I mean? They never show that kind of thing on Russian TV," old Nastasya said, shaking her head in disapproval. "Their folk sit around tables, act civilised, speak correctly. – But Sergeyich, maybe you ought to spend the night? It's getting late."

"Thank you, but no," Sergeyich said. He understood the old woman's words in his own way, taking them to mean that she wanted to go to bed, but would not do so while he was still there; so he bade his hostess a warm farewell, embracing her as if she were kin. He very nearly invited her to visit him, but managed to bite his senseless tongue in time.

The weight of the backpack pulled at Sergeyich's spine, but he stubbornly stooped as he walked, labouring to balance himself. From somewhere far behind him, past Svitle, came the sound of cannon fire. Around Gnutivka, probably, the beekeeper thought, and he picked up his pace.

# 15

All of a sudden, outside the window, the February sun began to shimmer and shine playfully, as if enjoying its first taste of freedom after long months of captivity. Sergeyich perceived this as soon as he opened his eyes. The silence in the house seemed off to him – somehow excessive. He listened closely, holding his breath, and came to understand the reason for his concern. His eyes went over to the soundless alarm clock on the windowsill: it wasn't ticking; its hands had stopped at half past ten. That meant he had slept late. But it was impossible to say how late. He couldn't even tell which half past ten he was looking at – yesterday evening's or this morning's.

Before getting out of bed (what was the rush, after all?), he thought back to the previous day's journeys. How much walking had he done? Something like twelve kilometres?

Sergeyich grunted proudly. He stayed in bed a little while longer, then got to his feet. Pressing a palm to the side of the potbelly stove, he found it was barely warm, so he added more coal. Then he looked back at the stopped alarm clock.

I'll go over to Pashka's and get the right time, he decided.

The sun had spread even more of its yellowness through the yard. The trampled snow had turned yellow, as had the fence, and the grey walls of the shed and the garage.

It wasn't that Sergeyich didn't like it – on the contrary. But he felt that the sun's unexpected playfulness, as appealing as it may be, disrupted the usual order of things. And so, in his thoughts, he reproached the celestial object, as if it could, like a person, acknowledge that it had acted improperly.

The artillery was whooping somewhere far, far away. Sergeyich could only hear it if he wished to hear it. And as soon as he went back to his thoughts, turning into Michurin Lane, its whooping melted away, blending into the silence.

As Sergeyich entered Pashka's yard, his right leg began to ache at the knee. The expression on his face changed as he approached the door. His lips were twisted in pain.

He knocked with his fist. No response. Then he remembered that he had had to wait a minute or two for Pashka to open the door on his last visit.

But that time Pashka had come to the door immediately, before walking away without opening it. Now, however, he hadn't even asked who was knocking.

Sergeyich knocked three more times. Again no response.

He pulled the handle: the door wouldn't budge – it was deadlocked.

Sergeyich limped out of the gate and looked in both directions: no-one in sight.

A mysterious thought crept into his head. Maybe he's . . .

And although the thought did not fully express itself, Sergeyich understood what it was driving at. He stepped back into Pashka's yard, went around the house, walked into the orchard, and saw fresh tracks in the snow leading out to the garden. He followed their path, and stopped at the edge of Pashka's land, where it bordered a field that sloped downwards a little, then rose up towards Karuselino, where the "Donetsk Republic" maintained its defensive position.

"So that's where he gets his bread," Sergeyich grunted. "The fool isn't afraid that some sniper might have watery eyes or an itchy finger . . ."

And then another, more terrible hunch pricked his thoughts.

"What if Pashka's the sniper?" Sergeyich recalled the bed of straw and the shells scattered in the snow. "That's why he isn't afraid – they don't shoot at their own."

Sergeyich suddenly felt cold. He thought he perceived a frosty wind blowing from over there – from Karuselino.

He returned to Pashka's house. His right knee still ached, and now he felt a tingling, poking sensation on the right side of his belly.

He raised his hand to his belly and grinned: the alarm clock was in his pocket, poking him with the small metal knob on its back.

Sergeyich remembered Pashka's weight-driven wall clock. Convenient – no need for any winding – just lift up the weight and on it goes, obediently and smoothly.

Sergeyich rolled Pashka's chopping block over to one of the windows, climbed up, and looked inside. The clock was hanging on the opposite wall, to the right. Thanks to the blazing sunshine in the yard, the house appeared dark inside, but he managed to make out the time: twelve forty-five. He pulled out his alarm clock, adjusted its hands, and wound it up. With the ticking object back in his pocket, he rolled the chopping block away from the window and limped home.

# 16

The restoration of time put Sergeyich's mind in order, subduing all his thoughts, except for one: that Pashka himself might be the sniper who kept taking shots at Ukrainian soldiers. And this notion, no matter how much Sergeyich tried to dismiss it, seemed more and more persuasive. After all, Pashka clearly had it better than Sergeyich, although they lived under seemingly identical conditions and on similar streets in the same God- and people-forsaken village. Only, Pashka had two potbelly stoves in his house, a fresh loaf of bread, lard, a charged-up mobile . . . Where did he get these things? Not from the Baptists, that's for sure. If they had brought Pashka aid, they would have done the same for Sergeyich. And, food aside, how about the electricity? Baptists can't deliver power as they do noodles or sugar. You have to go and get electricity. And where's the nearest source of power? In Karuselino – where the path through Pashka's yard, orchard, garden and field leads . . . Sergeyich's thoughts suddenly leaped from electricity over to his own mobile, which was charging somewhere far beyond Sergeyich's garden and beyond the indented field, among the Ukrainian soldiers. More likely, it was already charged – just waiting for an opportunity to return to its owner.

Sergeyich recalled the words of the soldier Petro, about hanging a rag from a tree in his orchard, as a sign that help was needed. So what – if I don't hang a rag, he won't bring my mobile back? he thought, smiling wryly.

But then he declared war on his wry smile. What, was Petro supposed to risk being shot by a sniper for the sake of Sergeyich's damned mobile? What if the sniper got him? On whose conscience would that rest?

The wry smile fled from Sergeyich's lips. His expression turned serious, gloomy. He reflected on the fact that trying to cross the snowy field might cost you your life. The guy with the earring, for example – he never did make it across.

The sun appeared to be weakening, as if its voltage had dropped. Sergeyich opened his wardrobe, and froze for a moment, his eyes fixed on Vitalina's ant dress. Then he opened the other door and rummaged through a pile of rags until he found a white kitchen towel.

He walked out of the house, the snow creaking under his feet, and stopped at the far edge of the orchard. The distance between this point and the end of the garden, beyond which lay the field, was about two hundred metres. He chose an apple tree and tied the white towel to one of its lower branches. Then he turned and looked at the horizon, which was hard to make out, since the field and the sky were so similar in colour.

He took about twenty steps towards the field, looked back, and sighed heavily: even from that distance, the towel was almost impossible to spot among the trunks of the apple and apricot trees.

Well, he said I should hang a rag, so let it hang, he thought. He'll see it. They have military binoculars over there – more powerful than Pashka's.

He returned to the house and prepared a simple dinner, a little millet.

While eating, he kept glancing at the alarm clock. It now occupied a place of honour – in the middle of the table, right beside the candle. Its soothing tick-tock flowed into the silence of Sergeyich's home. This silence was like a huge bottle of thick glass; it held many things, and if you brought your ear up to its mouth, you could distinguish these near-sounds, but just barely, with great difficulty.

But that was now, in February, when the silence was as fine as dust in a beam of sunlight. In a month's time, maybe less, he would release an entire army of bees into this silence. More precisely, in military terms – the comparison suggested itself – he would release six regiments of bees onto the wild and tame flowering fields. Indeed, how is a hive not a regiment? Or a barracks to house one? Sergeyich smiled at his thoughts and plunged into dreams of the coming spring. When these dreams dissipated, he looked out of the window and saw that dusk had already fallen. It was getting harder and harder for the candle to brighten the room. Darkness was encroaching, climbing in through the windows.

Now Sergeyich realised that he was not just sitting at the table, he was waiting for Petro, who was supposed to arrive with the fully charged mobile. The beekeeper added coal to the stove, then went out into the yard. He stood there awhile with his face turned up to the stars, imagining Petro stepping through the gate between the orchard and the yard. He must be very tired; it was no easy feat to cover the distance between the Ukrainian positions and Little Starhorodivka on foot. For a bullet, on the other hand, distance was no obstacle – zip and it's there. But trudging across the field, along the snowy crust – yes, Petro was sure to get tired. And it wasn't just a matter of trudging; he also had to be on guard, alert the whole time. After all, when crossing open terrain, in plain sight, anything could happen.

What if he's crossing the field right now, and that sniper in the straw on the edge of the Krupins' garden is waiting? Sergeyich asked himself.

The thought turned him cold.

He hurried in the direction of the church, towards the sniper's nest. He walked in darkness and silence, shushing his thoughts, so that they would not force him to turn back.

Sergeyich stopped in front of the Krupins' gate. The silence here seemed indistinguishable from the silence in his own yard. But you can't tell by ear if a sniper's around. You've got to lay eyes on him. He opened the gate, cautiously, and went around the house into the orchard. When he reached the last row of trees, he froze, peering into the snowy garden. He believed he saw the bed of straw. In the dark, surrounded by snow, it looked grey. Eyes, of course, can be deceived by

71

darkness; instead of seeing everything clearly, they may fill in what they haven't quite caught. But people are used to believing their own eyes, even if they are half-blind, even if what lies before them is obscured by nature or by smoke.

Sergeyich squatted down and, holding his breath and swaying like a duck, made his way towards the edge of the Krupins' garden. His right knee was aching again, but he chose to ignore its nagging. Having crept up to the sniper's position, he sighed with relief: no-one there – just straw and the same spent shells in the snow.

What if I had found the sniper – and what if he wasn't Pashka? Sergeyich wondered, and he felt his knees tremble. What would I have said to him? Would I ask him not to shoot at the soldier? Because he was bringing me a charged-up mobile? What a fool . . . Why in the hell did I come here?

Sergeyich felt like a prize idiot. He was too scared to keep on thinking, but his frightened imagination had already laid Pashka out on the sniper's bed. It was as if Sergeyich saw his childhood enemy lying before him, wearing that sheepskin coat of his, with the collar turned up. And then all fear fled from the beekeeper's body. After all, this was Pashka. How could he not listen to Sergeyich, who gave him honey and had helped him to install new windows? Of course he would listen! Yes, Pashka the sniper would respect Sergeyich's request. He would lay his scope-sighted rifle down on the snow, and maybe even get up and head home, back to Shevchenko Street. He might be glad not to have to lie there, in the dark and cold, waiting for some Ukrainian soldier to wander into his cross hairs.

Sergeyich went back to his house and sat down by the stove, allowing his body to soak up the warmth through his clothes. Then he took off his boots and his jacket. Eventually, his body and the air around it warmed to a mutually acceptable temperature. This was no great blessing; it was merely a return to domestic comfort. That comfort, of course, did not cover the whole room, just as the light of the candle did not reach the walls and corners. But what use did Sergeyich have for the walls and corners? His legs had long ago learned the perimeter of comfort, in the centre of which stood the stove. He only ventured beyond its confines out of necessity, to fetch or replace something.

A hand knocked three times at the door. "Who's there?" Sergeyich called out.

He thought he heard an answer, but he could not make it out; the voice was too soft.

Well, it can't be Pashka, the beekeeper concluded.

He opened the door, and there was Petro, in camouflage, with a rifle on his shoulder and a backpack at his feet.

Sergeyich nodded and stepped aside, letting his guest come in.

"Why don't they give you snow camouflage?" he said. "Would be safer."

"It's all the same in the dark," Petro said. "So what happened?"

"Nothing." Sergeyich shrugged, watching the guest untie his military boots. "I've just made some noodles. Let me fry them up for you, with an egg!"

"Oh, I thought you were starving . . . Brought you some food," the soldier said.

"Well, I was starving, the day before yesterday. So yesterday I went to Svitle, swapped some honey for a few eggs. And tomorrow – who knows? Come in, come in. Sit by the stove and warm yourself."

Petro sat down in a chair facing the stove and placed his feet, in their thick socks, right under its glass door.

Sergeyich used a fork to smear some lard on the bottom of a frying pan, then threw in the noodles and cracked an egg on top. The food hissed in the heat and filled the air with a delicious, salty aroma. Petro smiled. Stirring the egg and noodles with a wooden spoon, Sergeyich stared into the pan, wondering: would it be enough for two servings?

"A sip of honey vodka?" the beekeeper asked when the soldier was at the table, mashing his food.

"No, thanks – but I wouldn't say no to tea," the soldier said. The host set a kettle on the stove.

"Do they feed you over there, in the trenches?"

"Sure they do." Petro looked up. "And we don't sit in the trenches all the time. We have good dugouts, and we've taken over a couple of empty huts in the village. We've got everything we need – even a bathhouse."

An ambiguous question escaped Sergeyich's lips: "So you're planning to stay, then?"

The soldier shrugged.

"If it were up to me, I'd be sitting at home. They promised to give me leave – five days – to see the wife and kids."

"And what are their names?" the host said.

"My wife is called Svita, my girl Halyna, and my boy Ivan."

"Fine names," Sergeyich declared thoughtfully. "The kind I like. Did you choose them yourself – for the kids?"

"My wife and I chose them together. Agreed right away."

"You were lucky. My wife and I . . . Well, it didn't work out."

"What didn't work out?"

"Couldn't agree on a name for our daughter."

"So what did you end up naming her?"

"She's called Angelica now. At first I registered her as Svetlana, but my wife changed it when she left me and took her away."

"That's not the kind of name you want in a place like this," Petro agreed. "In the city, by all means: nobody pays attention to names there. But here, everything's so grey – and on a grey background, a name that bright . . ."

"Now listen," Sergeyich said, surprised and offended. "Grey can be plenty bright! What do you know about it? I can discern twenty shades of it. If I had a better education, I'd come up with a name for each shade, like they were all separate colours. And not everything around here is grey, either – I've got a Lada in the garage, and it's green."

"You mean no-one's nabbed it?" Now the soldier was surprised, but in a good-natured way.

"Nobody around to nab it," Sergeyich replied. "It's just the two of us here – me and my neighbour Pashka – and he never learned to drive. He's no criminal, either. I've got my father to thank for the car. He left me a scooter with a sidecar. I put it up for sale, and a buyer came out all the way from Taganrog. He brought me the car in exchange."

"You can't put a sidecar on a scooter!" Petro said, smirking, as if he had caught the host out in a childish lie.

"Fat lot you know about scooters! Ever heard of the Vyatka 200K? The guy who bought it off me said it was vintage, rare. Still ran too. I can show you photos."

Sergeyich leaped up, went over to the sideboard, and opened a door at the bottom, on the right. He extracted a large inlaid box and set it down on the floor, then pulled out two albums. After flipping through the first, he found what he wanted and returned to the table, laying the album in front of the soldier.

"Here, have a look! I'll make the tea."

The soldier gasped in surprise. "You're right. Never seen anything like it. They must not have reached our parts. Neat little rig!"

Petro cast a glance at the large, unusually patterned inlaid box on the floor by the sideboard.

"And what's in there? More photographs?" he asked.

"No," Sergeyich said, then bent down, put the box back, and closed the door.

"It's beautiful," the soldier said.

"It used to be a hobby of mine. Back in school, I even won a few prizes in arts and crafts competitions at regional and district levels."

"That's lucky – when a man's good with his hands," Petro declared, sounding almost envious. "I'm hopeless with wood. But I can fix a bicycle, no problem."

"So what's the news in Ukraine?" Sergeyich cut in, sounding fatigued, as though he was no longer interested in keeping the conversation going.

"News? Nothing much. They keep renaming towns and streets, as if we have nothing else to worry about," Petro said with a wave of his hand. "And it's so much work . . . There's sabotage. People refuse to take down street signs. Others want the flag flipped. If it were up to me, I'd rename the country first."

"And what would you name it?" his host perked up, surprised.

"Well, I don't know, exactly . . . I'm not a politician . . . 'The Ukrainian People's Republic', for example," the young man suggested uncertainly.

"No, 'People's' is a bad idea," Sergeyich shook his head. "You'll have all sorts of fools and criminals in power, like in these 'Dee-pee-arias'. . . Tell me, how come you're unshaven?"

"Me?" Petro said, running his fingers over his cheeks. "I'm waiting for the volunteers to bring us new razors."

"Wait." Sergeyich rose again and went over to the sideboard.

He returned to the table holding a small box.

"Here, take it – electric. It's old, but it works like a combine, doesn't miss a hair."

Petro pulled a rounded electric shaver from the box. It resembled a flattened pear and bore an ornate metal inscription on its red body: kharkov.

"I've got no use for it," the beekeeper told him. "No electricity."

"Thank you. I'll bring it back," Petro promised, returning the shaver to its box. Suddenly his eyes lit up, as if he'd remembered something important. "By the way, someone came and took the guy who'd been killed. Probably the separs from Karuselino. He's gone from the field."

Sergeyich grunted. "That was me," he said. "I covered him up with snow. Poor guy's still out there."

"Really?" the soldier said, amazed. "You certainly take risks . . . If someone had spotted you, they might've fired."

"I did it at night. Everyone was asleep."

They drank tea with honey. Then Sergeyich remembered his mobile and asked Petro if he had it.

"Sure, charged it up long ago – here he is," the soldier said, drawing both the charger and the mobile from his jacket pocket and laying them on the table. "And here's my number, just in case," he added, placing a piece of paper next to them. "Now you don't need to hang any rags on trees. Just send a text – or even call, if it's urgent."

"Thank you," Sergeyich said. "You're a man of your word. That means a lot around here. Listen, you sure you don't want a sip of honey vodka? For the road? To warm you up?"

The beekeeper discerned the struggle between doubt and desire in the soldier's eyes.

"Come on, no-one's ever got drunk off one shot. And I'll drink with you, so you don't think I'm trying to poison you! I hardly ever touch the stuff myself."

"Alright, alright," Petro said, surrendering to the mercy of his host.

Sergeyich fetched the bottle.

"I'll give you a glass the likes of which you've never seen," he said, opening an upper door of the sideboard. He took out a tiny crystal slipper. "We drank from this at our wedding, me and Vitalina. A gift from my ex-mother-in-law."

Sergeyich got himself a normal shot glass, but first he poured his guest's measure, and the yellow liquid sparkled joyously in the crystal slipper.

"Let's drink to a quick end to all this bullshit."

"The war, you mean?" the soldier said, wanting to be sure.

"That's right."

"Here's to that," Petro nodded, then wrapped the fingers of his right hand around the slipper's tall crystal heel, as if it were the stem of a wine glass. With cautious effort, he lifted the slipper to his mouth, then hesitated, trying to decide which part should touch his lips. He tilted the slipper back so that the liquid flowed to the heel and drank from it slowly, enjoying the sweet taste of honey. Sergeyich accompanied his guest out to the edge of the garden.

When the soldier had already taken a dozen steps into the field, the beekeeper remembered the sniper's bed. He called out, and Petro came back. Then Sergeyich led him along the edge of the gardens to the Krupins' place, to show him what he had found there.

"Saw it a couple of days ago," he said. "Thought I'd give you a heads-up."

The soldier, who had seemed a bit tipsy to Sergeyich a moment ago, was now stone-cold sober.

# 17

Sergeyich noticed the snowfall by chance. Before winding up the alarm clock and blowing out the candles, he put his face to the window and got the impression that the outer darkness was alive. The darkness was usually silent, but now he seemed to perceive a remote conversation, muffled by the glass. He understood, of course, that this was the rustling of snow, the jostling of snowflakes falling in dense proximity. He understood it, but just to make sure, he peeked out into the yard – without getting dressed, and only for a moment. As he pushed at the door, he immediately heard it scraping fresh snow from the threshold, clearing a neat semicircle.

The beekeeper closed the door, locked it, then checked that it was secure. He would not be able to sleep if he were not certain that it was. He extinguished the candles, shut his eyes, and fell out of life. When he opened his eyes again, the house was cool, and a new morning was dawning grey outside the window.

Sergeyich fed the stove with coal and put a kettle with water on top, knowing that it wouldn't boil for a good while. So what? He had plenty of time, patience, and coal – enough to last until spring, and maybe even until summer, should he need it. He had plenty of everything: especially time. Time was all his, now, and would be for the rest of his life.

He recalled how, a couple of days earlier, he had shown Petro photographs of his father. He had shown them, but he hadn't actually looked at them. Now he would. Over tea. Like a sweet. Why "like"? Memories really do sweeten life, even when you haven't got any sugar. The photographs were all old and peaceful. They covered everything from his father's days after the Second World War to his own days before the current war. There he would find Vitalina with his daughter, his neighbour's wedding, his trip to Sviatohirsk for the beekeepers' convention . . .

Sergeyich laid his two albums on the table. When the tea was ready, he began to leaf through the first one. Once again, his gaze lingered on the scooter, which was now zipping around Russia somewhere. A funny vehicle, that's for sure . . . No wonder people didn't believe such a thing even existed, a scooter with a sidecar. It's like a kid's toy. On the next page were his father and mother – not so old yet, but already decrepit, eyes dimmed. It was work that had done it. They'd had bad jobs. Mother had been a storewoman at the district hospital. She managed the bed linens, which always returned to her: a patient would recover or, conversely, be carted off to the morgue; the linens were washed, disinfected and ironed, then sent to her, then placed back on the beds for new patients. Father had loved light machinery all his life, but, to make money, he'd had to operate the heavy stuff. Once he even confessed to Sergeyich that he was scared of driving those hulking Kamaz lorries, afraid he might run someone over. "They're too big, too unwieldy," he said. What had made him happy was the scooter with the sidecar. Sometimes he would zip over to the hospital and pick his wife up after work. He died like most people who spend their lives in fear: from a heart attack. He didn't know he was having it, and so for once didn't even have time to feel scared. A good thing that Sergeyich's parents hadn't lived to see this new war. They were lying side by side, behind the bombed-out church, and knew nothing of what was transpiring on the earth above them . . .

The next pages in the album changed Sergeyich's mood for the better. Here he was in his element, among his fellow beekeepers. This was their farewell picnic by the river, followed by a bonfire in the evening. He was with his roommates: Akhtem from Crimea, near Bakhchysarai, and Grisha from Bila Tserkva. The three of them had had a grand time. Their room at the boarding house, where all the participants were accommo dated, had been small, but it hadn't felt cramped. Sergeyich still had their addresses and telephone numbers somewhere in his notebook . . . Once the war was over, he would have to get in touch, or, even better, get together with them. There might be another convention. But who would send him? The regional society of beekeepers? Unlikely. Was there a society in Donetsk these days? If there was, it wouldn't be the region's, it would be the "republic's", and that meant he was no longer a member. Of course, if the part of the region that remained in Ukraine had chosen Mariupol as its capital, then maybe there was a new society there. But Sergeyich was neither in the "republic" nor in the country. He was in the grey zone, and grey zones have no capitals . . .

Sergeyich's mood soured again. But just then there came a loud knock.

He started, but did not rush to the door. First, he returned the albums to the sideboard, laying them on top of the large inlaid box and closing the little door tightly.

"What took you so long?" Pashka said in lieu of "hello", as he entered the house.

Behind him entered a man of about fifty, a stranger to Sergeyich's eyes. The man was wearing warm camouflage trousers and a black canvas jacket that was puffy with insulation – either fake fur or fleece.

Sergeyich shut the door and turned to his guests with a look of befuddlement, unable to guess the reason for their visit.

"What's going on?" he said sternly to Pashka, ignoring the stranger.

"What's going on?" Pashka repeated, almost joyfully. "Greyich, don't you ever look at the calendar? It's Defender of the Fatherland Day – February 23rd! So we came to congratulate you! I mean, you were in the service, weren't you?"[5]

"I was, yes," Sergeyich nodded. "Drove a tank. But that was ages ago . . ."

A bottle of vodka flashed in Pashka's hands. It seemed that he hadn't been holding it when he came in. Probably had it stuffed inside his coat pocket. Sergeyich's gaze shifted to the unknown second guest.

Pashka made the introductions. "This is Vladlen, a friend of mine . . . So, let's mark the occasion. We figured it was wrong to celebrate without you, just the two of us."

Vladlen had a round face, a mole on his left cheek, and a thick but neatly trimmed moustache. Both the side pockets of his canvas jacket stuck out, as if there were a one-litre jar in each of them.

The guest, seeming to notice the host's interest in his pockets, pulled out two bundles.

"We couldn't show up empty-handed, could we?" he said, looking round for the table.

Now Sergeyich had to put out plates and knives and forks. Then the men unwrapped the bundles, revealing half-smoked sausage, bread and lard.

"You've got some pickled cucumbers and tomatoes?" Pashka said, hanging his sheepskin coat on the back of the chair he had chosen for himself.

"I do." Sergeyich nodded.

But first he retrieved some shot glasses from the sideboard.

"Greyich, maybe you'll give our guest that crystal slipper? Just for kicks?" Pashka suggested.

Sergeyich turned and his gaze instantly wiped the sly grin from his neighbour's face.

"We won't be using that," Sergeyich said. "It was a wedding gift." The beekeeper sliced the sausage and the lard, and placed a shaker full of salt on the table. Then he opened a one-litre jar of pickled cucumbers, as well as a half-litre jar of tomatoes. Pashka filled the shot glasses with shop-bought vodka and made the first toast: "To the Soviet Army!" All three drank.

"But you didn't serve," Sergeyich said, turning to Pashka with a piece of sausage in his mouth. "So what's the deal, drinking to the army?"

"I drink to our defenders! Like him," Pashka said, indicating Vladlen with his eyes.

Vladlen nodded in agreement. He hadn't said a word since they'd sat down, and this made Sergeyich uncomfortable. After all, a man reveals himself not only by way of his face, but also by way of his voice, or at least with a drunken song. It's not for nothing that any normal drinking session ends with singing. But, of course, they weren't yet drunk.

"You from over there?" Sergeyich looked Vladlen in the eye and nodded towards the window.

"Your window points in the wrong direction," Pashka cut in. "He's from my side, over there."

"I'm actually from Siberia," the guest said at last. "Volunteered and made my way over here. To defend you all."

"You're from Siberia?" Sergeyich said thoughtfully.

"That's right," Vladlen said. "Where it's colder this time of year, and prettier too."

"What's prettier?" Sergeyich said.

Vladlen looked at Pashka, who took the hint and refilled their glasses. "Let's drink to victory!" he proposed.

"Here's to that!" Pashka seconded the toast.

Sergeyich said nothing, just clinked his glass against theirs, and drained it, like them, in one gulp. Then he fished a cucumber out of the jar and popped it into his mouth.

"So what's prettier in Siberia?" Sergeyich said again, swallowing the last bit of cucumber.

"Maybe it's just the war," the Siberian guest began calmly. "But there isn't much colour around here. The fences are grey, no carvings or platbands around the windows . . . Everything looks sort of poor and run-down."

"That's the war, alright," Pashka chimed in. "After it's over, the place'll be pretty again, just as it was before."

"It wasn't ever pretty," Sergeyich objected. "It was just normal. Nothing too flashy."

Vladlen looked at their host in surprise, then shifted his gaze to Pashka, who poured more vodka.

After the third glass, Sergeyich grew calmer, making peace with his guests and the occasion. He finally began to hear the half-smoked sausage on his tongue; he hadn't had anything like it in a long time.

"Everything that used to be Soviet became Russian," a half-drunk Vladlen was explaining to Pashka, the whole time watching Sergeyich out of the corner of his eye. "And what did not become Russian soon will. Everything always returns to the beginning, to the starting point . . ."

It was already getting dark when Pashka pulled the second bottle out of his coat. The Siberian guest was still talking, but Sergeyich was no longer listening. He was sleepy. Vladlen's voice grated on his ears, and Pashka's demeanour, his constant kowtowing, made him want to spit. There was something toadyish, something unmanly about Pashka's face this evening.

Sergeyich's mouth gaped in a yawn. He didn't even have time to cover it with his palm.

"You know what," he declared to his guests. "I'm really not feeling well . . . Maybe you two could continue this over at Pashka's?"

"But I'm all out of vodka," Pashka said mournfully.

"I'll give you some for the road," Sergeyich offered.

Vladlen rose to his feet easily, as if he hadn't had a sip, and slapped Pashka on the shoulder. Pashka also rose.

Sergeyich handed them two bottles of Awesome – the same poison that had recently laid him out. He gave it to them without thinking, just to get them to leave.

"Hell, thank you – what a friend!" Pashka rejoiced. He had already put on his coat and so he immediately stuck the bottles into his side pockets. "Funny, isn't it? Came over with two bottles, and now I'm leaving with two!"

Sergeyich all but shoved his guests out of the door. And he didn't watch them walk away for long, either – five seconds at most. They were enough for Sergeyich to feel that the frost had subsided.

# 18

Anxiety swept over Sergeyich in the early morning, perhaps even during the night. After all, he had woken up twice before dawn, and both times from the same nightmare: that he was writhing in agony from alcohol poisoning, that his ankles were quivering and his stomach was twisted, that someone had stuck the nozzle of an air pump into his ear and was pumping away furiously. In his dream, his head kept getting bigger and bigger, until it was just about ready to burst. It was only in the morning that he realised what all that was about. He remembered that he had given his guests two bottles of that knock-off vodka, Awesome. By that point, they had already been pretty well plastered, having split two half-litre bottles between the three of them, and Pashka and Vladlen would no longer have cared what they were drinking, or how much. It was a sure bet they had finished both bottles of Awesome and were now laid out, racked with pain – if not worse . . .

Sergeyich found the open bottle of Awesome that had poisoned him after Petro's first visit. He gave it a whiff. Smelled like alcohol, of course, but not all distillations were alike: one might put you to bed, another into a coffin.

The beekeeper was horrified. He feared for Pashka's life. Vladlen somehow didn't come into it. The Siberian was Pashka's responsibility. Pashka had brought him to the door, when he could very well have left him out by the gate and gone to ask Sergeyich first whether he minded playing host to an unbidden stranger.

"Have to go and check on him," Sergeyich firmly commanded himself aloud, as if he knew that he would never leave the house without strict orders.

Fresh snow lay gleaming in the yard. He had to trample fresh paths to the gate, the bee-shed, the garage.

He glanced up at the roofs of the outbuildings; the snow there was almost knee-deep, thicker than at ground level.

Sergeyich was concerned. The roofs were old. He had to clear the snow, or they might fall onto the car and the bees.

His mind drifted away from Pashka and his guest. He raised a ladder to the roof of the bee-shed, climbed up, and began to sweep the snow off with a broom. Hard going. He swapped the broom for a broad snow shovel. That helped. Little by little, Sergeyich cleared both roofs. It took him a while to catch his breath. Only then did he hurry to Shevchenko Street.

When he stepped through Pashka's gate and saw the pristine snow on the threshold, he grew even more frightened. No-one had left the house all morning.

He went up to the door and knocked. Silence. Sergeyich thought he smelled death and went numb.

So I'm alone, then – alone in the village, he thought, unnerved. But then there was a noise behind the door. He heard footsteps. "Thank God," Sergeyich exhaled, feeling an unprecedented sense of relief.

"What's going on?" Pashka said groggily, when he opened the door.

"Nothing," Sergeyich said, somewhat at a loss. "Was just worried, that's all . . . Didn't know if you made it home – you were pretty drunk."

Pashka let Sergeyich in, and the two of them went into the main room. The host was in his underwear, his face blotchy and swollen.

"Head hurts?" Sergeyich inquired cautiously.

"Course it does," the host grumbled, pulling on a pair of warm sweatpants.

"So, where's your guest?"

"Took off. Got a call."

"When was that?"

"Who the hell knows? At night."

Sergeyich glanced at the weight-driven clock. The lighter weight had already risen almost all the way up, nearly touching the bottom of the wooden box. The mechanism might stop at any moment. Sergeyich hopped over to the wall, pulled down the weight, and looked back at Pashka.

"Don't do that again," he told him.

"Do what?" Pashka asked.

"Don't bring strangers to my house."

"Why not? Ain't you lonely? Ain't you glad to meet someone new?"

"Depends on who it is. New people are all different," Sergeyich said quietly.

"Well, this one's a good guy, a soldier – came over here to defend us."

"I don't need anyone to defend me. I can defend myself."

"Is that so? From Right Sector?"[6] Pashka smirked. "Those thugs'll show up, mow down your bees, take your car – and if you squawk, they'll put a bullet in your head. Shit, they might bump you off anyway, for no reason – just because you live on Lenin Street!"

"Don't tell me what to do!" Sergeyich shot back. "If you're so afraid, let 'em defend you – but I don't need 'em. Come over with a stranger again and I won't let you in. Got that?"

Sergeyich's gaze went under the table and found two empty bottles of Awesome.

"Whaddaya mean, won't let me in?" Pashka asked in disbelief. "You won't let in soldiers? With weapons? They'll break down your door and come in anyway – only it won't be a visit to one of their own, but to an enemy. If that happens, don't come crying to me—"

"What soldiers? Those gun-toting hoodlums that come over to your place? To hell with 'em! You wanna get the whole village bombed to pieces for their sake? Or do you go over there too? Huh? Did you sign up as a 'defender'?" The morning's anxiety and his present irritation had formed an explosive blend in his head. And so he blew up. "If you're going to bring them to our village, stay off my street!"

Pashka's eyes bulged. "You come over here, into my house, and shout at me? If you're hungover, just say so – I'll get a bottle, and we'll sit down and take care of it. But if you don't want to sit down, then get the hell out!"

Sergeyich did not respond. He stood still for a full minute. He was so angry that a shiver ran through his body. And in the shiver's wake came a wave of fatigue that almost knocked him off his feet. He sat down at the table.

Pashka took this as a sign of consent, went to the kitchen, and returned with bread, lard and a bottle.

The beekeeper glanced warily at it; the label was old and worn, which meant that it was moonshine.

He came home two hours later, staggering. After feeding the stove with coal, he lay down on the bed, on top of the covers, and dozed off. When the doze let go of him, Sergeyich heard a noise in his head. It was quiet but intrusive. He knew it well. It was the noise of moonshine, and it had to be endured. With time, it would die away of its own accord. And it still allowed him to think – just more slowly, with a bit more effort.

He should never have gone to check on Pashka. Devil knows why he was so worried . . .

Sergeyich turned his head to the side and stared at the flame behind the smoke-stained glass door of the stove. He immediately felt warmer. Amazing how your eyes can fool your body, he thought.

# 19

"Well, what can you do?" Sergeyich muttered, when he woke in the middle of the night and realised he would not be able to fall back to sleep.

The alarm clock showed half past two – which meant he had slept for more than twelve hours! True, in that time Sergeyich's head and body had been restored to normal working order: the noise of moonshine was gone, as was the knee-ache. All that was left was anger at himself for a day wasted. And all because of Pashka.

He had not erupted like that in a long time . . . maybe five years. And before today, only at his wife – who invariably responded with a few choice words of her own.

Sergeyich struck a match and lit a church candle that had burned nearly all the way down to the edge of its jar. There was almost no sense in using these church candles at home, since they gave little light and burned much faster than ordinary candles. But they did create a cosy atmosphere. You couldn't deny it. Ordinary candles were clearly more practical, and burned longer, but the smell wasn't the same – and besides, there was nowhere to buy them now.

The beekeeper sat down at the table. He had no desire to sleep. His appetite was in full swing, too, since he had eaten nothing since the hangover remedy at Pashka's.

Sergeyich cut himself a piece of bread from the loaf that the soldier had brought, which was already going stale, smeared it with butter and added salt.

He thought back to his quarrel with Pashka. "What an arsehole," he said aloud.

And as he was chewing his bread, he had an idea. Now he knew how to occupy himself until dawn. He would do what everyone in the country does. It's just that they don't do it at night – but he would. Special circumstances: there was a war on. He couldn't very well do it in the daytime, when someone along the horizon might be watching through a pair of binoculars, a periscope or an optical sight.

He drank some hot tea with honey, dressed up warm and went out to the garage. There he struck a match and, in the light of its trembling flame, extracted everything he needed from his toolbox and placed it in his backpack. The backpack, which had belonged to the guy with the earring, suited Sergeyich perfectly, being neither too small nor too bulky. Tools, of course, aren't made out of paper. The claw hammer alone weighed a ton.

The beekeeper's eyes quickly adjusted to the dark. He walked along his street to the point where you could no longer see the church – not even when it had still been standing. He reached the first houses, where the dirt road ran into the village, found the sign that read Lenin Street in white letters on a blue background, tore it off with his claw hammer, and wedged it into his backpack. The next sign was six houses down. He used to think that every house had the street's name on its fence, but no . . . Methodically, he made his way down the street, examining the fences, and almost missed a sign nailed directly to one of the houses.

Who lived here? he wondered, stepping into the yard. The Melnichuks?

He hooked the sign with the claw and pressed down on the tool's long handle. The sign proved stubborn – the master of the house had clearly fixed it to the wall himself, not sparing the ten-millimetre nails. Sergeyich spent some five minutes prising it off, and he couldn't avoid bending it a little.

By the time he reached the bombed-out church, he was running low on steam. There were now twelve signs in his backpack, along with the tools – quite a load.

He returned to his yard, pulled out the signs and laid them out on the snow, one on top of the other. He let out a hoarse laugh, then immediately raised his hand to his mouth.

Dammit, he thought. Only half done.

He trudged over to Pashka's street and prised six shevchenko signs off the fences. He could find no more, even though the two streets had an almost equal number of houses.

At first this surprised Sergeyich, but he quickly came up with an explanation: in Soviet times, Lenin had been more important than Shevchenko. Lenin's name was famous throughout the world, while Shevchenko was known only here.

So be it, he thought and waved his hand, driving away these considerations. Poets are harmless, unlike politicians . . . I'm going to live on Shevchenko Street.

First he nailed a shevchenko sign onto his own fence, to the left of his gate, then he replaced the sign at the start of the street, and finally he put one up in front of the last house on the right, nearest the church.

When he returned home, he checked the time: half past four – still hours before dawn. He went out into the yard again, got his hammer, nails, and the lenin signs, and marched back to what had been Shevchenko Street. First he nailed a lenin sign on either side of Pashka's gate. It didn't even occur to him that the hammering might wake the master of the house. Then he distributed the remaining ten signs along the length of the street. One each, of course, went up at the beginning and the end. The end of Pashka's street was pointless, like the end of all Soviet history. The only things there were the tumbledown cowsheds of the shuttered Iona Yakir kolkhoz, and beyond them some other buildings that had long ago been stripped of their slates, window frames, and a good number of the bricks themselves.[7]

At last the beekeeper came home, pleased with himself. His legs were protesting, true, but his right knee was silent, as if it approved of the cause for which Sergeyich had deprived it of peace that night.

# 20

If ever you lose the rhythm of life, it can take days, even weeks for it to knock you back into your usual routine.

And so it was with Sergeyich after his recent day-long doze. He had already forgotten about the moonshine and his quarrel with Pashka, but he was still stuck between sleep and wakefulness, unable to find a convenient position that would correspond correctly to any given time of day. One moment he might feel fine and go out into the yard to fetch some coal; the next moment, though the alarm clock showed half past noon and it was bright and sunny, all he wanted was to lie down . . .

So he did – but as soon as he shut his eyes, there was a knock at the door.

"Who's there?" Sergeyich said, hoarse and disgruntled.

"Who do you think?" Pashka's voice replied.

"You alone?" the master of the house wanted to know.

"Uh-huh."

Sergeyich let him in and closed the door. Then he shrugged, unable to determine what accounted for the joy he had glimpsed on his guest's face.

Pashka sat in front of the stove and stretched his hands out towards it, his fingers playing an accordion in the air, as if they were frozen.

"So, what brings you here?"

"Whaddaya mean, what? Felt bored and thought I'd visit my friend," Pashka said, grinning. "You don't mind, do you? I'm not mad at you, myself. Never been mad at you. Especially now that you've gone and done me such a favour! Really, I can't thank you enough – losing sleep over me like that . . ."

"What're you talking about?" Sergeyich muttered, staring at his guest as at a madman.

"No, no, I appreciate it – I understand." Pashka struggled to find the words. "I mean, I'm grateful. And don't go thinking that just because you yelled at me once I'll never forgive you – I know you're not the type to hold a grudge. But 'Lenin Street' – that's really something! What a gift . . . I'd had it up to here with that goddamn Shevchenko," he said, running a finger across his throat.

"Oh," Sergeyich said, having finally understood the cause of Pashka's joy. "Want some tea?"

"Sure, if you've got honey."

"So you're happy, then?" Sergeyich said, once they were seated at the table and drinking tea.

"Of course!" Pashka exclaimed in surprise. "How could I not be?"

"I guess now you're the 'Leninist' around here," the host said with a chuckle.

"Well, it certainly isn't you," Pashka chuckled in response. "You didn't like anything before, don't like anything now . . . But here's a question: what if people return to the village and demand we put the signs back where they were? That'd be a pity."

"They won't," Sergeyich said confidently. "Streets are being renamed all over the country and not just streets, but whole villages and cities. The main thing is that the residents agree to the change. And you agree, right?"

"Absolutely!"

"Well, I do too. We can take a vote now, to make it official, and then we can say the decision was unanimous." Sergeyich raised his hand.

Pashka's hand shot up and a smile exposed his uneven teeth.

"There we have it, then," Sergeyich said. "If people didn't show up to the meeting, that's their fault. And when the government comes back, we'll inform them of our decision."

"Seems maybe we should drink to it, no?" Pashka suggested cautiously.

"Another time," Sergeyich replied, and his gaze grew so stern that Pashka immediately changed the subject.

"And how about Michurin Lane? Unchanged?" he said.

"Why change it?" the host shrugged. "Michurin never did anyone any harm. And there are only two houses there . . ."

"Sure, let it stay. I don't mind, either," Pashka said. "And how're your bees? Awake yet?"

"They never really sleep, you know. If they fall asleep, they'll freeze. They've got to keep themselves warm, even in winter. Thirty-seven degrees. They heat their own hives, so they've got to stay awake. If I slept all winter long, I'd freeze too . . . Someone's got to put coal in the stove."

"And when it gets warmer, where will you send them for pollen? To our side, or over to the Ukes?" Pashka said.

"They'll fly wherever they want. I'll bring the hives out into the orchard, and then it's up to them."

"You should bring them out to my orchard. It'll be calmer over there. And more flowers in the field too."

"Thank you." Sergeyich nodded. "Once spring comes, we'll see where the flowers are."

This time they parted amicably, and Sergeyich even shook Pashka's hand at the gate. Then he went into the bee-shed.

"Remember," he said, looking at the metal-shielded hives. "We live on Shevchenko Street now. Same house number – thirty-seven – just a different street."

Sergeyich stood in front of the hives for another minute or two, listening attentively. He thought he could hear the bees buzzing in the shed's silence. And that meant they had heard him too. They must have.

# 21

The snow shovel scraped loudly against the hard layer of crust, which had been pulverised and packed tight by the beekeeper's heavy boots. The upper layer of snow, which had only recently fallen and had yet to grow heavy, was easy to remove, and Sergeyich was shovelling it off to the edge of the yard, towards the orchard's fence.

This activity, of course, seemed senseless to him – something of the order of morning stretches. All the same, clearing fluffy new snow off the old icy crust could be considered work. And Sergeyich missed work . . . Not the kind you have to travel to in packed minibuses, but the kind your hands itch to get done. Labour like that can distract you from idle sadness, and can even bring you joy, if it has an immediate goal – like the removal of snow, for example. Although Sergeyich wasn't actually removing the snow; only the spring could do that. But he was sorting it.

Sergeyich grinned, taking a moment to catch his breath. He remembered how he used to love fashioning those boxes of his – polishing them with sandpaper, applying varnish. A fine activity . . . And good for wintertime, too, like needlework was for women. Tools, carpentry glue, polished planks on the table, and beyond the window – autumn rain, winter snow, or even May thunderstorms. And when he was invited to a wedding, he arrived with a gift: a cherrywood box, its lid inlaid with two interlocked birchwood wedding rings. True, it was no fine china or a hundred hryvnias in an envelope, but it was warm, straight from the heart and soul. Everyone appreciated it – especially the newlyweds . . .

He cast a glance around the yard. Strangely quiet, he thought. And indeed, the silence in the yard was of the peacetime variety, rather than the military. One couldn't even hear the muffled roar of distant explosions.

Sergeyich rested his shovel against the fence and went into the bee-shed. After moving aside the protective sheet of metal, he placed his ear to the wall of the nearest hive. He felt the wall trembling, but heard no sound. A hive's wall is like an eardrum, only turned inside out, so that this trembling *was* the sound, as processed by the membrane.

"Good, good," he whispered, straightening up, and replaced the sheet of metal. "You'll be getting back to work soon."

He left the shed.

But where will they fly to? he thought, looking in the direction of the orchard, beyond which lay the garden and the field.

Without answering his own question, Sergeyich ducked into the garage. He unhooked the ignition key from a nail on the wall, climbed into his Lada, and placed his hands on the cold steering wheel. Once again, his mind turned to the coming spring. He was a calm, cautious driver – never took the car out in the winter, only in warm weather. And so now he imagined himself driving out of the yard in the springtime, right onto his newly renamed street.

He inserted the key and turned it, pressing the accelerator.

Silence. Total silence.

Sergeyich cursed, then remembered that the car's battery was in the house, warming itself by the stove. A battery is like a human being: when exposed to extreme cold, it first goes numb, then freezes to death.

He fetched the heavy box from the house, installed it under the bonnet, and attached the clamps. The engine started immediately – loudly, almost clangorously. A lazy, dreamy smile spread across Sergeyich's face. No-one, he thought to himself, could hear the noise of the engine – not because he had started the car inside the garage, but because there was nobody around. The sound would not reach Pashka on Lenin Street; it would, if Sergeyich drove out into the yard, but it was too early for that. The engine, in any case, was like a hammer: kicked into action with the first spark.

Sergeyich turned off the engine, removed the key, and the unusual peacetime silence was restored to all its former beauty.

But then it was invaded by a barely audible squeak.

Sergeyich listened. No, he had not imagined it. The sound was remote, but somehow familiar. Like the ringing of a telephone.

He took a few steps – and his eyes grew wide: it was his own mobile, ringing inside the house. For the first time in three years.

The beekeeper rushed into the house, grabbed the mobile and pressed it to his ear.

"Hello?"

"Hello?" a man's voice said in response. "Who is this? What's your name?"

"Why?" Sergeyich said, dumbfounded. "Who are you calling?"

"Anyone who picks up! Where are you now?" the unfamiliar voice replied.

"Home."

"And what's the address?" the stranger pressed Sergeyich.

"What's it to you?" the beekeeper demanded. "Are you nuts? Want my shoe size too? Get the hell out of here with your questions!"

He pushed the button to hang up, but his own shouts still rang in his ears. He was agitated, and it took him some time to catch his breath, as if he had been sprinting.

He looked down at the screen and checked the call list: private number.

"Hmm," he said doubtfully. And then he thought: Maybe I should call someone?

His mind turned to Vitalina, his wife. But he doubted she'd be happy to hear from him. She'd probably assume he needed something. No . . . Better call someone else. Maybe Pashka? But they had never called each other, in all their days. Why call when you can walk over?

Then he recalled the beekeepers' convention in Sviatohirsk again. He thought of Akhtem, the Crimean Tatar. Such a polite fellow . . . Not a drinker himself, but he would sit with the others when they were sipping honey vodka and munching on boiled sausages. Never touched the vodka – said that Islam forbade it – but he didn't turn down the sausages. And when Grisha from Bila Tserkva decided to needle the Tatar, telling him he was eating pure pork, Akhtem just laughed and said, "You really believe they put meat in sausages? It's all starch and Dutch food colouring!" After that, it was Grisha who lost his appetite, while Akhtem kept on munching.

What if I call him? Sergeyich thought.

The beekeeper got out his notebook, in which Akhtem had written both his telephone number and his address, found the number, and dialled it.

"No such number," a businesslike female voice announced. "What do you mean?" he said in surprise.

He tried again.

The same female voice responded, and this time he didn't bother hearing her out.

95

Aha, Sergeyich thought. The Russians must have changed all the Tatars' numbers when they took the peninsula. But Pashka said people still go to the beach down there, so there probably isn't any shooting.

Sergeyich grew gloomy. He was tired of the winter. If only spring would come tomorrow, with droplets dripping from the roof in the warm sun . . .

The beekeeper thought about springtime. And again he remembered a pre-war spring – not the last, or the one before that. He remembered that spring when the chairman of the village council told him that an important guest would pay him a visit at lunchtime, to sleep on top of his hives. The chairman warned Sergeyich not to invite anyone else – and then the beekeeper understood who the guest would be. He understood that the former governor had decided to come back from the capital to visit his native region, and, naturally, to drop in on Sergeyich for the third time. The beekeeper was delighted, and not only because the former governor was a generous man. Generosity aside, the man was pleasant to deal with on account of his straightforwardness, his openness. In fact, it was hard to work out how such a straightforward, kind-hearted guy could have managed to get all the way to the capital and rise to the upper reaches of the government. And so Sergeyich waited and waited. Lunchtime was over and the sun descended towards the west. Then, at around four o'clock, a black jeep pulled up – just one, not three or four like the last two times. Sergeyich understood that something was not right. He went out into the yard and was met by a big, muscular fellow in a suit, holding a plastic bag.

"Sorry," he said. "Change of plan. The boss wanted to come, but got a call from Kyiv. Things aren't looking good. Has to go back."

"Something happen?" Sergeyich said, worried.

"Uh-huh," the assistant answered. "Over there, something happens every day. Boss asked me to pass this on. A gift."

And he handed the bag to Sergeyich. The beekeeper looked inside and saw a box, the kind they sell shoes in.

"If you don't mind, I'll have a lie-down on the hives myself," the man said. "Never tried it before."

"Of course," Sergeyich said cordially. "Follow me."

He led the man into the orchard and covered the bee-bed's mattress with a thin sheet, which he had intended to lay out for the more important guest he'd been expecting.

The assistant lay down on his back. His wide-open eyes told Sergeyich that he was uncomfortable, perhaps a little afraid. The beekeeper grinned.

He's afraid the bees will sting his back, he thought. Through the roofs of the hives, and through the mattress, too . . .

"You just lie here a while, try to relax," he told the assistant politely. "I'll be in the house."

"No, don't," the fellow pleaded, loosening his tie. "I'll only stay a couple of minutes, just to see what it feels like."

And indeed, after about three minutes, he got down from the hives. The bees had filled the entire glade with their buzzing. The guest stepped away, brushing off his suit, although it was not at all unclean.

When the jeep drove off, Sergeyich returned to the house and took the shoebox out of the plastic bag. Inside he found a pair of those astonishing leather shoes, the colour of mother-of-pearl. He spread a newspaper out on the floor, put them down, slipped his feet into them – and felt like he was swimming: they were some five sizes too large. And so he realised that this was not a practical gift, but a keepsake – that these were the very same shoes his guest had worn, not just an identical pair. When Sergeyich had slipped his feet into them, he had heard the crunch of paper. Now he reached his hands into the toes and pulled out four hundred dollars – two hundred from each toe!

He never had spent that money. It was still in the sideboard, inside one of his books, along with the rest of his savings.

The beekeeper glanced at the dozen books standing behind the sideboard's glass door. He was glad he had remembered about the money. What if Pashka should come and ask for something to read? Sergeyich could have lost his savings . . . Pashka was like that – if he found something in a book, he would never admit to it. That would be that.

# 22

Five identical days flew by, just like crows. Sergeyich wouldn't have thought of these calm, monotonous days as crows, of course, had cawing not been the only loud noise he had heard throughout that time.

Maybe they'll bring on spring with all their cawing, he thought, vainly searching the surrounding world for other sounds.

A couple of times, he noticed drops falling from the edge of the roof. He wouldn't dare call that a proper thaw, though, because the sun was still barely visible, and a cold, damp wind still lashed at his face. The beekeeper would go out into the yard, but not stay there long – just long enough to look around, then back into the house.

And what was there to do in the house? Nothing much. Move from the bed to the chair, from the chair to the bed. Think and reminisce. But he was tired of memories, be they cheerful or gloomy. And like every man at this time of year, he felt the pull of the shot glass. Luckily, Sergeyich had a strong will, as well as an atypical approach to shot glasses: he could sit with one for two whole hours, looking but seldom touching.

"You should've been born in Paris," Vitalina once commented with a laugh, noticing this habit of his. "Frenchmen can sit for hours at a café, nursing a single glass of brandy."

This was when they were still doing alright. How did she know that about Paris? Must have seen it on television or read about it somewhere. She had never been abroad, if you didn't count Belarus, where she would go for cheap perfume and knitwear.

Strange that Pashka hadn't come around in a while. Sergeyich redirected his thoughts from his ex-wife to his friendly enemy. Was he ill? the beekeeper wondered. Maybe I ought to go check . . .

It was getting near dusk. The days were growing longer, but they still ended too early, giving Sergeyich no cause to call the gathering darkness beyond the window "evening".

The beekeeper dressed and put on his boots. Pausing outside his gate, he gazed at the sign: Shevchenko Street.

When he came to Pashka's gate, he stopped as well, and saw that the windows were dark. So he must be sleeping, or out wandering.

Sergeyich peered towards one end of the street, then towards the other: grey stillness.

He walked up to Pashka's door and knocked, for propriety's sake. The sound died away and the silence returned.

"Where could he be?" Sergeyich muttered as he examined the snow around the threshold.

His eyes followed the trampled path that led to the orchard gate. It was clear that Pashka went there more often than he went out to the street.

Sergeyich followed the tracks, which brought him out to the edge of the garden. The tracks continued into the field, down into the ditch and up again, but the beekeeper went no further.

He had already guessed that Pashka made trips over there, to Karuselino – for bread, vodka. And he had never asked Sergeyich to go with him. While all manner of "Vladlens" came to visit Pashka from that direction. Maybe he really was spying for them . . .

Sergeyich returned to Pashka's house, rolled the chopping block over to one of the windows, and looked inside. His gaze struggled through the grey darkness of the room and reached the wall with the clock. What he saw took his breath away: the heavier weight hung almost all the way down.

Son of a . . . Sergeyich swore in his thoughts. We could lose track of time for good that way!

The beekeeper jumped down from the chopping block, hurried to the door, grabbed the knob and pulled it, not quite daring to use his full strength.

"Where the hell is he?" Sergeyich whispered angrily.

And then he pulled again at the knob, no longer holding back. Iron rasped against iron, the lock's bent tongue leaped out of its groove, and the door opened.

Sergeyich hurried inside, grabbed hold of the lighter weight, and pulled it down; its heavier counterpart shot upwards and hit the bottom of the wooden box with a thud.

"Made it," the beekeeper wheezed.

He stepped out onto the threshold and tried to force the door back into its frame, but the lock's bent tongue would not let him. So he rolled the chopping block over from under the window and propped it against the door. Now the wind would not be able to blow it open. As for thieves – no need to worry about that around here . . .

# 23

Sergeyich slept for about three hours, his hands folded over the blanket so that he wouldn't get too hot. The stove had overdone it; even the kitchen was warm. He slept soundly, but a loud knock at the door forced his eyes open before he was properly awake.

"Who's there?" he asked sleepily.

"Open up! Quick! It's me – Pashka!" the familiar voice jabbered.

"Someone chasing you?" the beekeeper said, letting him in.

"Don't know, didn't look back – but they robbed my house – I think they're still in there – heard a noise!"

"Robbed your house?" Sergeyich said, lighting a church candle.

"Why's it so hot in here?" Pashka wanted to know.

"Did it accidentally," Sergeyich said, putting on his trousers and, out of habit, pulling a sweater over his undershirt. "So what happened?"

"They broke down the door – don't know what they were after . . . Food, maybe."

Sleep was just now retreating from Sergeyich's head. "The door, eh. So what?"

"Whaddaya mean, so what?" the guest asked, his eyes wide with fear. "They could have killed me! Who do you think is out there, wandering around empty villages? Bandits – human life isn't worth spit to them."

"Hmm." Sergeyich sighed. "Let's go have a look," he suggested after a pause.

"Are you crazy? We'd better do it in the morning. Let me spend the night, will you?"

"Fine," Sergeyich agreed. "Take the couch."

Sergeyich put out the candle. The guest lay down and was snoring within five minutes. It was a broken, clamorous snore too – the kind you get after drinking bad vodka.

In the morning they set out for Pashka's. Sergeyich took his axe, just in case. As they walked, he thought it would've made more sense to take the grenade Petro had given him. A grenade is a real weapon, while an axe . . . But where the hell had he stuffed it? Maybe it had rolled under the sideboard or the wardrobe? But he had checked all the obvious places – where could it have gone?

The door to Pashka's house was still held closed by the chopping block, only now the block lay on its side.

"Hey! Anyone in there?" Pashka shouted from the threshold. Then he pushed the chopping block away with his foot, opened the door, and shouted again. "You in there? Anyone?"

Silence. Only a crow flying by overhead, cawing.

"Nobody," Sergeyich mumbled confidently. "What would they still be doing in there, even if they had broken in?"

Pashka opened the door wider, peeked in, then entered the house. Sergeyich followed him inside.

Everything appeared to be in order. The drawers of the sideboard were closed, the door to the kitchen was shut – no signs of theft.

"Check your valuables again," Sergeyich said. "All safe?"

Pashka darted into the kitchen, shutting the door behind him to discourage his guest from following him through. He re-emerged almost immediately.

"Everything's where I left it," he said, bewildered. "I just don't get it."

"It's cold in here," Sergeyich said, turning around to face the wall clock.

Pashka added coal to the main room's stove, then placed two glasses on the table, poured some moonshine, and brought out a hunk of lard.

"This ought to warm us up," he said.

"You know," Sergeyich said after half a glass, gazing guiltily into his host's eyes, "the truth is . . . I broke your door – accidentally."

"How?" Pashka asked, stunned.

"I got scared – thought something might've happened to you. Couldn't find you anywhere. Came here and you were gone. Then I see through the window that your clock's about to stop – the weight's almost down to the floor. I tugged at the door and the lock broke. So I ran over and fixed the weight, then propped the chopping block against the door. If I hadn't, you could've lost track of the time . . ."

Pasha refilled their glasses. His mouth opened, as if he wanted to say something, but it took him a minute to respond to the revelation.

"You're a fool, Greyich. What the hell do I need the exact time for? It's just crazy – you keep track of minutes, but you don't notice days flying by. You didn't even know it was February 23rd, remember? If you ask me, it's the calendar that matters." Pashka pointed to the wall on the right, above the bed. "You see that there? I keep track of days and dates, not time."

Thinking things over, Sergeyich really did feel a fool.

"Listen, I'm sorry," he said. "I'll fix the lock. I don't know what got into me . . ."

The beekeeper kept thinking about the calendar. He didn't have one at home, be it loose-leaf, wall-mounted, or desktop. But days were, after all, more important than hours . . .

He drank another half-glass of moonshine, then walked over to Pashka's bed. He looked closely at the calendar and saw that all the dates on the current sheet, except for the last one, were crossed out in red pencil.

"So today's the 28th? Tuesday?"

"It's the first already." Pashka came over, knelt on the bed, and reached up with the red pencil. He crossed out the last day of February, filling its box with a thick, bloody X.

"The first of March! Got it?"

"Got it," Sergeyich whispered. "Again, I'm sorry."

"To hell with you," his host replied grumpily. "I've got a spare lock, I'll change it myself. – But I forgot to tell you something important." Pashka turned and sat down on his bed, making the springs creak. "There's going to be a ceasefire the day after tomorrow. Just one day. Postal."

"Postal? What does that mean?" Sergeyich stared at him. "That's what they're calling it: a postal ceasefire. They'll be going around delivering mail to all the villages in the grey zone.

They've got piles and piles of it by now, since the local post offices haven't been working. So it'll be quiet all day."

"But it's been quiet for a week now," Sergeyich said, deep in thought.

"What are you, deaf, Greyich? Didn't you hear them pummelling Melkobrodovka with mortars yesterday morning?"

"No, I didn't," Sergeyich admitted. He stuck an index finger into his right ear, as if to check whether it was clogged. "But Melkobrodovka's fifteen kilometres away . . . Could you really hear the shelling over here?"

"You've got it good," Pashka said, waving his hand. "I'd love that kind of life: hear nothing, see nothing, don't know what day of the week it is . . ."

# 24

On the day of the "Postal Ceasefire", Sergeyich awoke especially early; he had set the alarm clock for six in the morning. It was still dark outside as he washed with water from the large kolkhoz milk can, dried himself off with a hard waffle towel that had once been white but had yellowed with age, and decided, in honour of the special occasion, to cook himself two eggs for breakfast.

The stove now cooled down more slowly, even after the last bit of heat had escaped from the burnt-out coal. And it heated up more quickly, too, because the house retained its warmth longer now that spring was approaching.

He threw in half a bucket of coal, and after twenty minutes the water in the pot was already boiling, bubbling up around the eggs. Sergeyich didn't step away from the pot until it was time to take it off the burner. And where could he go, anyway? Out into the yard? There, despite the approach of spring, he would have felt chilly, shivery. February had gone to its calendric grave, taking the frost with it, but the air in the yard had not yet freed itself of the cold, though the March sun was trying to melt it away. The cool dampness of the yard's air still came right up to the threshold – but the potbelly's warmth would not let it into the house. And with each passing day, less and less coal was lost in the battle between domestic warmth and outdoor dampness. After finishing his breakfast, Sergeyich ventured out into the wet, grey morning, heading directly for the gate that led out to the street.

Pashka had been expecting him at his place, though they had not agreed that Sergeyich would come so early.

"Want some coffee?" Pashka asked his guest, instead of saying "hello".

The guest nodded.

They sat at Pashka's table until eleven o'clock, largely in silence, occasionally talking about nothing – that is, about the past – and suddenly trailing off as the conversation strayed to their present, peculiar life.

At about eleven, Pashka received a text, and this made Sergeyich flinch; it was the first time he had heard the sound Pashka's device made when it received a message. The sound turned out to be two tolls of a bell – and Sergeyich remembered that the village's church bell was lying on the ground, among charred beams and whatever else was left of the bombed-out church.

"Alright, let's go!" Pashka declared, after reading the message. Out in the yard, Sergeyich noticed that Pashka's coat collar, which had been turned up all winter, protecting his ears from the frost, was now pressed down over his shoulders. Yes, spring really is here, the beekeeper thought.

"We might have to wait," Pashka said, glancing back at Sergeyich. "They just now got to Karuselino."

"Wait, is Karuselino in the grey zone?" Sergeyich asked, surprised.

"Well, yes, on the map, but sure, in real life it's the D.P.R. – anyway, they must have made some arrangement. Maybe they paid them off. Everyone wants mail, right?"

It occurred to Sergeyich that he himself did not. He would enjoy reading a newspaper, of course, but he hadn't subscribed to any for ten years now. He used to get his news from the television, until it disappeared along with the electricity. Come to think of it, he didn't really need the news either. What difference would it make? Still, newspapers were a pleasure to read, helping to take your mind off your own troubles . . .

They walked to the start of former Shevchenko, now Lenin, Street, where it flowed into the road to Karuselino.

The snow had yet to melt from the fields, so you had to strain your eyes to make out the dirt road that ran between them. And even then, you could only guess at it from up close because it stuck up a little, and because drainage channels had been dug on either side of it. Now they lent the road a kind of shadow, emphasising its boundaries.

"You think it'll make it?" Sergeyich said, without taking his eyes off the road.

"Why not? There aren't any mines or anything," Pashka said.

Sergeyich was silent. He began to study the horizon, which he knew was full of trenches, dugouts, fortifications . . . Of course, when viewed from where he stood, with the naked eye, these were invisible. The horizon looked like any other.

"There it is!" Pashka rejoiced, his index finger telling Sergeyich where to look.

Sergeyich looked – and there it was, a moving dot beneath the horizon.

The distance between Karuselino and Little Starhorodivka was just two kilometres as the crow flies, three and a half by road. But the road was such that you had to drive carefully and slowly, so as not to slide off into one of the roadside channels. And anyway, you can't drive fast at this time of year no matter what road you take: safest to proceed at a funereal pace. Some five minutes passed before Sergeyich was certain that the mail was coming towards them – and not just the mail but a van, the body of which was painted in the yellow-and-blue colours of the Ukrainian flag. It was strange to see this van here, especially coming from the direction of the D.P.R. – strange at first, but then somewhat cheering, as if it were bringing peace rather than mail. But could such a vehicle really bring peace? That's more of a job for a tank . . .

"And what if they bring packages for people who've died?" Pashka wondered aloud.

"We'll send them back," Sergeyich replied with a shrug, surprised that his frenemy was ignorant of such basic postal regulations.

"Send them back right away, or check them first?" Pashka asked, turning towards him.

"That I don't know," Sergeyich said, shaking his head. "They'll probably tell us."

By now they could read the inscription above the cab: Ukrposhta. Sergeyich's eyes were glued to this word; he was overcome with joyful surprise, as if he had inadvertently fallen under a hypnotic spell.

The van stopped. In the cab were two fellows with frightened faces. The driver opened his door.

"Little Starhorodivka?" he said, clutching a piece of paper. Pashka nodded. "Right."

Both fellows got out of the cab. The four of them went around to the van's rear. The iron latch screeched as the driver lifted it out of the round hole by its welded-on ear. He opened the right-hand door. Inside lay yellow, waterproof bags. The driver pulled the nearest one closer and looked at its tag.

"This is yours," he announced, nodding towards the bag. Then he reached for the next bag and pulled it up to the edge.

"This one's going to Svitle," he said.

"What – only one for us?" Pashka said, disappointed. "What about packages?"

"We didn't keep any packages. Sent them back. Only kept the letters – because nothing inside them can go off. Sign here, please," he said, handing the piece of paper to Pashka. "Next to the X. And print your surname."

Pashka signed.

Meanwhile, the driver's companion unfolded a map and began to look for the road to Svitle.

"You just drive straight ahead," Sergeyich told him. "When you reach the end of the street, turn left, and then right again at the bombed-out church. Then keep going straight."

Suddenly Pashka took a keener interest in the driver's companion.

"Hey, listen, have you got some vodka in there?" he asked, as if he were addressing an old acquaintance.

The driver and his companion regarded him carefully, then exchanged glances.

"What would you pay with?" the driver said.

"Roubles."

"Then it's a grand a bottle," the driver proclaimed.

"You wouldn't sell us that fake stuff, would you?" Pashka said, reaching into the back pocket of his trousers and fishing out a wad of roubles.

"We drink it ourselves," the driver's companion said. "Got it in Sloviansk."

Pashka handed over the money, and the man fetched five bottles from the cab.

Pashka stuffed the half-litre bottles into his coat: two on either side, two in the inner pockets. Sergeyich didn't notice where he managed to hide the fifth, only that his hands were suddenly free.

"Anything else?" the driver asked, smiling solicitously. "Maybe cigarettes?"

"No, thanks," Pashka replied, shaking his head. "Smoking kills – vodka thrills!"

"Well, have a blast, then," the driver said with a nod.

All signs of fear and stand-offishness had vanished from his face. Obviously, these postmen had been expecting the worst. Now here they were, off to a great start: five bottles of vodka sold already!

Pashka and Sergeyich followed the van with their eyes until it drove out of sight.

Then Pashka hefted the bag of mail. He was clearly disappointed – either by its lightness, or by the fact that the postmen hadn't brought any packages.

"Let's go," he sighed. "We'll sort through it at my place."

Sergeyich's boots stamped along the mail van's tyre tracks. He walked about a metre and a half behind Pashka, reflecting on the fact that the van was the second vehicle to have passed through their village this year. His thoughts about the van were light and quietly joyful, but then his mind turned to the first vehicle, the one that had visited Pashka one winter night. He remembered the people who had supposedly offered Pashka a foreign car without papers, going cheap.

Anyway, in terms of normal vehicles, this is the first of the year, he said to himself, casting away unpleasant memories and turning his mind back to the mail van. And when this is all over, a van like that will drive through here every day, and no-one will pay any attention to it. Just like before. People aren't surprised to see the sun rise, are they? That's because it rises every day. I mean, they can admire it, but they don't drop everything and run to the edge of the garden to watch it, do they? No, they don't.

"Hey," he suddenly shouted at Pashka's back. "Where'd you get the roubles?"

"My buddies help me out," Pashka said, looking back without stopping. "I help them, and they help me! Got to survive somehow, right?"

# 25

Pashka insisted on untying the bag himself. The letters rustled in a pleasingly mysterious manner as they fell onto the tabletop. Their envelopes bore all sorts of handwriting, but the names of only two streets: Lenin and Shevchenko. And none of the senders knew that everything in the village had been reversed, that Lenin was now Shevchenko and Shevchenko Lenin.

Sergeyich smiled and immediately caught a puzzled glance directed his way. Pashka was already folding up the empty bag.

"Could use it around the house," he said, and carried it off to the kitchen, where he kept everything he could "use around the house" behind a door he never left open.

Returning to the table, the master of the house swept the letters that lay near the edge of the table towards the centre, turned the top letter address-side up, and looked at his guest again, this time calmly and seriously.

"We'll divvy them up by street," he said. "You'll deliver yours and I'll deliver mine."

Sergeyich nodded.

For a long while he stood beside Pashka, who carefully scrutinised each envelope as if he were trying to recall the faces of the addressees.

"Hey!" Pashka suddenly exclaimed and turned to his guest. "Look what I've got!" he said, indicating the letter in his hand with a dart of his eyes. "Give us a dance, Greyich!"

"What the hell are you talking about?" Sergeyich said, unpleasantly surprised. "What's the matter with you?"

"Why, this letter's for you!" his host explained.

"Well, in that case, hand it over."

"Oh no, have you forgotten already? If you want the letter give us a dance! Didn't you use to dance for Pistonchik?"

Sergeyich felt as though he had been doused with cold water.

He just stood there, blinking. Memories of their old postman, Pistonchik, swam up from the distant past – Pistonchik, who used to deliver the mail each morning having already hit the bottle. He wouldn't always show up drunk, of course; sometimes he wouldn't show up at all. But often, anyway. Regularly, is more like it. And yes, whenever he did bring something, especially if he'd already had a few, he refused to hand the letters over until the addressee danced . . . Everyone danced for Pistonchik, even old women bent double by life . . . Maybe it was a good thing; everyone needs exercise, but not everyone does it voluntarily in the morning.

Sergeyich also remembered Pistonchik's funeral. It happened about eight years back. The postman had gone fishing with his friend Vitek. They had taken a tractor, and on the way back the thing overturned. The fields around here go up and down. There's a ridge at the top and a ditch at the bottom, which sometimes floods. That's where the tractor tipped over, on the slope. Vitek survived, but Pistonchik was crushed to death. All the old women from the village came to the funeral and cried. To the younger folks, though, the postman was just a fool and a drunk – they didn't mourn him much. Besides, the new postwoman, Ira (she was from Svitle and would come to them on a bicycle) won everyone over immediately with her positive attitude and the deep-cut blouses she wore in the summertime. She drove the dead man from everyone's minds . . . In fact, this must have been the first time since the day of Pistonchik's funeral that Sergeyich had so much as thought about him. And he did so only because Pashka had brought him up.

"You gonna dance or what?" the master of the house persisted, getting angry, but only slightly, not for real, the way adults do with children.

Sergeyich twisted his lips. He felt like an idiot, and so, like an idiot, he jumped up and down a few times, spreading his arms, as if dancing to an inaudible accordion.

"Here, it's all yours!" Pashka announced, his big grin contorting the lower part of his face.

So as to show his indifference to personal mail, Sergeyich dropped the envelope addressed to himself on the edge of the table and went on watching Pashka's hands.

"Hey!" Pashka stopped and looked playfully at his guest again. "Looks like it's time for another dance!"

Sergeyich sighed, jumped up and down a few more times, and took the envelope from Pashka's outstretched hand – along with another one.

"A bonus! Also yours."

Sergeyich stuck all three letters in his jacket pocket.

They drank a glass of moonshine each, with a piece of bread and lard. Then Sergeyich said goodbye and left, taking with him a whole package of letters addressed to the residents of the old Lenin Street.

Once home, after adding coal to the stove, Sergeyich laid the letters out on his table and corrected the address on each envelope, changing all instances of Lenin to Shevchenko with a purple pen. He did this so that the addressees, whenever they picked up their letters, would understand that they lived not on the same street as before, but on a new one, and so that they would inform all their letter-writing friends and relatives of their new address. Wasn't that how it was usually done when streets were renamed?

By lunchtime, Sergeyich felt that this March day was already dragging on – perhaps due to the fact that it was filled with important events; possibly due to the ceasefire. Sergeyich became convinced that it was the latter, after listening closely to the yard's silence a few times. Even the crows were silent.

The beekeeper understood that the postman's job was not an easy one. He sorted the letters carefully once more. This cost him a lot of energy – more energy than time. But as he was levelling out the stacks – beginning with the high house numbers closest to the church and running all the way down, in decreasing order – his soul filled with a sense of pride and satisfaction. This was exactly what real postmen did when they received their bags from the regional or district offices and sorted through them.

He dressed, took a packet of letters (up to house no. 40), and went out to where the street started. He stuck envelopes into letter-boxes nailed to fences and slipped them under doors, feeling that he was greeting each of his neighbours as he went along: it was easy to imagine that he could see their faces, hear their voices. True, this made his heart heavy, since he knew practically nothing about where they had gone or how they were doing. But at least the letters would be waiting for them, instead of them waiting for the letters. They would be eager to come home as soon as the war was over . . . And for now, their village, Little Starhorodivka, was one of the lucky ones. Sure, the church had been bombed, but nobody lived there anyway – it was the house of God, and God has one or two such houses in every village. And yes, a couple more shells had fallen, but only one of them had done any damage. Everything else was fine – almost the whole village: come back and go on with your lives!

After slipping five letters under the door of house no. 36, he returned to his own, no. 37. He took a rest, sitting at the table for about ten minutes, then went out again with a second packet of letters.

When he returned home after performing his unexpected postal duties, he noticed that dusk was descending, foreshadowing evening. The air was growing less transparent, and houses were retreating deeper into their yards.

The alarm clock showed five minutes to five. Sergeyich wound it up, then put a pot of water on the stove; he had decided to make buckwheat.

He suddenly wanted to hear some music, and recalled, with a crooked grin, how he had jumped up and down like an idiot in order to get his letters from Pashka. And that reminded him of the letters, which he now dug out of his jacket pocket. He then lit two church candles, adding them to a third that was already burning in a jar on the table. After pulling the flickering light closer, he opened the first envelope. In it he found a New Year's card: *Happy New Year, dear Sergey! We wish you wisdom, health, and peace – may it come soon! Yours, Vitalina and Angelica.*

He reread the lines of neat, gentle handwriting one more time. Would have been good to see this earlier, he thought, remembering how boring his New Year's Eve had been, two months ago – how he had just sat there, waiting for midnight, then drunk a glass of honey vodka and gone to bed.

He slipped the postcard back into its envelope, then brought the envelope closer to his eyes and studied the cancellation on the stamp: *Vinnytsia, December 16, 2015.*

Sergeyich gave a heavy sigh. His thoughts emptied out. A blank silence filled his head.

He picked up another envelope and realised that it too was from Vitalina. The cancellation on the stamp read: *Vinnytsia, February 12, 2016.* The third envelope also turned out to be from last year, only with a December date.

Sergeyich opened both envelopes. In one was a card congratulating him on Defender of the Fatherland Day, 2016. The other offered another set of New Year's wishes, but fresher: *Happy New Year! Be healthy and happy! If anything happens, come to us! Vitalina and Angelica.*

Anything? Sergeyich asked himself. He could find no answer.

I never sent them greetings myself, he thought a minute later.

But how would I, from here?

Treacherously, his gaze turned his attention to the mobile that lay near the alarm clock.

Well, should I call? he wondered.

He picked up the mobile, found their number, and, almost accidentally, pressed the call button and brought it up to his ear.

"Hello," answered a clear, familiar, dear voice. "Who is this?"

Sergeyich wanted to say something, but a lump rose up in his throat. He tried to move it down by swallowing, but that was no use, it only brought pain – not in his throat, but in his heart. He hung up and lowered the palm that held the mobile to the tabletop. Tears came to his eyes. His lips took on a tortured look and grew heavy. Everything grew heavy; his eyelids pressed down on his eyes and a weight pressed down on his shoulders.

The beekeeper succumbed to this weight and bowed his head in his hands. But suddenly the mobile, still clutched in his right fist, began to ring. It rang pitifully, as if it were hurt, as if Sergeyich were holding it too tight.

He listened to this ringing for a long time, for several minutes. Then he realised that the mobile had already gone quiet, but that the ringing still sounded in his ears. And so Sergeyich listened to the echo until it too faded away, until silence was restored.

# 26

On the third day of March, the sun began to flex its rays like muscles, and black patches began to spread across the fields beyond the garden, emerging from under the melting snow, straightening their earthy shoulders.

Sergeyich had gone out to the edge of his garden twice that morning. More precisely, he had gone out to the orchard, to see how the buds on the branches were faring. And the garden was just a stone's throw away from the last trees of the orchard, the grafted apricots, so both times he went over there too. He had stopped at the boundary path, which was wide enough for carts or even tractors – stopped and looked at the windbreak of trees, which ran along the right side of the field from the direction of Svitle, then rose up towards Zhdanivka. His eyes searched for the dead man with the earring, but he could not see well enough without binoculars. And besides, the snow had yet to melt where the guy lay. The trees of the windbreak shielded him from the morning sun.

Of course, Sergeyich could have gone to Pashka and asked to borrow the binoculars, but for some reason he was now less interested in the dead man than he had been when the guy was lying on top of the snow. The beekeeper still pitied him in his heart, though, and whenever the guy and his earring found their way into his thoughts, he grew glum – glum and pained.

Having pottered about happily in the March sun, Sergeyich returned to the house. He held the front door open for a minute or two, so that the inside and outside air might mingle, then he closed, hooked and latched it.

He took off his boots, undressed, and sat down at the table. Then he took out and carefully reread the three postcards he had received from Vitalina. They did not contain many words, of course, so he studied the handwriting rather than the self-explanatory messages. He examined them with a smile, tenderly. Where did this tenderness come from? he asked himself. Probably from loneliness. And from the fact that his ex-wife, after three years of war, had not forgotten about him – and had signed the cards on behalf of their daughter too.

He looked closely at each letter on the first, oldest card. The handwriting was even, rounded, feminine – not at all like his own. With him, it was as if each letter was trying to escape from its line, which would first jut up, then slope down, just like the field beyond his garden.

On the second, the Defender of the Fatherland card, Vitalina's handwriting was a little different, as if she had dashed it off in a hurry. The letters were squat and leaned to the right, in the direction in which the line was heading. Maybe the power had gone out and she had had to write by candlelight?

The third card was like the first, in that the handwriting was even and rounded. But something distinguished it from both the first and the second. Sergeyich took a closer look.

"Ah," he said with a smile.

He realised that, on the first two cards, Vitalina had signed both for herself and for their daughter, but on the third Angelica had written out her own name. And the more he looked at his daughter's name, the more differences he saw between her handwriting and that of his ex-wife. Yet, at the same time, he saw that they had a lot in common. For instance, their As were equally small, like twins, but their Es were not at all alike.

Sergeyich grunted, strangely delighted at his discovery.

So what does that mean, then? he thought. Turns out that relatives don't only share features like noses and eyes, but also share the shapes of letters?

He propped the postcards up against the candle-jar – with the messages, not the pictures, facing out – and kept glancing at them as he ate his lunch. Then he decided that he needed to write Vitalina a postcard. After all, another red-letter day was approaching – March 8th, International Women's Day! He would congratulate her, and make it clear that he had not disappeared, that he was still alive.

He fetched a bag of documents that he kept at the very bottom of the sideboard, under the photograph albums and the inlaid box. Among the papers were his certificates from arts and crafts competitions, as well as all sorts of letters and postcards. He remembered seeing some blank postcards in there too.

Sergeyich laid all the papers out on the table and rifled through them, but found no suitable card.

His eyes went over to the two albums of family photographs. He picked one up, opened it, and saw Vitalina, pregnant, sitting on a bench. The colour snapshot brought quiet joy to his thoughts. He flipped backwards through the album's pages, towards the beginning. And his life rewound before his eyes, frame by frame, back to his wedding, like a spool of film.

The wedding photographs were what he was looking for. He peered at the smallest one – the size of a postcard. He and Vitalina were both so satisfied, so happy, as if they had had their fill of borscht. They beamed at the photographer, looking ready to eat him.

Sergeyich pulled the photograph off the page. I could write on the back, he thought.

He got out a pen, as well as the notebook which he used to record numbers from the electricity meter. He decided he needed practice, since he had written nothing by hand in quite some time. He couldn't afford to make a mistake, as none of the other photographs would fit in the envelope.

Dear, he wrote – and paused to think.

That word, written out, sounded awkward, somehow inappropriate: so many years of silence – and suddenly "dear" . . .

He crossed it out, and a minute later, on a new line, wrote, Esteemed. But then he paused again.

In what sense is she esteemed? he thought. I mean, of course she's esteemed, but by her colleagues, her neighbours, not by her husband, even if he happens to be an ex-husband.

Her husband would love her – that is, call her "beloved". But what should an ex-husband call his ex-wife? Maybe he ought to write two separate messages. One would be for Vitalina, whom he might as well call "esteemed", and the other would be for his daughter; her, he would certainly call "dear", since she had nothing at all to do with these conflicts between him and Vitalina.

No, that wouldn't be nice, he concluded. It would look as if I were separating them in my mind. But when our family split, it split into two parts, not three. And some day these two parts will be put back together.

This last thought excited Sergeyich. He rose to his feet and circled the table two times, then picked up Vitalina's latest card, from New Year, and reread it. His eyes came to rest on the two names at the end of the message. And then the solution dawned on him. He sat back down.

*Dear Vitalina and Angelica,* he wrote, then he thought for a moment and added the word "My" to the beginning of the line.

The congratulatory message turned out to be short, so he copied it onto the back of the photograph in large letters. Then he wrote his name on the back of the envelope, and also indicated his new postal address: *37 Shevchenko Street.*

Sergeyich grinned: Vitalina might assume that he had moved one street over . . .


# 27

The envelope with the photo-card lay on the table, signed and sealed, until early evening. All it lacked was a stamp – but much more importantly, the village lacked a postal service. The Ukrposhta van had left for Svitle and never returned. Its route, apparently, had been one way, entering the grey zone here, exiting there. The driver and his companion might have taken the envelope, had Sergeyich asked them and paid. But he hadn't even thought of mailing congratulatory messages at that point. He wouldn't have thought of mailing them now, either, had it not been for Vitalina's three postcards . . . So what was he to do? How could he get the envelope out to the "mainland", where they had working post offices and sold stamps?

Sergeyich grinned sadly. He realised that the word "mainland" had swum up in his mind out of an old movie about Soviet polar explorers. Only now it was much closer; he had gone out to look at the "mainland" twice just that morning. Well, not at the "mainland" as such, exactly, but certainly in its direction. It was right there, over the ridge, beyond the horizon. The horizon, one might say, protected it from the grey zone. But why would it need protection? The grey zone never attacked anyone, that's why it's grey – because nothing happens there. It's nearly deserted. Yet on the other side of the grey zone is another horizon, also armed. Both of these horizons had taken up arms against the grey zone, though neither of them gave a damn about it: they were just shooting through it, aiming at each other. And if both of them went away, the grey zone would become the "mainland" again . . .

What if I asked Petro? Sergeyich thought. He would post the envelope for sure.

He recalled that Petro had left him his mobile number, just in case. The beekeeper found it and texted a single word, "Come", then immediately second-guessed himself: should he have sent it? Petro would trudge over the thawing field, through the mud, and find out that Sergeyich had summoned him simply to mail a letter – a greeting card for March 8th . . . The whole way, he'd be thinking that something must have happened. But what could happen here? From over in the distance, far beyond Svitle, came the sounds of shelling. But here, it seemed, the postal ceasefire endured – only without a postal service.

Around midnight, when Sergeyich was already in bed, staring up at the dark ceiling, there was a knock at the door.

"So, how are things?" Petro asked as he entered the house.

He had a balaclava on his head, but otherwise wore the same camouflage as last time. And again, a rifle was slung across his shoulder, its short muzzle pointing down at the floor.

"Quiet," Sergeyich answered. "But they brought the mail."

He got dressed, struck a match, and revived one half-burnt church candle. It illuminated the table, the postcards and the signed envelope.

It also illuminated the two men's faces when they sat down opposite each other.

"Do you have postal service over there?" the beekeeper asked. Petro nodded.

"Then could you buy a stamp and mail this?" Sergeyich said, pushing the envelope towards his guest.

"Sure," the soldier replied, casting a glance at the address, then shoving the envelope into the inside pocket of his jacket.

"It's for my wife and daughter," the host explained and stifled an involuntarily yawn. "Well, how is it over there? Quiet?" he asked, out of politeness.

"If it were loud, you'd hear it," the young man replied. "My rotation's coming up soon. So we might not see each other again. Next time they'll probably send me someplace else."

"But not far, right?"

"Who knows?" Petro shrugged. "The front line's more than four hundred kilometres long, from end to end. I wanted to bring you a present, but I didn't have time to get it."

"What sort of present?" Sergeyich asked warily, again remembering the missing grenade.

"Alright, I'll tell you. The surprise is ruined anyway. I wanted to bring you a tin of green paint. For your fence. You know, to brighten things up."

"Oh, that's nothing," Sergeyich said, waving his hand. "While you were gone, I renamed the whole street – hung new signs and everything. It isn't Lenin's anymore!"

"Whose is it, then?"

"Shevchenko's."

"That's great!" the young man replied approvingly, with a smile. "Shevchenko is better than Lenin – he wrote poems. I wrote poems myself as a kid, but they didn't turn out great, just so-so."

"What were they about?" the host asked.

"A girl named Masha. She lived next door. I was in love with her."

"You know what, Petro?" Sergeyich said, lowering his voice to a confidential whisper. "Let me show you something. You've never seen anything like it."

The beekeeper took out the large inlaid box, which was already familiar to Petro, placed it on the table, and opened it.

"What is that?" Petro marvelled.

"I'll light a couple more candles and you'll see."

When the room grew brighter, the soldier leaned over the open box and saw a huge pair of strange shoes.

"You see how they shimmer?" Sergeyich said, also leaning over the box. "Made out of ostrich skin. A gift from the former governor. He used to come here to sleep on my hives to regain his strength."

"Is sleeping on beehives really good for your health?" the soldier asked, changing the subject.

"You bet it is!" Sergeyich assured him. "I don't know how many of my own problems I've cured with the bees' help . . . I sleep on the hives in the summertime. The trembling's good for the nerves – makes you young again. If they send you back here before the autumn, come over: I'll prepare the bee-bed for you."

"I will," Petro promised.

"Listen, I'm thinking of taking my bees away from here for a while. Do you know which road I should take? Which way's easier?" Sergeyich asked, struck by a sudden impulse.

"Which road?" Petro wondered aloud. "The one with fewer mines . . . You should probably go through Karuselino to the D.P.R. checkpoint, then the zero checkpoint at the line of contact, then ours – and you're out."

"But that's where . . . *they* are, right?" Sergeyich asked, taken aback.

"Sure, but they think you're one of their own, a Dee-pee-arian. You won't be able to get through our positions, and if you take a detour through Svitle and Gnutivka, you'll still have to turn right, towards Horlivka. Better go through Karuselino."

Sergeyich recalled that the Ukrposhta van had driven into the grey zone through Karuselino as well. So perhaps the soldier had a point.

They sat up until half past one, finishing a glass of honey vodka each.

Then Petro got ready to leave. Sergeyich wanted to accompany him to the edge of the garden, but the guest wouldn't let him go further than the threshold. "I'll be fine on my own," he said firmly, then suddenly grunted and reached into his jacket pocket. He handed his host a box of matches.

"I wouldn't come empty-handed," he said, then loped off towards the orchard gate.

# 28

After March 8th, the days began to move faster. Before that date, they dragged on, oozing slowly like Moment glue from a tube.

Sergeyich had already dug out his old summer shoes. He noticed that the right one's toe had separated from the sole, so he squeezed the last drops of Moment into the cavity and placed a kettlebell on top. The weight of the kettlebell had made his arm hurt, although he had only carried it from the kitchen to the main room.

"Old age is no picnic," he muttered, then immediately curled his lips in displeasure, disagreeing with his own words.

Forty-nine isn't old, he thought. I may be disabled as far as the pension fund's concerned, but I've got a long way to go before I hit old age . . .

But then he grunted doubtfully, surprised at this unexpected fit of optimism. What's driving me from one extreme to another? he wondered. He ascribed his emotional instability to March 8th, which he had spent thinking about his ex-wife and daughter. He had even decided to ask his wife's forgiveness when they next met, or to ask for it in writing – forgiveness for objecting to their daughter's name. He had made this decision not under pressure from his conscience, but under the influence of joyful reminiscence. The first thing he recalled was where and how he had met Vitalina. The trade union committee had given him a ticket to the Jubilee Sanatorium in Sloviansk. They had told him that the sanatorium didn't treat silicosis, but that, upon admission, the local doctors would surely find that he suffered from other diseases that fitted their profile. And so they did, prescribing a whole heap of procedures – mostly mud-related: mud poultices on the lower back, salt baths, muddy hydromassage. So off he went to the hydropathic clinic, which, he noticed right away, was full of women, with only a couple of men among them. This merry band of women in treatment took an immediate interest in him. After supper, they lay in wait in the main building's yard. "What's your name?" they asked playfully. He told them, at which point they peppered him with their own names, talking over each other: Masha, Ira, Sveta, and – all of a sudden – Vitalina! Sergeyich's jaw dropped. He stared at the unusual name's owner. Her eyes were also unusual – grey-green – her little nose was straight, and her eyebrows were like arrows. "As a man, you should treat us to champagne," one of the women joked. Why not? He made a run to the shop and returned with two bottles of red Artemovsk bubbly, and towards evening they all set off for the salt lake, to take a dip and drink from plastic cups. There, in the rays of the setting sun, he realised that Vitalina was the most interesting person present. In every respect.

He was staying in a luxury double room with a heart patient from Kherson. His roommate went home two days before Sergeyich was due to leave, so Vitalina moved in. They joined the beds. The wooden rib in the middle separated them, of course, but they spent both nights together. And these were the best nights of Sergeyich's life. He proposed to her, but she asked what he was being treated for. After learning that the doctors had found nothing more serious than slight angina pectoris and some trouble with his joints, she agreed to marry him. Only when they parted did he think to ask where she worked. The housing department, it turned out.

The evening of the night that would divide March in two had already descended upon the village, upon Sergeyich's yard.

He had fed the stove early that morning, not so much for the sake of warmth as for the sake of breakfast and tea. And now, in the evening, he fired up more coal, but also placed a little tent of branches from the orchard on top. The burner would warm up more quickly this way.

Burning wood gives off more heat than coal; it burns hotter and faster.

Sergeyich scooped out some of the home-made stewed pork he had received as a present in Svitle and threw it in a pot, which he placed on the burner. Then he thought about his reserves of food: they were diminishing. He would either have to go to Svitle again, or ask Petro for humanitarian aid, or just sit and wait for the Baptists – maybe they would come through again?

But suddenly his thoughts were blown to pieces by a loud explosion – close and powerful. The windows shook and rattled, trying to escape from their frames.

Sergeyich ran over to the nearest window, his ears still ringing. All he saw outside was darkness. He touched the glass with his palm: it was trembling. Must have been very close . . .

Sergeyich stepped out onto the threshold and looked round. Nothing new. And the rumbling had already passed. All that remained was the ringing in his ears.

I'll have a look in the morning, the beekeeper decided.

What was the rush? What could he see now, anyway? The main thing was that the shell had not landed in his yard, or in either of the neighbouring yards. Otherwise, he would have definitely lost his windows.

He ate his pork, though he had lost his appetite, and went to bed. He couldn't fall asleep for a long time, and only drifted off well after midnight.

He was woken by the sound of an engine and men's voices. Then came a knocking. It grew louder and louder, until he woke up and staggered over to the door.

"Who is it?" he asked hoarsely.

"Me, Pashka!"

As soon as the door was opened, two sinewy men in camouflage burst into the house. They didn't even take off their dirty boots. Pashka followed them in, but remained near the door. He just stood there, gloomy and silent, chewing on his lower lip.

Sergeyich went after the men. They had opened the doors of the sideboard and wardrobe, and one had dashed into the kitchen.

123

"What're you looking for?" Sergeyich shouted, not fully awake and feeling he was about to be seized with anger and irritation at the incomprehensibility of the situation.

One of the men returned to the front door, picked up Sergeyich's boots, and scrutinised their soles. Then he stepped out onto the threshold, leaving the door open, squatted down, and started dipping the boots in the mud.

"Got any white paper?" he asked, stepping back inside and glancing carelessly at his host.

"No," Sergeyich grunted.

The man peered into the open wardrobe, at the shelves of towels and linen. He pulled out a pillowcase, unfolded it, threw it down on the floor, and pressed the dirty boots against it, leaving footprints. The second man squatted down and stared at these prints, illuminating them with a torch.

"No," he concluded. "Not his."

"What's all this about?" asked Sergeyich, sensing that some unknown danger had just passed him by.

"Get dressed," the first man said, looking at Sergeyich. "You can give us a hand."

A black foreign car was parked outside the house. Both men got in – one behind the wheel, the other beside him. The passenger rolled down his window and shouted, "Come on, this way!" The car drove off towards the church.

Pashka went first, and Sergeyich followed. The mud squelched under their feet.

"So, what happened?" Sergeyich asked again.

"Vovka the sniper got blown to bits," Pashka replied without turning around.

"Who's Vovka the sniper?"

"You know – Vladlen, from Omsk. Vladlen was his call sign, but his name was Vovka."

"Ahhh," Sergeyich dragged out. "A direct hit, was it?"

"No, they put a mine under his position. He lay down last night and the mine went off, just like that."

Five minutes later they reached the car, which was now parked outside the Krupins' gate. The camouflaged men were in the yard, and one of them was unrolling and tearing off black bin liners.

"This is yours." He offered one to his companion. "This is yours. And this one's for you. Go on, fill 'em."

Pashka took his bag and stomped off towards the back of the house. Sergeyich turned his bag around in his hands.

"Kinda small," he said, displeased.

"Go on and fill it – we'll give you another."

The sniper's position was now a crater at least a metre deep. And the earth around it was all churned up, with lumps of it scattered here and there.

Sergeyich looked to one side of the crater, then to the other. Near the orchard he spotted a boot with a leg sticking out of it, up to the ankle; a white bone was poking out of red flesh. He turned away, feeling sick. Instinctively, he walked in the opposite direction, towards the field. Twenty steps later, he stopped and looked down at his feet. The earth was black and greasy; grass had begun to sprout, but it was still too weak and too thin to conceal all the blackness with its verdure.

He took two more steps, and his gaze fell on a human ear. It lay on the ground, turned to the sky and edged with blood.

Sergeyich looked at his hands, at his clean palms and fingers. He didn't want to pick up a scrap of a human being with clean fingers. He glanced round, to check whether he was being watched. Pashka and the second man in camouflage were scouring the garden, while the driver remained in the yard.

Sergeyich squatted down, took a lump of earth in his hand, and crumbled it. Then he grabbed the ear with his dirty fingers and tossed it into the bag.

"Get on with it!" the driver shouted from the yard.

For the sake of order and appearances, Sergeyich tossed a few lumps of earth into a bag; with just a single ear, it had seemed rather empty.

He returned to the yard. Pashka and the second man had full bags tied with blue cable ties.

"Enough," the driver declared, having surveyed the bags – two full, one half-empty – with an indifferent look. "Load 'em in."

They carried the bags to the car and lowered them into the boot. The two men in camouflage took their seats. Then, unexpectedly, Pashka climbed into the back.

"Come with us," he suggested to Sergeyich.

"Where to?" the beekeeper asked, surprised.

"Karuselino. We'll do some shopping!"

"No," Sergeyich muttered. "I've got things to do."

"Want anything from the shop?" his frenemy asked in a perfectly friendly manner.

"A couple of loaves of bread, maybe some pasta, a kilo of groats . . ."

"I'm not buying much – have to come back on foot," Pashka warned him before slamming the door.

The car drove up to the church and turned right.

Sergeyich set off for home. Silence reigned in his head, but when he decided to check whether it was the same as the outer silence, he realised it wasn't. The outer silence was louder; it was a war-time silence, and you didn't need to strain your ears to make out the sound of distant bombardment, of something hooting and banging, but far away. Somewhere past Svitle. Far beyond Svitle.

# 29

That same day, only late in the evening, when the alarm clock was already set and two church candles were burning in the jar, Sergeyich had another visit from Pashka. When the beekeeper opened the door, he was startled: instead of his usual sheepskin coat, Pashka had on a red jacket, which was too large for him and hung awkwardly on his frame.

"What the hell are you wearing?" Sergeyich said, but then his gaze travelled down from the jacket onto the shopping bag in his guest's hand. Two loaves were sticking out of it.

"The fellas got humanitarian aid and decided to share! All I've got for spring is my old leather jacket and raincoat. They got a whole lorryful of junk from Kuban – they can't use it all themselves. It's a good jacket too. I think it was made for a priest. Look, there's a white cross on the back."

Pashka turned round so that Sergeyich could check out the cross on his red back.

"Yeah, I see it . . . Take off your shoes," Sergeyich said, nodding knowingly. "We'll have a bite to eat."

"Good idea," Pashka concurred. "I only stopped by my place for a second when I got back, then came straight over."

Sergeyich pulled two kilos of pasta, a packet of millet and two loaves from the bag.

After finding a place for it all in the kitchen cupboard, he fixed his eyes on the last two of the eggs he had traded for honey in Svitle. There were hardly any noodles left either – maybe just enough for two, in fact.

He returned to the main room, tented some branches over the burning coal, put a pot of water on the stove, and, to liven and brighten things up, lit two more church candles.

"You know, Pashka" – he looked attentively at his guest – "tomorrow or the day after I'm going away. With the bees. Until August, probably."

Silence filled the air in the wake of his words.

"Where will you go? Vinnytsia?" Pashka said, coming to after a minute or two of gloomy silence.

"No, somewhere closer. Where there's no shooting. To let the bees fly."

"So what, I'll be all alone?"

"Why alone? You've got friends over there in Karuselino."

"Yeah, I had one . . . But he was killed – right here in our village . . . The rest of 'em are a bunch of arseholes, really – sometimes it's 'Hey, brother!' and sometimes it's 'Fuck off!' Let's drink to Vovka, eh? A.k.a. Vladlen. You got anything?"

Sergeyich silently got out the honey vodka and set it on the table with a pair of glasses. Then he poured the remaining noodles into the pot on the stove.

"Alright – may he rest in peace," Pashka said, raising his glass.

"Yes, let 'im," Sergeyich agreed, downing half his vodka. "I'll leave you a key," he declared after the customary pause. "Will you look after the place?"

"What's there to look after?" Pashka glanced round. "You've got nothing worth stealing, especially if you're taking your Lada." This wounded Sergeyich's feelings a bit. He decided to surprise Pashka.

"Let me show you something," he said, lending the words an air of significance. He lowered the shoebox onto the table and lifted its lacquered lid. "Take a look."

Pashka leaned over the box, and the curl of bewilderment on his lips turned into a smile.

"What're they made of? Crocodile skin?" he said enthusiastically, touching one of the toes with his finger.

"Ostrich. A gift from the former governor. He used to come visit me, you know – to sleep on the hives. Back before the war."

Pashka nodded. "So your neighbours weren't lying." Carefully, he drew one shoe out of the box. "Can I try them on?"

"Sure, but they're big. Wait, I'll get a little rug."

Sergeyich couldn't find the little rug, so he put a towel on the floor instead.

Pashka lowered the shoes to the floor, onto the towel, and inserted his feet.

"Well, they ain't that big," he said.

"What's your size?" Sergeyich asked, taken aback.

"Forty-four. But I've got fallen arches – that makes my feet bigger. Can I take a walk around the room?"

"Sure."

The guest carefully circled the table, constantly glancing down at his feet, or rather, at the shoes. Then he took his seat, removed them, and slipped them back into the box.

"Listen, let's exchange numbers, just in case," Sergeyich suggested.

"But I thought your battery was dead?"

The beekeeper bit his lower lip, so as not to say something he would regret.

"It is, but I'll charge it over there," he said, after a pause. "You just write yours down for me. Oh, and another thing – I'll be driving through Karuselino. Will your 'brothers' let me past?"

"Why wouldn't they? You'd better worry about the Uke checkpoint. I think you need a pass to get through there."

Sergeyich froze. "A pass?"

"Well, it's either a pass, or you need to come to some agreement. Maybe they'll let you through on account of your address, your passport? The main thing is, don't be afraid of 'em – stand up for your rights! If they mouth off to ya, just give it right back. But know when to stop and watch their hands. If one of them reaches for his rifle, shut up and apologise! Say the shelling's messed with your nerves."

# 30

Fiery birds flew into Sergeyich's dream in the dead of night. They flew in with a whistle and immediately flew out again. A whole flock of them. He turned from his right to his left side. And just then – from somewhere far away, where these birds had flown to in his dream – came a thunderous rumble. As soon as it began to subside, more birds burst into his dream; they whistled right past his closed eyes. And then came more rumbling, but not so far away. This time the rumble even seemed to rock Sergeyich in his bed, as a passing motorboat might rock him in his dinghy on the Donets.

Sergeyich opened his eyes and peered cautiously out of his dream into the darkness of the room. Something, somewhere, was buzzing, but he couldn't determine the cause of this buzz on account of his borderline state – a state between the dream and the real, but closer to the dream.

And then came the whistle again, now heavier, as if just above his head. And the house trembled.

Sergeyich, frightened, looked up at the ceiling, but he couldn't see it. It was dark, after all – the middle of the night.

And then came the rumble, only it was louder than in his dream, and felt even closer.

He got out of bed, dressed, felt around for the matches on the table, and lit a candle.

Once more, the house trembled from top to bottom. The floor under Sergeyich's feet shook so hard that he put his left leg out a little to keep his balance.

He went over to the window, which was open a crack, and the night breathed moisture into his face. Then a new whistle came through the crack. It seemed to have travelled down from above, from the lower part of the sky, but it flew into the house through the window. Together with the wind. And Sergeyich thought that it must have been the wind that had set the house trembling from the inside, as if trying to inflate it. He closed the window, and the room grew quieter.

The beekeeper slid his bare feet into his boots and stepped out onto the threshold. There, the terrible force of the whistling and rumbling froze him to the spot, paralysing him. Again, a whistle passed right above his head and whistled off towards his garden. After a few seconds – new peals of thunder.

"What the—?" Sergeyich looked back, in the direction from which these invisible fiery birds were flying. Are they firing from Karuselino? he wondered, but immediately rejected the notion. How could they be firing from there if the shop's still working? No, it's probably coming from Melovannaya – there's nobody left there.

Sergeyich grew nervous – and suddenly he realised that he was walking towards his orchard. It was as if his legs were leading him there on their own, while his thoughts simply weren't paying attention. He pulled himself together, uniting his thoughts with his body, but still only managed to stop at the edge of his garden. And what he saw there left him dumbfounded: on the other side of the field, where Zhdanivka hid behind the ridge, a red glow rose from the earth to the sky, constantly reinforced by new flashes followed a second or two later by a thunderous rumble.

A wind blew in his face – not strong, but strange, warm, as if it had been heated in a stove. The smell it carried was like that of burnt pastry, or of something else that hadn't been pulled out of the oven in time.

Once more, a heavy whistle passed above his head.

Probably getting even for Vovka the sniper, Sergeyich thought.

He shook his head, pitying the silence. He had grown used to it, with its occasional sounds of distant bombardment. But apparently its time was at an end.

He plodded back to the yard, dejected, and went over to the beeshed. It seemed to him that its wooden walls were trembling. He placed his palm against one of the walls to confirm it. He opened the door and an anxious buzzing burst into his ears. Thousands of bees were rushing about inside the darkened shed, beating against its walls. Several dozen immediately flew out of the door into the yard. One smacked into Sergeyich's unshaven cheek.

The beekeeper slammed the door shut.

"Scared out of their wits," he whispered. He felt powerless to help the bees in any way. There was nothing he could do to reassure them.

And so, being a rational, wingless creature, he returned to the house, where he sat down at the table and waited for the bombardment to end. It took a long time – about four hours.

At the first sign of dawn, everything grew calm, returning to normal. Only the morning birds refused to sing for some reason. And the echo of the night's rumbling still rang in Sergeyich's ears. He pulled his mobile out from under his pillow and texted Petro a single word: "Alive?"

After a minute or two, he received a reply: the same word, only without the question mark.

"Well, thank God." The beekeeper sighed, and set about gathering his things. It was time to go.

# 31

This time, getting ready for the road proved to be an unusually slow, difficult process, despite the fact that Sergeyich was an old hand at packing to leave. But, of course, there was getting ready, and then there was getting ready. If this were peacetime and he were going off to some sanatorium, then his travel bag would have been zipped in ten minutes flat – and any sanatorium nurse would have given him high marks both for the skilful selection of items and for the careful packing. Any item, any article of clothing taken on the road must serve its purpose. Sergeyich had learned this unconditional rule a long time ago, and a couple of times it had led to unintended consequences. More precisely, it had sometimes served to create a false impression of Sergeyich among people who did not know him well or had come to know him by chance. For example, towards the end of a stay at some sanatorium, he might find that he had only worn the T-shirts he had brought, which meant that his three or four dress shirts – each with its designated tie in a single colour (Sergeyich had no truck with playful ties) – had remained clean and folded. And so, in the last couple of days of his stay, he would wear one dress shirt with its accompanying tie from morning until lunchtime, and another set after lunch. Once, on the last day of a certain stay – when everyone was saying goodbye and wishing each other good health – he ran through four sets of shirts and ties, all different colours. That evening, the woman who sat next to him at mealtimes could not resist telling him that he had concealed his true nature too skilfully over the course of the preceding twenty-four days. She didn't explain what she meant, and so Sergeyich went home puzzling over the mystery of his "true nature", which he would have loved to solve, but never did.

Now, with no foreseeable sanatoriums in his future – either near or distant – it made no sense to worry about the variety of clean clothes. But his Lada estate was a roomy vehicle, which meant there was no need to limit the volume of luggage. It's like filling a travel bag halfway:

you always end up thinking, What did I forget? Besides, with this new bombardment, you never knew: a shell might fall on house no. 37. And then everything he hadn't taken with him would be turned to ash.

Three sweaters, two pairs of trousers, a pair of rubber boots, an armful of socks (ranging from woollen to summer), a scarf and a canvas fishing jacket (not as warm as the Chinese down jacket, but waterproof) all fitted easily in Sergeyich's large bag. But the first items he had put at the bottom of the bag were two books from the sideboard: his Nikolai Ostrovsky with the dollars in it, and his *War and Peace* with the hryvnias.[8]

Sergeyich started the car. While the motor came to life after a long period of inactivity, the beekeeper used a tube to fill up three canisters with petrol from an iron barrel.

When he drove his green Lada out into the yard, drops of rain began to fall. Sergeyich threw a glance up at the sky, and rain hit him straight in his open eyes. The drops had also fallen on his lips and tongue, and it seemed to him that they were salty. It was as if these were heavenly tears instead of rain – as if the sky were crying for him, for Sergeyich, because it too did not know whether he would ever return. And if he did, whenever that might be, would he find everything as he had left it?

To the sound of the raindrops, Sergeyich examined his native walls, trees and fences, his little world, in which he had lived through all his troubles and problems, day after day, night after night. It – the trees, the gates, the doors and the windows – had up to this point protected him like a fortress, like a bulletproof vest. And all these years he had thought the opposite: that he was protecting his home, his land, his world. No, he had been wrong. Only now, when it was time to leave, did he realise it.

He shut off the engine – warm enough, he reckoned. Now he needed to attach the flatbed trailer, which was propped upright against the wall in the garage. Then he would prepare the beehives for the road, closing the entrances so that the bees didn't scatter along the way. He would need to load the hives onto the trailer one by one, cover them with a tarpaulin to protect them from the rain, then strap them down nice and tight. Oh, and he mustn't forget to pack a dozen or so jars of honey. After all, honey is also money. It may even have more in common with money than sausages or clothing, since sausages and clothing fluctuate in value, while honey, regardless of whether it's buckwheat or motley grass, resolutely maintains its value. Like the dollar.

The rain didn't stop, but it dripped unobtrusively, calmly. And that was good for travelling with bees. Had the weather been warmer, he would have had to drive by night, because bees tend to get agitated by bumpy roads, raising the temperature in their hives. And if the hives get too hot inside, they might die – especially if it's also hot outside. But now the temperature was hovering around ten degrees, and the rain, though warm, still had a cooling effect. All in all, the conditions for travel were perfect.

Sergeyich stopped the car in front of Pashka's house. He came in to hand his frenemy the key to his front door, but Pashka insisted that his guest had some tea before leaving. He also urged him to raise a glass of something stronger, to toast his journey, but Sergeyich refused. In the end, Pashka persuaded Sergeyich to drive him to the end of his street, before the turning to Karuselino, so that he could see his neighbour off properly. He put on his red jacket with the white cross on the back.

However, when they reached the agreed place, Pashka decided he would accompany Sergeyich a little further down the road. He couldn't bring himself to say goodbye.

Sergeyich drove down towards the bend in the road carefully, constantly glancing back at the trailer.

"Stocked up on petrol?" Pashka said, sniffing the air inside the car. The driver nodded. "Yes."

Sergeyich stopped the car at the bottom of the slope, before the road began to rise.

"You'd better get out here. You'll have to walk all the way back through the mud," he said to Pashka.

Pashka sighed, looked up at the rainy sky, and climbed reluctantly out of the car. Sergeyich got out, too, and faced Pashka.

"You should paint it, or dirty it up a bit," he said, nodding at the red jacket. "Or you're sure to get shot. You're the only bright spot in the whole district."

Pashka looked down at his jacket, his lips pursed with displeasure. He was evidently rather fond of it.

"Well, then," Sergeyich said, extending his hand.

Pashka had tears in his eyes. He raised his right hand to meet Sergeyich's and his left hand rose up all by itself. They embraced as men do, tightly – clasping each other close, then immediately weakening their hold.

"You take care of yourself up there," Sergeyich said, nodding towards the village, which now seemed to be looking down at them through its orchards and gardens. "I left a three-litre jar of honey on the windowsill in the kitchen. That's for you. Alright, then." Without saying another word, he got behind the wheel. Slowly, the Lada drove off, pulling its trailer with six hives under a tarpaulin, its wheels smacking against the wet dirt road.

The white cross on Pashka's red jacket gradually receded in the rear view mirror. Pashka was making his way home, his head bowed either with grief over his new loneliness, or because he was carefully choosing a place for every new step amid the mud.

# 32

Sergeyich left Karuselino behind him. Was it living or dead? The yards seemed to be empty, but in one of them he had seen freshly washed linen fluttering in the wind.

Sergeyich drove slowly, so as not to disturb the bees on the trailer. The windscreen wipers were smearing raindrops across the glass with a lulling squeak, and he yawned to their music – when suddenly a man in camouflage came out from behind an old bus stop and pointed his rifle at the Lada.

Sergeyich stepped on the brake, stopping about twenty metres away from the armed man. His drowsiness vanished.

Here we go, he thought woefully, and waited for the camouflaged guy to approach.

But the man gestured with his hand, commanding the car to come closer.

Sergeyich obeyed, then rolled down his window.

"Where you coming from and where you going?" the man asked.

"From Little Starhorodivka. Getting my bees out," Sergeyich replied, nodding towards the trailer.

The camouflaged guy smirked. "Got everything else out already?"

"Why should I? I'm coming back. I live here. Want to check my passport?"

"Nah, no need, I recognise ya." The man waved his hand. "Just got no-one to talk to."

Sergeyich recovered his courage. "Listen, what's the best way to Zaitseve?" he said.

"Head towards Vuhlehirsk, but turn right before you hit the city limits. Then go straight, past the mines, and ask there. Funny, a fella from the village just took off for Zaitseve yesterday, to get his pension . . . If you'da known, you coulda just followed him." If I'da known? Sergeyich thought, driving away from Karuselino along a tarmac road. How could I have? I didn't even know until yesterday that I would be leaving today. And now I don't know where I'll find myself tomorrow . . .

An hour later he drove out from under the rain. The sky brightened overhead, and the slag heaps of the mines loomed in the distance. Sergeyich stopped the car and walked back to the trailer. He put an ear to one of the hives; its warm wall trembled with the bees' humming.

Two days on the road would be hard for the bees. He should hurry. But he couldn't go too fast, either. The tarmac was all torn up – hadn't been patched in three years.

He picked up a little speed anyway. Along the road to the right stretched the endless ruins of some factory, which had either collapsed on its own or got smashed during the current war. On the left stood the rusty frames of abandoned greenhouses.

No, the war's not at fault, Sergeyich realised. This stuff went to hell a long time ago . . .

Soon the roadside wreckage thinned out, and on the left the bee-keeper saw a white brick church with blue domes. Beyond the church was a lake, and on its shore stood a man with a fishing rod. The fisherman gazed at the green Lada as it passed by, then turned his eyes back to his bobbing float.

Sergeyich suddenly had a strange sensation – he felt as if he were driving inside a movie. He felt that everything around him was unreal, that it had been pre-recorded, and that he alone was alive and not on film.

He shook his head, chasing away the foolish sensation. But then another, even worse thought jolted him painfully – the thought that he had left his alarm clock in the house. He had wound it up yesterday evening, so today or tomorrow it would stop, fall silent. And then there would be no living time in the house until its owner returned and wound it up again. Maybe Pashka would do it? No, that would never occur to him. All he cared about was crossing days off his calendar, hours be damned . . . Was it worth calling and asking him to wind it? But then he'd have to do it every day . . . No, he wouldn't go to the house just for the sake of winding the clock, even if he promised to do so. It was foolish to worry about time, of course. Time plays a role when there's someone to keep track of it, to depend on it. And if no-one like that remains, then time, too, stops and disappears.

Another church, this time of red brick, passed by and then diminished in his rear-view mirror. And up ahead sat of a new pair of slag heaps, one of them levelled off to a plateau.

He recalled how he used to descend into the mines in cages, ruminating on the dangers and meaninglessness of his work. Health and safety inspections had to be carried out constantly, but what kind of health and safety can one expect in a mine? None. Still, all the mine administrators would feed him as if he were an honoured guest, treat him to vodka as if he were a brother, and bid him farewell as if he were a beloved relative. So each of his work trips had two tastes: bitter and sweet. Everyone deceived one another, and everyone embraced one another. They deceived out of necessity, embraced in drunken fellowship – and all the while the miners would stare at him with the same question in their eyes, which sometimes also contained an obvious threat, as if to say: "You're not going to do us over, are you?"

Time passed. The road kept veering a little to the left, a little to the right, and so on. Five-storey buildings would flash up here and there. Private houses hid behind grey fences. Sometimes there would be a building with no windows, or a pile of ashes in place of a house, but Sergeyich wasn't about to rubberneck at ruins. He would catch something out of the corner of his eye and keep going. Besides, there were now plenty of cars to keep his eyes on, though all the cars were cheap, like his – none of the shiny foreign makes that used to zip down the road, cutting everyone up, before the war.

It was already getting dark when the cars ahead of him sparked their brake lights and slowed down. He, too, pressed his brake pedal. About a hundred metres down the road, he saw that little concrete pyramids, painted yellow, were narrowing the lane. That's why everyone was driving so carefully, trying not to scratch their cars against the pyramids. He, too, drove cautiously, at about the speed of a hurrying pedestrian, and stared fixedly at the road. Out of the corner of his eye he glimpsed camouflaged men with rifles. One of these men took a look at Sergeyich's Lada, with its trailer of beehives, then pressed the talk button on his walkie-talkie and brought it up to his mouth.

Sergeyich did not like this. He kept his eyes on the rear-view mirror, watching the armed men. It seemed they were still looking at his car.

The beekeeper's unpleasant foreboding was justified ten minutes later, when yet another camouflaged man with a rifle on his chest commanded him with a wave of his hand to pull off onto a shoulder separated from the road by concrete blocks. The man then approached the car, opened the driver-side door, and looked inside.

"Where you going?" he said dryly.

Fatigue from the road and fear prevented Sergeyich from being able to bring his focus to bear.

"Taking the bees," he said uncertainly.

"Where?"

"To Ukraine."

"Why would they need your bees?" The man glanced back at the trailer. "They've got their own, don't they?"

"I'm from the grey zone, from Little Starhorodivka," Sergeyich finally began to explain more clearly. "They've started shooting over there. If I release the bees at home, they might get spooked by the shelling and fly away. I'd lose them."

"Aha!" The camouflaged man smiled, as if pleased to have learned something new. "So bees are afraid of blasts, are they? Interesting. Have you got your papers?"

"I do." Sergeyich reached into the inside pocket of his jacket.

"No, no need – I see you're one of ours. You'll have to show 'em over there, to the Ukes. But they might not let you through with the hives. Have you got papers for the bees too?"

Sergeyich grew confused. "No . . . Do I need them?"

"Who the hell knows?" The man shrugged. "Hey, got any cigs?"

"I don't smoke."

"Alright, go on – you might even make it by end of day," the man with the rifle said, ending their chat on a peaceful note.

Much relieved, Sergeyich started the engine and returned to the lane narrowed by the concrete pyramids. Soon the pyramids disappeared, but after another kilometre and a half or so he ran up against a queue of cars. Next to the cars stood people – some in pairs, some in groups of five – all of them talking and looking up the road.

He got out, approached the driver of the Tavria directly ahead of him and asked, "What is this – the queue to leave?"

The driver, who was smoking beside his car, turned round. "Yes, this one's for leaving – and then there's another, to enter."

The man explained to Sergeyich how it all worked – how they

would examine his papers, the customs check, and so on. He also told him about the preferential queue.

"Do they let category II disabled people in that one?" Sergeyich asked, his eyes lighting up.

"Probably." The man sighed thoughtfully. "They let all kinds of disabled people in. Give it a try."

Sergeyich returned to his Lada, drove around the main queue, and after about three hundred metres ran up against another, shorter one.

"What sort of goods you carrying?" asked the Dee-pee-aria's customs inspectors – two moon-faced guys, red-eyed either from vodka or from lack of sleep.

"No goods. I've got bees."

"And there's nothing in those hives aside from bees, eh?" one of the guys asked with a sly squint.

"You can go have a look."

"That we will," the squinter replied firmly, and they all walked back to the trailer.

"So should I take off the straps?" Sergeyich asked somewhat irritably, due to his tiredness. "Or will you just put your ear to them?"

And one of the guys did put his ear to a hive.

"Hey, those little bastards are really buzzin'," he said, looking back at his partner.

"Go ahead and put your ear to each one of 'em. There might be bees in the first three, contraband in the rest."

The guy went around to all six hives, listening to each of them.

After that, the inspectors left Sergeyich alone.

It took about ten minutes to get through passport control. The camouflaged man sitting behind a kiosk window took his passport and began to copy something from it into a computer. Then he stepped away, still holding the passport, and Sergeyich had to wait nervously for several minutes. He was anxious for nothing, however – his passport was returned, and one couldn't say that this was done in an especially hostile manner, or an especially friendly one either. A camouflaged hand simply lowered Sergeyich's passport onto the kiosk's windowsill. And now the officer wasn't looking at the beekeeper, but at those behind him in the queue.

When the Ukrainian soldiers at the zero checkpoint saw the trailer of beehives, they exchanged glances.

"Why are you all suddenly bringing out your bees?" one of them asked Sergeyich.

"All?" the beekeeper asked. "I'm travelling alone."

"You're the fifth one with bees just today," the soldier said. "Only the others had more hives."

"Well, maybe they're fitter than I am – I'm disabled, you know. Category II," Sergeyich said. "I've got silicosis, miner's cough." And he strained himself, forcing out a cough, which didn't sound very convincing and embarrassed even him.

"Don't worry, I know what silicosis is – I'm from Kayutyne. Show me your pass."

The word "pass" passed right by Sergeyich's ears because he had instantly remembered driving through Kayutyne. He had liked the name, and had seen a slag heap somewhere near there, and a mine-shaft tower.

"Pass!" the soldier repeated.

Now the beekeeper heard the soldier and he grew nervous. He broke out coughing in earnest, and this time his silicosis spoke at full volume, as if it wanted to prove its own existence to Sergeyich himself.

"But I don't live there," Sergeyich got out after the coughing fit subsided. "I'm from the grey zone. Little Starhorodivka, near Karuselino."

The soldier looked doubtfully at the beekeeper, then shifted his gaze to his partner and handed him the passport. The other man flipped through the document, found the stamp with the residence permit, and raised a walkie-talkie to his mouth.

"Vanya, check whether Little Starhorodivka is in the D.P.R.," he said into the little black device, which looked a bit like a box of soap, then immediately fixed his eyes on the beekeeper. "So why are you entering through the O.R.D.L.O.?"[9]

"That's what your Petro told me to do – said it was safer."

"Yeah, it's safer," the first soldier grunted.

"And who's 'our Petro'?" the second suddenly enquired.

"He's from your army, Ukrainian. Comes across the field to visit me."

"What's his surname?"

"Don't know . . . But he's from Khmelnytskyi."

"And he comes to visit you in the grey zone all by himself?"

"Yeah, just him. He also took my mobile and charged it, and he left me his number."

The stern soldier demanded to see Sergeyich's mobile and stepped away, taking the beekeeper's passport too. The other soldier commanded him to pull off onto a concrete-blocked shoulder, to make room for the next car.

Sergeyich's mood plummeted to his feet, while darkness spread through his head – and only at that moment did he realise that evening had set in, deep evening. The small windows of the strange military van shone with a yellowish light. The site of the checkpoint itself was lit by the headlights of all the queuing cars, which were innumerable: their luminous snake-chain ran off into the distance – the distance from which he himself had come.

Sergeyich went over to his bees and put his ear to the nearest hive. Their buzz sounded tired, despairing. He looked nervously in the direction the soldier had gone and saw him walking back towards him with tired, infirm steps. He handed back his passport and mobile.

"Drive," he said. "And show this piece of paper at the next checkpoint."

Sergeyich put his passport and mobile into his jacket pocket, along with the piece of paper, which he folded four times so that it wouldn't get crumpled or frayed.

"Thank you," he said, glancing round in search of the second soldier, so as to say goodbye to him as well.

But he couldn't find him.

Cars were parked along the side of the oncoming lane, their headlights off. People were wandering beside them, talking quietly, some were on their mobiles; while he, Sergeyich, drove cautiously in his lane, without accelerating, leaving behind all these wanderers whom the war had placed in a new queue. About ten minutes later, he passed the last car and in front of him lay an empty road, illuminated only by the low beams of his Lada. Nobody was driving towards him, and no headlights showed in his rear-view mirror either. Sergeyich switched on his high beams and felt a strange, almost joyful excitement. It was as if he were very young and had burst into the open, into freedom, into life, the borders and dangers of which he did not yet know.

Though he understood that this youthful, almost joyful excitement was false and unjustified, he nevertheless drew reassurance from it, the belief that everything would be fine. Both Dee-pee-aria and the Ukrainian army were now behind him, as was the roar of distant and nearby bombardment. He left behind him a war in which he had taken no part, in which he had simply happened to have found himself dwelling. Yes, he had been a resident of war – an unenviable fate, but one far more bearable for people than for bees. If it weren't for the bees, he wouldn't have gone anywhere; he would have taken pity on Pashka and not left him all alone. But bees don't understand what war is. Bees can't switch from peace to war and back again, as people do. They must be allowed to perform their main task – the only task in their power – to which they were appointed by nature and by God: collecting and spreading pollen. That's why he had to go, to drive them out to where it was quiet, where the air was gradually filling with the sweetness of blossoming herbs, where the choir of these herbs would soon be supported by the choir of flowering cherry, apple, apricot and acacia trees.

At the next checkpoint he was held up for three minutes, no longer. All they did was look at his passport and the piece of paper he had been issued with. Then he stopped twice more, in response to warning signs of increased road control. There too everything went smoothly. And two hours later his headlights picked out a large sign on the side of the road: you are now entering the Zaporizhia region. There was nothing particularly cheerful in these words – they didn't promise to fulfil some secret childhood dream or anything – but as soon as this sign was behind him, tears welled up in Sergeyich's eyes, as if a great weight had fallen from his shoulders. He glanced down at the speedometer and pressed the brake pedal again. "Don't rush," he told himself and stared with tired eyes at the deserted road, which was well lit by his high beams, and bordered on both sides by apricot trees – the usual companions of southern Ukrainian drivers, beside which, in two or three months, anyone who wasn't too lazy or had no other gifts for their kids would stop on their way home. They would stop and pick up ripe orange apricots from the grass – three in a bag or a cardboard box, and one in the mouth.

# 33

The warm, bright morning sun filled the inside of the Lada, in which Sergeyich had fallen asleep the previous night, sitting behind the wheel, after pulling off to the side of the road. If it weren't for the sun, he would be sleeping still, despite the uncomfortable position (he hadn't reclined the seat all the way back).

A lorry rumbled past, followed by a bus. They finished the job of waking the beekeeper.

He got out and looked round: the road and the fields, nothing more.

He poured a can of petrol into the tank, massaged his sleep-stiffened lower back with strong fingers, glanced back at the trailer, and immediately got back behind the wheel. His conscience propelled him further down the road.

A half hour later, a road sign offered a choice: Melitopol to the left, Vesele up ahead. He preferred Vesele, and not only because of the meaning of its name – "joyful". The lorries and vans in front of him were already blinking their indicators, signalling their intent to go to Melitopol. Since these were all bound for Melitopol, he was definitely going straight on. After the fork in the road, he spotted a cart drawn by a grey horse in the opposite lane. An ordinary-looking fellow was driving it, and behind him stood three big milk cans. Sergeyich smiled. He realised that he had chosen the right path.

He began to look at his surroundings more closely. The roofs of rural houses flickered first here, then there, beyond the fields. To the left, far away, flashed the dome of a church. Here it was: life in all its beauty, in its regularity and stability, in all its unhurried calm . . .

To the right, on the horizon, a little forest peeked out. And here was an exit onto a dirt road.

Sergeyich turned off and the car began to tremble, demanding that he slow down. The track was dry and hard, and every little bump made the Lada jump.

When Sergeyich reached the forest, he saw that it was well cared for, and catered for picnics. There was a crudely constructed wooden table with two benches dug into the ground, a rubbish pit, and a huge fire pit. The trees here were pines and birches, and beyond them he could make out a few tall oaks.

He liked the place. He drove a bit further, leaving the picnic table behind, and parked beneath the nearest oak. Then he hurried back to the trailer and put an ear to one of the hives.

"Hold on just a little while longer," he whispered.

Sergeyich removed the straps from the hives and pulled off the tarpaulin. Then he edged a hive that stood in one corner away from its neighbour, so that he could grab it on both sides. He filled his chest with air, hoisted the hive up from the trailer bed, and froze for a few moments – long enough for him to realise that he wouldn't be able to transfer this hive anywhere. The strength was gone from his hands, his collarbone ached, and his shoulders hurt. He lowered the hive back into place, but gently, without dropping it.

No problem, he thought. Just need a little rest. Second time lucky. Sergeyich strolled through the forest, his gaze picking out dry pine and birch branches that would be suitable for a fire. He decided he might as well get the iron tripod, with its hook for the kettle, out of the Lada's boot – and the camping kettle itself, while he was at it – but his thoughts drifted back to the bees. He had to get the hives off the trailer first. But he couldn't do it alone.

He needed help.

He unhooked the trailer, pulled an empty twenty-litre plastic water canister from the boot and put it in the back seat, then got behind the wheel and drove back the way he had come for a couple of kilometres, until the domes of the church he had seen earlier flashed in the distance. He quickly found the road leading to the church, and it turned out to be tarmac, not dirt. Sergeyich took it.

It led him to a village, as he had anticipated, only it entered this village from the wrong end, as it were; the first thing a visitor encountered was the cemetery, then the church, and only then did one begin to see the houses with their orchards and gardens.

The sight of a dozen or so fresh graves covered with wreaths and flowers suggested that either the village was a large one or its residents died with unusual frequency.

A few minutes later the road ran into a small, roundish square. A solid one-storey building made of white brick appeared before Sergeyich's eyes. It had a sign, which read Nadya's. To the right of this little shop, on a bus stop's awning-covered bench, sat two men. And further to the right was a little lane, but its surface resembled Rossiyskiy cheese – all covered in small dips and holes.

Sergeyich parked between the bus stop and the shop, locked the car, and approached the men.

"Greetings!" He saw that each of them was holding an open bottle of beer.

"Greetings," one of them answered.

"Listen, I need a hand. Have to get some beehives off a trailer," he explained. "It's not far – just down the highway. I can pay you in honey."

The one who had responded with a greeting now shook his head.

"We won't do it," he said.

"You waiting for the bus?" Sergeyich enquired, just to keep the conversation going. He hoped that a chat might warm them up.

"Nope. Waiting for a friend. The bus from the district centre won't come till the evening."

"I'd drive you there and back – and give you a kilo of honey each."

The second, thus far silent one wearily lifted his indifferent gaze towards Sergeyich. Then he brought the bottle of beer to his mouth and took a couple of sips, keeping his eyes fixed on the stranger.

"Visiting your family?" the first man asked, casting a glance at the Lada's licence plate.

"No."

"Refugee, then?" the first continued his interrogation.

"What refugee? I came from the grey zone, to give my bees a break from the shelling."

"We had three refugees around here." The second man had suddenly come to. His voice turned out to be reedy, like a schoolboy's. It didn't at all go with his face, which had been tempered by the wind and the sun and eroded by rural life. "And we put up with 'em, till they started stealin'. Then the cops nabbed 'em and took 'em off somewhere."

"I tell you, I'm no refugee. I won't be here long," said Sergeyich, growing uneasy.

Why should I justify myself? he thought. And switching to a dry, businesslike tone, he asked, "What about water? Is there a standpipe?"

"Nope," the talkative one replied. "Go and ask at the shop."

He gave the men a silent nod, got the plastic canister from the car, and entered the shop – a regular village shop· bread, groceries, a glass fronted refrigerator with butter, cheese and sausage on the shelves. Behind the counter stood a round-faced woman in a headscarf. She gazed at her new customer evenly, without enquiry.

"Are you . . . Nadya?" Sergeyich asked awkwardly.

"Nadya died. Shop belongs to her husband now. I just work here."

"Oh, I'm sorry." Sergeyich sighed heavily. "Listen, can I fill up on water?" He raised his canister, to indicate what he meant.

"You can fill up, but you can also buy," the woman told him good-naturedly.

Then she took the canister and disappeared into the back room. The beekeeper calmly examined the goods in the counter, behind the glass, then looked at the shelves lined with canned fish and meat.

He searched for honey among the goods, out of habit. The prices on jars of honey usually boosted his self-confidence. Unlike ordinary

147

customers, he liked it when the price of honey in the shops increased markedly. But he didn't see any honey here.

The saleswoman returned from the back room, walked around the counter, and put the canister of water on the floor in front of him.

"You can drink it right away." She nodded towards the canister. "Our water's artesian. From a well."

"Thank you," Sergeyich said. "The men around here are very strange," he blurted out, turning towards the front door for a moment. "I asked them for help, but they turned me down. They're just sitting there, drinking beer."

"The ones at the bus stop?" the saleswoman asked him. He nodded.

"You found a fine pair to ask for help." She chuckled without malice. "All those two ever want is a bottle of vodka in the evening and a couple of beers in the morning."

"Maybe you know someone else who might lend me a hand? Someone who lives nearby?"

"What sort of help do you need, exactly?"

"I've brought my beehives here. Found a place about six kilometres down the road, by the forest. But I can't get the hives down from the trailer by myself. I could manage it with one other person. And I'd pay in honey."

"We haven't got any honey," the saleswoman said thoughtfully, casting an eye over the shop's holdings. "We've got a beekeeper, but he takes his honey all the way to Odessa. Says they pay more over there. Listen, if I help you myself, how much honey will you give me?"

This turn in the conversation was not what Sergeyich had expected. He began to move his dry lips, as if he were calculating some amount in his mind.

"I'll give you three kilos!" he exclaimed. "And I'll drive you there and back. I can wait till the shop closes."

"Why wait?" The woman shrugged and fixed her colourful headscarf, which was tied at the back so as to hide her light-brown hair. "Better go now, before the bus arrives. Won't have any customers before then."

They drove in silence. And it felt somewhat strange for Sergeyich to have a woman sitting beside him in the passenger seat – pleasant, round-faced, with eyes that were either grey or grey-blue. She wore a jacket that reached down to her knees, like a coat. And she had retied her headscarf in a different fashion before getting into the car, so that she no longer looked like a saleswoman.

"What's your name?" Sergeyich asked hesitantly.

"Galya."

"I'm Sergey. We'll take care of this quickly – one, two, and we're on our way back."

When they heaved the first hive off the trailer together, Sergeyich was stunned by her physical strength. The thing felt as light a feather, and this meant that Galya had taken most of its weight, and that of its inhabitants, herself. They carried the hive to the spot Sergeyich had marked out. The rest of the hives were just as easy to move. They arranged them like checkers on a board: three closer to the forest, spaced about two metres apart, and the other three a couple of metres in front of the gaps between them, so that all bees would have roughly the same view all around.

Sergeyich got two one-litre jars of honey from the Lada's boot.

"That's exactly three kilos," he nodded at the jars. Then he squinted thoughtfully. "Maybe you'll take some to sell?" he asked. "I've got more."

"Well," Galya said noncommittally, before falling silent for a few moments. "Why don't I pay you for the honey in groceries. You've got to feed yourself somehow, haven't you?"

Sergeyich nodded. "What price will you set for the honey?"

"Will seventy hryvnias per kilo do?"

"Certainly," Sergeyich agreed. "And how much will you take?"

"Well, to begin with, ten kilos – we'll see how it goes."

Having returned a second time from the village in whose centre stood "Nadya's" shop, and having eaten his fill of bread and sausage and drunk his fill of artesian water, Sergeyich reflected on his day – which was now in its last hours – with a sense of peace and warmth. The exchange of honey for groceries was a pleasing one. He hadn't been able to choose enough food to balance out the price of the honey, so Galya told him that he now had a line of credit at the shop, like in a bank. That was as good as money! Five hundred and sixty hryvnias, to be exact – and he could redeem them in groceries any day he chose. Credit like that was like the key to the refrigerator. The unusual – or rather, forgotten – sensation of stability swept over him and drove away the fatigue that had settled onto his shoulders especially heavily several times that evening. He relaxed, still hearing the echo of the bees' buzzing in his head. For no less than half an hour he had sat on the grass beside the hives, glancing first at one entrance, then at another, watching the bees emerge, look around, perform brief flyovers, explore their new surroundings and reassure themselves after their long, painful journey. Their buzzing seemed to have changed that day, to have grown a little quieter, just like a human heart, which pounds like a madman after a run, but then, when the runner stops and crouches down, gradually returns to its normal, infrequent rhythm.

Darkness fell from the sky onto Sergeyich, the hives, and the forest – thick, slightly damp darkness. The beekeeper started a fire beneath the iron tripod and hung his kettle, full of artesian water, on the little hook. He had decided to drink some tea before going to sleep.

And he had also decided to spend the first night in the car. True, there was a tent in the boot, but it lay under a pile of other things. He would put it up tomorrow morning. This night he'd spend as if he were still on the road. His driver's seat reclined as far as he could, right onto the back seat. He'd fall asleep in no time – how could he not, with such fatigue on his shoulders?

# 34

The buzzing of bees, sweet to the ears, filled the air around Sergeyich.

Beneath the sun's rays, the beekeeper dreamed that he was lying on a straw-filled mattress on top of the hives in his orchard. He dreamed he was sleeping and gathering such energy and strength from the bees that he could build a house single-handed or dig a pond with a shovel. He dreamed he was sleeping sweetly and alertly, inextricably bound to his honey-bearing wards.

But when something tickled his nose, instead of bringing his hand to his face, he opened his eyes. The thin shell of his sleep, weakened by the sun's rays, cracked too easily, releasing him into the new day like a chick from an egg. And what he saw on his nose was a bee, tired and motionless. He looked closer and realised it wasn't a worker bee but a drone. Drones have huge eyes and better vision than ordinary bees, but they only see what they need to see. Sergeyich waved the drone off his nose and it fell on the grass.

He looked from side to side, struggling to piece yesterday evening and this morning together in his mind. They didn't fit very well. When he sat up on the ground, he realised that he had awakened in a sleeping bag beside the hives. And then, if only foggily, he remembered how he had got out of the car in the night, rubbing his aching lower back, and had taken the sleeping bag out of the boot. He also remembered that this had required pulling out the tent, since the bag had been packed underneath it.

Sergeyich got out of the bag, bunched it up, and left it on the grass. Then he set up the tent midway between the hives and the trailer. He rolled up the sleeping bag and put it inside the tent, along with an icon of Saint Nicholas the Wonderworker, which he had retrieved from the Lada's glove compartment. He designated a place for the divine piece of painted cardboard in the far left corner of the tent, placing a jar with a candle in front of it. After that, he put fresh wood on the ashes of his fire and filled the kettle. Sergeyich took his time over breakfast, savouring his food amid the silvery music of his bees. He cut some of the bread and sausage he had received from Galya in exchange for honey into rough pieces, so they would give him the satisfaction of resisting his teeth. And he chewed the thick, soft sandwich with unusual ease, chewed it and thought that he had now begun a new life: a peaceful, springtime life, beneath the sun and the trees, not far from harmless, sometimes even friendly, people, and very close to his bees, which were hard at work even now, while he was chewing. They worked for him, and they asked for virtually nothing in return – just love and care. And he had given them plenty of love, plenty of his knowledge and experience, and, of course, plenty of care. In fact, he had probably cared more than most beekeepers. After all, he had worried about his bees all winter, protecting them from the war, from the noise of explosions, from the cold. He had protected them both in his thoughts and in reality, over which, in the end, he had precious little control.

After breakfast he lifted everything out of the boot of his Lada, arranging it on the ground beneath the open, skyward-facing rear hatch. At a leisurely pace, he began to sort through his belongings. He carried a bag of kitchen utensils to the tent, then arrayed his one-litre and half-litre jars of honey on the grass and counted them. It seemed he had brought a good amount of sweet currency with him – in terms of kilos. In terms of money, however, it didn't come to all that much. And even that was assuming he would be paid in money, not in sausages and bread. But then he decided that everything was fine – much better than it could have been – and that there was really no reason for concern. After all, spring was already in full swing, the sun was warming the earth, and so he wouldn't have to pay for heat. The bees, meanwhile, were scouting the area and establishing their routes; now they would have nothing to worry about, aside from flying to work.

A little later, Sergeyich found himself wanting to visit the village again. At first, he even composed a shopping list in his mind, consisting for the most part of various cereals – a kilo of each – so that he could make porridge. But then he began to suspect that he didn't so much want to get groceries as to see the woman in the shop. And to bolster his resistance to this desire, he calculated how much petrol the trip would cost him. The amount was paltry, of course, but you can't pay for petrol in honey. And even if they did take honey at some station or other, the petrol would seem very expensive indeed. Sergeyich decided against it.

He would postpone it until the next day, by which time he would have run out of cheese and sausage and be hungering for fresh bread.

Having calmed down, the beekeeper spread out the old bedspread he used to conceal things in his Lada from prying eyes, lay down on it, and dozed off.

In the evening, when the twilight had lowered the sky towards the ground, a noise other than the bees' buzzing entered Sergeyich's aural environment. It grew steadily louder, until it forced Sergeyich to rise to his feet. Beyond the trees, on the road along which he had come to this cosy nook, flashed the bright yolk of a motorcycle's headlight.

Sergeyich frowned. He went over to the fire, where his little trail axe lay on the grass. Who knew who might be riding around out there in the dark?

Meanwhile, the headlight had already traversed the dirt track towards the forest. It now shone directly at Sergeyich's hives, his tent, his entire "summer camp". And the rumble of the engine now overwhelmed the buzzing of the bees.

When the beam of the headlight reached Sergeyich, he quickly stepped out of its path. Then, suddenly, the headlight went dark, the engine went quiet, and out of the ensuing silence came Galya's voice.

"Seryozha! You there?"

"Uh, yes," he said, approaching her and awkwardly hiding the axe behind his back.

The fire was burning, and in its scattered light the beekeeper saw that Galya had lowered a bag to the ground, placing it by her feet.

"I thought I'd bring you some potatoes. You're probably down to bread and not much else."

"Thank you," Sergeyich said, voicing his shocked gratitude. "I hadn't expected this. Hadn't expected anyone . . ."

He moved the old bedspread closer to the fire. They sat down together. Galya pulled something wrapped in an old jacket from her bag, uncovered it and handed it to Sergeyich.

"There's a spoon in there and everything," she told him.

Sergeyich removed the lid from the aluminium pot, found the spoon, and began to scoop up the boiled, still hot, generously buttered potatoes. He ate greedily, thinking all the while of Galya's kindness, about her concern, which had made her bring him hot food after work.

"You live alone?" he said suddenly.

"Yes," she replied, not taking her eyes off the fire.

"No husband?"

"Had one. He died."

Good, Sergeyich thought but didn't say. Yet even the thought made him feel ashamed, and he squinted at the woman sitting next to him, as if to check whether she had heard it.

They said nothing for about three minutes.

"How are things at the shop?"

"The usual." She shrugged. "Not enough bread for everyone, but the sausage isn't moving like it used to – the price went up."

"And why isn't there enough bread?" Sergeyich said. "Does the army requisition it?"

"No, we just don't stock up on it – otherwise we'd have to throw out what we don't sell. I'd rather disappoint those who come late."

"That's right," the beekeeper agreed. "If you want bread, you have to get up and buy it in the morning."

"That's how it used to be . . . Well, the grannies still come in the morning. And they're the ones who buy up all the bread. They don't need sausage."

The next silence lasted longer, and Sergeyich had no wish to break it, because the crackly, unobtrusive music of the fire was now accompanied by a barely audible chorus of bee-wings emerging from the hives. And this music made Sergeyich feel so cosy that he did not dare draw his unexpected but caring guest's attention to it with his words, even with a whisper. But she herself seemed to be taking pleasure in the silence. And that meant she could hear the music, regardless of what she might be thinking about.

# 35

After three simple but warm scooter-delivered dinners – the last of which had especially touched the meat-starved Sergeyich, with its sumptuous steamed turkey cutlets – Galya said that she could not bring him the next meal she had planned. This wasn't because she lacked the wish to do so and it was tiring to ride her scooter down the road in the dark, but because it was impossible to deliver the planned dish in an acceptable condition. Sergeyich only realised what she meant when the sweet word "borscht" fluttered out of her mouth.

They were sitting on the bedspread in front of the fire, as usual. Galya was silent, and he was devouring his noodles and cutlets, when she suddenly broached the subject of the following evening. Her voice sounded so beautiful in the half-dark; it seemed as though it were separate from her, floating there all by itself, as in some fairy tale. And Sergeyich was listening to it as if it were music, until she uttered the word "borscht" and the music became speech.

"Don't worry about it," he said, thinking that Galya was making excuses for not coming tomorrow and feeding him.

"That's not what I mean," she said, softening her voice, as if at that moment her interlocutor had become a child whom one had to address more gently. "I was thinking you might want to come and visit me. The neighbours slaughtered a calf and I've bought a shoulder off them. I'm planning to cook it up properly, with beans, simmering it over a low heat – I'll run out of the shop to check on it every now and then . . ."

"Well, why not?" Sergeyich said plainly and happily, with a little sigh, and a smile lit up his face.

Galya waited until he finished his noodles and cutlets, then slowly got ready to go. The rumble of the scooter subsided in the distance. The fire was dying down and Sergeyich did nothing to keep it going. He climbed into his tent, got into his sleeping bag, and drifted off straightaway.

The next evening he arrived in the village earlier than they had agreed. He brought with him his powerless mobile and the charger.

The shop was open. A homely light shone from its two barred windows.

After parking his car in his usual spot, between the shop and the bus stop, he entered the establishment. Galya was serving two women. Both were wearing coats, one of which was short, while the other was longer.

"So which sausage would you like, Evreyskaya or Brusilovskaya?" Galya asked her customers.

"Whichever is fresher, as long as it isn't too fatty," one of them replied.

"Is it really 'anti-alcoholic'?" the second one asked about something that Sergeyich could neither see nor understand.

"Sure is. It's got young stinging nettle," Galya assured her.

"I'll take a jar."

"Do you need a bag?" asked Galya.

"Brought one."

The women stuffed their purchases into a homemade bag and left.

"You're early, you know," Galya remarked to Sergeyich.

"I had nothing to do. My bees are fine."

His gaze slid across the counter and stopped on the half-litre jars of honey that stood in even rows to Galya's right. The price tag pasted on one of the jars reported that it was ANTI-ALCOHOLIC HONEY. 76 HRYVNIAS. Sergeyich looked closely at the honey and saw green crumbs in it.

"What's this?" he said. "Someone else gave you honey to sell?"

"No, it's yours." Galya smiled. "All I did was prepare it for sale. Scalded some nettle leaves with boiling water and crumbled them in. You know, to make it more attractive ..."

"And why is it 'anti-alcoholic'?" the beekeeper asked, expressing his bewilderment.

"I told you: to make it more attractive. I bought a book recently – *How to Sell*. Learned a lot. Care to borrow it?"

"No." Sergeyich shook his head. "I don't like selling."

"Of course." Galya nodded understandingly. "But I've got no choice. Anyway, the book has all sorts of rules, and one of them is: 'Don't sell products simply as products – sell them as what people want to buy.' That means you've got to think up new properties for your product to increase the buyer's interest. For instance, people don't just buy sausage, they buy sausage that helps them lose weight. You get it?"

"I've never worked in trade," Sergeyich said, as a means of politely refusing to engage with the subject. Although a question immediately arose in his mind: wasn't the price on his honey a bit high? But, of course, when it came to prices, Galya knew better.

"Let me take you back to my place. You can sit there and get some rest until I finish up. I've got a TV," the saleswoman suggested.

They walked to her house, which wasn't far. She opened the door, switched on the light in the hallway, and hurried back to work. Left alone in someone else's house, Sergeyich froze for a moment, attuning his ear to the little noises, to the house itself. Then he took off his shoes and stepped into the living room. At first, once he had switched on the light, the large square room put him off, with its cleanliness and the artificially emphasised warmth of its decor. Dark red rugs hung on two of the walls, and another huge specimen lay on the floor; to the right, in the corner, a bulky television sat on a fragile-looking coffee table, whose little legs slanted outwards for added stability. The dining table was covered with a red tablecloth, and in the middle of it lay the remote control. The sideboard was almost identical to his own, and near it stood a wardrobe with a mirrored door. In other words, a familiar setting, only with more rugs.

Sergeyich sat at the table, put his hands on the tablecloth, and suddenly his nose caught the aroma of borscht. The scent led him to the kitchen.

On a gas stove – next to which stood the little red cylinder that fed it – a large enamelled pot was cooking borscht in its belly, over a small flame. Sergeyich lifted the lid and a surprising aroma hit his face, filled his nostrils, and stilled his thoughts.

He replaced the lid, stepped back from the stove and licked his dry lips. Then he returned to the living room, where he found an outlet and plugged in his charger and mobile.

After waiting a quarter of an hour, Sergeyich turned on the phone and checked his text messages. The latest was the single-word note from Petro: "Alive".

Hope he's alright, the beekeeper thought.

He clicked reply again, typed the word "Alive", adding a question mark, sent the message, and returned to the table.

About five minutes later, the mobile beeped, announcing the arrival of a response.

"Alive," Sergeyich read, and he nodded, relieved.

•

Galya's borscht slayed Sergeyich. There were dried porcini mushrooms swimming in it, and beans, and pieces of veal. He ate it steadily, unhurriedly, occasionally gazing up at her; this was, after all, the first time they had dined together – not like their evenings by the fire, when she had fed him without eating herself.

There was a bottle of shop-bought vodka on the table, to accompany the meal. Sergeyich and Galya drank without toasting, half a shot glass at a sip. Galya had also peeled several cloves of garlic, which lay on a saucer beside the bottle and a dish of salt. They ate these cloves in turn – first he would take one, dip it in the salt and place it in his mouth, then she.

No conversation arose; there was no need for talk. After the third bowl, Sergeyich realised he had had enough, although, at the same time, he felt he could have overcome a fourth bowl in order to please his hostess. He decided that if she offered another serving, he would not refuse. But Galya, having finished a second bowl herself, yawned and gave him a guilty look.

"I feel so tired, for some reason," she said. "Too much running around today . . ."

"Well, in that case I'll be going," Sergeyich said, preparing to get up from the table.

"But you can't drive now – you've had a few drinks . . ."

"Have you got traffic police in the village?" he asked, in a serious tone. Then he glanced at the bottle and saw it was empty. That meant they had drunk half a litre of vodka each.

"Not in the village, but they sometimes park themselves out by the highway. You had better stay."

He stayed. Galya turned off all the lights, and he found it so easy to undress and get into bed that he himself was surprised. He was even more surprised to sense the warmth of her body on his skin.

Don't suppose she lay down for nothing, he thought, turning to face her in bed.

Her hands gripped Sergeyich's shoulders and pulled him towards her, almost hoisting him onto her warm body. And he managed to follow her lead so obediently that he left all his thoughts behind, giving himself over to her desires, which he could read with surprising ease both through her movements and her touch.

And then the energy of love withdrew from them. It was over.

Now he just felt hot, and when Galya's palm pressed insistently against the left side of his torso, he toppled onto the sheet. He lay beside her, his right palm still resting gently on her stomach.

After waking in the dark a few hours later, Sergeyich anxiously, cautiously climbed out of bed and tiptoed out of the bedroom. He picked his mobile up from the floor and checked the time: half past four. Sergeyich thought of the bees he had left unattended – the bees, rather than the trailer or his other possessions, which would have been much easier to steal. It was the bees that worried Sergeyich, because without them, the meaning of his life, the sense in his departure from Little Starhorodivka would be lost. The meaning would evaporate, abandoning him to a meaningless state. It frightened him even to imagine such a state, the likes of which he had never found himself in before. He dressed in the living room – having brought his trousers, shirt, sweater and socks out of the bedroom – and put on his shoes in the hallway. Then he shoved his mobile and its charger into his jacket pocket and, his hand tightly squeezing the car keys, left the hospitable house, shutting the door carefully behind him.

# 36

The cold woke Sergeyich in his tent. His hand crawled down in search of the blanket, which must have fallen off his body, and stumbled upon his jacket pocket. It turned out he had fallen asleep in his clothes, and not inside his sleeping bag but on top of it. Before he even opened his eyes, his hand slipped into the pocket and stopped when its fingers embraced the warm mobile, as if they craved its warmth.

He got out of the tent and walked over to the car, to check the door. It was open; he closed it and only then turned towards the hives. It was at that moment that the sonic world arose around him, as if some- one up above had turned on his hearing, which had been switched off for the night. The world began to buzz, subtly and unobtrusively. And this buzzing coincided with the movement of the bees, who flew from the entrances easily, almost weightlessly. As usual, he trained his eyes on a single bee and followed it as it rose half a metre from the entrance, then flew in a straight line towards the field.

Sergeyich grew calm. He kindled the fire, then filled the kettle with water and hung it on the tripod's hook. His mind turned to Galya. He thought about the preceding evening, the aromatic borscht full of large beans, the veal bones with their tender meat, and the message from Petro that contained the most important of words: "Alive".

And then, cautiously – as if someone were liable to peep into his mind and spy on his thoughts – he remembered how he had undressed in Galya's room and lain down on the bed, remembered the heat of her body and the strength of her hands. Of course, he also remembered his flight. Although he at once crossed out the word "flight" – crossed it out, but did not replace it. He couldn't find another word. So he left it in the air, and turned his next thought in another direction, rejoicing that he could think as he wished, without giving in to inner prompts. He began to think that Galya might have taken offence: it wasn't very mature, was it? Leaving a woman's bed so quietly, without saying goodbye.

I have to apologise, he decided. I mean, why did I leave? Because I was worried about my bees. I haven't got a guard dog, haven't got anyone to look after my things and my hives . . . She'll understand.

And she really did understand. He arrived at twelve, bringing a jar of honey and three church candles as a gift (he had nothing else to give), and tried to explain himself, haltingly, right there in the shop, when it was just the two of them – but she stopped him with an understanding smile and reassured him.

"Go back to my place and have lunch. There's still some borscht left. I'll meet you there in a little while," she said, handing him the key. "Take this too. Cut yourself off a piece and put the rest in the fridge."

Sergeyich took the key and the stick of smoked sausage, and plodded off to Galya's house.

Along the way he bumped into a man with a familiar face and was at first taken aback by this sense of familiarity, but then his memory caught up with his eyes. It belonged to one of the two locals who had refused to help him.

Sergeyich nodded to the fellow as they passed one another, and the fellow nodded back without slowing his pace.

This time Galya's home seemed warmer to him. He took off his shoes and his jacket, and immediately went into the kitchen with the sausage. He opened the valve on the gas cylinder, lit one of the burners, got yesterday's pot of borscht from the refrigerator, and set it on the stove.

Galya arrived about ten minutes later.

They sat at the table to have lunch, as if he lived there. No vodka this time.

"Everything alright at the campsite?" she said in a businesslike manner.

Sergeyich nodded as he finished chewing a piece of meat. "Ran out of water. I should fill up a canister."

"Well, go ahead. Fill it up."

"Canister's in the car."

"So drive up to the gate. That way you won't have to carry it so far."

After lunch they had tea, and Sergeyich smeared a thick layer of butter on a piece of bread to go with it, as if he hadn't had enough food already.

"Where will you go from here?" Galya asked all of a sudden.

"When? In the autumn?" he asked her, then, without waiting for an answer, said, "Home."

"Home?" she said, sounding surprised. "What, you think the war will be over by then?"

"Doubt it," Sergeyich sighed. "But I've got to look after my land."

"Did you plant things?"

"No," he said, levelling a thoughtful gaze at her. "I don't plant anything in my garden anymore. Too afraid. There could be unexploded shells down there. You know how easily they sink into the earth? And it closes over them right away, so you can't even see where they went. Over in Svitle – that's a village not too far from ours – some poor old coot was pottering around in his garden and blew himself up. But they're stubborn, the folks in Svitle – they keep on planting things."

"Horrible, horrible . . . Why go back?"

"I don't know . . . That's where home is, and you've always got to come home . . . I'm like that. If I were different, I'd be living the good life in Vinnytsia."

"Vinnytsia?" she echoed tactfully. "But how would you get on there? That's no village."

"My ex-wife lives there. With my daughter. They left me, before the war. She was homesick too – couldn't get used to the village . . ."

"Has she married again?"

"Who knows?" Sergeyich shrugged. "Hasn't told me, if she has."

While Galya was washing the dishes, Sergeyich turned on the television and found the news.

"The queue for biometric passports forms at five in the morning," proclaimed the newsreader, and the screen showed a serpentine queue in front of a modern office building with large windows.

Sergeyich turned off the television, out of pity for the people standing in the queue.

"So, what's going on in the world?" Galya asked, peeking out of the kitchen.

"Nothing good," Sergeyich said. "Government's torturing people, just like before. Only now there's a war on too."

# 37

The onset of summer slowed the passage of time. There was more noise in nature now, the birds sang more loudly in the morning hours, yet the ringing of bee-wings was not lost amid it all. Sergeyich considered that ringing to be not only proof of the presence and health of his bees, but also proof of his own presence. He wasn't merely the owner of an apiary, after all – he was the representative of the legitimate interests of its bees. The bees, of course, had just one interest: gathering nectar and pollen. Sergeyich regarded the internal rules of their life (relations between the worker bees and the drones, all that petty, everyday nonsense) to be their personal business, the same as with people. It was no concern of his. The only thing that would concern him would be the unexpected death or loss of one of the queens, but, thank God, all was well on that score; the queens lived, reproduced and died as and when nature ordained, passing their batons to their replacements, who were born in the same hives. Sergeyich only kept watch over the health of the bees, driving out and exterminating wasps, who repeatedly tried to move into their hives; using a metal scraper to uncap the honeycombs, so that he could extract the honey and pour it into jars; collecting wax and bee pollen. It was by these means that his work and his life's meaning were bound into a single whole – and there was more meaning in it than work, since most of the latter was carried out by the bees themselves. They never asked his advice on what to do or how to do it. They didn't need his advice, or his permission.

Galya's commercial fabrication – the claim that his honey was "anti-alcoholic" – proved successful even in the neighbouring villages. Money began to accumulate in the glove compartment of his Lada (which played the role of a wallet and could be locked with a small key), allowing him to look to the future with greater confidence. Galya would ride her scooter to his campsite whenever she hadn't seen him for more than three days. But she did not come often, because he tried to pop into the village two or three times a week. He would fill up his water canister, have dinner at Galya's, and stock up on tea, sausage and cheese – no longer using the honey credit, which had long ago run out. After Galya sold the first batch, she began to pay for the supply in advance, using cash. But this did not change their relationship into a business arrangement; it remained warm and friendly. Galya herself felt out an acceptable distance with her mind, so as not to seem clingy, while getting everything she needed, emotionally and bodily, from the man she had chosen. The beekeeper put up no resistance. He would have accepted more, but the state of semi-independent equality that had been established between them was entirely to his satisfaction. He didn't live in two houses – that is, his tent and her house – but only in one, his own. The land beneath and around his hives also seemed to be his own, temporarily, and it would have been inappropriate for him to stray too far or for too long. And there was no doubt that Galya understood this. She understood it, but still, from time to time, accidentally said things that made her secret wish clear. That wish was for Sergeyich to bring his bees and come and live with her: he would move into her house, the bees into her orchard.

When the bees began to seal their combs with wax, Sergeyich began to worry: he hadn't brought his honey extractor. He asked Galya to introduce him to the local beekeeper, the one who sold his honey in Odessa. Turned out to be a decent fellow. A couple of days later he brought his extractor to Sergeyich's campsite on a flatbed trailer, peered into the hives with interest, and helped to extract the honey – almost a hundred kilos, all told. Sergeyich paid him in cash, since it would have been silly to offer a brother-in-bees honey. But the fellow took only fifty hryvnias of the proffered sum – "For petrol," he said. And at parting he gave Sergeyich a manly handshake and looked him in the eyes with warm sympathy, though he hadn't asked the newcomer a single question about his life. So Galya must have told him the basics.

In the evening, left one-on-one with his new honey and his old bees, Sergeyich sat down on his bedspread by the fire. He had taken a bottle of honey vodka from the boot, along with a plastic cup and his mobile. It was already getting dark, which made the fire seem brighter. He poured himself half a glass and dialled Pashka's number. For some reason, he was sure that he would never be able to get through to their village from here, outside the "zone". But after three beeps, something clicked.

"That you?" Pashka's hoarse voice asked, surprised.

"Yes, it's me. Where are you? Home?"

"Yes, home – watching TV."

"You mean they turned on the power?" Sergeyich exclaimed.

"Naah, I'm just pulling your leg – there's no power," Pashka hastened to reassure him. "Nothing's changed. Only more shelling."

"What're they shelling?"

"Take a guess. Each other. At night. Sometimes that stuff flies so low you can see it . . . scary . . . and then, on the other side – bang!"

"I see," Sergeyich sighed. "You been to my house lately?"

"Why should I, when you ain't there?"

"Well, to see if everything is alright," Sergeyich suggested, sensing irritation creeping up on him.

"Eh, don't worry," Pashka responded. "I stopped by a week ago. Everything's alright, nothing's broken – just smells of mice. No cats in the village now."

"You might air it out a little."

"You either gotta do that really late or really early, when the air's fresh. Most of the day, it's stuffy as hell around here. I'll air it out next time, no problem. I keep thinking of going down to the quarry, out past Svitle, to take a swim."

"You crazy or something?" Sergeyich exclaimed. "They'll kill you for sure! Look out for yourself, will ya? I've got some ginger vodka at the bottom of my sideboard, behind the documents. Take it – it's all yours."

"Thanks for that," Pashka said. "I've run out of everything. And the guys in Karuselino have a new commander. Tough as nails, from Kuban. So they don't come around no more, and I'm afraid to go there myself . . . When you getting back?"

"I've got it good here," Sergeyich said, and he immediately felt guilty. "Bees are comfortable. Honey's easy to sell. I think I'll stay for a while. But when I do come home, I'll make sure to bring you something."

"OK, but don't stay away too long, you hear?" Pashka pleaded. The call saddened Sergeyich. He had expected more, it seemed – either more news, or more joy from Pashka at the fact that he had thought to call. But he'd received no news, heard no joy. A useless conversation. Pashka was probably mad at him. He was having a hard time of it, all alone, with shells flying overhead and no-one to talk to.

I should call Vitalina, Sergeyich thought a minute later.

But the mobile was already in his pocket, and the beekeeper didn't want to take it out again.


# 38


In the morning, Sergeyich was awakened by the familiar rumble of the scooter.

He climbed out of the tent. There was, as usual, no sign of the sun in the sky, which was covered with clouds.

"I boiled a couple of eggs for you," Galya said, lowering a bag, the contents of which were clearly not limited to two eggs, onto the grass by the extinguished fire.

She pulled a box of matches from one of the pockets of her warm blue jacket (Sergeyich had never seen this jacket before), then gathered a bundle of thin branches and lit them skilfully, with a single match. Once the fire got going, she began to take packages out of the bag and lay them out onto a newspaper.

Infected by her vigour, Sergeyich set to work straightaway. He added water to the kettle, went over to the woods, and brought back thicker branches for the fire. Then he fetched the rolled-up bedspread from the tent and spread it out in its usual place.

The boiled eggs, still warm, reminded the beekeeper of his trip to Svitle, of how he had tramped along that frozen, snow-swept road to exchange honey for twenty of Nastasya's finest. But then Galya also laid out sausage sandwiches, sliced cheese, a plastic bowl of strawberries and two matchboxes: one filled with salt, the other with sugar.

They ate together, but Galya kept glancing at her little wristwatch.

"Are you in a hurry?" the beekeeper said.

"I've got goods coming in just after seven. Have to be back at the shop."

"What are they bringing?"

"Sausages and milk in the morning, canned fish and alcohol at lunchtime."

"And what about the honey – still selling?"

"Is it ever! I could take a couple of jars from you now to save a trip."

"Great." Sergeyich nodded. "And thanks, by the way, for introducing me to that other beekeeper. I was planning on driving over to his place to get the honey extractor, but he brought it out here himself – and helped me crank it too."

"Yes, he's alright," Galya agreed. "Only a touch greedy, but you won't get by these days without a little greed. – Why don't you ever call me?" she said suddenly.

"I just . . . I mean, I . . . I can't," Sergeyich admitted. "I'm really no good at talking on the phone. That's probably why I'm afraid to call. Can't even call my ex-wife. I tried, but it didn't work. Called my friend back at home, but it turned bad – a stupid conversation. If I actually had something important to say, then maybe . . ."

"Yeah," Galya agreed. "It's better to talk when you're with a person, anyway – when their voice isn't torn loose from their body, when you can see them."

Sergeyich noticed that the kettle was steaming and he rose to his feet. He looked up at the sky, as if he wanted to follow the steam's unfolding fate.

Actually, he was interested in the clouds. He gave a passing thought to the rain, which would fall, if not now, then certainly before lunchtime.

Soon Galya got ready to go. The beekeeper helped load a bag with two one-litre jars of honey onto her scooter's pannier, securing it with rubber straps. He also gave her his mobile and its charger, asking her to plug it in at the shop and promising to drive over before lunch.

The rain finally came at around eleven, but it turned out to be so light that even the fire paid it no heed, let alone the bees. The temperature, of course, did fall a bit, so Sergeyich dug a sweater out of his belongings, as well as an orange cap that bore the words F.C. SHAKHTAR DONETSK. He pulled the cap down to his ears; it was enough to protect him from the drizzle. Suddenly he wanted to look himself over in the mirror – but where could he find one? His eyes turned to the car. He got behind the wheel and adjusted the rear-view mirror so that he could look at himself. He looked, but he did not examine what he saw too closely – he seemed far too old. And his hair stuck out unkempt from under his cap, as if he were some kind of drifter . . .

The drumming of the drops on the windscreen grew louder. Sergeyich started the engine, switched on the wipers, and drove to the shop to the sound of their squeaky music.

Galya gave him a piece of fresh brawn, plenty of sweet tea and money for his two kilos of honey.

"Have you got a barber in the village?" he said, stuffing his charged mobile into his pocket.

"No, we don't. There are a few in the district centre, up in Vesele. Just off the highway, to the right, look out for a bunch of five-storey buildings. About a fifteen-minute drive."

"And what if I need a wash?" Sergeyich's voice sounded sadder and more pleading. "Maybe they've got a bathhouse in Vesele too?"

"Who needs a bathhouse?" Galya said, giving him a condescending look. "I've got a water heater – you can take a warm shower at my place."

The invitation to shower perked Sergeyich up. He began to bustle about.

"Great, great – I'll drive over and get a haircut now, then come back and shower!"

"Alright, go on then," Galya smiled. "What is it, your birthday or something?"

Sergeyich shook his head.

About twenty minutes later he saw a sign on the side of the road that read Vesele and featured a coat of arms with two bulls' heads. Up ahead were several five-storey buildings. The first on the right was not on the main road, but on a parallel street. He found a hair salon without difficulty. There were no customers inside, and a slender young woman in a blue robe who was sitting at a manicure table tore her gaze away from her tablet when she heard the door open.

"Maybe you'd like a shampoo as well?" she suggested, when he was already in the barber's chair.

"No need," Sergeyich answered.

"And what style would you like?"

"Short, so I don't have to brush it."

The girl chose a nozzle for the electric trimmer, and about eight minutes later Sergeyich was admiring his updated image in the large mirror opposite his chair. Almost everything in this image suited him, except for the uneven stubble on his cheeks and chin.

"A shave, perhaps?" the young hairdresser guessed. Her customer nodded.

Sergeyich stepped out onto the street feeling refreshed and rejuvenated. His cheeks ached pleasantly from the sting of the cologne, as did the nape of his neck, which the young woman had also scraped with a razor and sprayed with the contents of a green bottle. He was even a little embarrassed by the fact that all this – the haircut and the shave – had only cost him thirty hryvnias.

He got back in his car, started the engine, and caught himself thinking that it was wrong to come all the way to the district centre and see only the outskirts. He decided to drive around a bit, acquaint himself with the town.

The beekeeper returned to the main road and drove past a wooden church with gilded domes. He also passed a bank. A supermarket with the funny name Vakula flashed by. Soon he reached the opposite end of town and turned back.

Less than an hour had gone by before he was sitting at Galya's table, clean from head to toe. A key to the house lay on the tablecloth – a key that Galya had once again entrusted to him without qualms, as if he were her husband. She had handed it to him, asking him to wait at her place until she returned from work and promising to whip up a quick dinner. Galya's hands really were quick, which is why she was the hostess she was. Everything she made was delicious and quick – everything except the borscht, to which she devoted as much time as necessary, because you can't cook good borscht in a hurry.

It happened every time: when he was in her house, he couldn't help thinking about her. And there was always plenty to think about. She offered simple, understandable reasons for reflection. Women always offer more food for thought than men.

Yes, she's a good woman, Sergeyich thought. Cooks well. And it isn't fair that she has to live here alone. A pointless life, without a man . . . But she's awfully plain. Even her name is plain – Galya. Life with her would probably be too plain for my taste.

All on their own, these thoughts called up another face from Sergeyich's memory: that of his ex-wife, Vitalina. He remembered her outfits, her strange Vinnytsian complaints about him, his native village, their life together. Suddenly, everything that had once irritated him in his ex-wife's behaviour came back to his mind like the antics of a child – antics that, years after they're played, prompt a parent's nostalgic smile.

Sergeyich sighed and exchanged his thoughts for the television. He found a detective series with no beginning and no end, and began to watch its heroes, who were shooting at and chasing after each other, as always. A smooth calmness filled his head. He waited amid the sound of shooting and screeching brakes, and eventually Galya appeared.

Neither before nor during dinner did Galya express the desire with which Sergeyich was now familiar. This surprised him somewhat. She liked his new haircut and stroked the little spikes with her palm, smiling, until he grew annoyed and stopped her. Then she pressed him about his trip to the district centre: What did he make of it? Did he see the monument to the horseshoe? Did he stop to look in any shops?

Sergeyich praised Vesele, so as to make her happy. And he added that "the people there are nice", having in mind not the population as a whole, but the friendly young hairdresser.

"Yeah, we're a nice bunch. Over there, and back here too. About thirty folks from the village go to work at the Prodmash machine factory in Vesele, maybe more – they're expanding."

She went on praising the district centre for a whole five minutes – without neglecting her village, either – and only fell silent when Sergeyich got up from the table, indicating that he was about to leave. At that moment, her face showed confusion. She must have been expecting him to stay until morning. Apparently, she had taken it for granted that any man who showered at a woman's house planned to spend the night there.

Instead, Sergeyich thanked her both for the hot water and for dinner, said goodbye warmly, almost like a member of the family, and, with the words "Till next time", walked out of the house.

Beyond the gate, by the fence, stood his green Lada. The night had nullified its colour. Now the car was simply dark, reflecting the light of the nearly full moon with an occasional dull gleam. From somewhere nearby, out in the street, came the sound of a loud conversation. Two men were arguing about football. Sergeyich caught the word "Dynamo" and his hand shot up to his hair, to check whether he was still wearing his orange Shakhtar cap. Even as he was groping for it, he was laughing

*171*

at himself, because he remembered perfectly well that he had tossed the cap into his tent before coming.

He was driving towards "Nadya's" when a figure with a raised hand appeared in the glow of his headlights. The beekeeper slammed on the brakes and the car seemed to stumble; his chest hit the steering wheel.

Sergeyich got out of the car, angry, ready to lay into the idiot who'd tried to throw himself under his wheels.

The man who'd spoiled his mood was shorter than him, and had difficulty standing upright.

"Gimme a ride to Vesele, bruvver," he said.

"I can take you as far as the highway," Sergeyich said, his anger giving way to pity. There was no sense in staying angry at a drunk.

"No-one'll pick me up there . . ."

"If I drive you all the way, who will pay for the petrol?"

"For petrol?" the drunk repeated. "What, you out of money? Yer from Donetsk, ain't ya?" Sergeyich was stunned.

"Get in," he said, after thinking it over briefly. "I'll give you a ride." That last word sounded like a threat.

But the man didn't notice. He flopped down in the passenger seat.

"Who told you I'm from Donetsk?" the beekeeper said when they were out of the village, having left both the church and the cemetery behind.

"Fuck, everyone knows," his passenger shrugged. "You're a smooth one, aren't you? All slick. My pal Klim's been puttin' the moves on Galya for a year, now – nothin' doin'. But you show up and – bam – she's all yours! You don't got any women in Donetsk these days, do you?"

The passenger yawned.

"So what are you saying?" asked Sergeyich. "If I'm from there, that means I'm no good?"

"Who knows?" the passenger said, with a wave of his hand.

"Well, if I'm no good, how come I agreed to give you a ride to Vesele, even though I wasn't going there?"

"Listen, I didn't say you were no good – I just said you were from Donetsk . . ."

172

The passenger yawned, dropped his head onto his shoulder, and dozed off.

They drove onto the highway and turned towards Vesele. There were more cars now. The headlights of oncoming lorries dazzled the beekeeper's eyes. Just after crossing the city limit, having spotted the bright windows of the five-storey building where he had got his haircut, he stopped the car and nudged his passenger awake.

"We're here," he announced.

The passenger threw up his head, peered into the windscreen, and turned to him.

"Drive a little further, eh? Know where the supermarket is – Vakula?"

Sergeyich grinned. You couldn't make this up, he thought: first he came here in the morning, on Galya's advice, to get a haircut, and now he's back here in the evening, delivering a local drunk, like some taxi driver.

The beekeeper took his passenger to the supermarket. And the drunk surprised him when they parted, handing him ten hryvnias for the petrol.

"What's your name?" Sergeyich asked the man as he climbed out of his car.

"Alyosha," he said, turning to Sergeyich, who examined his face more closely. An ordinary face. He had obviously shaved that morning.

"Alyosha, I'm not from Donetsk. I'm from the grey zone. You understand? I worked in the mines my whole life – never killed anyone, never stole anything."

"What're you tellin' me for?" Alyosha shrugged. "I didn't say nothin' . . . It's them," he nodded over his shoulder, "that're doin' the talkin' . . . And on the TV, too . . ."

Sergeyich took his time driving back. He was thinking about Galya, her village and her fellow villagers, who, he now knew, had been discussing him.

The headlights of oncoming cars were blinding him again. He was afraid he might miss the turning onto the dirt road, so he leaned on the steering wheel, peering ahead.

# 39

Another summer week went by – a week full of humming bee-wings and sunshine, a week that included three meetings with Galya and her borscht, which was cooked over a low heat without regard to time and contained large white beans that first burst between the teeth, then melted away on the tongue. Their dinner that evening consisted of borscht alone, but, of course, she had served it properly, with black rye bread, vodka and garlic. It was Friday, and Sergeyich was beginning to feel so good in Galya's home that he got scared. He was afraid that, after two or three more dinners of this kind, he wouldn't want to return to his tent anymore, where, every night, through the thin shell of his sleeping bag and the rubberised canvas bottom, the earth kept jabbing him in the ribs with its firmness. He would settle in at Galya's silently, without asking the hostess for permission. After all, he already knew what she wanted. And her desire for him was perfectly legitimate. Such was the law of nature: all living things want to live in pairs. Except for bees and their ilk.

As they sat at the table, rain gurgled outside the windows. It was as if the raindrops were tapping anxiously against the glass on purpose, so as to spook Sergeyich into spending the night with Galya. And that's precisely what happened, all by itself. Nor did he suddenly wake up in the night as before, out of concern for the bees. The rain took care of that, too, for he knew it would keep them in their hives. Bees don't like rain, and so they sit at home getting cross. It's best for the beekeeper not to peek into the hives when it rains – they're liable to sting. And the reason they grow angry is that the rain prevents them from working.

Sergeyich didn't hurry back in the morning, either. After breakfast, Galya asked him to give her a hand in the cellar. A flight of concrete steps led Sergeyich about two metres down, into a large underground space, where a dim bulb lit up beneath the round arch of the ceiling.

At his hostess's request, he moved three empty barrels from one corner to another, and carried three wooden boxes (also empty) up into the yard. Then he went back down the steps, having realised that she didn't actually need his help. She could have done all this on her own without much effort. Did she simply want to show him her cellar? Must be . . .

His guess was further confirmed by what he saw when he came back down: in the dim light of the bulb, on an empty wooden shelf, stood a bottle and two glasses filled with a dark liquid.

"Cherry vodka," Galya announced sweetly. "Made it last year. Try it."

They emptied their glasses of sweet, weak liquor at one gulp. Then Galya embraced him, bringing her sweet, cherried lips up to his. The beekeeper didn't resist. He returned her embrace, pressed her close. For some reason he suddenly felt sorry for her, as if someone had hurt her needlessly.

"You're so calm," she whispered in his ear. Her breath was warm. "I'd be happy with you."

# 40

Early on a rainy morning, Sergeyich heard the familiar rumble. He stuck his head out of his tent, thinking that Galya had brought him breakfast. He also had time to think that, in such weather, they'd have to eat inside the tent, not by the fire.

Leaving her two-wheeled rumbler under a tree, Galya almost ran to the tent. As Sergeyich made room for her, he gazed at her hands, bewildered and perplexed. They held nothing – no bag, no package.

"We've got to be there at nine!" she blurted out in one breath.

"Vitya Samoylenko was killed in Donbas . . . have to go greet him."

"What do you mean, greet – if he was killed?" the confused bee-keeper asked.

"Haven't you seen it on TV? How the Western Ukrainians greet their dead? They all line up kneeling along the road. Are we any worse than they are?" Galya explained after catching her breath. "The whole village is coming!"

"Well, if it's the whole village . . ." Sergeyich responded meekly and nodded.

At about half past eight, after a short ride in the rain, Galya and her passenger reached the turn off the highway. They parked the scooter under an apricot tree and lingered there for a while, so as not to get soaked again. Dark, wind-fallen apricots lay on the wet grass at their feet. Sergeyich picked up a couple that were still intact, wiped one with his palm, and held it out to Galya. She deftly broke the overripe fruit in half and the pit jumped out all by itself.

"Sweet," Galya said, licking her lips, and gazed at Sergeyich warmly.

Several cars drove up from the village and pulled over to the side of the road. Sergeyich looked round and grew anxious: rows of people wearing dark jackets and capes and holding umbrellas were approaching both from the direction of the village and from that of the district centre – which wasn't very close, after all, if you weren't travelling by car. Then Sergeyich recalled that, further down the road, there were signs for other villages. Maybe these people weren't from Vesele.

He felt uneasy, cold. And this seemed to have nothing to do with the rain, which wasn't a cold one.

"What happens after?" he asked Galya.

"After what?"

"After we greet the man who was killed."

"We'll head to the cemetery. Funeral service, burial, wake, the usual."

Galya's words – not even the words themselves, but rather her kind, warm voice – reassured Sergeyich. But not for long. Three women in dark shawls ducked under the branches of their tree. One of them shot a hostile glance at Galya and Sergeyich.

The beekeeper averted his eyes but continued to sense the women's presence. The crowd of greeters grew by the minute. Most of them stood in groups of five or six, though some were alone, and all kept looking at the highway, in the direction from which Sergeyich had come not long ago, and from which the dead man would soon arrive.

"Maybe we can skip the wake?" whispered the beekeeper, turning to Galya.

"We'll just stop by – half an hour, at the most. They've covered the whole yard with a tarpaulin."

Sergeyich sighed. This was the first time he had felt so alienated, so out of place here. These people (there were hundreds of them now) all knew each other, and they knew the man who was returning to them for the last time, to be honoured with a ceremony and lowered into his native soil. While he, Sergeyich, had nothing to do with any of it. The beekeeper did not wish to violate their grief with his presence – after all, the death of a friend or acquaintance could give rise to a variety of emotions. It would have been better for him to stay in his tent, near his rain-angered bees. He had grown unaccustomed to mass gatherings. Three years in an abandoned village with Pashka had taught him that one could have few, very few people around, and nothing bad would come of it. On the contrary, such near-isolation could help one better understand oneself, one's own life. But now he was surrounded by hundreds of strangers, all of them interconnected by long cohabitation and companionship. And who was he to them? Of what use?

The people standing on either side of the road began to fold their umbrellas. Sergeyich's gaze was immediately drawn to them. A movement – or rather, an excitement – animated the faces of the dead man's greeters. The little groups split up, and those who had been hiding under the trees went out to the road. Galya tugged at the sleeve of Sergeyich's jacket.

"Let's go," she whispered.

Sergeyich looked towards the highway. Those standing just past the turning to the village were already getting down on their knees; this was happening gradually, not like in church, where everyone drops down at the priest's command, their knees hitting the wooden floor with a thud.

He and Galya stopped at the edge of the tarmac, on the road to the village, about fifty metres from the turning. Opposite them were a row of men and women with wet, gloomy faces. One of these men wore

177

a green hood detached from a jacket, instead of a cap. He was already kneeling, as were the women either side of him. Sergeyich froze. He was still standing, though Galya had already knelt on his left, and a boy of about fifteen had done so on his right, as had what must have been the boy's parents – also young.

"Come on," Galya urged him.

But the beekeeper turned in the direction from which the dead man was expected to come. A dark-green "pill" (an old minivan) was crawling down the road, followed by several khaki-coloured jeeps. Sergeyich stared at the pill, which slowed almost to a stop at the turn.

Galya's hand pulled nervously at Sergeyich's trouser leg. He bit his lip. Why should he kneel with them? In the dirt? A long time ago, when he was still a boy, he used to have to get down on his knees whenever his father punished him for fighting at school. And he had also knelt in church a few times. Only the weak go down on their knees. In church, everyone is weak before God – so that makes sense. But even there he didn't much like it.

"Seryozha!" Galya's tense, angry voice reached him from below. Sergeyich sighed again, heavily, and sank down to Galya's level.

At that point he realised that several pairs of eyes were looking at him. The cold, hostile gaze of the people on the opposite side of the road dug into him like pitchforks. The boy on the right was also looking asquint at him, grimly – but then the green minivan drove up and they all lowered their heads and fixed their eyes on the tarmac. Sergeyich bowed his head too, and immediately went limp; he felt as if all the strength had fled from his body, casting him down to the ground – as if the muscular hand of God had pushed him from behind and he had fallen, collapsed, become nobody, lost his name, his pride.

He remembered the words someone had written on the bus stop in Karuselino three years ago: "No-one can bring Donbas to its knees!"

Well, the fuckers finally did it, he said to himself, and immediately shook his head, frightened by this thought, which seemed so alien and dangerous to him.

What's wrong with me? These people are grieving, he thought, examining his reflection in a puddle. The image was cloudy, dark, gloomy – like this day itself, on which the sun refused to warm and illuminate the human world. Refused or failed.

The pill was moving away, towards the village. Everyone, including Sergeyich, was watching it go. They were in no hurry to rise from their knees. All down the road, along which Sergeyich's gaze was now travelling, men, women and children were kneeling, motionless, only lowering their heads as the minivan carrying the dead man approached.

Time froze. The rain, to which no-one had been paying any attention, had stopped, but the clouds did not disperse. Footsteps began to smack against the wet tarmac: some people were walking towards the turning to the village, others were rising to their feet, groaning, and shaking themselves off. The latter too began to follow the pill, or first retrieved the bicycles, scooters or mopeds they had left under the trees. Those who had come by car took their time; they were already inside their Ladas and Moskvitches, but had not yet driven them onto the road.

Sergeyich rose hastily and helped Galya to her feet. She shot Sergeyich a look full of compassion, but said nothing. They walked back to the scooter under the apricot tree. The expression on her face was gloomy. He found another overripe but intact apricot, picked it up, wiped it and offered it to Galya, but she shook her head. So he ate it himself, and his mouth was filled with the sweetish taste of fermentation.

"I'm not going," Sergeyich said firmly, after swallowing the last bit of fruit.

Galya nodded. About five minutes later, when the cars began to leave the roadside, she rode off on her scooter.

Sergeyich walked along the highway to Vesele. A bus drove past, followed by two lorries. The noise from the passing cars assaulted his ears, oppressing him. Only when he turned onto the track that led to his bees, to his little forest, did his surroundings grow quieter. It felt good to walk, all alone, down a dirt road that led nowhere but to the fields. This was his road – the road to his temporary shelter and to the shelter of his bees. There was no-one else here, and that was as it should be.

He pictured hundreds of people with wet, gloomy faces walking along the tarmac towards the cemetery and the church. He pictured Galya walking with them, her head lowered. And this pained him, as if each of the walkers was intentionally stepping on him as he lay on the tarmac, having been thrown under hundreds of feet for some unknown sin.

# 41

In the far left corner of the tent, in front of the cardboard Saint Nicholas the Wonderworker – which was the size of a postcard and usually rode with him in the Lada's glove compartment – the church candle burned in its jar. Large raindrops rattled against the soft tarpaulin roof. Sergeyich kept lifting his head and listening closely to the bad weather, but then his eyes would return to the cardboard Wonderworker, whose bearded face was enlivened by the playful flame's tongue.

Surrendering to sorrow, the beekeeper wandered in thought through the ruins of the church at the end of his native street, through the empty, lifeless houses of neighbours who had fled, around the big shell crater by the Mitkov place on Michurin Lane, which was the shortest route from Lenin to Shevchenko Street. It had always been the shortest route, even before the streets were renamed. Then the road to Karuselino and the parting with Pashka swam up in his memory. And Karuselino itself sailed past exactly as it had that day, when he had driven through it cautiously, fearfully, dragging his obedient trailer loaded with hives.

The candle burned uncertainly, dimly. The tarpaulin, wet with rain, breathed its damp breath at the flame, pushed away the light, kept it in the corner where Sergeyich had placed it. And only Nicholas the Wonderworker, it seemed, had reason to rejoice: thanks to the small flame, his face was more visible than that of the beekeeper.

Sergeyich tried to focus his sorrow on Samoylenko, the fallen soldier, about whom he knew nothing save for the fact that he had been killed in Donbas. He tried, but his thoughts kept jumping to the soldier Petro, who had come into his home with the gift of a grenade. They then jumped to the soldier with the earring, who had lain dead on the field half the winter, and whom neither one side nor the other wanted to retrieve and place in the ground, which would have been the decent thing to do. He also recalled the explosion that had torn apart the sniper from Omsk, who had built himself a battle nest on the edge of the Krupins' garden. The beekeeper shook his head and sighed. He took out two glasses and a bottle, then filled one glass to the brim and put it in front of the cardboard saint. He poured a little less into the second and drank it himself.

"May he rest in peace," he whispered.

And it seemed to Sergeyich that a peculiar echo picked up his words. His whisper seemed to be repeated – first behind him, then to the right. He looked round cautiously with eyes adjusted to the gloom, then turned back to the candle.

Its flame was down to the rim of the glass jar. In no time at all its yellowish trunk would slide down, come to rest against the wall beneath the rim, and burn out.

And then his thoughts jumped, unbidden, to the slain, unknown Samoylenko.

Sergeyich began to imagine him, but all that appeared in his mind's eye was a soldier in uniform, lying dead – no face, no sprawled-out arms. The soldier was lying on the black earth, which had just been freed of snow. And the beekeeper imagined he saw grass pushing through the earth, saw the earth's blackness disappearing. The grass rose and fluffed itself up, scattering its verdure and blotting out the blackness. The soldier, too, vanished, merging with the grass that grew over him, becoming invisible, indistinguishable.

Sergeyich unrolled his sleeping bag, just as the candle went out. He closed his eyes and recalled kneeling by the roadside – recalled the endless rows of people, himself, Galya.

What was all that for? he thought. It's not like he's some kind of hero, some cosmonaut . . .

A funeral from long ago surfaced in his memory, when the body of a fellow villager had been brought back from the war in Afghanistan. The whole village had shown up that day. There were long eulogies at the cemetery, lots of talking, but no-one had gone down on their knees. Everyone remained standing. The dead man's mother alone had tried to fall onto the fresh grave, to embrace it. But those around her had kept her upright. They held her back and led her away, and while she was surrounded by friends and relatives, the soldiers fired their automatic rifles into the sky and covered the grave with wreaths.

The Lord is with him, Sergeyich thought, both about the soldier from the Afghan War and the one from the war in Donetsk. They merged in his thoughts.

The beekeeper dozed off. A mine cage lowered him down into the mine of his dreams. And he saw himself in this cage, standing beside a group of regular miners – only he was wearing a black cassock, with a silver cross on his chest. There was a belt around his waist, from which hung a gas mask and a one-litre flask of water, both clipped on with carabiners. The cage crawled down for about ten minutes before it reached the mine's black bottom. The miners stepped out first, and the cassocked Sergeyich followed them. Suddenly he heard the manly voices of a church choir. They were praising God. The voices were loud, drawn-out – even rude, offended, angry – but they sang everything correctly, word for word.

Sergeyich listened.

The choir continued: "In Your mercy cut off my enemies, and destroy all those who afflict my soul; for I am Your servant."

Then incongruous voices reached Sergeyich through his dream, penetrating the ground – voices that didn't chime with the choir, screaming voices. Sergeyich looked round, and his eyes met the mine's uneven walls of black coal and the dark faces of the miners in the choir, each of whom wore a gleaming silver cross the size of a man's palm over his black clothes. No, all the miners were opening their mouths simultaneously, adding equally to the psalmody.

The voices that didn't belong to them were coming from an

*182*

invisible height – from the surface of the earth. The beekeeper glanced up and fixed his gaze on the mist, beyond which a searchlight seemed to shine through a cloud of dust.

"What the fuck's wrong with you?" the sharp male voice said, sounding even louder. "Come on out, you piece of shit!"

These words forced the beekeeper's eyes open, and he gazed out of his dream. His sense of the world slowly followed the direction of his gaze.

"Who's that?" he said hoarsely.

"Come on out and you'll see!" answered the voice.

Sergeyich rose up and glanced into the corner of the tent, where the cardboard icon stood invisible. He struck a match, got out a new candle, lit it, and placed it in the jar; now there were two of them in the tent – with illuminated faces.

In the darkness of the evening, someone grabbed his hand and, intent on speeding his emergence from the tent, yanked it. Sergeyich almost fell, but then managed to free his hand with a sharp movement. He staggered back, trying to understand who was in front of him, and how many of them there were. Two figures stood silhouetted against the dark-blue sky.

"What do you want?" the beekeeper asked in a cold voice, without a hint of fear.

"I'll show you," one of the figures responded in a drunken youthful voice and, staggering, tried to reach Sergeyich's face with his fist.

The fist might well have reached the beekeeper, but the second fellow, who seemed to be older, pulled his staggering companion back, trying to keep him from starting a fight.

"Why the hell are you out here? It's on account of you that Sashka was killed, you fucker!"

"Valik, calm down!" the second fellow demanded.

"And why should I, Mikhalych?" the younger one asked, turning to his elder. "Was it *you* who lay in them trenches, gettin' shelled? No, that was *me*! Did *you* get a concussion? No! You were too busy telling kids stories at school! Well, I *did* get a concussion, you fucker! And where was *he*? I'll *tell* ya where he was – on the other side of the front!" The young fellow almost choked on those final words.

Sergeyich's eyes had already got used to the dark. Now he could see his uninvited guests' faces.

"I was at home. Never fired a shot at anyone." Sergeyich squeezed out the words hoarsely. His nose picked up the scent of vodka.

"At home, eh?" the young one repeated, cocking his head again. "So why didn't ya stay at home, back in Donetsk? Why the hell did ya come out here?"

"I'm not from Donetsk," Sergeyich responded. "I'm from the grey zone."

The older one repeated the beekeeper's words. "You hear that? He's not from Donetsk!"

"Hell, the whole of Donbas is a grey zone!" the drunken Valik declared, turning to Mikhalych. "And why didn't he come to the funeral? Didn't have a drink at the wake?"

"I'm a stranger here," Sergeyich explained. "Didn't feel right . . . But I commemorated the fallen, paid my respects . . ."

"Where did you commemorate him?" the young fellow said, his lips twisting incredulously. Sergeyich noticed a long scar on the young fellow's right cheek, running from under his ear to the bridge of the nose.

"In there." Sergeyich nodded towards his tent. "I lit a candle too – did everything right."

And then the beekeeper noticed that the young fellow wasn't listening to him; he was staring at the axe lying by the fire pit. Only the older man was listening – the one the young fellow had called Mikhalych.

"Come on in and have a look," Sergeyich offered, then turned and climbed into the tent.

The sounds behind his back told him that his invitation had been accepted.

The beekeeper sat down on his sleeping bag and Mikhalych perched beside him. But the young fellow remained outside, beneath the night sky.

Mikhalych glanced at the candle, then at the icon. His eyes softened.

"He's not coming in?" Sergeyich said.

"He's probably having a smoke," Mikhalych said. "He used to be alright, you know. I taught him history."

"Should we commemorate the fallen?" the master of the tent proposed.

Mikhalych agreed. He was younger than the beekeeper by five, maybe seven, years. Sergeyich got out the bottle and a glass, which he filled and handed to the history teacher.

Mikhalych crossed himself, then drained the glass in one gulp and handed it back. Sergeyich poured himself a glassful, turned to the candle-lit cardboard Nicholas the Wonderworker, crossed himself, and drank it down.

A strained cry broke into the tent: "Fuckers!" The beekeeper shuddered and cast a questioning glance at Mikhalych.

The history teacher shook his head, sighed, then waved his right hand, as if to say, "Nothing we can do . . ."

And then they heard a loud bang – a bang and other strange noises. It sounded like someone striking thick cardboard with a stick, or perhaps striking something thicker, like sheet metal, with a crowbar.

Sergeyich leaped up, but the teacher, who had also risen to his feet, blocked the beekeeper's path.

"Don't! Stay here," he said. "Out of harm's way . . ."

"But what's he hitting out there?" Sergeyich said, and then, before the teacher could answer, realised that the "counterterrorist" was wrecking his car.[10]

Sergeyich tried to move the teacher aside, but he grabbed the beekeeper by the shoulders and pushed him back down onto the sleeping bag. It turned out that Mikhalych's hands were stronger.

"I'm begging you," the teacher said in a tense, nervous voice. "He's shell-shocked, totally nuts. You won't stop him now."

"And what if he goes after my bees?" Sergeyich cried out. "I'm just supposed to sit here? Hide? Not a chance – I'm not afraid of him!"

185

Sergeyich managed to push the teacher aside and almost made it out of the tent, but then Mikhalych continued the struggle, grabbed the beekeeper by his left hand, and pulled with all his might. Sergeyich crashed back down onto the sleeping bag, and the teacher immediately sat down beside him.

"Let's have a drink," he said firmly. "We'd better have a drink. Commemorate."

He reached out and, to the beekeeper's surprise, picked up the glass of honey vodka that had been placed beside the candle for the fallen soldier.

"Pour yourself a glass. I'll drink for him – to his memory. He was my student too, Sashka was . . ."

Breathing heavily, nervously glancing at the tarpaulin flaps, Sergeyich filled his glass and, as he was filling it, noticed that his hand was trembling.

The ruckus outside suddenly abated. The beekeeper, without bringing the glass to his lips, tried to get up again, but the teacher shook his head in the negative.

"Don't," he pleaded. Pleaded – not advised or ordered.

Sergeyich resigned himself, sighing, then took two small sips and one large gulp, which emptied the glass.

"Let's sit and wait a while," Mikhalych said. "I know what he's like. He's smoking now, calming down. Give it ten minutes or so. Then I'll go out there and take him home."

Sergeyich gazed into the teacher's eyes in the half-dark – gazed into them with bitterness and distrust.

"And you – you really had better leave," Mikhalych said. Unable to bear the beekeeper's gaze, he turned away, lowering his eyes.

"Ahh!" Valik wailed sharply, like the siren of a fire engine, outside the tent. "My eye! Fuck! My eye!"

Mikhalych burst out of the tent. The beekeeper rose up from his sleeping bag, but, upon realising that Valik was howling rather than screaming, chose to stay inside.

He heard the sound of car doors slamming. Then an engine

started, and, responding to a foot's excessive push on the accelerator, roared. The noise of the unfamiliar engine began to fade into the distance, until all that remained in Sergeyich's ears was a strange, white, painful ringing, which sometimes transformed into a whistle.

Blood pressure? the beekeeper thought, taking fright.

At long last, he climbed out of the tent. The stars shone high above, and among them hung the thin horn of the moon, like a sickle that had been tossed into the sky and got stuck there. Now the night didn't seem dark at all. Sergeyich could make out the trees, the tent. After taking a few steps in the direction of the hives, he saw his Lada, but he did not recognise it. He came closer. The shell-shocked "counterterrorist" had smashed all the car's windows with the axe. Shards of glass jingled plaintively underfoot. Only fragments of the windscreen remained in place, bent inwards at the top and bottom by the blows. The driver-side window was totally gone, as if it had never existed. The window behind it was cobwebbed with cracks.

Sergeyich walked around the Lada with stabbing pains in his heart. He looked back at the hives and listened closely. It seemed to him that the dear, familiar buzzing of the bees reached his ears. Then he noticed a single, faint axe mark on the edge of the nearest hive. Apparently Valik had spent all his strength on destroying the car.

"Thank God for that," Sergeyich muttered.

All on their own, his hands reached for the pieces of the windscreen that still jutted out along the sides of its metal frame. The glass came out easily, without resistance. Sergeyich had no idea why he was bothering: what was the point? Nevertheless, after finishing with the windscreen, he started on the driver-side door. Mechanically, without hurrying, the beekeeper pulled out all the broken glass that hadn't been scattered by the blows of the axe. He sliced open his right palm and doused it with honey vodka. The wound started to close up, but still dripped blood onto the ground. And so Sergeyich lifted the Lada's hatch (which had also been deprived of its glass), got a tuft of cotton wool from his first-aid kit, and pressed it to the cut; then he found a latex glove and pulled it over his hand. That stopped the bleeding – but suddenly the taste of blood appeared in his mouth, on his tongue. And the beekeeper concluded that this taste, which was so recognisable from childhood, when every fight outside school had ended in a busted lip, had appeared on his tongue as a reminder that he was still in danger: the shell-shocked "counterterrorist" might come back, or someone else might show up with the same drunken bone to pick.

"You really had better leave . . ." Those had been the parting words of the teacher who had brought his former pupil to Sergeyich's apiary.

The beekeeper got out his mobile and checked the time: just after midnight. He dialled Galya's number.

"Well, look who it is," the familiar, sleepy voice replied. "I was already asleep."

"Galya, can I come over? I really need to," he pleaded.

"Sure, come on over – I'll put on the kettle."

He got behind the wheel. The car started easily and obediently, as if it weren't at all offended by the fact that some stranger had taken out all his rage, all his pain and hatred, on its body.

# 42

As Sergeyich was approaching the village cemetery and could see the outline of the church against the dark sky, an ambulance came speeding his way, lights flashing and siren wailing. Sergeyich had time to pull over to the side of the road, letting it pass, and it seemed to him that he recognised Mikhalych the teacher in the passenger seat.

That's odd, he thought. Why's he going to hospital?

The beekeeper parked the Lada beside Galya's fence, got out, and cast a pensive glance at the street lamp. The gate opened with too loud a creak, so Sergeyich took extra care to close it gently behind him – it was the middle of the night, after all . . .

An hour later the gate creaked again when Galya and he stepped out into the street. Galya's eyes were wet, and tears were streaming down her cheeks.

"How are you going to make it? With a car like that?" she whispered bitterly.

"He tried to smash up the hives, too, but he didn't have the strength," the beekeeper said, without answering her question.

"Nothing but trouble," Galya said. "He'll be the death of us. You know, a week ago, he tossed a grenade into the yard of the village council's bookkeeper. A good thing it didn't go off. He's deep in debt to the council, for water. But when he hits the bottle, he starts yellin' about what *we* owe *him* . . ."

"So what should I do?" Sergeyich asked yet again.

He had already posed that question twice, in the house, over tea. But Galya had only shrugged and gazed at him sadly, as one gazes at a departed loved one's body.

"You'd better get out of here, at least for a while," she finally advised him. "Maybe they'll arrest him, put him in prison . . . I'll call and let you know right away. Just don't go too far, OK? There are plenty of nice places around Melitopol, with sanatoriums, a little river . . ."

Sergeyich turned his pensive gaze from Galya to the street lamp, which shed a cone of light onto the road and onto part of Galya's fence and gate. The same street lamp also illuminated his battered car, which brought him shame and pain. Along with the shame and pain came a sense of umbrage, which seemed to pressure him both from within and from the sky above. It made him stoop. He was afraid in advance of glances from other drivers, afraid of traffic police, afraid of plain old passers-by, who, catching sight of his windowless Lada, might pick up a stone and lob it in his direction.

I've got three hours before dawn, and there aren't too many cars on the road in the first few hours of the morning, either, he thought. Have to hurry . . .

He drove back to the hives, listening to the rumble of Galya's scooter, on which she was following him, through his broken windows. They set the trailer down on its wheels. Sergeyich shut all six entrances, then he and Galya loaded the hives onto the trailer, wall to wall, and strapped them down. The rest of his belongings went into the Lada's boot.

"Have a look around later," the beekeeper asked Galya. "If there's something I missed, keep it safe for me. I mean, I'll be back, right?"

"Of course you'll be back," Galya reassured him.

Only after hearing her response did he realise that he had meant to reassure her, not to ask for reassurance. But apparently something had gone wrong in his head.

And again, only more slowly and cautiously, the beekeeper drove out to the main road. He stopped at the turning and shut off the engine.

He and Galya embraced at the side of the road. They held each other for a minute or two, surrounded by the night's silence, saying nothing.

"Call me when you find a place to stay," Galya whispered in his ear at last. "If it's not too far, I'll bring you some food."

He nodded and ran his nose across her temple, touching her cold little ear and sensing the extra chill of her gold earring. The bittersweet scent of her hair was so distinct that, at this moment, he felt Galya was the closest, dearest person in his life. He didn't want to let her go, but his arms loosened and she emerged from their embrace.

He got behind the wheel, looked back at Galya and her scooter, waved goodbye, and drove off.

The empty road had a calming, almost lulling effect on Sergeyich, but he had no wish to sleep. Soon he reached a fork: Donetsk straight ahead, Melitopol to the right. He had driven past junctions which might have led to quiet, secluded corners, where he could have pitched his tent and set up his hives, where, in all likelihood, no-one would have interfered in his and his bees' calm, harmless existence. But the desertedness and nighttime compliance of the road propelled him onward, further and further, as if "further" meant "better". Then, suddenly, a large sign flashed up in the beams of his headlights, and on it, at the very top, above the arrow indicating the main road, was the word Simferopol.

I'm . . . almost in Crimea? Sergeyich thought, with a jolt. But the shock was a happy one, like when you find ten hryvnias in the street.

190

And he remembered the Crimean Tatar Akhtem, whom he had befriended at the beekeepers' convention all those years ago. He had thought about him just recently, in the winter, and he had even tried to call him. Apparently, it was meant to be . . .

Why don't I pay him a visit? the beekeeper thought. I've got his address in that notebook, in the boot, with all my other papers. They say Tatars are hospitable folk, even though they aren't Christian – I'm sure they won't turn me out. And it's not as if I'd be asking to stay in their home . . . I just need a place to pitch my tent and set up my hives.

This idea gave Sergeyich a surge of confidence – confidence that he knew the road ahead, as well as what awaited him at the end of that road. After all, Crimea had fields, and forests, and mountains. And the air down there, Akhtem had told him in Sloviansk, was wonderful. And the people were peaceful, well behaved. No war, either. They – the peaceful Crimeans – had summoned the Russian army themselves, and it had come, and had stayed to protect their peace. Didn't this sound like paradise for his bees? And for him? He picked up speed, in order to get as close to Crimea as possible before the road filled up with lorries and holidaymakers, who were also going to Crimea, but for different reasons, and transporting their human, not their apian, families. Of course, Crimea was glad to welcome any sort of family – but especially an apian one. It was a sweet place. Sergeyich had never been there, but each time he mentioned the peninsula, he could taste it on his tongue. It tasted of honey, of sugar.

# 43

Sergeyich passed through the checkpoint at Chonhar pretty quickly. The compassionate people in the queue of cars at the administrative border with Crimea had kept glancing at his mutilated car, at his licence plate, and at his gloomy face, which seemed to belong to a man who was experiencing his own death in his mind. Time and again, the word "refugee" had reached his ears in a whisper, or even at full volume, always accompanied by a look or a gesture in his direction. This had made Sergeyich feel even worse. The absence of a windscreen (indeed, of any window) left him vulnerable both to stones and to words. But while only a few pebbles had flown into his Lada from under the wheels of the cars directly ahead of it – and none of these pebbles, thank God, had hit him in the face – the word "refugee" had flown in a few dozen times, and each utterance lingered, linking up with its fellows. They all buzzed in his ears like mosquitoes, like annoying midges that are hard to drive out and against which there can be no defence in a car with missing windows.

Sergeyich had driven past the cars in the queue at a crawl, so that he could stop, apologise, and return to the back at any shout of "Where do you think you're going?" But no-one had raised any objection. There was always the same look of surprise, followed by sympathy. The first glance would land on his face, the second on the licence plate, as if the licence plate could explain the cause of his misfortune. And, of course, that's just what it did – maybe not in detail, or very specifically, but still . . .

The Ukrainian border guard leafed through his passport, paused over his address, and glanced at the car with its trailer, which stood nearby, where it was being examined by two customs officers, who seemed a little excited and even scared.

"Planning to stay long?" the guard asked. Sergeyich shrugged. "Maybe a month."

"Go ahead. Only don't pick up any hitchhikers on the way to the Russian side. That's not allowed. You might get fined."

As soon as Sergeyich opened the driver-side door, the customs officers moved away and turned their attention, with apparent relief, to a brand new dark-blue Volvo, which had driven up to their post behind the windowless green Lada.

Yet Sergeyich remained tense. Fear pooled in his trembling fingers, making him grip the steering wheel harder and stare straight ahead, where people with carts, suitcases, bags and backpacks were walking in both directions on both sides of the road. He drove past them, attracting various glances, ranging from pleading to compassionate. After crossing the bridge, he saw the broad silvery canopy of the border post, which bore the words: Russia. Dzhankoy checkpoint. He remembered the transformer box he had noticed at the entrance to Chonhar, on which someone had written in black paint: 18 km to the Russian occupiers.

"That was only eighteen kilometres back?" he thought.

In his peaked cap and neatly ironed shirt and trousers, the officer at the Russian post indicated with a nod of his head where Sergeyich ought to park. The beekeeper noticed how, as the officer approached the Lada, the expression on his face changed from stony indifference to stony perplexity.

"Why is your car in this condition?" he asked sternly, coming up on the driver's side.

"Someone smashed my windows. Haven't had time to replace them," Sergeyich began to explain in a trembling voice.

And then he guessed the officer's thoughts and how he would proceed. The latter took a couple of steps back and trained his eyes on the Lada's licence plate.

"Fell into the Banderites' hands, did you?" he said.[11]

Sergeyich nodded — not so much in response to the question as to the suddenly friendly intonation.

"Show your documents over there," the serviceman said, pointing with a glance to a window beneath a sign that read border control.

The border guard lazily took the beekeeper's worn Ukrainian passport from his hand. He leafed through it, scrutinised the address, and only then looked up at the document's owner, squinting. This border guard was no older than thirty, and the serious expression he wore on his face didn't suit him, as if he were straining to hold the grimace. It seemed that at any moment he might relax his pursed lips and they would immediately form a smile.

He got up from behind his computer desk and looked through the window at the Lada and its trailer.

"That yours?" he said.

"Yes."

"And this village – Little Starhorodivka – is it in the Donetsk Republic or in Ukraine?"

"Between the two," Sergeyich answered cautiously. "In the grey zone."

"That so? Huh," the border guard declared, as if surprised, though his face remained unchanged. Without saying another word, he stepped out of his container and disappeared.

Sergeyich heard footsteps and voices behind him and turned round. He saw that his movable property – that is, his car and trailer – was being inspected by three soldiers at once. And a German shepherd, under the watchful supervision of its handler, was sniffing around his trailer. The handler himself was probing the axe mark on the scarred hive with his finger.

Sergeyich was getting nervous. He looked round to check whether all the cars were being inspected and sniffed like this, or just his. But the Russians weren't devoting such attention to anyone else.

He walked away from the window, then considered approaching his car, but decided against it. Best not get in the soldiers' way, he thought. Let them do their job. I've got nothing to hide.

Just then one of the soldiers turned round, as if he had heard the beekeeper's thoughts.

"Move the car over there," he commanded in a cold voice, pointing to a spot some distance from the canopy.

As he drove to the spot, Sergeyich nearly grazed a red Mazda with plates from Dnipro.

"Watch where you're goin', Donetsk arsehole!" he heard someone shout from behind, but he didn't look back.

Having left the car where he had been told, the beekeeper returned to the window. And then there came the sound of footsteps, again from behind him.

"Sergey Sergeyich, follow us."

He turned and saw two men in civilian clothes – also young, with the same serious expressions on their faces.

Together, they went over to a one-storey prefabricated building, which must have just been brought there and lowered to the ground by a crane.

"Could we have a look at your mobiles?" one of the men said.

Sergeyich obediently handed it over.

"This the only one you have?"

"Yes."

One of the two went off somewhere, mobile in hand. The second invited Sergeyich into the building.

Inside the little office, the man in civilian clothes sat down at a desk and, with a glance, indicated the chair opposite. He was holding the beekeeper's tattered passport.

"Where exactly are you going?" he said, leafing through the document and not looking up.

"To Crimea," Sergeyich responded.

"That much I guessed. But specifically?"

"I . . . I have an address. A fellow I know. Lives near Bakhchysarai. He's a beekeeper, like me. I'm not going for myself, you know – I'm going for my bees, so they can fly in peace, make honey . . ."

"Alright, well, what's this fellow's name? Address? You do understand that you're entering another nation, right? That this is Russia?"

"I've got the address . . . Here it is," Sergeyich said, unfolding a page he had torn from his notebook and folded in four. He handed it over.

"Good, good." The office's occupant nodded. "Now, what happened to your car?"

"They smashed my windows. I stopped in the Zaporizhia region, near Vesele planned to spend the summer there."

"And you received a poor welcome?"

Sergeyich nodded.

"Because you're from Donbas?"

The beekeeper nodded again.

"Yes." The man sighed. "What you people are going through up there is horrible, horrible . . . Thank God we managed to get to Crimea in time . . . Would you mind speaking to some journalists about this incident?"

"Journalists?" Sergeyich echoed.

"That's right – we have to speak out about these things."

"Sure," the beekeeper said, but none too confidently.

"What did they attack the car with? Bats?"

"An axe," the beekeeper said. "Got the beehives too."

"Will you wait here one moment? I'll be right back."

The man stepped out. A second later a woman in a military uniform came in and set a cup of tea and a sugar bowl in front of Sergeyich.

The beekeeper stirred two spoons of sugar into his tea. His fear and confusion faded away. The tea also drove the unusual, unpleasant coldness of his thoughts from his body – a coldness that was purely psychological and independent from the temperature of the air under the bright summer sun.

Sergeyich drank the tea, enjoying every sip. It calmed him. That's why he was able to greet the man in civilian clothes with a peaceful, friendly expression upon the latter's return.

The office's occupant laid out a map of Donbas on the desk. "Please, enjoy the tea . . . And have a look here. Find your village on the map. The journalists will come round in about twenty minutes."

Sergeyich found and pointed to Little Starhorodivka. The office's occupant circled it in red pencil and continued their conversation, asking about life in the grey zone and about Pashka, whom Sergeyich mentioned.

In the course of the conversation, Sergeyich tensed up several times. He decided not to tell this obviously non-civilian man in civilian clothes about Petro, the Ukrainian soldier. Nor did he say anything about the guy who had lain dead in the field all winter long. He did talk, however, about the sniper from Siberia who'd been blown up by a mine, and about the guys from Karuselino who used to visit Pashka before they got a new commander. He also mentioned the strangers who had tried to sell Pashka a stolen car – and the fact that, in the neighbouring village, which was also in the grey zone, everything was different: there were still lots of people, and even kids running around in the streets.

The office's occupant listened attentively, nodding and occasionally jotting something down in his notebook. Sergeyich warmed up, relaxed. A couple of times, while sipping his sweet tea, he even forgot where he was and why he was there. It was just like a chat on a train: two chance companions telling each other tales – some true, some tall.

The chat ended when the female officer poked her head into the office again and nodded. The man hopped to his feet.

"The journalists are here," he announced.

They went out into the warm sunshine and walked around the canopy, beneath which border guards were inspecting cars and people waiting to enter, and the white office containers with windows for passport control.

About five people were busying themselves beside the beekeeper's green Lada. Two men with cameras were filming the car, trailer and hives from different angles. A young woman with a microphone in her hand perked up when she spotted Sergeyich; it seemed she already knew who was who.

"Are you ready to tell your story?" she asked the beekeeper as soon as he approached.

"Yes," he said.

"Alright, get out of the way," she commanded her colleagues, and then she turned back to Sergeyich. "You stand there, in front of your car. Right here. Ready?"

The last question was addressed to the two cameramen.

"So, Sergey Sergeyich, you came to us from Donbas. Tell us why."

The question set the beekeeper back on his heels. He half-turned to the trailer and pointed in its direction.

"Uh, well, my bees – you know . . . I'm from the grey zone . . . There's a war on and people are shooting. You've got the Ukrainians on the one side, and on the other, Russians."

"Stop! Stop!" The voice of one of the young fellows standing nearby broke into the interview. "No, that won't do. Repeat what you said, but without 'Russians'. How could you have 'Russians' over there?"

"You've got the Ukrainians on the one side," Sergeyich repeated a little more hesitantly. "And on the other . . . from Karuselino . . . separatists . . ."

197

"And what happened to your car?" the young woman said, interrupting him, and her microphone immediately zipped over to his mouth.

"They busted it up," Sergeyich breathed out, painfully and sincerely. "In the Zaporizhia region. I stopped there for a short time—"

"How many of them were there? And why did they attack you?"

"Just the one guy, actually. Shell-shocked. Got drunk at a wake. They were burying a soldier who got killed by the Russians."

"Stop!" the young fellow said. From Sergeyich's point of view, he seemed too young to be interrupting his elders or strangers in that tone. "That's enough, Lyuda – no live interview. We'll just get some footage. And make sure you record the bees buzzing. Here, get a close-up of the axe mark," he said, pointing to the damaged hive.

The young woman nodded, lowered the hand with the microphone, and, saying nothing to Sergeyich, walked away.

The beekeeper watched the two cameramen scour his car and hives with their lenses. They poked their cameras through the Lada's broken windscreen and kept casting strange, dry glances in his direction – glances devoid of sympathy and even of interest. At the same time, a border guard approached the trailer with a device that looked like a miniature sapper shovel. He began to run this thing along the hives, listening closely to its electronic squeaks. "You're in our way," the young journalist told him. "We've got a couple more minutes."

The border guard retreated.

The journalists left without saying goodbye, and the man from the office brought Sergeyich his mobile, his passport and the piece of paper bearing Akhtem's address, then asked him to return to the same window and fill in an immigration card.

The beekeeper's stay at the checkpoint was clearly coming to an end. He got a little nervous as he filled in the immigration card, but the border guard looked it over quickly, stamped both parts, separated them, and handed one back to Sergeyich along with his passport, wishing him a safe journey and warning him not to lose the insert.

Having already got behind the wheel and breathed a sigh of relief, the beekeeper noticed, out of the corner of his eye, that the man who had just dismissed him was trotting over to his car. The fellow was waving his hand, asking him to wait.

Just in case, Sergeyich climbed out of the Lada.

"Sorry," the man said, after quickly catching his breath. "This is for you." He reached into his jacket pocket. "The journalists pooled some money – for car repairs." He handed Sergeyich a fistful of banknotes. "They said they'd be in touch, for the programme 'Then and Now'. Well, have a nice stay."

The bewildered beekeeper leafed through the roubles, trying to figure out how much money had been collected. But his head wouldn't work; his thoughts got mixed up with his feelings.

"Thank you!" he shouted at the man, who was making his way back to his prefabricated office.

The man turned his head, gave a nod, and kept on walking.

# 44

Sergeyich's eyes were warmed by the sign indicating the turn to Sevastopol and Bakhchysarai. He had no business in Sevastopol, but the very fact that he was approaching that legendary city brought him joy. Bakhchysarai, on the other hand, was the ultimate goal of his journey – well, not Bakhchysarai, exactly, but the nearby village of Kuybyshevo, where Akhtem lived.

The sun shone now on his hands, which were turning the steering wheel, now on the passenger seat. The road did not let him get bored, winding to the right, then to the left.

The beekeeper's attention was drawn to a Volga with a strange trailer that was parked on the side of the road. Beside it, on a folding chair, sat a dark-skinned Tatar. There was a cylindrical container on the trailer, which bore the inscription "samsa".

Maybe it's "hamsa"? Sergeyich thought, digging up the only word he knew that resembled the one he saw.[12]

*199*

In any case, it was clear to him that the Tatar was selling something edible out of this cylindrical contraption. And suddenly Sergeyich wanted a snack . . . *Hamsa, samsa* – anything would do, as long as it was salty. But he had already driven some distance beyond the Volga and its trailer.

He now began to watch the side of the road more closely. Common sense told him he might encounter other sellers of edible goods.

And about ten minutes later the beekeeper did indeed spot a now familiarly shaped container on a trailer attached to a U.A.Z. jeep. Beside it stood another lean, dark-skinned man of eastern appearance, smoking. The man wore a pair of shorts, a long-sleeved shirt, and a cap that protected him from the scorching sun.

Sergeyich stepped on the brake.

"Samsa?" asked the Tatar.

"Uh . . . what is it? Fish?" the beekeeper asked, seeking clarification.

"No, bird!" The Tatar laughed. "It's a pie, with meat. Very tasty. Hundred roubles."

Not yet knowing how to react to the price, Sergeyich pulled out the money he had received to replace the car's windows. They were thousand-rouble notes.

"Take two?" the Tatar suggested.

"No, just one."

And right there, standing beside his Lada, Sergeyich ate the first *samsa* of his life. It was juicy and satisfying, and left a taste of rich broth on his tongue. And indeed, the beekeeper couldn't resist buying another one, which he also savoured before the satisfied Tatar's eyes.

"Do you happen to know the way to Kuybyshevo?" Sergeyich asked the *samsa* seller before getting back in his car.

"Albat? Of course. Drive through Bakhchysarai and you'll see a sign for Yalta. Follow that road for about twenty kilometres, and you're there."

Bakhchysarai was already looming in the distance when, suddenly, a light breeze brought a bee into the Lada. It flew in heavily, with a cargo of yellow pollen on its legs, and seemed to freeze in the air from fright – right next to Sergeyich's left ear.

One of Sergeyich's hands reached for the handle to lower the window. Then he laughed at himself. That's habit for you: the hand doesn't know the window's gone.

The bee must have been spooked by his laughter, as it flew away. Or maybe the breeze carried it off.

Sergeyich glanced back, wanting to follow its trajectory, but instead caught sight of his own hives on the trailer behind him.

"You just wait a little while longer, friends. I'll let you out soon," he told them.

# 45

"Akhtem?" asked a woman of about forty, dressed in a black sweater that was too warm for the summer and a black skirt that reached down to her feet. A purple scarf was tied around her head. "You mean . . . you don't know?"

"Ah . . . know what?" Sergeyich said, his eyes going back and forth between the mistress of the house, who had opened the door at his knock, and the brown mutt who was still barking at this unexpected guest, jumping and tugging not very insistently on the chain that bound him to his kennel. It stood beside the path that led from the gate to a tall cosy canopy covered with grapevines, under which stood a rectangular wooden table that appeared to have been painted blue fairly recently. When the beekeeper had passed by the kennel, the mutt had been sitting inside it, not even exposing his wet nose to the sunlight.

"Where are you from?" the woman said, gazing at the stranger with shy, not especially confident eyes.

"From Donbas."

"You mean," she said, sounding frightened, "from Donetsk?"

"No, my house is in the grey zone. So what happened to Akhtem? Where is he?"

"How do you know Akhtem?" the woman said, now more calmly, but ignoring his questions.

"We met at a beekeepers' convention, in Sloviansk. Shared a room there, at a boarding house. I'm also a beekeeper – came with my hives . . ."

She cast a glance behind him, at the red brick path leading back to the gate.

"Anam, kim anda?" came a sonorous voice from inside the house, and a girl of about seventeen – long-haired, slender, in jeans and a T-shirt – peered out from behind the woman's back.

"Donbastan babanıñ tanışı keldi,"[13] the woman replied, and immediately switched to Russian. "Akhtem is gone. They took him. It's been twenty months now."

Sergeyich froze, then took a step back and looked round. His eyes met those of the mutt, which started barking again.

"What did you want from him?" the woman said.

"I . . . I thought I'd set out my hives somewhere around here, so that my bees could fly in peace. I'd stay with them, in a tent."

"We have an apiary behind the vineyards, near the mountain," the woman said in a kinder voice – kinder and softer.

"Those are Akhtem's bees, aren't they?" Sergeyich said.

"Yes. Aisha and Bekir look after them," she said, nodding behind her, where her daughter had just flashed by. "But mostly Bekir, our son."

"Forgive me," Sergeyich offered, feeling awkward. "I didn't know about . . . Akhtem . . ."

He sighed, waved uncertainly, and turned to leave. The woman stopped him. "Wait. What's your name?"

"Sergey."

"I'm Aisylu. Why don't you stay? You can put your hives next to ours. I'm sorry, it's just that Akhtem never mentioned you . . . Maybe you'd like to have lunch with us?"

"No, thank you, I've already eaten. I need to let my bees out as soon as I can," Sergeyich responded, with genuine concern in his voice.

"Yes, yes." She nodded. "Wait a minute, I'll just have a word with my daughter and then I'll show you the way. I'll ride with you – it isn't far."

"What happened to your car?" Aisylu said, throwing up her hands as soon as they left the yard and stepped out onto the street.

"Oh, just some drunk," Sergeyich explained reluctantly. "Shell-shocked in the war... There was a wake – his pal was killed – so he took it out on my car."

Aisylu climbed into the car cautiously, with trepidation, and then immediately fastened her seat belt.

"Go straight, towards the mosque, then turn left," she instructed him.

An old woman came walking down the road in their direction, leading two goats. She stepped aside, clearing the way for the car, nodded to Aisylu, and cast a curious glance at Sergeyich.

"That's Savie, our neighbour," Akhtem's wife explained. "

Aisylu, Savie," Sergeyich said. "Unusual names."

"Yes, you really won't find too many Aisylus these days," his passenger said with a barely noticeable smile, as if recalling something. "My mother named me after her younger sister, who died during the deportation. She was still very small. Here, turn left."[14] He did so, and an extraordinary mountain rose up before their eyes. Its sides were covered almost entirely with a dense green forest, while its top was of bare yellow rock.

Sergeyich couldn't hold back a "wow".

"Mangup," Akhtem's wife uttered sweetly. "That's where my grand-father hid, under the Germans. The Soviet soldiers caught him after the war. They shot him over there, near the Kadyrov clinic, where they treat drug addicts."

"You have a lot of addicts around here?" the beekeeper said, surprised, turning his eyes to his passenger and away from the massive mountain, which, though distant, still seemed to tower over them in all its strange enormity.

"No, not around here. They would come from other cities. It was a private clinic. Dr Kadyrov would treat them. They say that when the Russians came he moved to Kyiv. The Russians refused to let him treat addicts. Here, see that building on the right? That's where the clinic was."

"What's in there now?"

"Nothing."

The mountain, it seemed, was still far ahead of them, but the road kept going up – steadily, almost imperceptibly. To the right were the vineyards, running off into the distance in even, slender rows. And further on, where the vineyards ended, began the forest. "There, to the right. We're nearly there," Aisylu said, pointing the way.

When the car rose above the vineyards, the road turned right and broke off, transforming into a path. What had looked like a dense forest from below revealed itself as a gentle slope lined with almond and fig trees, beneath which stood yellow, blue and green beehives. Sergeyich counted at least two dozen of them.

"Well . . ." Aisylu nodded. "We made it."

When they got out of the car, Sergeyich immediately began to look for a place to put his bees. Akhtem's hives stood further off among the trees, in three uneven rows. He could put his own there, only a little closer to where the road turned.

"I'm sorry, but could you help me unload the hives?" he asked Aisylu.

"Yes, of course."

He drove the Lada a little further, parking closer to Akhtem's apiary. Aisylu followed on foot. The two of them took the hives off the trailer and arranged them as Sergeyich wanted. Then she showed him the little shed where the tools of the beekeeping trade were kept; it stood behind the apiary, and was hidden by a bushy Turkish hazel tree.

"Here, take it." She handed him the key to the padlock. "You'll find everything you need. And there's a spring nearby." She pointed towards the mountain. "Follow that path and you'll see it – about three hundred metres away."

"Thank you," Sergeyich said, looking at Aisylu gently, faithfully, like a dog that has just been fed after three days of hunger. And then he asked: "Didn't the police look for Akhtem?"

She laughed bitterly, and tears flashed up in her eyes.

"The Cossacks grabbed him. For all I know, they sent him off to

Russia. Three of our people were taken that day. They had all gone in the same car to the mosque in Bakhchysarai. That was the last we heard of them. The car was sitting there, empty. A little boy saw them being shoved into a minibus . . ."

"They can't do that," Sergeyich blurted out, but he realised how helpless his words sounded – helpless and foolish. He also felt personally helpless, as if nothing in his life depended on him. It was as if he were sitting in the snow-covered field beside the murdered young man with the gold earring; there were shells falling all around, some bursting far away, some closer, and some so close that the explosive sound poured into his ears like molten iron.

"If you need anything, just come over. You know where we are," Aisylu said in farewell, looking at him as if he were a child. Perhaps she had also sensed his helplessness.

She walked away towards the turning in the road and set off down the hill. She walked beautifully and slowly, while the air gradually filled with the buzzing of bees. This buzzing brought Sergeyich back to his senses. He realised that these were Akhtem's bees, flying free – and that he had yet to liberate his own.

His legs carried him swiftly towards the hives, towards his long-suffering refugee bees.

# 46

The sun hung in the sky for a long – a surprisingly long – time. The earth had already turned away from it, lying down on its side, and so the sun now hung not in the middle of the sky, but at the edge. Yet it went on shining, as if it had decided not to retire until Sergeyich had set up his new abode. Having driven iron pegs into the rocky ground and stretched the corners of his tarpaulin abode with ropes, the beekeeper was now retrieving his clothes and belongings from the car.

The warm evening silence was suddenly pierced by the cry of a bird, as resonant as the blast of a Young Pioneer's bugle.[15] Sergeyich looked up at the nearby trees. He tried to imagine the bird that had uttered this cry, but he just couldn't. The birds he knew did not cry like that. The birds he knew did not cry at all – they cawed, tweeted, trilled and whistled. The cry had awakened the beekeeper's curiosity, reviving his mind; he tuned his ears to the colourful, sonorous silence of the world around him, the now silent flying-crying creature suddenly forgotten. Into this silence were woven the whisper of foliage, the breeze's breath, the buzzing of bees – all the tiny sounds that constitute the peaceful silence of summer.

As he listened closely, Sergeyich noticed that the sun had finally departed. The silence grew louder, more evident. One could stroke it, as one would a cat or a dog; it was warm, and it brushed up against Sergeyich gently, pleading for his involvement, his participation in its life, its sounds. And so, when his eyes had got accustomed to the sun's absence, the bee-keeper began to supplement the silence by searching for kindling. Having gathered some branches, twigs and even two planks from a wooden box, Sergeyich struck a match – and the sound of it also blended into the silence, becoming its property, an integral part of it, a note in its endless music.

And then the kettle suspended over the fire came to the boil. And Sergeyich, overstimulated by his journey and the beauty of his new surroundings, wandered around, gathering more branches for the fire.

In the morning, the beekeeper opened his eyes and no longer doubted that he had entered paradise. He found himself in a fairy tale, where nature not only serves people but dotes upon them; where the sun waits to depart until people have finished their daily tasks; where the air rings with countless unseen bells; where one can be free and invisible; where every living thing – every tree, every vine – has its own voice.

The path Aisylu had pointed out led him to the spring, and there he washed and awoke entirely. The birdsong near the murmuring water sounded even louder. The voices of the birds filled Sergeyich with inexplicable confidence, an assurance that everything bad was firmly behind him, while ahead of him lay well-deserved peace and a life in harmony with his bees, and therefore in harmony with nature.

He brought back two flasks of spring water and placed them by the car, whose green colour was now lost amid the brighter greenery of nature. He hadn't taken the plastic canister with him, as he didn't have the strength to carry twenty litres from the spring to the tent. Suddenly, he felt the desire to wash the Lada, to wipe off the dust and dirt of the road, so that it might sparkle. But there was really no good reason to scrub the car clean. You wash a car when it's new, when you need to go to the city or pay someone a visit. But the Lada, if it were alive, probably wouldn't want to make any public appearances or attract attention in its current state – just as a grown man who'd been socked in the eye while out drinking might not want to go out and display his shiner the next morning.

Then Sergeyich recalled the money for repairs that had been given to him by the journalists as he entered Crimea. He also recalled the indifferent, impudent journalists themselves. The money and the journalists somehow didn't add up . . . But, of course, one never knows . . .

I'll fix it, he mentally pledged to the strange benefactors who had pitied him. First we'll get settled, and then I'll fix it.

Sergeyich smiled, having caught himself thinking at one and the same time for himself, his car and his bees – as if they were one single family and spoke the same language. But that's how it was: the bees really were the only family he had left. The car was a hunk of metal, of course, while what remained of his human family lived far away, in Vinnytsia, and didn't complain about his absence. Still, he remembered them, and not only that but held them in his heart – both his wife and his daughter. And if his wife could be called "ex", his daughter certainly could not; children are yours for ever, wherever you live and no matter how much you quarrel with them. Angelica was already sixteen . . . She probably had a boyfriend . . . He wondered what she told her boyfriend about her father . . .

The day was heating up quickly. Sergeyich felt it on the crown of his head and fished out his orange cap. He turned it around in his hands, recalling how he used to watch every Shakhtar match on television. Where do they play now? he wondered. Definitely not in Donetsk. No time for football there.

In the afternoon, the beekeeper felt an urge to wander. He decided to go down to the village, to Kuybyshevo. It didn't seem too long a walk from Akhtem's apiary, next to which he had placed his own hives. After all, it had taken Aisylu and him only ten minutes to drive up there the day before. Sergeyich stepped out onto the dirt road and saw the whole village before him, bathed in hot, yellow-orange sunshine. The village trembled, its air melting beneath the sun. The roofs of its houses refused to stand still. Now Sergeyich began to feel that he wasn't so close to Kuybyshevo. He felt he was standing very high up on the mountain. It was only the obvious ease and straightness of the road that called him onward, despite his sudden doubts. He didn't care to think about having to make his way back up here later. Besides, given his age and that his disability (which Sergeyich sometimes doubted, not without cause) was unobtrusive, he was still quite fit. He hadn't had a single serious cough since entering Crimea – in fact he hadn't had any problems breathing at all. The air here was like butter tea: you could breathe it, drink it, even eat it. He wished Pashka were with him . . . His frenemy would start looking for something to complain about, as usual. He'd start looking, but then would feel like a total fool, because there was nothing to complain about, nothing wrong with this place. The people, the landscape, the air and the sun – all good . . .

Tiring of the imaginary presence of Pashka, the beekeeper put the man out of his mind and instead dragged his wife and daughter into the vineyards. He imagined them gazing at the equally beautiful land all around them. Vitalina would surely also be searching for something worthy of criticism, but their daughter (who did not take after her at all) would be doing the opposite: she'd be dancing with joy at having found herself in such a place. Angelica was an impressionable girl, and when her mother wasn't telling her how to behave, you could read all her feelings and thoughts on her face . . . Then, suddenly, the company Sergeyich had gathered in his imagination – formerly his family – was joined by Galya, who stepped out from behind the nearest maple tree. She gazed pensively at Sergeyich and the others, and her face expressed neither joy nor peace of mind. Something was troubling her, and this made the beekeeper uneasy. He wanted to know why she was in such a mood, what had happened. But he didn't feel right talking to Galya while his wife and daughter were there. Just then his mobile rang in his pocket. Sergeyich pulled it out, looked at the screen, and was dumbfounded: it was Galya – as if she had sensed from a distance that he had been thinking of her.

"Yes, hello, it's me!" Sergeyich blurted out, all in one word.

"Hello, Seryozha! Where are you?"

"In Crimea – Kuybyshevo. Near Bakhchysarai."

"You know why I'm calling? Valik's gone blind. One of his eyes was already no good, on account of the concussion."

"Who's Valik?" Sergeyich said.

"You know, the fellow your bee stung in the eye – the one who smashed up your Lada."

"Oh." The beekeeper breathed out. "So what?"

"I just thought you'd better not come back here . . ."

"I wasn't—" Sergeyich began, but stopped short. He wanted to say that he wasn't about to come back, but then thought that this might sound like he wasn't planning on returning to her at all.

"Is it beautiful down there?" Galya said, without waiting for him to say more.

Sergeyich's gaze again descended to the village, the cypress trees, the roofs of the houses.

"Yes, very – and the sun's so hot."

"How are the bees?"

"The bees like it too. They're buzzing around. Why don't you come down? It's not all that comfortable, of course, sleeping in a tent . . . But it's nice here, peaceful."

"It's nice and peaceful up here too," Galya said, and her voice grew even warmer. "My boss at the shop won't let me go on holiday until September, and in September I'll have to dig up my potatoes, pick my tomatoes . . . But I'd really like to come for a week," she added dreamily, like a little girl.

"Well, let's make a plan," Sergeyich said, bolstering Galya's dream.

# 47

This was Sergeyich's third visit to Akhtem's home – or, more precisely, to the home of Aisylu, Akhtem's wife. For the third time, quite unexpectedly, the twenty-year-old Bekir had driven up in his father's blue 4×4 and said that Aisylu was expecting the beekeeper for dinner. And Sergeyich had no choice but to get in the car. Two weeks before, on his first visit to their home, he hadn't been able to shake his sense of awkwardness. It was no doubt down to the absence of the man of the house, although no-one had mentioned Akhtem at the table. But then again, no-one had mentioned much of anything; Aisylu had merely explained to the guest, in a couple of words, what *yantıq* and *imam bayıldı* were.[16] The awkwardness may have also arisen from the fact that Aisylu hadn't asked Sergeyich a single question about himself and his life; he had expected that she would, and had thought long and hard – while rattling down to the village in the 4×4 – about what he was willing and eager to tell her, and what he'd prefer to withhold. Bekir and Aisha maintained a polite silence throughout the meal. Their mother alone talked, and only about household matters, and about their neighbours. She told the beekeeper that Bekir would drive him to the sea, to Kacha, where summer cottages owned by people from Sevastopol hung beautifully from a cliff above the water; it was the nearest coastal village, with the most sparsely populated beaches – although nowadays, of course, there weren't many holidaymakers anywhere along the coast.

Aisylu had already brought up the Black Sea more than once, and whenever she spoke of it her voice took on a strange, gentle ring. She had mentioned that she herself would like to go to the beach, but that somehow it never worked out. And another time she admitted that she hadn't been to the beach in five years, although Akhtem had offered, and had driven his friends from St Petersburg down to Kacha. These friends had come to visit four years ago, stayed at a campsite, and went hiking in the mountains. They brought a big box of Turkish delight from Russia and gave it to Akhtem and Aisylu as a gift, which triggered a lot of laughter. Turkish delight was easy to find in St Petersburg, in any shop, and so they had grabbed a box. It hadn't occurred to them that it might seem ridiculous to bring "eastern" sweets from the north to the south, especially as a gift for Crimean Tatars.

And this time too, as soon as Aisylu mentioned the sea, Bekir nodded decisively.

"We'll go soon – right after the weekend," he promised. "You'll come with us and Aisha will stay here, look after the house and the animals."

At the mention of animals, Sergeyich's ears pricked up. He raised his head.

"When do you folks extract the honey around here? Isn't it time?" he said.

"Yes, have to do it this coming week," he admitted. "I can extract yours too."

The beekeeper nodded. "That would be great. Only I'm out of jars."

"We've got plenty," Bekir responded with a wave.

"And what do you do with the honey? Sell it?" Sergeyich was lingering on the subject that most concerned him.

"A few of the shops around here are owned by Tatars," the young man said. "I give them as much as they'll take. The rest goes to resellers – they pay less, but they buy more."

Sergeyich felt it would be inappropriate to try and sell his honey at the Tatar-owned shops, since that would mean taking bread out of the mouths of Aisylu and her family. Nor did he want to sell his honey to resellers on the cheap – but perhaps he'd have to? And then he remembered that he still had roubles, a lot of roubles: money that had been given to him at the border for car repairs. Of course, he might actually need to spend it on the Lada. After all, the journalists had said they'd track him down for some kind of television programme, hadn't they? But what did he need to be on television for?

Sergeyich's thoughts made him nervous. Aisylu noticed.

"We'll help you," she assured him gently. "Maybe one of our shopkeeper friends will take it, or someone who does business along the highway to Sevastopol. The Russians love our Crimean honey – it has that mountain taste. If they're travelling by car, they might buy three jars at once."

"Crimean" . . . "mountain taste" . . . These words echoed in Sergeyich's mind and distracted him from his anxiety. He thought about taking this Crimean honey back to Ukraine and selling it there. It might fetch a better price.

The guest's face brightened, and Aisylu relaxed. Suddenly, her eyes were very focused.

"Sergeyağa," she said, almost in a whisper, and Bekir and Aisha froze, knowing that their mother reserved that voice for matters of extreme importance.

"Yes?" Sergeyich threw up his head.

"I want to ask you something . . . You're Russian, from Donbas . . . maybe . . . you'd be willing to go to the F.S.B. in Simferopol, ask them about Akhtem? They'll tell you the truth. I'd be turned away at the door, but they'll talk to you. I mean, you're one of their own . . ."

Sergeyich, who had been tackling a meat-stuffed pie, stopped chewing. Three pairs of eyes were staring at him intently, fixedly, expectantly. And one of the pairs – Aisha's – sparkled with tears. He, for his part, felt frightened. It was a strange, almost inexplicable fear, in that it was purely physical, paralysing his facial muscles but giving rise to no thoughts whatsoever. He sat like that for a minute or two, then he shrugged, and thereby came to understand that his fear had begun to pass.

"But I'm not Russian . . . I'm Ukrainian," he said quietly and not very clearly.

"But you speak Russian over there," Aisylu said, her voice sounding a little louder.

"Well, yes," he responded. "But I . . ."

Sergeyich tried to find words that might better explain his fear, his unwillingness to visit the powers that be – and not just the powers that be, but the Russian powers that be. What could he do over there? What would those people make of him, with his Ukrainian passport and smashed-up car?

"I don't know the way," he mumbled at last.

"Bekir could take you," Aisylu said. "But if you can't, don't worry..."

This dinner ended earlier than usual, and Sergeyich, having declined tea with baklava, also refused Bekir's offer to drive him back to the apiary. He told them that he would prefer to walk.

Bright stars shone above Kuybyshevo or Albat. The stars did not care above whom they shone, whose night their tiny spotlights illuminated. The village was quiet. From time to time a dog barked, and two or three more would bark in response.

Sergeyich walked over to the mosque, which he had only seen from above. Up close, it turned out to be as beautiful as a fairy-tale palace, but not very large. The warm wind intensified and blew in his face. And in the flavour of the wind, Sergeyich caught the salt of the sea. He thought about the fact that, in just a couple of days, he would lay eyes on it: the Black Sea. He might even take a dip. He hadn't brought swimming trunks, but who would care if he went into the water in his underpants? No-one. Who bothers to look at old men, anyway? Who needs them, other than they themselves? Well, maybe his bees needed him. But nobody else. Not even his ex-wife. And, it appeared, not even his daughter – otherwise she would call now and then to ask him how he was.

The mountain's dark shadow hung over the village, and the bee-keeper walked slowly towards that darkness, as if he were native to it, as if he could find his tent and his bees with his eyes closed.

A Volga came out of the darkness, blinding him with its bright lights. Loud music poured out of the car – music and laughter. He stepped off the road and waited for the Volga to pass, then followed it with his eyes as it took the music and laughter to the other end of the village, towards the Belbek River.

When he returned he made a fire, hung up his kettle, lit a candle in the tent, and, for some reason, decided to drink his tea inside, as if he were afraid someone might be watching him in the dark. It seemed to him that, after tonight's dinner, Aisylu wouldn't invite him over anymore. And she wouldn't have Bekir bring him *äyrän* and *samsa*.[17] They might not even take him to the beach now.

Then his thoughts redirected themselves to Akhtem, to their meeting at the beekeepers' conference in Sloviansk all those years ago. The aim of these thoughts, it seemed, was to prove to Sergeyich that no special friendship had arisen between him and the Tatar. He and Akhtem had merely been roommates, had sat beside each other at mealtimes, and had gathered in the evenings with the same crew to talk, drink vodka and tell jokes. Only Akhtem, as he recalled, did not tell jokes and didn't drink vodka. But he had listened and laughed. He must have been about twenty-five back then, as was Sergeyich. Which meant they were about the same age now too. If Akhtem was still alive.

Is he alive? Sergeyich wondered, feeling a stabbing in his heart. He thought of Aisylu, of how her husband had been missing for nearly two years.

He swallowed some tea, then glanced at the burning candle and realised that it was missing something. It was missing the cardboard icon of Saint Nicholas the Wonderworker.

What happened to Nicholas? Sergeyich asked himself.

Then he remembered how he had gathered his things in a hurry and tossed them into the Lada's boot.

"Must be somewhere in there," he muttered. "Tomorrow," he pledged – either to himself, or to the candle, or to the Wonder worker.

# 48

As lunchtime approached, rows of woolly little clouds rolled across the sky, sometimes obscuring the sun.

This day did not really differ from those before it, but Sergeyich just couldn't stop marvelling at the routine of Crimean summertime contentment, and so it seemed to him that the world rang with greater happiness each morning, that the bees and birds flew more joyously.

On his way to the spring, Sergeyich nearly tripped over a loitering hedgehog. He squatted down and rolled the creature, which had balled itself up out of fear, to the side. By the time he came back with two full flasks, there was no trace of the hedgehog, but a red squirrel scampered across the path.

Before his midday meal, Sergeyich peeked into his hives. The bees had already filled and capped most of their cells.

He opened Akhtem's hives and saw the same thing.

The beekeeper gave it some thought and decided that if Bekir didn't come that evening, he himself would go down to the village the following morning.

But Bekir hadn't forgotten about the honey. At about three, the hottest time of day, Sergeyich heard the rumble of an engine and went out to the edge of the apiary. The blue 4×4, trailer in tow, climbed steadily up the sun-dried dirt road. A cloud of yellow dust rose up behind it and floated off into the even rows of the vineyards.

Bekir and Sergeyich easily lifted out the honey extractor – and the wooden board to which its legs were screwed for stability – from the trailer.

Having found a spot where the ground was even, they set the machine down. Bekir walked to the shed behind the Turkish hazel tree and brought back four plastic thirty litre cans and a stack of about a dozen little buckets, also made of plastic. They tackled Sergeyich's honey first.

"I don't need a big can," he told Bekir. "I'm used to small containers."

They took turns cranking the handle. Sergeyich watched with a smile as the amber honey was flung out of his combs and landed on the steel inner wall of the extractor. His sweet gold filled up six five-litre buckets and two one-litre glass jars. Then they turned their attention to the hosts' hives.

Akhtem's honey was darker. Perhaps that's why it seemed heavier to Sergeyich. He wanted to sample it, for comparison's sake.

A convenient moment to do so, however, only came hours later, after they had cleared all the hives. Bekir managed to fill up three plastic cans and half a bucket with Akhtem's honey. Then he carried the half-full bucket over to the bedspread by the fire, and set an empty one under the extractor's tap. A thin yellow thread still oozed from the steel honey gate, glinting in the sun like pure gold. The young man brought a bag of flatbreads from the 4×4, broke one in two, dipped it in the half-full bucket, and handed it to Sergeyich, who put the honeyed edge of the flatbread into his mouth and began to chew, paying close attention to the flavour. "Do all the people around here bake their own bread?" he asked Bekir later, when they were having tea.

"We Tatars do, yes. Russians and Ukrainians buy theirs from the bakery."

"Does it taste bad – the bread from the bakery?"

"It tastes alright," Bekir said. "But it's cemetery bread."

"What do you mean, 'cemetery'?"

"They built the bakery over our old cemetery."

"Ah." Sergeyich drew the sound out in an understanding tone.

"Go ahead – dip, eat," Bekir said, nodding towards the bucket of honey and the bag of flatbreads.

Sergeyich dipped and ate with pleasure, washing it down with tea.

"You know," he said suddenly. "Tell your mother . . . Tell her I can do it . . . I mean, go to Simferopol, to ask about Akhtem."

Bekir's eyes lit up.

"I'll tell her! Thank you! I'll drive you myself!" he rattled away excitedly. "But make sure you take your papers – they won't let you through without papers!"

# 49

Sergeyich hadn't ridden in the 4×4 in a long time. And now, sitting in the front seat next to Bekir, the beekeeper felt insecure and uncomfortable. It seemed to him that he was too high up, and that Bekir's turns were too sharp. The car kept turning and turning – left, right, left, over and over – because the road ran along the Belbek. Wherever the river went, the road went too.

"No need to hurry," he urged the young man. Akhtem and Aisylu's son smiled, but he slowed down.

"It's a stable car," Bekir said, glancing at his passenger. "Just right for Crimean roads."

When they drove out onto the Sevastopol highway, Bekir had to reduce his speed yet again, although the road was actually much straighter. They easily slid into the dense convoy of vehicles moving towards the Crimean capital, but soon they were stuck, inching along. In front of them was a lorry, and behind them was a jeep with a Chinese jet ski mounted proudly on its trailer.

"Is this the way to the sea?" Sergeyich said, indicating the jet ski behind them.

"Yes – from Sevastopol the road runs to Foros, then to Yalta. And if you turn right, to Kacha."

Sergeyich nodded. But then the capital's five-storey buildings appeared ahead, and the beekeeper grew nervous, recalling the purpose of their journey.

"What's . . . the best way to talk to them?" he asked the young man.

"I don't know." Bekir shrugged. "The main thing is, don't try to be funny. They don't get jokes. I'll park a couple of blocks away, so that it doesn't look like I'm loitering."

For the next quarter of an hour, they rode in silence down the city streets. The lorry was gone; what they now saw in front of them was a tram, wagging its poles. At the next intersection the tram turned left, and they turned right.

Soon the blue 4×4 drove onto a calm, shady and quiet street,

"Well, here we are," Bekir announced, pulling up to the kerb. "This is number one." He pointed to the corner house on the right. "And they're number thirteen. When you go in, say you're looking for reception."

The first steps along the pavement proved difficult. Sergeyich even began to cough, either from excitement or from fear. It was as if his body wished to elicit its owner's pity, and, in so doing, to plead with him not to act foolishly – most of all, not to speak. And so the beekeeper, assailed by a cough and by fear, walked uncertainly, looking down at his feet. Out of the corner of his eye he saw that there were no houses on the right – only trees. But these trees seemed to be walking in step with him, not staying where they had been planted. Sergeyich stopped abruptly and looked first at the trees, then behind him. No-one there. He shook his head, getting a grip on his thoughts and feelings. Then he set off again, this time with surer step, but still checking on the behaviour of the lime trees and acacias out of the corner of his eye. The trees now remained in place – in other words, fell behind – which meant that Sergeyich was making progress towards his goal.

That goal was a huge, but not tall, building, which sprawled out to the sides like a spider with a red belly and a white back. Its address was 13 Ivan Franko Boulevard.[18] At its centre, beneath a portico that extended some two metres out into the street, was the main entrance. Sergeyich hesitated momentarily on the steps, but then the building's plastic, inexpensive, flimsy doors swung open and out popped a grey-suited little fellow with a folder in his hand. He walked past the hesitant beekeeper and disappeared down the street.

Was it this funny, pitiful little fellow who made Sergeyich smile inwardly? Was it the cheap doors? In any case, the beekeeper easily overcame the last two steps that led up to this serious institution, and was inside before he knew it – face to face with an armed man in uniform.

"What do you need?" the man said coldly.

"The reception room," Sergeyich recited from memory.

"To make a report or a complaint?"

The visitor had no answer, but the guard wasn't waiting for one. Maybe it was this functionary's special joke, which had arisen after hours of dull, monotonous standing.

"Papers."

For this, Sergeyich was prepared.

"Ukraine?" the guard said, surprised. He began to leaf through the tattered blue passport and stopped at the address: "Donetsk region?"

Sergeyich nodded.

The guard then studied the insert, which documented the beekeeper's entry into the Russian Federation.

"They won't give you asylum," he declared, as if he knew exactly why this visitor had come to the F.S.B. "Ninety days and that's it. Got it?"

"I'm not asking for asylum. I'm here for something else."

"What, then?" the guard said, with a note of fatigue in his voice.

"A man is missing. Two years, now. He was kidnapped."

"That's a matter for the police."

"His wife asked me to come to you."

"His wife asked you?" the man in uniform repeated, perking up. This was clearly not a common line of argument around here. "Alright, what's his name?"

"Akhtem Mustafayev."

"A Tatar?"

Sergeyich nodded.

The guard's lips curled in an odd way.

"What's your relationship with him? Or is the relationship with his wife?" he said, then looked again at the visitor's Ukrainian passport and flipped to his marriage record. "Wait here," he said in a commanding tone, and walked away, motioning another guard to take his place.

Sergeyich stood there, feeling restless, and listened to the creak of the doors opening and closing. Everyone who went through them wore heavy civilian clothes – suits and ties – despite the hot summer weather. The guard nodded at them, idly glancing at the papers they presented.

The beekeeper felt a buzzing in his legs. His eyes darted around in search of a chair or a bench, but found nothing. He smacked his lips with displeasure, drawing an inquiring look from the guard. Sergeyich sighed. No wonder he hadn't wanted to come here . . . But what now? They had taken his passport, so he had no choice but to stand there and wait.

The first guard reappeared about fifteen minutes later, by which point the unpleasant sensation in Sergeyich's legs had been joined by a nervous feeling of hunger.

"Follow me," the guard called to Sergeyich from the other side of the turnstile. "Let him through. I've already got his name." These last words were addressed to the second guard.

After going up a few steps, Sergeyich followed the guard down a long greyish corridor lined with tall wooden doors. At the end of this corridor they turned left and walked past a dozen more doors before the uniformed man stopped in front of another door, knocked, then immediately opened it and stuck his head through the crack.

"Here he is, Ivan Fyodorovich."

The guard then showed the weary visitor into a spacious office, but he didn't follow him. On the contrary, he shut the door behind Sergeyich, leaving him alone with a man sitting behind a desk. This man wore a dark-blue suit with a light-blue shirt and a red tie.

Sergeyich looked back at the closed door.

"Please, come, come closer," the office's occupant politely invited. "You wanted to have a talk, didn't you?"

"Yes . . . but he has my passport," the beekeeper responded in his confusion.

"Your passport's right here," Ivan Fyodorovich said, pinching the document between his thumb and forefinger and waving it over the table. "Have a seat."

Sergeyich sat down on his side of the desk. The chair, with its armrests, immediately felt too stiff.

"So, tell me – how do you know this Akhtem Mustafayev?" Ivan Fyodorovich enquired.

Not without some fatigue in his voice, Sergeyich told the story of the long-ago beekeepers' convention in Sloviansk, of the room in the boarding house, of the evening gatherings.

Ivan Fyodorovich listened and nodded, staring at his computer monitor.

"Tell me – do you have another acquaintance, by the name of Petro?" he cut in.

Sergeyich was dumbfounded. "Petro?" he said. "Which Petro?"

"The one you've been texting," Ivan Fyodorovich replied, moving the right side of his monitor a little closer to his face, as if he were reading from it. "You asked him: 'Alive?' And he answered: 'Alive.' This happened several times . . ."

"How do you know that?" Sergeyich blurted out. Ivan Fyodorovich grinned.

"Well, think about it. I'll give you a hint: do you remember handing over your mobile and your passport when entering Russian territory? Yes?"

The beekeeper rummaged through his mind. He recalled every last detail of that entire day: the transformer box with the inscription 18 km to the russian occupiers; Chonhar; the prefabricated office in which the man in civilian clothes had kept him talking for a whole damned hour; the journalists milling around his Lada's broken windows; the money for repairs . . .

"So who's this Petro, eh?" The office's occupant repeated his question.

"Oh, a friend of mine . . . From a neighbouring village. They're getting shelled too," Sergeyich said, checking his trouser pocket with his right hand: the mobile was in there.

"And who's shelling them?"

"Well, you know . . . our side . . . the separatists," the beekeeper said uncertainly.

"Your side . . . the separatists!" Ivan Fyodorovich asked in a thoughtful tone. "I suppose that means Petro isn't a separatist? Since the separatists are shelling him . . ."

"No, he—" Sergeyich began to answer but stopped, realising that he might stumble into revealing a truth upon which no-one around here would look kindly. "He just lives there . . . But that's not my reason for coming here. Why are you interrogating me?"

"What do you mean?" Ivan Fyodorovich said. "No, no, this isn't an interrogation – it's just a conversation. Since you've come all this way to see us, why not ask a few questions? Try to understand . . . You're a foreigner here. You've come from a war zone. See what it says?" He nodded at the monitor, which was invisible to Sergeyich. "'Admitted for humanitarian reasons.' In other words, we took pity on you and your bees, and let you into Russia. So now I would urge you to watch your words . . . You don't want anyone to accuse you of base ingratitude."

"No, no, I'm not complaining – I keep to myself, quiet as a church mouse. All I do is look after my bees!"

"Go on and stay, then. Keep to yourself. But no longer than ninety days. As for this Akhtem of yours, tell his widow to speak to the police. This case concerns either Crimean Self-Defence or the Cossacks."[19]

From all that he heard, the one phrase that immediately stuck in Sergeyich's brain was "tell his widow". A cold sweat broke out on his forehead. He stared into the eyes of the office's occupant, who had fallen silent. Ivan Fyodorovich's eyes turned out to be cornflower blue.

"So she's a widow?" Sergeyich asked for confirmation.

"I misspoke." Ivan Fyodorovich tried to grin, and almost succeeded. "The case isn't closed. And there are at least two dozen such cases in the hands of the police. But they're out of our hands. So please be on your way. Here's your passport."

Sergeyich got up, took the document, and checked whether the insert was still there.

"Take a right at the end of the corridor, then another right," Ivan Fyodorovich advised him.

It wasn't easy for Sergeyich to walk down the long corridor alone. He felt that at any moment one of the doors on the right or the left might swing open, allowing some faceless, strong-armed entity to drag him inside. But the doors swam slowly and steadily past, and although he walked carefully, as if across a minefield, he either did not have time or would not allow himself to raise his eyes to look at the names and ranks engraved on the plaques that decorated each of them. For some reason, out of his distant childhood, there came the sound of his grandmother's voice. Until her dying day, his grandmother spoke in the same amazing voice, by which one couldn't have guessed her age. "Never look Ustim in the eye. It's dangerous."

Ustim was the village madman, and he was mostly harmless. But it was true: as soon as anyone looked him in the eye, he would stick to them like glue. He'd follow them around for hours, and if they should go home, Ustim would park himself on their doorstep and sit there until threats and screams drove him away.

The second corridor still lay ahead. There the beekeeper picked up his pace and kept his eyes on his feet until he had descended the steps to the guard's post.

When he was already ten metres clear of the doors, Sergeyich looked round. He noticed that he was still clutching his passport with its insert, so he tucked it into his pocket. Then he took out his mobile, wanting to check the time, but the battery was dead. Without hurrying, he made his way towards the start of the boulevard, where Bekir was waiting for him – waiting for him, and expecting some kind of news. But what news did the beekeeper have? None . . . Except that this Fyodorovich had called Aisylu a "widow". True, he later claimed he misspoke. But do people in his position ever misspeak?

No, Sergeyich thought as he walked. That's precisely what he wanted to tell me . . . He probably had no right to say more. Really, how could anyone call a woman a "widow" accidentally, for no reason?

The blue 4×4 was where he had left it. Bekir himself was close by, hiding from the sun in the shade. The young man was eating an ice cream, and when he saw the beekeeper he bit off a large piece of the cone, so as to finish it faster.

"The door's open – go ahead and get in!" he shouted.

About three minutes later, they were on the road. The front windows were down, on account of the heat, and the noise of the city burst into the car along with the warm wind.

It was difficult to speak, with all that noise.

When Bekir turned onto the Sevastopol highway, he raised his window and the car grew a little quieter.

"What did they tell you?" he said.

"Nothing concrete," Sergeyich responded, having decided not to mention the word "widow". "I spoke to a fellow in civilian clothes. He said to contact the police – that there were two dozen such cases, and that the Cossacks and the Crimean militia were to blame."

"Nothing else?"

"No." Sergeyich shook his head.

"Well . . . Thank you, anyway," Bekir said with a sigh. "Mother called and said she's expecting us for dinner . . . She also asked whether you'd help us unload some coal."

"Coal?" Sergeyich perked up. "Of course! But what do you need coal for?"

"We use it in the winter."

Sergeyich closed his eyes and recalled his coal reserves. His hands, resting on his knees, could almost feel the warmth radiating from his potbelly stove. The beekeeper smiled and dozed off, overcome by a sudden fatigue – which was both nervous, thanks to the office building with its long corridors, and physical, thanks to the heat.

# 50

Only one who has dealt with coal since childhood can easily determine how many tons of it are lying in a heap on the ground after being dumped by a tipper lorry. And such connoisseurs needn't measure such a heap's radius or its height; they can just take a look and weigh it up in their minds, comparing it with heaps of coal they've burned over time.

"Five tons for sure!" Bekir said, refusing to give up, as they shovelled the coal into a wheelbarrow so as to roll it off to the back of the house and pour it into a cellar with a trap door and a sloping concrete floor, which had been constructed by someone who knew and understood all the intricacies of living with solid fuel.

Sergeyich shook his head again. He had first calculated that the heap was a little over four tons, but now, having seen how much waste rock there was, and having subtracted its weight, he revised his estimate to absolutely no more than four. In light of how vehemently Bekir defended his judgment, the beekeeper decided not to mention the waste rock. After they had rolled another ten wheelbarrow loads to the cellar – taking turns – he stopped beside the door to rest his aching hands and waited for Bekir to approach.

"Is your coal always like this?" he said.

Bekir, of course, understood the meaning of the question. He wiped the sweat from his forehead with his palm.

"Sometimes we get the good stuff – clean, from Rostov," he answered, "but it costs almost twice as much. This stuff's from Donbas. They promised there'd be no rocks . . . But what can we do now? They took the money in advance, and the driver just dumped it and left. Who can we complain to?"

Sergeyich nodded, gripped the wheelbarrow's handles, and pushed it down the sloping concrete ramp, to the left of the steps.

Only the steps reached down to the floor of the cellar, not the ramp. The beekeeper dumped the coal. He and Bekir waited for the dust to settle, then went down the steps and shovelled the lumps away from the entrance, to make room for more loads.

By seven in the evening, their work was done.

At the dinner table, Aisylu kept throwing inquiring glances at Sergeyich. Sometimes she'd exchange a few words with her son and daughter in Tatar, but quietly, almost in a whisper, so as not to make their guest uncomfortable.

"They didn't tell you anything at all?" she said later, over tea, pushing a plate of baklava closer to Sergeyich.

He shook his head and sighed.

"It's good that you went anyway," Aisylu said, looking at him. "Once words are said, they don't disappear – especially questions. The people you spoke to will now be thinking about Akhtem."

Sergeyich glanced anxiously at his hostess, then turned his eyes towards his mobile, which was charging on the floor, in the corner, on the edge of a thick dark-red carpet.

Have to remember to take it, he thought.

And again the voice of Ivan Fyodorovich from Simferopol echoed in his memory: "Tell his widow . . ." Sergeyich returned his gaze to Aisylu. He wanted to say something to her, something good – but what? He felt a dull ache in his shoulders, a heaviness. And his palms hurt. Hauling coal wasn't child's play, after all.

"I'll drive you back," Bekir offered, when dinner had come to an end.

"No need," Sergeyich insisted. "A walk will do me good. My hands worked today, but my legs didn't – so let them get a little exercise."

Aisylu walked with him to the door and, on the threshold, handed him a sheaf of roubles.

"This is for your honey," she said. "We sold it at a good price, both ours and yours."

Sergeyich shoved the money into his pocket without counting it.

He stepped out of the yard and went off down the familiar road towards the mosque, where both he and the road would turn left. The sky was getting lower and lower, the dusk was thickening, but real darkness – of the kind Sergeyich had known since his boyhood in Donbas – never came to these parts.

Somewhere a dog was barking. A female voice reached the lone traveller, a voice that was calling someone – maybe a dog, maybe a cat – by a strange, unclear name.

When he was already going up the mountain, passing the vineyards, Sergeyich stopped and shook his head in dismay. He had indeed forgotten his mobile . . . But he had neither the desire nor the strength to turn back now. He didn't really need it, anyway . . . It was like carrying around the keys to a house one has left far behind: they may seem like an important object, but in fact they are useless.

Sergeyich's thoughts travelled to his native village, to his house, to Pashka. Behind him, the lights of Albat – which all the signs called "Kuybyshevo" – trembled as they receded into the distance.


# 51

Sergeyich couldn't sleep that night. At first, the hedgehogs kept bothering him, snuffling and snorting too loudly. Then restless thoughts got into his head – or just one thought, really: had Ivan Fyodorovich

226

of the F.S.B. called Aisylu a "widow" by accident or on purpose? And for some reason it was then, in the middle of the night, that Sergeyich finally came to believe the F.S.B. official's words, to believe that Akhtem was no longer among the living. And it wasn't Akhtem he began to feel sorry for – he barely remembered his fellow beekeeper, and if he did he was remembering a very different person, twenty years younger . . . No, he began to feel sorry for Aisylu and her children. Although, if her husband had already been missing for nearly two years, how could she actually cling to the hope that he was still alive? She was an intelligent woman. She must have understood that, if they kidnapped him and abandoned the 4×4, then what they needed was his life, not his car or his money. And if someone had needed his life, then they must have taken it away. Otherwise, he would have found a way to let his family know that he was still alive.

Sergeyich turned over on his side, then on his stomach – he just couldn't find a comfortable position. He lay on his back again. Now he felt too hot inside his sleeping bag, though it was already half open. He sat up in the dark, and remembered that he had wanted to dig out the cardboard Nicholas the Wonderworker, so that his church candles would not burn in vain in the evenings. The beekeeper climbed out of the sleeping bag and groped for his torch. He moved the beam of light around the cramped tent, pausing for a moment on the jar with the extinguished candle. Then he turned off the torch, climbed back inside the bag, and fell asleep only because he was tired of thinking. He didn't sleep long at all, maybe three or four hours. And when he awoke, thousands of needles of sunlight were poking at the tarpaulin. They poked at it, but they couldn't pierce it, and so they didn't trouble the beekeeper's eyes.

He pulled on a pair of tracksuit bottoms and a T-shirt, then left the tent and found himself under the blinding sun. He squinted, picked up his bedspread, and settled in the shade beside the nearest hive. It was there, listening to the bees' quiet buzzing, that Sergeyich awoke completely. He then lit a fire and filled the kettle with water from one of his flasks. The smoke tickled his nostrils and he sneezed. Nature sounded louder in his ears, as if they had suddenly been unclogged. The birdsong seemed closer, the bees buzzed more resonantly.

Against this background of noisy nature, he made out another familiar sound – that of an approaching car engine. He went out to the road and recognised the blue 4×4.

Bekir stopped the car right beside Sergeyich and handed the bee-keeper his mobile and its charger, as well as a bag of flatbreads and vegetables. He reported that the power had been shut off in the village, then drove back.

Sergeyich returned to his fire. He ate the hearty flatbread with tomatoes and herbs, washing it down with tea. When he was full, he picked up his mobile and noticed that it had registered a missed call. He was more than a little surprised to see that the call had come from Russia: a plus, a seven, and a long unfamiliar number. The bee-keeper shrugged. Must have been a misdial, he decided. Just in case, he checked his text messages. Nothing new there: "Alive?" and "Alive". But Petro hadn't responded to the latest message, so Sergeyich decided to resend the usual one-word question. And then, not yet ready to release the mobile, he called Pashka. "What're you calling for?" his neighbour asked in a surprised voice.

"Miss home," Sergeyich confessed. "How are things?"

"Quiet, lately – last two weeks. Before that, shells and more shells… Hey, the priest paid me a visit! Gave me an icon and promised they'd rebuild the church. Then the Baptists came and said they'd bring coal for the winter at the end of August – for free!"

"Bring it for you?"

"For me and for you, if you're back by then. They said they'll only bring it for those who've stayed."

"I'll be back, I'll be back." Sergeyich grew audibly anxious. "Is my house alright?"

"Why shouldn't it be? I go over sometimes. By the way, I tried on those moccasins again – the ones you keep in the box. Those sonsabitches are so damn soft – like slippers."

The beekeeper smiled. "Just be careful with them."

228

"You think I'm an idiot?" Pashka said. "You been to the beach yet?"

"I'm pretty far from the coast, here, but they'll take me. They promised."

"Alright, then – you keep calling, OK? I hate being alone . . . A good thing the guys from Karuselino started coming by again. Their Russian commander got killed. They got a local one. I go over there too, once in a while, for some bread and a bottle. Otherwise I'd go nuts."

After talking his fill with Pashka, Sergeyich was tempted to call Vitalina, but he couldn't think of anything to say.

While he was talking to his neighbour, he had managed to find Nicholas the Wonderworker in the Lada's boot, and had set it down in the far left corner of the tent, in front of the candle-jar. He also came across two thick bundles of church candles, which he hid behind the pillow in his sleeping bag.

The day was flying by like a bird overhead. Pashka's voice kept piping up in Sergeyich's mind, telling him the news. It was especially pleasant for the beekeeper to think of his good-for-nothing frenemy putting on the governor's shoes again. That meant they were still safe, in their special box.

I just hope he doesn't wear them to Karuselino, he thought. His separatist buddies might knock him out and take the shoes for themselves. Wouldn't put it past them.

When it got dark, he lit a candle in front of the Wonderworker and rekindled the fire outside, so that there'd be light in both his temporary homes. The candle inside the tent, of course, gave a more homely light than the bonfire in the clearing. But the "big home" didn't really need the bonfire's illumination. That fire existed to provide comfort and warmth, and so that Sergeyich might make tea or porridge. Before going to bed, the beekeeper walked over to the road that led down to the upper rows of the vineyards, in order to gaze at the evening lights of Albat. He stopped at the usual place, but saw no lights. This evening, there was no village – none that he could see, anyway. But Sergeyich didn't take his eyes off the invisible settlement, whose street lamps and sparkly windows usually lifted his mood before sleep, marvelling at how Albat, unilluminated by electricity, gradually emerged in the dense southern darkness. It emerged like something unalive, like distant ruins. In fact, this was probably how his native Little Starhorodivka looked at night, when seen from Karuselino or from Zhdanivka.

He recalled Bekir telling him earlier that the power was out. Apparently it still was.

The beekeeper reflected on his own life without power. It had been strange at first, of course, even painful . . . And the most painful part – more so than the unplugged refrigerator – was the television's dark screen. But eventually he got used to it. After all, bees did just fine without electricity, so why couldn't people? Were people any worse than bees?

Sergeyich considered this for a moment. Yes, people are worse than bees, he concluded.

Then he recalled Aisylu and her children: some people were worse than bees, and some were as good as bees. But better? Unlikely. He decided he would bring Aisylu some candles. Who knew when the power would come back? Maybe tomorrow, maybe in a week . . .

Sergeyich retrieved one of the bundles, lowered it into a bag, and hefted the pleasant burden. The bundle was thick and weighty – about fifty candles. He set off for the village, enjoying the unexpected evening coolness.

The first houses of Albat-Kuybyshevo gave him a bit of a fright, with their mute, dark windows. A couple of times, the beekeeper threw up his head to look at the street lamps, hoping to see at least a hint of light. But darkness reigned all around him. And though his eyes, having grown used to it, helped him to navigate, the absence of light added a sense of threat to the evening silence. The village seemed too quiet, now, as if it were hiding in fear, as if it had withdrawn into itself. Not a single dog barked, not a single car drove down the street . . .

Sergeyich's legs carried him to the mosque. There he turned right. When reached Aisylu's yard, the beekeeper listened closely: the world was holding its breath. He stepped up to the threshold and put his ear to the door: creaking floorboards – they hadn't gone to bed yet. He

wanted to knock, but suddenly changed his mind: They'll ask me inside
... Hospitality...

He placed the bag of candles at his feet, struck the door three times with his fist, then hurried back to the gate.

When he was out on the street, Sergeyich heard someone open the door and pick up the crackling plastic bag.

He felt lighter on the way back, and not because his hands were free. The joy of having done a good deed filled his thoughts and even seemed to lend him strength, so the climb up to the apiary troubled neither his body nor his mind.

# 52

That night rain began to drum on the tent's tarpaulin roof. At first, Sergeyich took it for a dream – and he breathed easily in this dream, inhaling its fresh air. But when he opened his eyes in the morning, he heard the same rain and inhaled the same moist freshness. The joy that he had felt in the night suddenly evaporated; he realised, for the umpteenth time, that while dreams are nothing but movies, their soundtrack is often drawn from real life.

He had experienced this so often since the war began. Sergeyich recalled a distant dream from late spring in 2014, when there was still light in Little Starhorodivka's windows, but explosions were already booming nearby. He recalled how he had dreamed that he was still a child, running home barefoot across a ploughed field. The wind and rain were at his back, and there were heavy clouds in the sky. Someone up there was driving the clouds towards him, speeding them on with thunder and lightning. And so he ran across the ploughed and sown land, his feet sticking in the mud, but the fear helping him pull them out in order to save himself. Then he turned his head and saw fiery zigzags of lightning sinking into the earth. They looked so close and, at the same time, so far away. The earth seemed to tremble with every strike, and he felt these tremors as he ran. When he turned his eyes back to his village, he saw other explosions, not at all like lightning bolts, throwing enormous clods of earth into the air. Then he stopped and looked round, thinking: Where can I run now? At that very moment he woke up in the spring of 2014. His dream had vanished, but the explosions remained. And they continued to thunder until dawn.

The beekeeper rubbed his temples and ran a palm across his short, grey hair, which he had had trimmed only recently at the Vesele district centre. Then he climbed out of his sleeping bag, becoming calmer.

He left the tent and stood barefoot on the grass. The first drops of rain scorched his shoulders and chest, but pleasantly, with freshness. The rain wasn't cold at all. How could it be, in summery Crimea?

Approaching the wet fire pit, the beekeeper realised his tea would have to wait.

Then, all of a sudden, he heard voices, footsteps, crackling branches. He looked round. A few guys and girls wearing backpacks and transparent ponchos were making their way up the path that led from the vineyards to the spring. They stopped when they noticed Sergeyich. One of the girls pulled out a smartphone and photographed the beekeeper in his boxers. Then she smiled guiltily, looking him in the eyes.

"Sorry to bother you. We're tourists," one of the guys said to Sergeyich. "Is this the way to Bashtanovka?"

"I don't know," Sergeyich replied. "I'm not from around here."

"Oh? So where are you from?"

"Donbas."

The guy tensed up, cast a nervous glance at the tent, then nodded either to Sergeyich or to his comrades and walked on.

The tourists rustled past the beekeeper in their ponchos without giving him another look.

Now Sergeyich felt a chill. Something creaked in his chest and burst out in a familiar cough. He quickly climbed back into the tent, dried himself off with a towel, and got dressed. Then he noticed that the candle in front of the cardboard Nicholas had burned out, but he didn't light a new one.

By evening the rain had stopped and the grass was dry again. The sun even managed to warm the air for the night before setting behind the mountain. And once it had set, Sergeyich went out to the vineyards, having decided to gaze out over Albat. Once again, not a single light shone from the village.

What's going on? the beekeeper wondered anxiously. He set off downhill, not quite understanding why, but with a firm desire to go up to Aisylu's house and peer through the windows.

That evening – perhaps because of the day's rain, or perhaps because it wasn't so very late – there was audible, visible life in Albat. As soon as he entered the village, Sergeyich saw two cars on the road, both sweeping their headlights across fences and houses. Then someone holding a torch passed him in the street. Dogs were barking. And a bat flew over his head, flapping its wings, not like a bird, but crisply, as if they were made of oilcloth.

Sergeyich entered the familiar yard and paused inside the wide, comfortable arch beneath the grapevines. The leaves above him rustled in the breeze.

He came up to the window nearest the door and saw that there was light in the house – a dull light, but sufficient for evening living. Then he got up on tiptoe and peered inside: three church candles stood burning on the table.

Once again, the warmth of a good deed done filled the beekeeper's heart. A smile appeared on his lips, and he quietly left the yard.

Out on the street, Sergeyich looked back at Aisylu's house one more time.

That's the life, he thought. Warm, quiet, grapes . . .

Then he set off for his tent – stopping to look around now and then, and stepping off to the side of the road when he heard an engine behind him or saw blinding headlights approaching up ahead.

If I could sell my place there, buy one down here . . . he fantasised, having already left the village.

And he looked back again at the cosy, peaceful darkness into which the absence of power had plunged Albat.

But how could I sell my place? he asked himself. Who'd want to live there?

Strangely, even this thought, which sought to blot out his sudden fantasy, didn't really upset him.

"That's alright," he said to it in a whisper, already hiking up past the vineyards to the apiary. "There's a buyer for everything. You just have to be patient . . ."

# 53

When the sun lay down on the mountain, Sergeyich walked out to the road, as usual. The last, wearily yellow rays of light still fell on Albat. Like a magnifying glass, they seemed to bring the village closer, to enlarge the roofs of its houses – some of grey slate, some green, some red – as well as its squat mosque and church.

The day dimmed its light slowly. The setting sun gradually draped the valley with the mountain's shadow – the shadow of the passing summer day.

The village receded, while Sergeyich stood on the hill over the vineyards, lost in thoughts. He emerged from them when, down in the half-darkness of the valley, street lamps began to come on, one by one. And in their wake, here and there, lights appeared in the windows.

"Thank God," Sergeyich said to himself.

And he had the strange sense that it was he who had somehow restored the village's power. He felt it had not been for nothing that he had stood there for half an hour or more, until the sun went down and the air lost its transparency. He had stood there, he felt, in order to control the delivery of night-time light to Albat. Illuminated by this night-time light, the village looked much more romantic and attractive than it had in sunlight. The glow of the street lamps emphasised the lines of the roads, as well as the considerable size of Albat, which contained at least two dozen streets and lanes. Now, Sergeyich felt, in the light of the street lamps, he could actually see the village that bore the unusual, enchanting name of Albat, which was not indicated on any road signs. It seemed to him that Albat now lived, breathed, and spoke its Albatian language behind the luminous windows of its houses. During the day, on the other hand – or in the evening, before the darkness settled and the lights came on – what he saw down there was Kuybyshevo. That place spoke Russian – that is, Kuybyshevan – and differed little from Little Starhorodivka, if one ignored the southern vegetation . . .

This thought captivated the beekeeper and led his mind onward. It occurred to him that, when this village was deprived of power, it remained Kuybyshevo at night. On such nights, the "non-cosiness" he knew so well could only be driven away by lighting candles.

Then Sergeyich's thoughts jumped of their own volition to his home in the grey zone, and a brief sadness arose in his eyes. He remembered the potbelly stove in the middle of the room, remembered the warmth it gave him all winter long and into the spring. But he knew that the potbelly stove and the house were far away, being looked after by Pashka, and the lights of Albat managed to dry the sadness in his eyes, returning him to a calm, joyful mood. Such a mood puts life in balance and creates the illusion that calmness is in itself happiness.

After taking his fill of illuminated evening Albat, Sergeyich turned round and began to carry his calmness and tranquillity back to the tent and the apiary. But then a distant siren drew his attention. And it wasn't just one siren, but a few of them – if it wasn't a trick of the mountain echo. He turned again and, far away, on the road that led to Albat along the Belbek, he saw flashing red lights. Several cars were speeding towards the village. Now he definitely heard multiple sirens, and their noise, though distant, grew louder and louder.

The cars flooded the road with the bright glow of their headlights. The convoy turned left, drove through the streets, and, after two more turns, came to a stop. The sirens fell silent. The red lights ceased their flashing. Albat grew quiet again, but Sergeyich found this new silence unnerving.

Looking intently at the cars, which still had their headlights on and so were clearly visible, the beekeeper concluded that they had stopped somewhere near Aisylu's house. His anxiety intensified. The convoy's incursion into the peaceful silence of Albat alarmed him.

His mobile showed that it was half past ten – not especially early, not especially late, but exactly the hour when all sorts of misfortunes tend to occur. They occur, these misfortunes, due to human vulnerability in the face of the darkened world, the world of night.

Why so many cars? he wondered. Paramedics, maybe? But why so many?

An unpleasant foreboding left a bitter taste on his tongue.

I'll go down and find out, Sergeyich decided – and he did it firmly, so that the fatigue he had accumulated throughout the day could not challenge his decision.

But first he added a few branches to the fire, to make it clear that he was still nearby. He didn't want some tourist wandering around the Crimean mountains to climb into his tent, thinking it had been abandoned.

Down in the village, walking along the first street, Sergeyich had a strange sense of his own foreignness. Albat seemed to bristle against him, although everything looked much the same. The street lamps were on, there was light in the windows – perhaps in even more windows than usual at this hour. But there was something else in the air that he hadn't noticed before, or that simply hadn't existed. He heard too many small, sharp noises: doors slamming, voices shouting words he couldn't understand (apparently in Tatar, but too loud for this dark time of night). Then suddenly three men overtook him, talking loudly, also in Tatar; they passed the lonely wanderer, paying no attention to him, then disappeared, almost at a run, around the next corner.

And before he himself could turn at the same corner, heading towards Aisylu's house, Sergeyich came to feel even more alien. Another group of men caught up with him, one of whom was wearing a white fez. They spoke in hushed tones, and lightly pushed Sergeyich aside. This might have been inadvertent, but it gave the beekeeper a fright and stopped him in his tracks. Standing there, beside someone's fence, he saw yet another group of men heading in the same direction, to where the speeding cars had stopped.

He stayed there a little while longer, but then continued on his path, sticking to the edge of the pavement, so as not to get pushed aside again.

He came up on a crowd of about fifty people, right outside Aisylu's house. The cars were there too, and beside them was a cluster of policemen in mottled uniforms of uncertain colouration, all with black bulletproof vests.

Now Sergeyich understood that something quite serious had happened, and he desperately wanted to find out what it was. But whom should he ask? The Tatars, who were talking animatedly in their own language? Or the armed men, whose native language was clearly Russian?

Sergeyich touched the shoulder of the nearest Tatar, who turned round.

"What's going on?" the beekeeper asked.

"What's it to you?" the Tatar said. "They brought back the body of one of our men."

"Akhtem?" Sergeyich guessed.

"You know him?"

Sergeyich nodded.

"Yes, Akhtem. Found him buried somewhere in the woods. Killed long ago," the Tatar explained.

Sergeyich bit his lower lip. He stared at Aisylu's house. There was light in all the windows.

"But why all the police?" the beekeeper asked, seemingly addressing himself rather than the Tatar, and never taking his eyes off the window of Aisylu's living room.

"They're staying a few days," the Tatar replied, his voice turning cold. "Until the funeral is over and everyone goes home. They're afraid."

"And when is the funeral?"

"Tomorrow morning," the Tatar responded. Evidently intending to end the conversation, he moved over to another group, which included the man in the white fez.

237

Sergeyich also stepped aside. In the yard, behind the closed gate, stood the blue 4×4. He listened closely, thinking that if he could focus his attention, he might hear Aisylu crying inside the house. But the night was filled with too much extraneous noise, like the faint rumbling of car engines. Immediately outside the entrance was a Kamaz police van, its headlights striking the assembled Tatars with aggressive reddish-yellow beams. But the crowd ignored this, lowering their eyes to their palms, which were turned heavenward, and whispering a prayer in a multitude of low voices. Three more men walked past Sergeyich, who was holding his breath. Two of them were carrying a wooden stretcher, and the third held a green blanket or pall folded many times over.

The beekeeper began to feel that his presence was superfluous. He turned to walk away, but then heard footsteps rushing up behind him.

"Hold it," a man's voice commanded him in unaccented Russian.

The beekeeper turned and came face to face with a muscular man in black trousers and a windcheater of the same colour.

"Passport," the man demanded.

"What for?" Sergeyich said in surprise. "My passport's up in my tent."

"Where's your tent?"

"Up there," the beekeeper gestured towards the vineyards. "Near the apiary."

"You a beekeeper?"

"Well, yes . . . But not a local beekeeper. I'm from Donbas."

"Ah . . ." The man drew the sound out, as if he already knew all about Sergeyich. "Why'd you come down here?"

"To see what was going on. I heard sirens."

"I see. Just curious, then." The man nodded, yet, to Sergeyich, the expression on his face looked neither kind nor calm. "Go on, then, back to your hives. This is no place for an Orthodox fellow to be hanging around."

As he made his way up the street, Sergeyich looked back, to check whether the muscular man was still watching him. But he was gone, while the crowd of Tatars had grown.

"No place for an Orthodox fellow to be hanging around." Sergeyich looked down at his feet. Did he mean all of Crimea? That can't be . . . There's a church right here in Albat . . . Or did he mean I shouldn't be hanging around Tatars?

Sergeyich grunted and turned his eyes to the vineyard beside the road leading up to the apiary.

When he reached the spot from which he liked to gaze at Albat, the beekeeper stopped and cast down a final glance before going to bed. He cast it down, but there was nowhere for the glance to fall. The void at the site of the village indicated that the power had gone out again, reducing Albat to Kuybyshevo.

# 54

Early the next morning, after washing with spring water from one of his flasks, Sergeyich hurried down to the village. He made it halfway without thinking about anything other than the funeral, but when he approached the first houses, he stopped and examined himself. The beekeeper brushed down his unironed trousers and tucked in his white shirt again. He wasn't satisfied with his light sports jacket; its grey colour didn't suit the occasion, but he had no other jacket.

After turning onto Aisylu's street, Sergeyich noticed that the blue 4×4 was now parked outside. Behind it, where the police cars had pulled up the night before, stood a single vehicle, the towering black Kamaz, and near it were three Berkut men, in uniform but without helmets. They stood there looking bored, chatting amongst themselves. The black rubber batons attached to their belts swayed peacefully beside their left legs with every movement.[20]

The people gathering for the funeral milled about Aisylu's yard.

The door to the house was wide open, and people kept coming in and out, speaking softly in Tatar. Sergeyich, standing midway between the gate and the house, looked for Bekir or Aisha. He was simply too scared to come closer to the house, let alone to enter it. But then he spotted Bekir on the threshold and rushed over to him. "Bekir! Bekir!" he called out, seeing that Akhtem's son was about to go back inside.

The young man looked round, saw the beekeeper, and hurried in his direction.

"Is it OK if I come to the cemetery?" Sergeyich enquired cautiously.

"Let me go and ask the imam. Wait here," Bekir said, and he disappeared into the house.

Sergeyich stood at the door for about five minutes, trying not to get in the way of the Tatars who went past him, but sensing that he still would, no matter where he went. He began to feel like a bee in an unfamiliar hive, and he knew all too well what bees did to strangers . . . But then Bekir re-emerged.

"You can come," he said quietly. "But when we start to pray, you'll have to move back from father's grave."

"Emir Allahtan, başıñız sağ olsun," an elderly Tatar pronounced, coming up to Bekir.

"Dostlar sağ olsun,"[21] Bekir said, turning away from Sergeyich. A broad bench was brought out of the house and placed in the yard. Then the stretcher – which now bore Akhtem's body, wrapped in a green pall embroidered with golden Arabic script – was lowered onto the bench. The visitors surrounded the stretcher, leaving some space between themselves and the deceased. Sergeyich noticed that all the men were wearing fezzes.

Indeed, Sergeyich was surprised to find that all those who had come to say goodbye to Akhtem were men. He didn't even see Aisylu or Aisha near the deceased.

By then the imam had come out to the stretcher. The yard resounded with his stern, sorrowful voice, speaking in a language of which Sergeyich understood not a word, yet every word of which he could feel in his body, on his skin. Nor did he need a translation when the Tatars bowed their heads towards their upturned palms and recited their prayer, as if intending their entreaties to bounce off their palms and fly skywards towards the Almighty.

From that point on, everything Sergeyich experienced he experienced as a bee in an unfamiliar hive. He brought up the rear of the funeral procession, before which friends and neighbours took turns carrying Akhtem's body on their shoulders, supporting the stretcher with bent arms. In the cemetery he stood a little to the side – not as far away as an outside observer, but not as close as someone who had been near and dear to the deceased. He heard only Tatar spoken, and it sounded more and more distinct to his ears; he even began to distinguish individual words, though their meanings remained a mystery.

He watched three men hop down into the grave, which seemed exceedingly narrow. They accepted the body wrapped in green cloth, and their heads dipped smoothly beneath the edge of the grave, disappearing below the level of the ground.

It was getting hot. The sun hung directly over the cemetery. Somewhere nearby an indefatigable cricket was rasping out its immortal melody on an invisible violin.

The beekeeper listened, allowing the cricket to hypnotise him, to carry his thoughts off to some unseen, faraway realm. A sense of lightness arose in his head, as if it were empty – not just of thoughts, but of everything that weighs on one's life, of memories and experiences that pile up over the years and bring a pain that threatens to squeeze tears from one's eyes.

"Allah rahmet eylesin,"[22] he heard.

Sergeyich returned his gaze to Akhtem's grave, and heaviness returned to his head, along with thoughts.

The men were again reciting prayers into their upturned palms. When their prayers were done, they began to move away from the grave and Sergeyich noticed two wooden posts in the ground – one at the foot of the mound, the other at its head.

Falling in step with the others, Sergeyich began to question the appropriateness of his presence at the wake. And then he suddenly wondered: did Muslims even have wakes? Maybe everything was different . . . After all, their funerals were not at all like those of Slavs . . .

And when all the other mourners filed back into Aisylu's yard,

*241*

Sergeyich remained outside. He stood there for a minute or two, his eyes searching for Bekir.

Meanwhile, the same phrase kept reaching his ears from the yard – the phrase he had heard at the cemetery: "*Allah rahmet eylesin.*"

The Tatar men would repeat these words to each other, then go over and exchange them with other men.

Just like bees, Sergeyich thought.

He decided to return to the apiary, to his bees and to those that were not his, but whose buzzing he understood equally well – and better, needless to say, than Tatar speech. But first he turned his back to the yard, so that no-one would see him, and crossed himself three times, thinking of the deceased.

# 55

A week had passed since the day of Akhtem's funeral. The weather grew better and better. Sergeyich was first awakened by the birds, then the sun finished the job as he climbed out of the tent and went up to his hives to check how his bees were getting on. He also looked in on Akhtem's hives and saw that his bees were working too, undisturbed by their owner's death.

He drank some tea, had some breakfast, and realised that it was time to do a little shopping: his reserves were running low.

He walked down the road, deep in thought. What worried him was the fact that Bekir hadn't come to the apiary since his father's funeral. It was as if the connection between Akhtem's family and Sergeyich had been ruptured, as if they had turned away from him when Akhtem's sad fate became apparent. No matter how much thought Sergeyich gave to this, he kept arriving at a dead end, unable to work out what to do . . . How should he regard Aisylu and her children now, and how should they regard him – a man of a different faith and from a different land? He had, of course, come to them for help, and not alone, but with his bees. Despite their grief, they had given him help, and continued to give it, not only in the form of flatbread and dinners, but also in the form of spiritual support. He had grown attached to them, like a stray dog grows attached to kind passers-by, following them around, wagging its tail. But suddenly death intruded on their relationship. And that was it. Silence. No-one to talk to. As if they had forgotten all about him.

An empty backpack dangled from his shoulders. In the pocket of his trousers was a wad of roubles – those he'd been given for car repairs upon entering Crimea and those he'd received from Aisylu for his honey. Yes, they had also helped him by selling that honey, so they must have cared about him before the funeral . . . Maybe he had offended them by tagging along to the cemetery? He had been the only outsider there; none of the local Slavs had come to pay their respects.

Sergeyich shook his head. Maybe I should call on them anyway? he thought.

Obviously, he wasn't on their minds. They were in mourning. But he didn't know how Muslims mourned. Maybe their way of mourning precluded them from seeing any outsiders, any people of a different faith.

Well, then they'll politely turn me away, the beekeeper decided. They'll explain at the door. Yes, I'll stop by their place first, then go to the shop . . .

Sergeyich began to count the days that had passed since the funeral, bending his fingers one by one. And suddenly he realised that he wasn't counting the days but the nights, and not even the nights but his dreams. He remembered the last of these dreams, which he'd "seen" the night before: a terrible dream – terrible and stupid. He had dreamed that he lived underground, in an abandoned mine. Somehow, miraculously, there was still electricity powering the dim lights. And the bed in there was just like the one at home. Maybe it was the same bed: an iron frame, with a chrome headboard taller than its chrome footboard, and with round, shiny knobs at the top of each post, which one could unscrew if necessary. And near the bed, about three metres away, all six of his hives were lined up in a row. Bees kept flying out of them, but

Sergeyich had no idea where they were going . . . He dreamed he was sitting by the hive closest to the bed, watching its entrance. He saw the bees fly out, saw them return, plopping down heavily under the weight of the pollen they'd gathered. Only this pollen was black, like coal. Sergeyich looked at the bees, scrutinised them, but could not understand; maybe it was the dimness of the light, but they looked grey, or even black, like big autumn flies. The buzzing alone – which he could never have mistaken for the noise of other insects – told him that they were bees.

When the beekeeper's legs brought him past the mosque, he drove last night's dream from his head. He turned onto Aisylu's street and saw, right by her fence, a dark-blue minibus and a jeep of the same colour with flashing lights (now at rest) mounted on its roof.

As he approached Aisylu's gate, a Slavic guy emerged from the minibus and stared inquiringly at him. It looked as though this guy was about to call out to him, but the beekeeper hastened through the gate, hurried up to the door, and knocked.

It took a long time for the door to open. Sergeyich was about ready to turn back when he heard footsteps.

"Oh, it's you," Bekir said.

"I thought I'd stop by," Sergeyich whispered as he entered. "Wanted to give your mother my condolences."

They sat the unexpected guest at the table and treated him to tea.

"I'm sorry if I came at the wrong time," Sergeyich said, examining his hostess's face and trying to determine how it had changed. Aisylu looked unwell, as if she hadn't slept for days. Her eyes glowed with a strange, cold tranquillity. Aisha sat down at the table, but only for a moment, then took her cup and left the living room. Now it was just the three of them.

A familiar church candle was burning on the dresser. If the mirror had not been draped with a dark cloth, it would have reflected the little flame, which was entirely superfluous in the bright sunlight that spilled into the room through the large window.

"Please accept my condolences." Sergeyich turned his gaze from the candle to his hostess. "And forgive me for disturbing you, for intruding . . ."

Aisylu nodded.

"Thank you," she said quietly. "And thank you for going to Simferopol. If you hadn't, they wouldn't have returned Akhtem."

Sergeyich shrugged.

"They knew," he whispered, looking into Aisylu's eyes. "I didn't want to tell you before . . . The person I spoke to, he called you a widow . . ."

The hostess accepted her guest's words with surprising calm. "You can't call someone a widow if her husband hasn't been buried," she said. "I'm a widow now, though . . . You should come tomorrow, to the wake."

"Has it been nine days?" Sergeyich said, somewhat confused.[23]

"Six," she answered. "Tomorrow it will be seven."

"You do it on the seventh?"

"On the third, the seventh, the fortieth – and the fifty-first," Aisylu said, lowering her eyes to her untouched tea, then turning to her son. "Will you pick him up tomorrow?"

Bekir nodded.

About five minutes later Sergeyich got ready to go. Neither Aisylu nor Bekir had touched their cups during their short conversation, so the beekeeper decided not to finish his own tea either.

Akhtem's son escorted the guest to the door.

"Tell me, why didn't Aisylu come to the funeral?" Sergeyich asked, before leaving.

"Our women and children don't go. They say their goodbyes at home," Bekir explained. "I'll pick you up tomorrow, around one."

# 56

The next day, the first thing Sergeyich looked for at the mourners' table was alcohol. But he found none. Only lemonade and compote. He knew about the Muslim prohibition against alcohol, of course, but he had thought that maybe at wakes . . . That was, after all, a special case . . . The other guests had fallen silent when he'd come in. They glanced at him and nodded. Then they got up and, by the looks of it, started saying goodbye to the hostess in Tatar. This gladdened Sergeyich; perhaps now he would be left alone with Akhtem's family, and they'd be able to speak in Russian. But just as he was thinking this, two more men entered the room. Sergeyich recognised one of them – the one who had led the prayers at the cemetery. This man now greeted the beekeeper in Russian and shook his hand. Then all the guests began to speak Tatar again. Sergeyich shrank into himself. He felt uncomfortable.

To make things worse, he had developed a nervous appetite. No longer looking at the guests, who had all taken their seats at the table once more, he reached for a piece of flatbread topped with cheese and herbs.

Suddenly the imam – the man who had led the prayers at Akhtem's grave – addressed Bekir and Aisylu in an unexpectedly loud and, it seemed to Sergeyich, stern voice. Hearing it, even Aisha peered out from behind the door, entered the room, and began to listen.

The imam then pointed to the burning candle, explaining something to those present. Aisha ran to the dresser, bent over the candle, and blew out its little flame.

The imam cast an approving glance at the girl.

He left about five minutes later, and, as he was walking out of the room, shook Sergeyich's hand again, which calmed the beekeeper's nerves a little.

After the door slammed shut behind the imam's back, Aisylu rose from her seat, went over to the dresser, struck a match, relit the candle, and returned to the table.

Then the voices of still more guests reached Sergeyich's ears from the corridor. He rose, gave the hostess a mournful look, caught her attention, and, nodding goodbye, left the living room. In the corridor he stepped aside to let two men and one woman pass on their way to the mourners' table.

This time two minibuses were parked by the fence. There were

Berkut men in the one nearest the gate, with black bulletproof vests over their uniforms.

For some reason, as he walked past the vineyards, Sergeyich kept thinking of these policemen in body armour. He reflected on the fact that bees and ants also had their guards, who maintained order and protected families from foreign incursions. He also thought that people might learn a thing or two about maintaining order from bees. After all, bees alone had managed to establish communism in their hives, thanks to their orderliness and labour. Ants, on the other hand, had only reached the stage of real, natural socialism; this was because they had nothing to produce, and so had merely mastered order and equality. But people? People had neither order nor equality. Even their police were useless, just loafing around by the fence . . .

Sergeyich might have thought of nothing but bees, ants and the Berkut stationed outside Aisylu's house until he reached the apiary, but his attention was suddenly drawn by a group of tourists hurtling downhill on heavy mountain bikes. The one riding out front, who wore a yellow backpack, loudly greeted the beekeeper. "Good afternoon to you too!" Sergeyich shouted in response.

Then he stopped and followed the whole group of bike tourists with his eyes.

At about five, just as Sergeyich returned from the spring with fresh water, his mobile rang in the tent.

The beekeeper, surprised, ducked inside and looked at the screen.

"Galya?" he whispered.

"Seryozha? Can you hear me?"

"Yes! Yes!" the beekeeper replied, pressing the top of the device to his ear.

"Well, how are you?"

"Not bad. It's hot down here. And you?"

"We've had a . . . a bad time," she said in a flustered voice. "Valik killed himself. The one your bee stung in the eye."

"What do you mean? How?"

"Blew himself up with a grenade. He'd been out of it, lately. Kept bumping into things, on account of his blindness – into lamp posts, people. He'd bump into someone, then pick a fight. Well, this morning we hear a big blast. The whole village comes running – I left the shop open – and we see him there, in his yard . . ."

Sergeyich sighed. "I'm sorry. That's awful."

"Yes, of course, it's awful," Galya agreed. "But what I'm calling to say is – you can come back. No-one will bother you now."

"You really think so?"

"I'm telling you, come back. Things will be better with you here . . ."

# 57

In the evening, Sergeyich retrieved his bottle of honey vodka from the boot, took the enamel mug he used for tea, and sat down beside the hives – but not his own hives. Akhtem's bees didn't seem to object to his presence. He sat, mug in hand, and listened to the music of bee-wings. Then he took a sip of the vodka, and a warmth filled his mouth, along with a bitter aftertaste (this happens when alcohol and honey fail to find a common tongue). The honeyed bitterness made Sergeyich think of Akhtem. He understood that what had happened to the Tatar was no accident. He must have got into politics, must have gone against forces from which one ought to run and hide. After all, it wasn't for nothing that the Berkut were keeping watch over his house even after his death. "Why didn't you protect him?" Sergeyich whispered, looking at the nearest hive's entrance, where, despite the approach of evening, bee-life was in full swing. "Why did you let him leave you?" He sat there, feeling sad, occasionally pouring more vodka onto his tongue in order to refresh the honeyed bitterness. He glanced at the Tatar's other hives and thought about Bekir. "He'll manage," the beekeeper whispered to himself. And suddenly a sharp pain pierced his heart like a knife. He felt envy for the late Akhtem. It occurred to him that he himself had no son, and if something should happen to him, his bees would be orphaned. They would die of disease or parasites, or simply waste away from neglect. He had a daughter, of course, but in actual fact it was his ex-wife, Vitalina, who had her. And his daughter took no interest in bees, anyway – a love of bees isn't transmitted through mother's milk. That strange thought startled Sergeyich. What did mother's milk have to do with anything? It wasn't as if Vitalina cared a whit about his bees . . . He sighed, then took another sip.

Galya's call came to mind.

She's waiting, after all, he thought. I mean, I can't stay here. Ninety days and you're out . . . And if not back to Galya, then where? Home? I could . . . should, even. The Baptists will bring free coal in late August . . . And Pashka said they'll only give it to those who are there to receive it.

Sergeyich wanted to pour more vodka into his mug, but he saw that the bottle was empty.

He looked down at the entrance again. The bees, returning home with pollen on their legs, were pushing and shoving one another, each trying to get inside before the others.

"Come now, don't act like people," he reproached them.

# 58

Most evenings, as darkness descended, Sergeyich would stroll out to the road overlooking the vineyards and Albat. He wanted to feast his eyes on the life of the village, illuminated by glowing windows and street lamps – but, lately, no such luck. The district seemed to be having serious problems with electricity. Instead of enchanting Albat, what he saw was the black hole of Soviet Kuybyshevo. He would look down into the murk, sigh, and head back to his tent.

On the other hand, the beekeeper found it easier to fall asleep these days. Yet he would wake up anxious – and this anxiety was triggered by thoughts of honey. The combs both in his and Akhtem's hives were nearly full. Before you knew it, the bees would start to seal them with wax. It was time to ask Bekir to bring his extractor again, but the

249

young man hadn't come up to the apiary since his father's funeral. And Sergeyich, for his part, hadn't gone down to the village. He had enough food, and he didn't want to impose on those grieving for Akhtem.

The beekeeper would have liked to know, of course, how long Muslims were expected to mourn for their dead. Aisylu had told him that they held wakes on the third, seventh, fortieth and fifty-first days, but he hadn't thought to ask her about the period of mourning. There was no-one around to tell him now: he couldn't very well ask the bees, could he? And what if Bekir didn't come in the next few days? The honey had to be extracted, otherwise the bees would think they had all they needed. Then they'd have no reason to fly off and work. How was he supposed to explain to them that it was just a mistake, that they had to keep flying all summer long? Didn't Bekir sense it was time? Akhtem would have sensed it. Maybe, Sergeyich thought, he should go down and try to find another beekeeper among the locals. He didn't want to trouble Aisylu and Bekir. And any beekeeper would help a brother in need, wouldn't he?

The next morning Sergeyich went out to the road and caught sight of a young woman pedalling uphill, giving it her all. He watched her from above, a little perplexed: tourists usually travelled in groups, but this one was all alone.

And so the beekeeper stood there, warming his head in the rays of the sun, which had yet to start burning in earnest, and watching the stubborn young cyclist, who had jumped off her bike and was now walking it up the road. He stared and stared, and at last recognised Aisha. From far away her face didn't look eastern at all. Only up close could you see that she wasn't Slavic, thanks to the shape of her brown eyes. She had never come up to visit him before, so most likely she was just passing through; there was no end of trails around here, leading this way and that.

Still, Sergeyich stood there and waited.

And when Aisha spotted the beekeeper, she picked up her pace. He could see how hard it was for her to push the bike.

"Hello," she gasped, stopping about three metres away from him.

Sergeyich walked up to the young woman and waited for her to catch her breath.

"How have you all been down there?"

"Mother needs to see you," Aisha said. "As soon as possible."

"She does?" Sergeyich said, puzzled. "So you came here to get me?"

The young woman nodded.

"I'm such a fool – I should have given you my number," the beekeeper said quickly and nervously. "You wait here!"

Then he walked back to the apiary, to his tent, cursing himself along the way, trying to understand why he hadn't immediately set off for the village with her, why he had asked her to wait, as if he had to take something with him. And why hadn't he given them his number?

Ducking into his tent, he calmed down.

Of course, he decided. I can't come empty-handed, can I? They're probably running low on candles by now. I'll bring some more . . .

He pulled five candles from a bundle and left those for himself.

The rest he wrapped in paper and put into a bag.

About halfway down, Aisha asked whether he minded if she rode her bicycle. It was silly, of course, to push a bike downhill when you could ride it.

"Go ahead!" said Sergeyich.

And so she took off down the dirt road – cautiously, pumping the brakes.

When the beekeeper turned right at the mosque, the first thing he noticed was that the Berkut were gone. In fact, Aisylu's street was deserted – no people, no cars with flashing lights. This should have eased Sergeyich's mind, but it had the opposite effect. He couldn't get to the grapevine-covered yard fast enough. Once inside, he didn't even bother closing the gate behind him, just made straight for the house.

Aisylu opened the door and led him into the living room. He shot a glance at the mirror above the dresser: it was still draped, and there was still a candle burning in front of it – but a candle of different sort, made of stearin.

"They've arrested Bekir," Aisylu said, in a voice weighted with weary, crushing pain, now that a new grief had been added to one that had already sapped her of all her strength.

"What for?" Sergeyich said, staring dumbly into her eyes.

"They searched the house. The detective said that Bekir had robbed the church, that he had stolen some candles." She glanced at the small flame fluttering in front of the mirror. "But someone left those candles at our door when the power went out. Bekir was away that day. How could he have robbed the church when he was in Qarasuvbazar?"

Sergeyich became tense.

"No, he didn't steal them," he said after a pause. "I'm sure of it. I brought you those candles. They're mine. No-one stole them. Our church was bombed back at home, and I went in and took them . . ."

Aisylu's eyes lit up.

"It was you who brought the candles?" she said, as if she could not believe his words.

"Yes, and look, I've brought some more." He pulled the paper bundle out of the bag, placed it on the table, and unwrapped it.

"Praise Allah!" Aisylu exclaimed with a sigh of relief. "Then you'll tell them? Yes? You'll tell them you brought the candles?"

"Of course, of course – but who do I tell?"

"Go to the police station in Bakhchysarai. That's where they took him."

# 59

That same day, with Aisha beside him in the passenger seat, giving him directions, Sergeyich arrived in Bakhchysarai.

"How can I help you?" asked the policeman at the desk.

"I need to speak to your chief. About a young man from Albat, named Bekir."

"You mean Mustafayev?" the policeman said, grinning wryly. "What's Albat? He's from Kuybyshevo. And what's he to you?"

"No-one," Sergeyich answered, feeling a little confused. "I just wanted to say that I gave them those candles. He didn't rob any church."

"That so?" the young policeman asked, looking intently into the visitor's eyes. "I see. So why ask for the chief? You need the lead detective. Show me your papers."

The beekeeper handed over his battered Ukrainian passport.

"Why didn't you get a Russian one?" the policeman asked with some surprise as he accepted the document. Leafing through it, he stopped at the address and gave the visitor a look of even greater surprise. "Where's your immigration card?"

Sergeyich handed him the insert, which he had folded in four.

"You should show more respect for documents," the policeman said, shaking his head. "Wait here," he added, and off he went into the depths of the corridor.

He came back accompanied by another man of about forty, with close-cropped hair, wearing black trousers and a blue shirt. In his hands the man held Sergeyich's passport and its insert.

"Well, then," said the man, after glancing at the document and returning his gaze to the beekeeper. "Sergey Sergeyich, let's go and have a chat."

There were three desks in the office to which the detective brought him, all littered with folders and papers.

The detective introduced himself indistinctly, sat down at a desk by the window, and pointed the beekeeper to a chair opposite.

Tritonov? Grifonov? Sergeyich thought, still trying to decipher what he had heard, as only the first word – "detective" – had been spoken clearly.

"So tell me," this Trifonov or Grifonov commanded, staring straight into his eyes.

Sergeyich explained about the candles, about his village and the bombed-out church, about his bees. And the detective listened and nodded, but his face remained stony, indifferent, as if he didn't believe a single word. And so Sergeyich grew ever more nervous.

"That's the truth," he added, after his story seemed to have come to a natural full stop.

"You gave Muslims candles from an Orthodox church? What brought you to such extremism?" the detective said in the voice of someone genuinely horrified by something genuinely terrible.

"What's wrong with that?" Sergeyich shrugged. "Their power was out. I use the same candles back home. We haven't had electricity for three years."

The detective turned and fixed his eyes on an icon of the Mother of God that hung on the wall.

Sergeyich swallowed nervously. He too looked at the icon, then shifted his gaze to a portrait of the Russian president, which hung to the right of it.

Trifonov-Grifonov took several sheets of paper and a pen from the drawer of his desk and cleared a space in front of his visitor.

"Write down everything you told me," he said. "In detail." Sergeyich began to puff over the first sheet of paper.

"I might make some mistakes," he said, looking up at the detective.

"Don't worry, we'll sort them."

It took the beekeeper some twenty minutes to retell his story. The detective waited patiently. At the end, he picked up and read the three sheets covered in uneven handwriting.

Then, without saying a word, he left the office with the papers in his hand.

Sergeyich decided that the detective had gone to get Bekir.

He'd bring the young man out and let them go.

But about five minutes later the detective returned alone: no Bekir, and no papers either.

"You can go now," he said indifferently.

"So . . . I should wait for him outside?" Sergeyich said.

"What do you mean?" the detective said, his eyes widening.

"Well, I mean, you'll be letting him go now – and I came by car, so I can drive him home . . ."

The detective shook his head, looking baffled.

"You're an odd one, you know that?" he said after a while. "Why do you feel the need to get mixed up in other people's affairs? And do you think we got this Mustafayev on the candles alone? He's a brazen little guy – been driving someone else's car for two years without official permission, mouthed off to the authorities . . ."[24]

"But it's his father's car!" Sergeyich interrupted indignantly. "And his father was killed. You know that."

"Yes, the car is registered to the father, and the father never gave official permission to his son. That means the son has been flouting Russian law for two years."

"But how can a dead man give official permission?" the beekeeper said, spreading his hands and looking at the detective as if he were an idiot.

The detective seemed to read Sergeyich's mind. His eyes flashed with anger.

"Your Tatar has two options," the representative of Russian legality squeezed out through his teeth, his whole face exuding contempt for Sergeyich. "Prison or the army. If he's smart, he'll choose the army. They'll teach him to respect authority, or at least to fear it. If he's not, then . . ."

The detective did not finish. He seemed to have decided that he had given Sergeyich more than enough, and that he was not going to honour him with another word.

"So what should I tell his mother?" the beekeeper said, this time more quietly, fearfully.

"Tell her whatever you want," the detective snapped. "Remember, you're a foreigner here," he added, returning the visitor's blue Ukrainian passport with its insert. "And if you don't leave the territory of Russia in eleven days, you'll be brought here yourself – and not to an office, but to a cell."

On the road back to Albat, Sergeyich kept glancing at Aisha, wondering whether to tell her what he had found out. That whole time he did not say a word, nor did she ask him anything. She just sat there quietly, tense, almost as if she were afraid of him. It was like that all the way to the village.

When Sergeyich told Aisylu about his conversation with the detective, she could barely hold back her tears.

"They want to break us," she said quietly. "They were going to drag our neighbours' son off to the army, but they bought his way out. They got the money from family. Now he's in Chernihiv, at the university . . ."

Aisylu fell silent, rose from the table, and went into the kitchen. Sergeyich raised his head and looked at the lit chandelier. Then he turned to the dresser: a stearin candle was still burning in front of the mirror.

"Would you like a drink?" Aisylu said, returning to the living room with a plate of sandwiches.

"You mean – you drink?" Sergeyich asked dubiously.

"No, but we have some."

He nodded. Aisylu placed a shot glass on the table, and then an open bottle of vodka appeared in her hands. She filled the glass and took the bottle away.

Sergeyich reached for a sandwich. He had got so used to home-made flatbread – both here and at the apiary, when Bekir would bring him provisions. And now: white bread, cheese?

"I have no strength left," Aisylu sighed, noticing her guest appraising the sandwich. "None . . . Aisha and I are all alone now . . ."

"Maybe you could buy Bekir's way out?" Sergeyich suggested. "If the neighbours did it . . ."

Aisylu shrugged.

"I wanted to ask for something else," she said, looking more intently into her guest's eyes. "I'd like to get Aisha away from here."

"Where would she go?"

"Home with you . . . You people have it better up there."

"We do?" Sergeyich said, looking at Aisylu as if she were mad. "There's shooting and shelling, and no power . . ."

The beekeeper grew nervous and felt his hand begin to tremble, along with the sandwich he was holding. He took a bite, then reached for the glass with his left hand, brought it quickly to his lips, so as not to spill any vodka, and emptied it in one gulp.

As he chewed, the flavour of the white bread struck him as strange. "This is from that bakery that's at the cemetery?" he said.

"We don't have any other," Aisylu said. "I'll bake some flatbread tomorrow. They say it's going to rain . . ."

"May I have a little more to drink?" the beekeeper asked.

The hostess rose to her feet, brought the bottle, filled his glass, and took the vodka back to the kitchen.

I don't know whether to laugh or to cry with these Muslims, Sergeyich thought, watching Aisylu walk away. He shook his head, and when she came back to the table, empty-handed, he raised his glass again.

"I wasn't talking about Donbas," the hostess said calmly, in the tone of a teacher addressing a pupil. "I want to send Aisha to Ukraine, to get an education. But I don't know where would be best. I came back from Uzbekistan when I was still a girl, and I haven't left Crimea since – I've been too afraid . . . Where do you think she should go?"

Sergeyich thought for a moment.

"I haven't done much travelling myself . . . Horlivka was a fine place, and Donetsk . . . That was then . . . But Vinnytsia – Vinnytsia's still good, that I guarantee."

"Vinnytsia?" Aisylu repeated. "Do they have a university?"

"Of course. It's a big city. My ex-wife's over there. With my daughter."

"So maybe I'll send her to Vinnytsia?" Aisylu said, addressing herself more than her guest.

"Why not?" the guest agreed.

"We'll raise some money," said Aisylu. "And we'll get her to the border, but on the Ukrainian side . . ."

She looked inquiringly into Sergeyich's eyes.

"I've got to go back soon, anyway," said the beekeeper. "Seems to me they're counting the days till I leave . . . I'd be happy to take her to the border."

"And maybe you'll help her on the Ukrainian side too? Put her on a bus to Vinnytsia?"

"Maybe," Sergeyich said uncertainly. But then, catching the

hostess's questioning look, he nodded and said more affirmatively, "I'll do it."

# 60

In the morning Sergeyich drove down to Albat in his car, trailer in tow. He asked Aisylu for the extractor, saying he would happily take care of both their apiaries.

"All by yourself? No – I'll help," she responded firmly. The bee-keeper did not put up a fight.

They lowered onto the trailer the wooden board to which they would screw the extractor in order to maintain its stability on the ground. The extractor itself went on top, further secured with straps. Then Aisylu retrieved some plastic thirty-litre cans and a stack of a dozen five-litre buckets from her shed. Their lids were in a separate bag, which she loaded into the boot.

When they were getting in the car, Aisha came running out of the yard. She handed her mother a cloth bag that contained something round, like a pot.

They drove away from the house. Sergeyich kept turning around to check on the trailer, and every time he did so, a warm, pleasant odour teased his nose.

"What smells so good?" he wondered aloud.

"Aisha baked us *samsas*. We'll have them later."

A warm wind blew in their faces, going straight through the Lada and carrying the smell of warm *samsas* out into the open air.

The car shook its way up the dirt road, past the vineyards. "You didn't have to come. I would've managed it myself," Sergeyich said.

"It'll be quicker this way," Aisylu replied quietly.

As he watched Aisylu deftly screw the extractor's legs to the wooden board, Sergeyich realised she was far from a novice. She must have helped Akhtem too.

They took turns cranking the centrifuge's handle, and started with Akhtem's hives. After they had cleared thirty honeycombs or so, the centrifuge grew stiff. Aisylu placed one of the plastic cans under the honey gate, filled it almost halfway, and set it aside.

They sat down to eat after filling two cans.

Sergeyich munched on the little pies stuffed with juicy chopped lamb, savouring them, and thought: how come he and Aisylu didn't talk while they worked? When he and Bekir had been at it, they had talked nonstop, about everything and nothing. Their mouths hadn't closed for a second. It helped pass the time, made the job easier. But with Aisylu, it was all done in silence – just "hold this", or "enough". And yet they worked quickly enough – quickly and smoothly.

Maybe it's for the best, the beekeeper thought. I mean, what would I talk about? Vitalina? Petro? Pashka? No, she wouldn't understand . . . There's no sense in talking about Galya . . . And me, well, I wouldn't understand anything about their lives, either. For instance, why do they bury their dead without coffins?

Sergeyich recalled Akhtem's funeral: the body on the stretcher, wrapped in a green pall embroidered with golden Arabic script. Was that any way to bury someone?

He found no answer to his question. If that's how they did it, then it was one way to do it.

Maybe that's why the F.S.B. and the police don't like them, he thought. He had felt this dislike in Simferopol, when he had inquired about Akhtem, and at the police station in Bakhchysarai, when he had tried to free Bekir. He remembered the detective's question: "Why do you feel the need to get mixed up in other people's affairs?"

It was Aisylu who was cranking the honey extractor now – tirelessly, as if she did it every day.

The sun was sinking towards the mountain, foreshadowing the approach of evening.

They had worked their way up to Sergeyich's hives, and it seemed to him that his bees had made less honey than Akhtem's.

This upset him, and he began to crank the handle more aggressively.

"Let me help," Aisylu offered, noticing that Sergeyich looked tired and had paused to catch his breath.

"No need," he protested stubbornly, gripping the handle again.

Three full plastic cans stood by the car – a harvest to be proud of. Only there was no-one to take pride in it. After all, the person who ought to take pride in a harvest of honey is the beekeeper, not his wife. But Akhtem was dead and buried. Maybe that's why Aisylu's face showed only tiredness. It suits her, Sergeyich thought, and he felt an urge to comfort her. But how? Embrace her? Lend her a shoulder to cry on? No, she wouldn't cry, that much was clear. And he couldn't embrace her, either: she wasn't allowed to have such close contact with other men. It was all so different with her people . . . In a word, they lived by different laws.

Sergeyich had extracted seven five-litre buckets of honey from his hives – a little over a can. No mean amount, considering the fact that he only had six hives, while they had three times as many. So why had he felt that there was less honey in his combs?

The sun set on the mountain. If it had legs, it would now be dangling them, all bright and fiery, from the mountaintop.

"We ought to clean out the extractor," the beekeeper suggested. "I've got water here."

"Don't worry." Aisylu stopped him. "I'll do it at home."

Working together, they unscrewed the extractor's legs from the wooden board. Then they brushed all the grass and dirt from the board, lowered it onto the trailer, and set the extractor on top. The three cans of honey came next.

Sergeyich put his little buckets in the boot of the car. "Sell it," he said. "And use the money to free Bekir."

They arrived at the house at dusk. Aisylu stepped out of the car, opened the gate, and Sergeyich drove into the yard.

Windows glowed from within. And the street lamps were on.

That evening, there was power enough to light Albat.

# 61

Stoking the fire, Sergeyich thought back to the previous August: very different, not at all like this one. The sun had blinded Donbas mercilessly . . . The heat had been unbearable . . . The birds would sing only in the early morning, then fall silent, as if their little throats had grown parched. But then they would start singing again before the following dawn, at the top of their voices. One would think they were still happy, despite it all, about the start of a new day, about the new heat. Sergeyich smiled, recalling the birdsong that used to wake him in the mornings. Yes, of course they were happy – of course they were. They were happy that a new morning had begun, that they were alive to greet it. And, listening to them, he too was happy, for the same reasons. Although he sometimes felt that this happiness of his was foolish – not human but animal, birdlike. Some weeks earlier, Pashka had brought back news from Karuselino: the separatists and the Ukrainian army had agreed to move their artillery further away from Little Starhorodivka, widening their native grey zone, which would now include Karuselino, Zhdanivka and a few other villages besides. Life would be peaceful and normal, as in Svitle, where there were still families with small children. And indeed, for almost a whole month, not a single shell exploded, not even at night. All was quiet. Out of happiness and renewed courage, Sergeyich even took to sleeping in his orchard. He'd drift off to the chirping of crickets and wake up to the trilling of birds. The bees flew freely in the fields. There was less honey in the middle of August, of course – the flowers were withering, drying up in the sun – but then, that's why God gave bees wings, so that they could search for sweet pollen both near and far. It was then, in the middle of August, that he had extracted the last of the year's honey. It hadn't been much. Then he had cleaned the combs, prepared the hives for the winter. By that time the bees were already driving out their drones, also preparing for the winter. But here in Crimea, it seemed, the honey season would last longer. Although the sun this morning was warning him of autumn's approach. That's the way it ought to be, with nature itself issuing warnings – rather than a man in a suit counting out the days before your departure.

After breakfast, Sergeyich checked on his hives. He lifted their roofs, sniffed for moisture, then squatted beside the one the late "counterterrorist" had attacked with an axe, and saw that one of its corners had come loose. He ought to fix that; otherwise, when it came time to load the hive onto the trailer, its bottom might come off. There was a hammer in the car, and probably some nails too.

His thoughts seemed to gravitate towards his departure. And though the summer sun was again as hot as could be, and its rays had already dried the moisture that had gathered on the ground throughout the night, Sergeyich could not force his mind to stray far from the autumn and the road.

As evening drew near, clouds began to crawl across the sky. A light rain fell. And whenever a cloud would block the sun, even for a moment, Sergeyich's eyes would darken and he would yawn – either from fatigue, or because of the humidity in the air. Tomorrow I'll go see Aisylu, Sergeyich decided. And I'll call Vitalina to tell her about Aisha. Maybe she'll have some suggestions?

The rain kept stopping and starting. The beekeeper made a fire and hooked a little pot of water onto the tripod above it. His plan was to cook some buckwheat.

But suddenly he heard the sound of an engine – still far away, but coming closer. He joyfully leaped to his feet, thinking it was Bekir.

They let him go! He hurried out to the spot overlooking the vineyards.

He wondered, along the way, whether Albat had power that evening.

When he came out to the road, he sighed with relief: the street lamps were on, and there was light in the windows. A car was slowly climbing towards the apiary, its headlights probing the ground. Sergeyich couldn't yet make out what kind of car it was, but he saw that it wasn't a 4×4, and so it wasn't Bekir.

Seven or eight minutes passed before Sergeyich himself was caught in the headlights, which belonged to a large minibus.

Pulling up to the beekeeper, the vehicle stopped. Its right door opened right in front of Sergeyich, almost hitting him. He took a step back.

"Good evening," said the man emerging from within.

The voice seemed familiar to Sergeyich, and this puzzled him. After all, he hadn't made any friends here: he had barely even spoken to anyone other than Aisylu and her children. He might have occasionally exchanged a few words with some locals down at the shop, or with some tourists walking or cycling past the apiary, but, come the night, those random voices, heard once, would sink into the abyss that swallowed all the day's unimportant sounds. This voice, on the other hand, was not like that, was not random.

"Don't you recognise me?" the man said.

Sergeyich strained his eyes, but the man's face, partially obscured by darkness, told him nothing.

"You came to see me in Simferopol," the man prompted him. "Ivan Fyodorovich, in case you forgot."

Sergeyich tensed up. He remembered the endless corridors of the F.S.B., the tall doors and the office where he had spoken with Ivan Fyodorovich.

"Oh ... what ... brings you here? Passing through?" the beekeeper said, unable to square the presence of the newly arrived officer with his bonfire, his tent and his apiary.

"Not exactly," Ivan Fyodorovich responded in a perfectly friendly voice. "We came to pay you a visit. A short one. Whereabouts are you staying?"

"Over there," Sergeyich said, pointing. "See the fire?"

"Alright, then, you walk back, and we'll drive," said Ivan Fyodorovich.

The door of the minibus slammed shut, and the vehicle drove towards the tent and the fire. It stopped with its headlights trained on the beekeeper's green, windowless Lada. As Sergeyich walked up, he noted that his long-suffering car looked even more miserable when bathed in yellow light.

Now the driver emerged from the minibus too, leaving the headlights on.

Ivan Fyodorovich loomed up in front of the beekeeper.

Sergeyich spotted a military emblem on the minibus's door. This surprised him. He was also surprised to see that the minibus had no windows, except for those at the very front – which meant it was made to transport cargo, not people.

"This is Vasily Stepanovich," Ivan Fyodorovich said. "He's not really a driver. It's just that there's too much work and not enough people to do it, so I asked him to drive. Well, where are your bees?"

The beekeeper pointed. "Over there."

"Let's have a look," Ivan Fyodorovich said, exchanging glances with his companion. The two of them set out for the hives, and the owner of the bees hurried after them.

Vasily Stepanovich turned on a torch and began to lift the hives' roofs, peering inside. His behaviour alarmed Sergeyich.

"What this about? What are you looking for? I've already extracted the honey," he rattled off nervously.

"That's precisely why we didn't bother you earlier," Ivan Fyodorovich said, turning to the beekeeper. "We'll have to take one of these with us . . . just for a couple of days. Run some tests."

"What sort of tests?" Sergeyich said, dumbfounded.

"When you entered the country, you violated the rules. The department of health and sanitation didn't clear your bees. You know, of course, that bees can transmit diseases, putting the local Crimean bees at risk."

"But . . . nobody said anything. They just let me through."

"Yes, they were being humane. But now they've realised their oversight. In any case, it's nothing to worry about."

In the meantime, having examined all six hives, Vasily Stepanovich stopped beside the third one from the fire. He directed the torch at the entrance, then lifted the roof again and reached inside.

Sergeyich realised that he was shutting the entrance.

"We'll take that one," Ivan Fyodorovich declared, nodding towards the hive beside which his companion was standing. "Lend us a hand?"

Sergeyich and Vasily Stepanovich lifted the hive and carried it to the minibus. Ivan Fyodorovich had dashed ahead to open the door. They placed the hive inside.

"But I'm . . . leaving soon," the beekeeper said, sounding somewhat confused.

"I know, I know," Ivan Fyodorovich replied. "Don't you worry, we'll bring it back in a day or two – if the bees are in good health, that is. And if they aren't – well, you'll forgive us, but we'll have to confiscate all the hives . . . Never mind that for now, let's not get ahead of ourselves."

Watching the minibus recede into the distance along the invisible dirt road, seeing only its headlights and red taillights, Sergeyich felt depressed and broken.

"Confiscate all the hives? And what – destroy them?" he said in a trembling voice.

On the one hand, everything was clear. He himself regularly checked his bees' health, made sure there were no signs of disease. But he did it himself, without involving any outside inspectors. And his bees were fine – he had examined the hives just a little while ago. Couldn't he tell a sick bee from a healthy one? If a bee isn't well, you can see it right away. No, these people were just trying to scare him . . . They'd have a look and return the hive. Nothing to worry about. They would bring it back tomorrow or the day after. What do they need his bees for, anyway?

And yet these thoughts weren't enough to calm Sergeyich. What occurred to him now was this: even if Vasily Stepanovich really was a veterinarian and a specialist in bees, why did Ivan Fyodorovich come along with him? Ivan Fyodorovich – who had an office on the ground floor and, though he preferred to wear civilian clothes, obviously kept an officer's uniform at home . . . What did the F.S.B. have to do with his bees?

He searched for some simple, reasonable explanation, but could find none. And so he got out the honey vodka and had a drink. But this didn't make him feel better, either. He added wood to the fire and sat down beside it. Now his back was too cold and his chest was too hot. The evening brought moisture to the ground. The rain had stopped an hour earlier, but its cool, clammy smell still filled the air.

He took another sip from his enamel mug. The bitter sweetness spilled across his mouth, pinching his tongue.

The sooner I go, the better, he thought.

# 62

Sergeyich couldn't sleep all night. He was chilled to the marrow of his bones. Nothing could keep him warm – neither the sleeping bag nor the sweater he had pulled onto his naked body. And so, not having slept a wink, the beekeeper clambered out to the extinguished fire. He now felt that it was colder inside the tent than outside. He rekindled the fire, pulled the bedspread closer, and held out his palms. But shivers kept running down his spine maybe from the cold, maybe not. Some sort of inarticulate fear had taken root in him – a skin-freezing fear.

He raised his head to the sky, as if in search of salvation. The sky was clear, sprinkled with stars, and the moon was huge and bright, almost full.

The beekeeper was puzzled. It seemed to him that the sky was much brighter than the earth. When he looked down in the direction of his hives, he was met with such a murk that memory, not vision, gave the best indication of the nearest hive's position. And the second hive was entirely obscured by the darkness, as was the spot where the third had stood.

Where did they take it? Sergeyich began to wonder again about that confiscated hive. And they knew just when to come too – in the evening, when all the bees were back from the fields, when the whole family was home . . .

He shook his head. It was true: that second guy knew his way around bees.

And along with these thoughts came a noise. It was a strange noise, somewhat reminiscent of a headache – a rare experience for Sergeyich.

But if this Vasily Stepanovich was a beekeeper, then he must have seen, with the help of his torch, that Sergeyich's bees were healthy. They had no disease, no parasites. And why did he choose that particular hive? What did he see in there? There wasn't anything special about that bee family . . . Maybe they had something else in mind . . . What if they planned to infect his bees, to get back at him for asking about Akhtem and Bekir? The detective had warned him, after all, about getting "mixed up in other people's affairs" . . .

And so Sergeyich sat there, thinking and mechanically tossing branches into the fire. His hands grew warmer and warmer, and his eyes were already accustomed to the night's darkness. Now he could easily make out the wall of the second hive. The main thing, he realised, was not to look up at the moon; after you met its gaze, everything below appeared pitch black.

Something rustled nearby, drawing the beekeeper's attention. He turned and saw a hedgehog hobbling lazily towards the fire. The little creature stopped and glanced round at the level of its eyes – not raising its snout, not seeing the human being. It stayed there for a while, then rustled away across the grass in the direction of the hives.

And when the rustle died down, birds began to twitter – quietly at first, then louder. Dawn approached. As the sun's first rays reached the tops of the trees, the birds began to trill, their song more strident than the little whistles Sergeyich remembered from his childhood.

The beekeeper, on the other hand, was anything but wakeful. He sat hunched over after his sleepless night; his head felt heavy, as if he were wearing a lead hat. At one point he staggered towards the fire and almost fell into it. The proximity of the flames frightened and invigorated him for a moment, gave him the strength to push his palms against the moist earth and straighten himself. He struggled up from the bedspread, climbed back into his tent and sleeping bag, and dozed off.

Sergeyich slept until noon, when he awoke in the heat, sweating. Once more, he was overcome with fear, unable to understand his condition.

Am I sick, or what? he wondered as he clambered out of the tent into the heat-shedding sun. His left arm was numb, disobedient, just dangling at his side like a stick.

Sergeyich remembered that he had woken up on his back, so he couldn't have crushed his arm in his sleep. In any case, the right one was fine, so he used it to wash himself. He placed one of the five-litre flasks on its side and loosened its plastic lid, allowing the water to flow down in a thin stream, as from a proper tap.

When he was done, his legs carried him out to the spot where a square of crumpled, yellowish grass indicated the former location of his confiscated hive. He stood there a while as bees from other hives flew past, buzzing busily. Then he approached the hive that needed repairs, and thought of getting his hammer and nails from the car – but how would he manage with his right hand alone?

Sergeyich sighed. He twitched his left shoulder, paying close attention to the numb hand, trying to revive it with the power of his thoughts and his bitterness. It seemed he could feel it, but it just wouldn't obey his commands, hanging there like a leafless branch.

It'll come good, he thought hopefully. Must've crushed it in my sleep after all.

Sergeyich turned his attention to the rest of his body. He didn't seem to be running a fever; the sweat had dried from his forehead. Yet he still felt broken, powerless, as if he had aged twenty years during the night.

A nap on the hives would fix me up, he thought, recalling how he used to sleep on his bee-bed beneath the trees in Little Starhorodivka, and how he would wake up feeling recharged by the power of several hundred thousand bees. He remembered the joyful smile that shone on the former governor's broad face when he climbed down from the bee-bed, lumberingly, after several hours of sleep. If he himself could do that now . . . His arm might come to life, his strength might return . . .

He surveyed his five hives, thinking that, for a proper bed, he'd need all six. But he could probably make do with five, if he only used one to support his head.

These thoughts eased Sergeyich's mind, strengthened his faith in the restorative power of his bees. Now he just had to put his hives together – but even if his left arm should come to life, he'd never be able to move them by himself . . .

After considering the matter, the beekeeper decided to go down to Albat, to Aisylu. Maybe she'd take him to the local doctor?

He hid his head from the hot sun beneath his orange F.C. Shakhtar cap. Instead of his sweater, which would have been too warm, he pulled on a blue T-shirt, and it seemed to him that his left arm obeyed him reluctantly as it poked itself through one of the short sleeves. He set off down the road without his former lightness of step, but with a sense of purpose that easily replaced true strength and vigour.

# 63

Aisha opened the door.

"Where's your mother?" the beekeeper asked, looking behind the girl and expecting Aisylu to peek out into the corridor at any moment.

"She went to the kindergarten on Kolkhoznaya Street – Fairy Tale," Aisha said. "She's looking for work, and they have an opening for a teacher."

Sergeyich took off his shoes in the corridor and stood still, wondering what he should do.

"Will she be back soon?" he said.

"Yes, any minute now. It was only an interview."

Aisha led the guest into the living room, seated him at the table, and went out to the kitchen, saying that she would make some tea. Sergeyich, sitting in the same chair in which he had sat more than once, glanced round. Something in the room had changed, but at first he couldn't tell what it was. An unusual, unpleasant odour tickled his nostrils – not unbearable, but not the odour he was used to. Still puzzled, he turned his head and looked at the dresser: the mirror was still covered. Then he looked down and saw a burning stearin candle, but it wasn't the same as last time; this was the cheapest kind, grey.

So that's it, Sergeyich realised. They've run out of mine, or they're too scared to light them. And those bastards from the police probably pocketed the ones they found during the search. Of course . . . They're a lot better – real beeswax.

The young woman brought the tea and was about to leave for her room.

Sergeyich stopped her. "Aisha."

She turned and looked at him with bashful eyes.

"Would you sit with me?" the beekeeper said, pointing to the chair beside him.

Aisylu's daughter sat down hesitantly – and not in the chair beside the guest, but in the one opposite him.

"Don't be afraid." The beekeeper spoke softly. "I just wanted to ask about the candles. You light them in memory of your father, yes?"

Aisha nodded.

"How long will you keep lighting them?"

"Forty days," she said quietly.

"I'm sorry," Sergeyich said, biting his lip, wanting to pose his next question but afraid to do so. In the end, he asked: "I mean, your father was killed a long time ago – no-one knows when, exactly . . . So how do you count the forty days? Not from the date of his death?"

"From the date of his funeral," Aisha said, her quiet voice sounding calm. "That's what the imam told us. He scolded mother for the candle." She looked at the little flame that could not find its reflection in the mirror.

"Why?"

"He said that Muslims don't light candles for the dead. So mother hides the candle when he comes."

Sergeyich sighed, pulled out his mobile, and checked the time. His heart began to ache. He wished Aisha would go, leaving him alone, but the young woman sat there silently, as if waiting for more questions.

270

The beekeeper sipped his tea and again glanced back at the candle. Then he ran his eyes along the walls, the rug hanging over the sofa, and the glass-fronted sideboard that held many bright, beautiful dishes and plates.

"My people put the candle in front of a photograph of the departed," Sergeyich said. He wanted to add that they also put a glass of vodka covered with a piece of bread beside the portrait and candle, but realised that it might be inappropriate to mention vodka.

"The face isn't important," the young woman said, in a barely audible whisper.

"What did you say?" Sergeyich said, not sure if he had heard correctly.

"The face isn't important," Aisha repeated, a little louder. "Allah has no face, but he exists."

"But . . . but . . ." the guest stammered. "If it's the face of a loved one . . ."

Aisha shook her head.

"Faces change," she said, again in a whisper.

"That's why people take photographs – to remember," Sergeyich pronounced abstractly. He shrugged, trying to understand Aisha's words. "Or don't you take pictures?"

"Of course we do," she said, her face expressing surprise.

She rose from her chair, went to the sideboard, looked through the bottom drawer, and returned to the table with a book in her hands. When she opened it, Sergeyich realised it was a photograph album.

"Here." She pushed the album towards the beekeeper. "Our photographs. Father too."

The beekeeper drew the album closer with his right hand and leafed through it.

The first picture showed two newlyweds: Akhtem and Aisylu, young and happy. He was wearing a blue suit and a white fez. She had on a white dress gathered by a blue belt, and also wore a fez, but hers was blue and taller than the groom's.

Sergeyich turned the page: the young people were now leading a horse through the field. He looked closely at Akhtem's face. Strange – he didn't recognise him. The beekeeper only knew that the young man was Akhtem because he was standing next to Aisylu. Of course, Aisylu herself had changed since the picture was taken.

Aisha's quiet voice echoed in his head: "The face isn't important."

He began flipping more quickly through the thick pages, no longer paying close attention, until it seemed to him that he had flipped past something familiar. He returned to the photograph that had caught his eye – the only group shot he had come across, in which about fifty people, or even more, were lined up in three rows. They stood on the colonnaded steps of a beautiful old white building. And the building, too, looked familiar, as if Sergeyich himself had been there.

He thought for a moment, shutting his eyes.

"What a fool," he whispered to himself. "It's Sloviansk – the beekeepers' convention!"

He bent over the photograph and began to examine the faces. But the faces were small, and instead of becoming more distinct as he came closer, they blended and merged.

"Aisha, could you point out your father?" he asked, raising his eyes to the young woman.

She walked over, took a close look, and confidently pointed to a man standing in the second row, on the left.

Sergeyich stared helplessly at Akhtem's face.

"Do you have a magnifying glass?" he said, looking up at Aisha again.

She brought one. Sergeyich took it by the handle, held it above the photograph, and peered into Akhtem's face. Yes, that was him: slim, with high cheekbones, and with a moustache so neatly trimmed it looked as if it had been drawn on with mascara.

All on its own, the beekeeper's hand swept the rest of the faces with the magnifying glass. He could recognise none of the other delegates.

Well, it was a long time ago, he thought, and suddenly he froze in fright. But I must be somewhere in here too . . .

He scanned the faces once more, then gave Aisha a bewildered, pleading look.

"Could you help me?" he asked. "Try and find my face? I should be in there . . ."

She came closer, pressing her right shoulder against his left arm, and squinted at the picture. Then she turned to Sergeyich and carefully examined his face.

The beekeeper smiled, very faintly, because his left arm had actually registered the touch of Aisha's shoulder.

Meanwhile, her finger indicated the figure of a man in the upper row, on the right.

"Here you are," she said firmly, and took a step back.

Sergeyich pointed the magnifying glass at the spot Aisha had shown him. He saw a young, short-haired man with a round, clean-shaven face, who was wearing either a grey jacket or a grey suit – hard to say, as the trousers were hidden from view.

"Is that really me?" Sergeyich voiced the doubt in his mind. "No, I don't think so . . ."

He turned his head towards the dresser

"Do you have another mirror? I want to have a look at myself."

"In the bathroom," Aisha said.

The beekeeper switched on the light and entered the cosy bathroom. He held the magnifying glass under his left arm and the photograph album in his right hand. Stopping in front of the sink, he fixed his eyes on the mirror above it and began to examine his unshaven, weathered face. Then he lifted up the album and pointed the magnifying glass at the face he had had as a young man.

"Yes," he breathed out in a whisper. "That's me, alright."

He heard a door open in the corridor, stepped out, and saw Aisylu. She was already putting on her slippers.

# 64

Over a simple dinner, which was more like a snack, Sergeyich complained to his hostess about his mood, his sleepless night and his left arm.

Aisylu listened half-heartedly, thinking of something else but nodding, and smeared soft butter on half a piece of flatbread.

The guest looked into her melancholy eyes and fell silent.

What am I doing? he asked himself harshly. Her husband was killed, her son is under arrest, and here I am, telling her I've had trouble sleeping . . .

"I'm sorry," he said in a firm tone. "I shouldn't have come to you with my nonsense . . . You have more serious things to worry about."

"What's the trouble with your arm, exactly?" Aisylu said, as if waking up from her thoughts. "We've got a hospital here. You could see a doctor."

"I'd rather put the hives together. Use my own method . . . The bees have treated me more than once . . ."

"And it helped?"

"It'll help, alright. I just need a hand putting them together. It's better with six hives, but the F.S.B. men took one away – to check the bees for disease, they said. – And I wanted to ask about that: do they often take your hives for inspection?"

"I don't remember them ever doing that," Aisylu said, looking confused. "Let me call and ask . . ."

She took out her mobile and made a call. Sergeyich listened to the murmur of Tatar without understanding it. Several times he heard the unfamiliar word "köpekler".[25] And when he heard "balqurtlar" and "balqurtlar sepeti", he perked up.

"Balqurtlar" means bees, "balqurtlar sepeti" means hive, he repeated to himself, recalling how Bekir had taught him these words at the apiary.

"No, this is something new," Aisylu told Sergeyich when she hung up. "No-one in Albat has ever had their hives taken away."

After the moment of silence that followed, Sergeyich asked for help in constructing his bee-bed.

"Let's go," Aisylu said.

"It's too early," Sergeyich responded. "Have to do it at dusk, after the bees return, so that they don't get lost. They get used to the hive being in one place . . . And we'll have to bring someone else. It's a two-person job, and I'm no use now . . ."

"I'll ask Server, the neighbours' son," Aisylu said, gazing at the beekeeper with pity and, in so doing, briefly awakened his self-pity. On the way back, Sergeyich stopped at the shop and bought boiled sausage, a roll and some buckwheat. He carried the bag in his right hand, very much wanting to shift it to the left, so as to give the right a rest, but the left – though he could now feel all the way down to the tips of its fingers – still refused to obey him fully. In order to distract himself, the beekeeper began to add up the days until the expiry of his permitted stay in Crimea. He kept losing count and starting again.

When he reached the spot overlooking Albat, he was mouthing the number six. He turned round and saw that the village, flooded with sunshine, looked friendly and peaceful.

"Well, I made it," Sergeyich said to himself, smiling and thinking of how, that evening, Aisylu and her neighbours' son would arrange his hives into a bee-bed, and of how healthy and, God willing, restorative his night's sleep would be.

# 65

At first, the missing hive created some complications. After all, in terms of size, six hives placed together didn't differ so much from an actual bed, but if there was only a single hive at one end you needed to adapt, to decide what you would put on this narrow edge: your head or your feet. Sergeyich tried it both ways and, in the end, decided that he would use the fifth hive for his head. Instead of a straw-filled mattress, he topped the bee-bed with his sleeping bag. He lay down on his back and looked up at the dark sky perforated by stars.

The bees, it seemed to him, were too calm. At any rate, Sergeyich didn't feel the usual vibrations beneath him. What he did feel, though, was a growing sense of peace and of oneness with the world, which had retired for the night.

He remembered how diligently Aisylu and the young Tatar fellow – a friend of Bekir's, it turned out – had worked to construct the bee-bed, placing little stones and branches beneath the two hives at the one end, so that the surface would be smooth and level. The ground was uneven, now rising, now falling. Server was a clever young man. He had asked to lie on top of the bees for a moment, then jumped right down.

"Interesting," he had declared. "Never tried that before."

"Do you keep bees yourself?" Sergeyich asked him.

"My uncle has a big apiary – thirty hives – near Küçük Süyren. That's not too far from here."

"You can make some money from this," Sergeyich said. "Before the war, our governor himself used to come visit me, sleep on my hives. Paid me in dollars. And you've got a flood of tourists coming through . . ."

Server nodded. "We had a flood before the occupation. Now it's a trickle . . . But if my uncle's willing, I'll give it a try."

Good guy, enterprising, Sergeyich thought now, closing his eyes.

And as soon as he ceased to see the dark heavenly sea above him, with its stars and moon, he felt the vibrations from the hives beneath his back and feet. He also heard muffled buzzing, as if shutting his eyes had sharpened his ears.

The warm air of the Crimean night carried within it the aromas of herbs and juniper.

He fell asleep, breathing deeply, his chest rising to the starry sky with every inhalation, sinking with every exhalation. Warmed by the Crimean air and lulled by the vibrations of his healing bed, he had a dream. In it, he lay sleeping on top of his six hives in the orchard of his home in Little Starhorodivka. The governor and five of his bodyguards were waiting for him to wake up. The guards were trying to rouse Sergeyich, to shove him off the bee-bed and clear it for the governor – after all, the man hadn't driven nearly an hour for nothing, had he? But the big, tall governor was just sitting in a chair under a pear tree, gesturing to the guards, trying to calm them, to keep them from disturbing the master of the hives and the orchard. When Sergeyich awoke in his dream, he saw the governor and the guards, immediately felt embarrassed, and clambered down from the bee-bed, ceding it to his guest. They changed places: the governor lay down, and Sergeyich sat in the chair. And the beekeeper felt such peace in his heart that it was as if heaven had descended to earth. Most remarkable of all was the fact that his left arm did not hurt a bit and obeyed him, behaving like a dog, not like a cat. At the very slightest mental signal, his hand would rise to touch his shaved chin, his nose or his ear.

Sergeyich smiled in his sleep, but no-one noticed. There was no-one around. Even the birds were silent and asleep. And so were the crickets. Even the owls. Only the bees in their hives were awake. They kept on buzzing – not as loudly as during the day, but still quite audibly and palpably against the background of Crimea's nighttime silence.

Meanwhile, the dream continued, and the governor, having slept his fill, carefully climbed down from the bee-bed, put on his violet-coloured leather shoes of astonishing birdlike softness, and sat back down in the chair vacated by the master of the orchard. He was waiting for tea, and Sergeyich hastened to his house, into the kitchen, to make it and bring it out to his guest.

After tea, the governor and his guards drove away in two large black cars. The beekeeper stroked the dollars he had received with the pads of his fingers and felt their pleasant, authenticating roughness; he carried them into the house and hid them in the sideboard. Then he climbed back onto the bee-bed and fell asleep. And the dream he had then, as evening arrived, was different from an ordinary dream. In it he only heard sound, saw no movie. He heard his neighbours singing songs after dinner at the table in their yard. Then they started arguing about the war – the old war – and Hitler. They were debating whether he'd managed to run away to Argentina, because they'd seen photographs in the newspaper *Top Secret* that seemed to depict a very aged Hitler sunbathing next to a young blonde on an Argentinian beach. But soon the argument died down and all the beekeeper heard was the clatter of the dishes being cleared from the table. And suddenly there came the sound of explosions. They drew closer and closer, grew louder and louder, making Sergeyich, still asleep on top of the hives, shiver. Upon hearing these explosions, the bees, becoming nervous, buzzed louder. Sergeyich felt the hives heating up beneath his back and rolled over on his side, but that felt uncomfortable, so he lay on his stomach instead. He listened to the bees with his stomach and chest, while the explosions got louder and louder, closer and closer. They seemed to be booming not in his dream, now, but over it, over the orchard, over the world.

And then Sergeyich rolled over on his back again, biting his lower lip, regretting that the explosions were driving away his dream. He tried to cling to it, to hold on, but it was hopeless . . . He opened his eyes, and the sky above him began to shimmer with the Northern Lights, which he had never seen – to sparkle with all the possible colours except black and white.

Fireworks! he realised in amazement.

Then he felt someone's presence nearby. He turned his head in the direction of this presence and saw Pashka, his frenemy.

"What's this about?" he asked Pashka.

"Victory!" Pashka replied joyfully. "Victory!"

"And who won?" Sergeyich asked, then froze in fear when he saw another rocket explode and rain its little fires down onto him. He pressed his back into the bee-bed. But the fires died out long before they reached the hives.

"Don't know," Pashka said. "Doesn't matter. Main thing is victory – the war's over!"

"But which war?" Sergeyich said, remembering his neighbours arguing about Hitler in his dream.

"The future war," said Pashka.

"Future war?" Sergeyich repeated in confusion, and he began to rise, pushing against the bee-bed with his palms. He sat up slowly and turned to face Pashka, but Pashka was gone. And maybe he had never been there . . .

Silence all around. The fireworks were over. The only sound was the quiet buzzing of bees beneath Sergeyich.

He opened his eyes. The moon had already made it to the other side of the sky.

Sergeyich understood that he was lying on his back. This meant he had dreamed sitting up after talking to Pashka.

He tried lifting his left arm, and it rose.

Sergeyich sighed with relief. His hope had been realised. The bees had cured him. He was two-armed again, not disabled, and life could go on as before. So he had only dreamed of victory, then. Victory was a long way off.

# 66

Only when he was fully awake did Sergeyich feel a strange burning sensation on his cheeks. He felt them with his palm and realised they needed a shave. He also realised they stung to the touch. The sun must have scorched him as he lay sleeping, lulled by the bees' buzzing.

A splash of cold spring water cooled his cheeks and restored his vigour. And Sergeyich's thoughts filled with joy again, because he was washing with both hands. The left, having mended its ways, was trying to fulfil its duties as ably as the right.

Sergeyich rolled up his sleeping bag and put it back in the tent, where there was so much light that one might think he had cut windows into its tarpaulin walls.

His gaze wandered to the silent church candle and the cardboard icon of Nicholas the Wonderworker. Sergeyich recalled that he still had five candles left, and there was no sense in lighting them now. He planned to spend the nights until his departure under the Crimean sky, on his bee-bed – as long as it didn't rain, of course. Luck and the Lord willing, he would take his remaining candles back with him. And he would save the one in the jar too. Why waste it, if his home was no longer a tent but the world around him, with all its mountains, trees, vineyards, birds, hedgehogs and bees? He sat down in the tent on the sleeping bag, which he'd unfurled again, touched his cheeks, and grinned: how did he manage to get burnt like that?

Then he heard the crackle of branches and flinched. He wasn't expecting anyone. Or at least, if he was, it would be the men who had taken his hive, but they would have arrived by car, not on foot.

Sergeyich took a peek outside and his anxiety fell away. It was Aisha.

"Good morning," she said. "Mother asked me to bring this." She handed the beekeeper a plastic bag.

"Thanks very much," Sergeyich replied happily.

"She also asked me to invite you to dinner tonight. She bought some meat."

"Alright." Sergeyich nodded. "Listen, do my cheeks look burnt?" Aisha fixed her eyes on the beekeeper's face.

"Yes, they're red – crimson, even! Did you fall asleep in the sun?"

"Well, I woke up in the sun," Sergeyich admitted. "They really are sore..."

He walked Aisha back to the road, and only when he returned to his tent did he realise that he hadn't yet called his ex-wife, Vitalina, to talk to her about Akhtem and Aisylu's daughter.

"What a fool," he snorted at himself. Then he got out his mobile and dialled.

"It is really you?" a familiar voice answered.

Not even a hello, he thought, resolving not to be so uncivil himself: "Hello. How are you two?"

"Fine, fine. And you?"

"It depends. Listen, I have a request... actually, a question. You have a university over there, right?"

"Not just one. Why, do you want a degree in beekeeping?" Vitalina said, with irony in her voice.

"No. There's a girl down here – daughter of a Tatar I knew – who needs help. The man is dead, and his son was arrested, so the mother wants to send the girl to live in Ukraine, to study. They have money . . . But she'll need some help – maybe someone to take her to the university, show her round . . ."

"How old is she?" Vitalina said, the irony in her voice giving way to anxiety.

"I don't know for sure . . . Finished school . . . About sixteen or seventeen. I can put her on the bus to Vinnytsia, but someone would have to meet her . . ."

"Of course, of course," Vitalina said agreeably. "I'd be happy to do it . . . If need be, she can stay with us for a while . . ."

Sergeyich felt that his ex-wife was actually worried, which meant she had taken his request seriously. And that, in turn, meant that she had taken him seriously.

He smiled.

"How's Angelica?" he enquired

"She's alright. We had a fight yesterday, but we made up over breakfast. She has a boyfriend – ten years older . . . I keep asking her to introduce him to me, but she won't . . . I'm afraid he's married – you know what I mean?"

"Yes, I get it," Sergeyich said, realising that he ought to say something significant; he was the father, after all. "You have to find out, one way or another – maybe even spy on them."

"Well, if she doesn't introduce us, I will," Vitalina assured him. "Will you be going back soon?"

"Yes."

"Maybe you'll come to Vinnytsia? It's nice this time of year. Very pretty. We've got musical fountains, with lights . . ."

"Maybe. Anyway, I'll call you as soon as I get Aisha – that's the girl's name – on the bus, tell you when to meet her. She's shy, easy to recognise – skinny, with hair like yours, dark brown."

"Mine's white. I've been blonde for a year now," his ex-wife informed him.

"Well, then, hair like you used to have ... Say hi to Angelica for me. And tell her I said she should listen to you."

"I'll pass it on, I will," Vitalina promised. "And you be careful on the road, you hear? Thanks very much for the greeting card, by the way."

"What greeting card?" Sergeyich asked.

"You know, Women's Day."

Although he had already put the mobile back in his pocket, Sergeyich couldn't get the conversation out of his head. His cheeks were burning, and he kept thinking about his ex-wife. She seemed to have changed somehow. She had never sounded so warm on the telephone before – so warm and serious. It was as if they weren't separated, as if he were calling from some work trip to some mine somewhere, rather than from a past life.

He sat on the bedspread under a fig tree, hiding from the sun.

I should spend all these roubles, no sense in taking them back with me, he thought, in order to get his mind off the conversation with Vitalina. I'll buy some food for the road – and not just for the road. Plenty of space in the car. I can stock up for the autumn. He got out the pack of Russian money and counted it: a little over five thousand. The figure was large, but when he recalled the price of food, it immediately seemed smaller.

Late in the afternoon, Sergeyich set out for the village. He walked lightly and briskly, but he was not empty-handed. He had decided to give his remaining candles to Akhtem's widow. Let her light them in memory of her husband. Beeswax candles were far nobler than those made of stearin; no wonder they were used in holy places to pray for health and peace. And he was also bringing Aisylu the news that his ex-wife was willing to help Aisha.

Sergeyich hadn't expected Vitalina to agree so readily. He hadn't been forced to plead or anything ... But she was a good person, at heart. The only problem was that they were just too different. She came from a city with fountains, and he came from a village in Donbas, where some people didn't even have wells in their yards, never mind fountains ...

It seemed to Sergeyich that he had never tasted such tender stewed lamb as he had at Aisylu's that evening. The three of them ate together.

As soon as he had entered the house, the beekeeper had shared the news from Vitalina – both that she would meet Aisha, and that the young woman could stay at her place for a while. Akhtem's widow was delighted. She kept smiling. Only her eyes remained sad and tired.

How can two different moods get along on one face like that? Sergeyich wondered.

After a moment, she told him that she had been to Bakhchysarai that morning, to see Bekir. They had let her be with him for half an hour, for three thousand roubles. He had looked very thin; it was obvious they had been beating him. They wanted him to accept a service card, to sign up for the army. They said that if he accepted it, they'd let him come home for two weeks. But he refused. So if Aisylu didn't buy his freedom, he would wind up in prison.

"But for what?" Sergeyich said bitterly. "I wrote out an explanation about the candles."

"They're still accusing him of robbing the church. They say that it wasn't just the candles – that he also took icons and donations. But why would we need icons?" Aisylu asked, and her sad eyes flashed with tears.

"God willing you'll buy his freedom," the beekeeper said, trying to reassure his hostess.

She was already wiping away her tears.

Not wanting to make her uncomfortable, Sergeyich looked away, shifting his gaze to Aisha. The young woman was sitting quietly, with neither joy nor sorrow on her face.

Maybe she doesn't want to go to Vinnytsia, the beekeeper thought. Well, perhaps that isn't for her to decide. But then what? Aisylu will be left all alone.

Sergeyich's eyes returned to his hostess. He felt great pity for her, but he didn't want her to see that.

"May I have a little vodka?" he asked politely.

Aisylu went out to the kitchen, brought back a full shot glass, and set it in front of her guest.

"Well, here's to Bekir – may it all turn out well!" he said as he raised the glass. Then he drained it at one gulp and glanced guiltily at his hostess. He felt embarrassed. "I'm sorry, I can't drink without a toast . . ."

"Why are your cheeks so red?" Aisylu said.

"Sunburnt. Slept too long in the morning."

"And how's your arm?"

Sergeyich raised his left hand and waved it around. "The hives helped! They help with a lot of things."

"You had better go on Wednesday," Aisylu told him. "The queues at the border are shorter midweek. You can drive Aisha up to the exit. She'll pass through the Russian and Ukrainian controls on foot, and you can pick her up on the Ukrainian side. Is that alright?"

Sergeyich nodded.

"But I'll need a little help," he said after a pause. "To get my hives onto the trailer."

"Server and I will give you a hand," Aisylu promised.

As dusk descended, Sergeyich began to make his way up to the apiary. The noise of the village faded, allowing the beekeeper to sink into thoughts of home, of Little Starhorodivka, of Pashka and of Petro. He walked slowly, thinking that he would soon be driving along familiar roads. Recalling the checkpoints through which he would have to pass in order to enter his grey zone, he sighed joylessly. He also recalled that Petro had not responded to the last two or three of his one-word texts. And that could only mean one thing: that there was no more Petro, that he had been killed . . . This thought fell like a heavy weight on Sergeyich's heart, knocking his breath out of rhythm and making the climb to the apiary difficult, tiring. He tried to drive Petro from his mind and began to think about Pashka. Now his breath came back, and it was easier to walk. To cheer himself up, Sergeyich looked back at Albat, studded with lights, where all sorts of things were happening, of course – both good and bad. Life flowed on there. A plain, ordinary, peaceful life – the kind of life one could get used to.

But life flowed on in Little Starhorodivka too – a life that was, to him, ordinary and familiar. He was used to it. Yes, it was just him and Pashka now. No more shops, no mail. No fresh bread, except for when

Pashka's separatist friends brought some from Karuselino, or when Pashka went and got it himself. Not that it was as tasty as the old stuff... Yet life flowed on. Like a river. What else could it do but flow and flow, until it flowed into death? Sergeyich imagined Little Starhorodivka as it had been before the war, with lights glowing in the windows of its huts and houses. He even used his imagination to transport it here, to Crimea, and set it where his tent and apiary now stood. He imagined he was walking from Albat straight to his native village. And this felt so good – the road from Albat to Little Starhorodivka was so short... Well, why not? he thought. Little Starhorodivka comes with me wherever I go. I'm here now, so it's here too!

Suddenly the beekeeper heard the rumble of an engine behind his back. He turned round and saw two headlights.

He stepped off to the side of the road, close to the vineyards, having decided to let the car pass. But a question arose in his mind: the road ended up ahead, transforming into a dirt track... Was that where they were going? To see him?

A minute or two later, the car drew level with him. It was that windowless minibus, with the military emblem on the door.

"Hey, wait!" Sergeyich cried excitedly. "I'm right here!"

But the minibus had already stopped. The window in the door was down, and Ivan Fyodorovich looked out of it, his face expressing calm curiosity.

"Sergey Sergeyich?" he asked, for confirmation.

"Yes, yes," the beekeeper said, approaching the door. "Have you brought back my hive?"

Ivan Fyodorovich nodded.

"Great! Can you give me a lift?"

"Not allowed. We've got secret equipment on board. We'll wait for you up there."

Sergeyich hurried after the minibus. His breathing was off again; he couldn't adjust it to this quicker pace. When he finally reached the tent, Ivan Fyodorovich and Vasily Stepanovich, the bee specialist, were standing beside the minibus, smoking.

"So?" Sergeyich addressed them. "Everything good? My bees are healthy?"

"Yes, you could say that," Ivan Fyodorovich replied. "We'll just finish our cigarettes and then we'll bring out the hive."

"May I . . . make you some tea?" the beekeeper offered, feeling the joy of his bees' return and wanting to share it.

"Thank you, but no. We're pressed for time, and you'll have to kindle the fire . . ."

After stubbing out their cigarettes, the two men carried the hive out of the vehicle and placed it on the grass.

"Let's go – I'll show you where," Sergeyich summoned them.

"Where are the others?" the bee specialist asked, somewhat surprised, when they had manoeuvred the third hive onto the spot where it had previously stood.

"I made a bee-bed," Sergeyich told him, pointing in the direction of the fig tree. "Now I sleep up there, for my health. My left arm went numb, but now I can carry bags and everything."

"Really?" Ivan Fyodorovich asked sceptically. "Can I give it a try?"

The three of them approached the bee-bed. Vasily Stepanovich lit another cigarette, while Ivan Fyodorovich climbed on top of the hives and lay down on his back.

"Not very comfortable," he said under his breath.

"Well, I use a sleeping bag," Sergeyich explained.

Then Ivan Fyodorovich froze, as if listening to the life of the bees with his back.

"How is it?" Vasily Stepanovich enquired.

"Interesting."

"We've got to go," Vasily Stepanovich announced, with notes of impatience in his voice.

"Yes, you're right," Ivan Fyodorovich said, jumping down from the bee-bed. "Let's go."

For the next minute or two, Sergeyich listened to the receding noise of their vehicle's motor, and then everything grew quiet. A peaceful silence descended, with its rustling, with its barely audible echo of the past day's sounds, ground down by the breeze.

286

The beekeeper pulled his sleeping bag out of the tent and unrolled it on top of the five hives. Then he approached the hive that had come back, lifted its roof, and listened. The bees were unusually quiet, as if they were motionless, holding their breath. He thought about examining them with a torch, but that would only frighten them further.

He reached inside, opened the entrance, and carefully lowered the roof. Then he strode lazily back to the other hives, still sensing the warmth of the bees on his right palm.

# 67

After waking, Sergeyich lay still for a while, with no sense of time or place, as if he were alone in the world. He listened to the birds and bees, hesitating to open his eyes. But then he got down from the bee-bed and went straight over to the newly returned hive, to check on its residents.

Life in the hive seemed to be humming along. Bees always get to work with the first rays of the sun, and now here they were, landing near the entrance, delivering legfuls of pollen to their common household. They landed heavily, sometimes awkwardly, pushing away sisters and brothers who lingered too long.

This bustling at the entrances never failed to captivate Sergeyich. He could easily stand there, observing the activity around the bees' airfield, for a full half hour. Sometimes he felt he could even recognise certain apian faces. And sometimes he felt the bees were showing him a movie – like now, as out of the entrance came several drones. They were being evicted, weakened and unable to resist because the guard bees had blocked their access to food. The drones did not come out or even stumble out – they fell out. And after them came strong guard bees, confident in their might and right, pushing the drones to the left of the entrance. Like little winged bulldozers, the guards shoved the drones all the way to the edge and down onto the grass.

That's the end of them, Sergeyich thought, without particular pity.

After all, you've got to pay for your pleasure . . . Some bees fly, gather pollen, build honeycombs – live like the proletariat from day to day, from birth to death. Drones, meanwhile, just consume and consume. Can a worker bee ever really respect a drone? No . . . And so they drive the spongers out before the cold sets in, so as not to waste honey and syrup . . . When the time comes, the queen will give birth to new spongers and new workers.

It was the wisdom of nature that fascinated Sergeyich. Wherever this wisdom was visible and comprehensible to him, he would compare its manifestations with human life – always to the detriment of the latter . . .

One of the drones that had fallen onto the grass was no longer moving. They obviously hadn't let him feed for quite some time. He had even lost his bright colour, turning grey.

Sergeyich left the bees to their own devices, had a quick breakfast, and decided to load his things into the Lada. He placed the jars of honey under the rear seats, then glanced at the empty jerrycans; he would need to put those closer to the door, so they'd be easy to reach at the petrol station.

Once the beekeeper was done packing, he began to think about honeycomb foundations. He had managed to collect a bit of wax that summer, but it was dirty, unrefined, mixed with comb caps – no-one would accept it in exchange for new foundations. So he would need to buy them, or his bees wouldn't have anything to build on.

He didn't want to bother Aisylu. She was probably helping Aisha get ready. It must all be very hard for her – she'd be left alone. God knows whether Bekir would ever be allowed to come home . . .

He decided to go down to the village shop and ask the woman there. Women who work in rural shops always have more answers than any information desk.

Sergeyich locked the car, then looked at its broken windows and laughed soundlessly.

He went down to Albat and into the shop.

"Does anyone around here keep bees?" he asked the saleswoman, who looked bored for lack of customers.

"Do we ever!" she answered in a lively manner. "My husband, for one. You need honey?" Hope tinkled like a jingling bell in her voice.

"No, I've got honey of my own. What I need is honeycomb foundations, but I don't know where to get them . . . I'm not from around here."

"Yes, I know you're not from around here," the woman said innocently. "You're chummy with the Tatars but you avoid us Orthodox folk. Did you convert to Islam, or what?"

"God, no." Sergeyich dismissed her assumption. "I didn't convert to anything."

The woman, however, didn't seem to be listening to him. She was calling someone on her mobile.

"Zhora, that guy that's pals with the Tatars is down here. Says he needs something. You know, the one who sleeps in the tent, out past the vineyards. Here, ask him," she said into the mobile, then handed it to Sergeyich.

Zhora turned out to be solid fellow, ready for quick business. They settled on a price and Sergeyich waited for him right there in the shop.

While he waited, he began to make small talk with the woman. There was no avoiding it: she was really desperate to chat.

"Well, how are things up in Donetsk? Prices are probably sky-high . . ."

"I'm not from Donetsk," Sergeyich explained. "I live in a village. We haven't got a shop, so there aren't any prices. But where the shops are still open – there's one in Karuselino, just up the road – there the prices are high, alright."

"What about shooting? Lots of shooting?"

"There's some shooting. But mostly above our heads."

"Those Tatars of yours, they're getting kicked out," the woman said, suddenly changing the topic. "They don't like us, you know."

"What do you mean, they don't like us? They've been helping me."

"Well, you're not us. We're Russian. And they don't respect Russian authority. So the people in charge will probably make 'em go back to their Uzbekistans and such . . . That's where they should of stayed, anyway . . . What did they have to come down here for?"

"Well, this is their land," the beekeeper offered timidly.

"The hell it is!" the woman said indignantly, but without malice. "This land's been Russian Orthodox since time immemorial! Russians brought Orthodoxy from Turkey, brought it to Chersonesus, back before there were any Muslims. It was later that the Turks sent in the Tatars, along with their Islam. When Putin was here, he told the whole story – this is sacred Russian land."

"Well, I haven't looked into the history," Sergeyich shrugged. "Who knows what happened?"

"What happened is what Putin says happened," she insisted. "Putin doesn't lie."

# 68

That night Sergeyich felt cold in his sleeping bag. He brought a blanket out from the tent and draped it over himself.

After a little tossing and turning, he dozed off again. And he awoke to what he took to be the light ringing of sunlight. It wasn't the sunlight that was ringing, of course, but life itself, which the sun's rays had been warming for two hours, readying it for the day to come. They had been warming and preparing him as well, apparently.

He walked briskly over to the officially inspected hive – and took fright at what he saw. There wasn't a single bee at the entrance. He carefully lifted the roof and peeked inside: silent and empty, as if someone had sucked all the bees out with a vacuum cleaner . . . He looked round, listening closely. A buzzing reached him from the direction of the bed, and a bee flew past his face.

"What the . . ." he exhaled in distress.

He checked under the hive, then went over to a nearby elm tree, where again he tuned his ears to the sounds of nature. His gaze stopped on a wild pear tree, closer to Akhtem's hives than to his own. He approached it and breathed a sigh of relief, as he now heard the familiar choral buzzing of a swarm.

"So that's where you went," he grumbled.

However, the joy of having found his missing bees quickly gave way to concern.

How do I get them back to the hive? With my bare hands? Sergeyich wondered. I don't even have a ladder, much less a swarm trap . . .

He stared up at the bees, which were densely packed around the tree's trunk about two metres off the ground. If he could only find something to step on . . . Sergeyich realised he needed to hurry, before the swarm flew off. Strange, though: why had they all fled the hive? Usually, in cases like this, half the bees remain inside, and only half leave, with their old queen. Besides, that only happened if the family grew too big, too crowded – but these bees weren't pressed for space. He would have noticed.

Several bees flew up to the swarm from various directions and began to waggle beside it.

Scouts, Sergeyich understood. Telling the rest where they've been and what sorts of places they've found for relocation . . .

Sergeyich's gaze drifted over to the bushy hazel tree, behind which stood Akhtem's shed, with all its beekeeping tools. There he could probably find a spray bottle, as well as a swarm trap. Swarming was a common enough occurrence, after all.

The beekeeper recalled that he had already searched for the key to the shed, which Aisylu had given him on the day of his arrival, many times now . . . Where could he have put it? Such a shame – just like Petro's grenade, he had tucked it away somewhere and forgotten all about it. But he needed that key . . . If he didn't hurry, the swarm would fly away.

Sergeyich went up to the shed and fixed his eyes on the padlock. He placed his palm under the lock, lifted the curved piece of iron that ran through two rings, and pulled it towards himself; the door creaked, but the rings held tight.

So what do I do now? he said to himself, growing more and more anxious.

He pulled at the lock again, but this time more forcefully, with both hands. The rings still resisted, and even seemed to pull the lock back towards them.

The beekeeper scurried around the shed, looking down at his feet, searching in vain for anything that might help him open the door.

And suddenly it dawned on him. How could he not have thought of it earlier?

He ran over to the fire pit, yanked the iron tripod out of the ground, and took it back to the shed.

The legs of the tripod were strong, made of steel. You couldn't buy such tripods in shops. Welders made them and gave them as gifts to their friends, or sold them privately.

He thrust one of the legs into the rings and pulled. The lever worked – the lock and rings flew off, and the door swung open. Sergeyich's eyes glowed with joy. He saw everything he needed, all at once: a ladder leaning against the back wall of the shed, a plastic spray bottle, two smokers (which were useless to him now), a scraper to uncap honeycombs, and, most importantly, a round swarm trap with a lid!

How do I get them in there, though? he asked himself. But then his hand reached for the long handle of a dustpan. That'll do. Probably why it's in here. Can't imagine Akhtem spent much time sweeping up grass . . .

The swarm on the pear tree's trunk was humming louder than before – thousands of bees warming up their wings before flight.

"No," the beekeeper said confidently. "Won't get away that easily."

Using the spray bottle, which he had filled with water from one of his flasks, he began to mist the bees from below. Droplets condensed on their wings, making them heavy. Watery powder burst into the air and glittered in the sun. The buzzing grew quieter.

It was clear that none of the bees would fly away now, but Sergeyich kept misting them until there was no water left in the bottle. Only then did he lean the ladder against the trunk, climb up two rungs, squeeze the trap between the tree and his stomach, and begin to sweep the swarm into it with the dustpan. The bees collapsed into the trap in two large trembling clusters. A little under a hundred remained on the trunk, but he didn't have to sweep these in: they quickly crawled down into the trap all by themselves. They were afraid to be left without the swarm, without their queen. Sergeyich raised the trap higher, to make it easier on them. He watched with great concern as the last of the bees descended, then covered them with the trap's lightweight, clothlined lid, took hold of its leather strap, and climbed down to the ground.

Walking back to the empty hive, he hefted the swarm.

No more than three kilos, he thought. Why would a small family like that want to fly away?

He carefully tipped the bees back into their house. They plopped down heavily – wet wings, after all.

Before lowering the hive's roof, Sergeyich paused. Something seemed odd. He bent over the bees again.

They look a little greyish, he thought. Maybe it's just the water?

# 69

Sergeyich felt a pain in his collarbone at every turn of the steering wheel. From time to time he would glance at Aisha in the passenger seat; she too hadn't had enough sleep, but that wasn't why she looked so unhappy. With the windscreen gone, the wind threw cool, refreshing gusts at their faces. The bright morning sun shone high above their heads, but not down at them or at the road; it shone upward, whitening the sky with its rays. In a little while it would peep out from behind the mountains on the right and roll those rays down into the valley.

A good thing she's not the crying kind, Sergeyich thought, casting another sidelong glance at Aisha.

Aisylu and Server drove behind them all the way to Bakhchysarai. At the exit from the Tatar capital, they signalled for the beekeeper to pull over. Then Aisylu hugged her daughter for the last time, holding her close and whispering something hurriedly into her ear, in Tatar. Server did not leave his car, but Sergeyich climbed out of the Lada. He stood there watching the mother, who wore a modest long black dress, which was more like a robe, and the daughter, who wore jeans and a dark-green sweater over a black turtleneck whose collar rose almost to her chin.

In parting, Akhtem's widow nodded to Sergeyich, as if to say, "Go on." Then she looked at the trailer with its hives and shook her head.

Sergeyich understood. Last night, when he and Server were loading the bees onto the trailer, the bottom wall plank of the hive with the axe mark had come loose. The beekeeper had pressed it back into place with his palm and checked to make sure there were no cracks for the bees to sneak out of.

The road swayed from side to side. Cars occasionally came zipping towards them. Some of these had Ukrainian plates; some even had plates from Donetsk and Luhansk. If Sergeyich happened to notice the letters of his native region, he would stare inside the passing car. Families with children were driving towards the sea.

He thought of Bekir, who never did manage to show him the Black Sea, and sighed with regret – regret about both the young man's fate and the unvisited sea.

He glanced at Aisha again. He wanted to reassure her, but he didn't know how. Then he looked back at the green suitcase sandwiched between the car's ceiling and his belongings.

She'll have to pass through passport control on foot, he thought. Her backpack's heavy enough – does she really need to carry that suitcase too? Maybe it should stay in the car? Maybe the customs officers won't even notice? But what if they do – and they order me to open it – and find women's clothes?

The road turned right and merged into the Sevastopol highway.

Sergeyich looked back at the trailer, remembered the damaged hive, and chose not to press too hard on the accelerator.

"Are you hungry?" he said to the young woman.

"No," she answered. "We'll eat later, after we cross the border. They'll still be warm."

"Warm?" the beekeeper repeated in a puzzled tone.

But then he remembered about the bag of *samsas* on the back seat.

"I see," Sergeyich nodded, and now he felt the desire to step on the accelerator again. He wanted to reach the border faster, to taste the hot, juicy *samsas*.

The sign for the airport, its arrow pointing left, was now behind them. But they were on their way to Dzhankoy – they didn't need the airport.

"You didn't forget your passport?" he said, turning to Aisha, when they had driven past the suburbs of Simferopol.

She shook her head.

An hour later Sergeyich began to feel uneasy, sensing the approach of the border. They drove past a convoy of military vehicles that had stopped on the side of the road. Two of these were attached to tarpaulin covered artillery pieces.

Aisha tensed up when she saw them. Fear flashed in her eyes. Sergeyich pressed the accelerator in order to pass the Russian soldiers as quickly as possible. About three minutes later he slowed down, remembering the hive that could fall apart if shaken by the journey.

The familiar silvery canopy loomed up ahead. The beekeeper's foot automatically pressed the brake.

Pulling up at the side of the road, he looked inquiringly at Aisha. She understood right away and got out of the car, then took her backpack from the back seat and pulled its straps over her shoulders.

"Should I take my suitcase?" she said.

"Is it very heavy?"

"It has wheels."

"Then you'd better take it," Sergeyich said.

He looked back from the road. Aisha was already on her way, the green suitcase rolling behind her. She stepped lightly, but the expression on her face was dulled, as if she were making her way to a funeral or towards some imminent disaster.

There were about a dozen cars up ahead. The queue was moving along. Sergeyich again caught sight of Aisha in the stream of pedestrian border-crossers. She walked past him, without turning her head, and approached the passport control windows.

Having parked beneath the canopy of the border post, Sergeyich took his documents and, a little nervously, went up to the window himself.

"Why did you crumple up your insert?" the border guard asked him reproachfully, unfolding the piece of paper he had found in the beekeeper's passport.

The officer's face bore the stamp of concern. His lips moved silently, as if he were counting or saying something in his mind. Then he shook his head and looked up at the owner of the documents. "Eighty-nine days," he declared. "You definitely took the longest rest you could, didn't you? In proper Russian style. Even got sunburnt," he added, examining Sergeyich's red, weathered cheeks. Suddenly a man in civilian clothes appeared behind the border guard's back. He bent towards the window, cast a quick glance at Sergeyich, and put his hand on the guard's shoulder. The guard raised his head and immediately got up from his chair. Both men left the booth together.

The beekeeper grew nervous. He took out his mobile and checked the time.

Then the border guard's face reappeared.

"Move the car off to the side," he told the beekeeper. "Someone will meet you there."

Having made room for the next car in the queue, Sergeyich drove over to the spot indicated. He remained behind the wheel, steeped in bitterness and uncertainty, expecting nothing good to come from this delay. His passport and licence had been taken away. Who was he now? No-one. No documents, no rights.

He recalled the place where he had been forced to park when he entered Crimea. That delay had ended with the arrival of the journalists and his receiving money for car repairs.

Sergeyich looked round his "convertible", which felt windier than nature itself when he drove.

Yes, he hadn't fixed the car. And the money was mostly gone . . . There were still a few roubles in his pocket, but the greater part of the sum had been turned into petrol, of which he now had three cans. Petrol was better than money.

For about a quarter of an hour, long thoughts wandered through the beekeeper's head, trailing off in ellipses . . . They wandered around, brightening up the expected resolution of his fate. And then two customs officers came up to the car, along with a man in camouflage accompanied by a dog. One of the officers was holding Sergeyich's documents. The man in camouflage led the dog around the trailer.

The customs officer holding the documents fixed his eyes on the car's licence plate, then at the old, tattered registration.

"How did they let you in here?" he said.

The curved line of his lips showed both dissatisfaction and arrogance.

"In where?" Sergeyich asked, taken aback.

"Russia. Crimea," the customs officer responded in a cold, slightly raspy voice, "Your licence and registration are Soviet. And so's your licence plate. At least your passport isn't . . . What, are you still living in the U.S.S.R.?"

Unable to come up with a quick answer, the beekeeper shrugged.

"No-one told me . . ." he mumbled. "No-one told me to change anything. I've been driving with them the whole time."

"Where have you been driving, exactly? Ukraine?"

"At home, in Donbas."

The officer shook his head in surprise, but something kind awoke in his eyes at that moment. Sergeyich read that something as fleeting mercy.

A black stick with an upturned mirror appeared in the second officer's hands. He began to examine the Lada's undercarriage, then suddenly turned to its owner.

"You'll soon be braking with the soles of your shoes," he said. "You can't be driving around like that . . . Have to weld the undercarriage."

"Yes, yes, of course, I will." The beekeeper nodded, frightened. "It's just that I'm from the grey zone, you know . . . Hard to get cars repaired . . ."

Upon hearing the words "grey zone", the customs officers stared at Sergeyich in silence. The dog handler turned to stare at him too.

Even the German shepherd stopped sniffing the hives on the trailer and turned towards him.

"According to the rules, drivers must empty the boot of their vehicle for inspection," the second officer pronounced vaguely, after the longish silence. Then he looked at the hives.

Sergeyich's spirits sank.

There's so much stuff back there, he thought. And if they see the honey, they'll give me trouble . . .

"Shall we inspect the hives?" the second officer asked the first.

The first turned to the cars waiting under the canopy, and his eyes lit up at the sight of a large rooftop cargo carrier, beneath which glistened a Land Rover Discovery with Kyiv plates that looked as if it had just left the showroom floor.

"No, we won't," he said. "Let him count his own bees . . . Look how much work we've got left," he added, indicating the Land Rover with a glance.

He handed the documents back to Sergeyich.

"Safe travels," he said dryly. "Don't stop in the buffer zone. Not allowed."

Sergeyich's sharp change of emotions triggered a fit of coughing, which led to a stabbing pain in his heart. He started the car and hid his passport, licence and registration in the glove compartment – he would have to take them out again soon.

The beekeeper drove slowly through the buffer zone, overtaking those travelling on foot. He peered at them, looking out for Aisha. She must be somewhere among them by now – or maybe she had already made it to the Ukrainian border. After all, what was there to check? A glance at her passport, a quick look inside the suitcase, and off she went.

"Well, have you had a good holiday?" the Ukrainian border guard asked with an unkind irony in his voice. "You've got to watch out for that sun . . ."

He too had noticed the beekeeper's burnt cheeks.

The Ukrainian customs officers inspected the Lada without particular interest.

"Driving with bees?" one of them asked, poking a finger in the direction of the trailer.

"Yes. I'm a beekeeper," Sergeyich said.

"A bee-driver, you mean," the talkative officer jokingly corrected him, then, catching the strict glance of his partner, he wiped the smile from his face, and fell silent.

On leaving the Chonhar checkpoint, Sergeyich saw a crowd of people up ahead, as well as clusters of cars parked haphazardly on either side of the road. He drove at a crawl, searching for Aisha. There was no place to stop, and the drivers behind him were hooting impatiently.

Ahead of him, a Volga pulled out onto the road, and the beekeeper hurried into the empty spot. He didn't fit completely, but the trailer, nearly a metre of which stuck out over the tarmac, wasn't blocking the traffic.

Leaving the car, Sergeyich hastened back to the crowd of drivers and those whom they were meeting.

When he was very close, he spotted Aisha. She was trying to break out of this anthill, but a couple of men stood in her way. It seemed to Sergeyich that she had spotted him, too, peering over these men's shoulders as though over a fence.

"A hundred hryvnias to the train station," a thin, bearded man in a brown jacket excitedly offered Aisha. "We leave right away. I've already got three people in the car – one seat left."

"He ain't got no-one in that car," insisted a competitor in a T-shirt and tracksuit bottoms. "You'll just be sittin' there, waitin' for him to round up three more. Me, I've already got two!"

Sergeyich parted the taxi drivers like an icebreaker, extended his hand, took Aisha by the elbow and pulled her towards the car. More precisely, he pulled her through the phalanx of warring taxi drivers, then took the handle of her suitcase and rolled it behind him, its wheels bouncing over the pebbles and debris. Aisha walked by his side.

# 70

The line to the ticketing window moved fast. "Any seats left to Vinnytsia?" Sergeyich asked.

The grey-haired woman in a purple blouse on the other side of the window tapped on her computer's keyboard and stared at the monitor.

"Strange – looks like there is," she said, not looking at her customer. "Seems someone gave up a seat . . . Number eighty-six, corridor carriage, upper level. Carriage number 5. Departs in forty minutes."

"We'll take it!" the beekeeper announced, delighted.

"Your passport," the woman demanded.

Aisha held out her Ukrainian passport, which looked brand new.

"Two hundred and sixty-three hryvnias and forty kopecks." Aisha handed the cashier three hundred-hryvnia notes.

"And when will it arrive?" Sergeyich asked. "I need to arrange for someone to meet her."

"Tomorrow morning, at five-forty. A seventeen-hour journey."

The beekeeper expressed his surprise. "That long?"

When they stepped outside, he noticed a smile on Aisha's face, and that made him happy.

"When you get to Vinnytsia, don't leave the platform. My wife will meet you there. Her name's Vitalina," Sergeyich rattled off when they were already standing beside the fifth carriage. "Here's her number, just in case . . ."

Aisha loaded her suitcase and backpack onto the train, then again stepped down onto the platform.

"Don't be afraid on the train. Our passengers are OK," Sergeyich said, feeling the urge to reassure the young woman before the start of her long journey.

"It's all women in there," Aisha said, as if she herself wanted to reassure the beekeeper. "I'll be fine."

"Oh, and tea – make sure to order tea from the conductor! They'll do it. They always have hot water."

Aisha nodded.

"All aboard," a plumpish, matryoshka-like conductor announced in Ukrainian, clearly addressing Aisha.

Fear flashed in the young woman's eyes again. She gave Sergeyich a pained look, as if they were family members being forcibly separated. Before he realised it he was embracing her, pressing her close.

"Don't just stand there like you're frozen!" the conductor said, almost indignantly. "The train won't wait!"

A voice boomed through the station: "Number eighty-six, Novooleksiyivka–Lviv, departing from platform one."

Sergeyich released Aisha.

The last of the carriages swerved out of sight, and the beekeeper was left alone on the platform. He staggered a bit, as if he himself were on board and not Aisha. Bitterness swam up in his heart – bitterness and regret, as if he had done something wrong, as if he had missed his chance to get on the train.

"Damn," he whispered, wiping his eyes with the back of his hand. It seemed to him that he might be crying.

He called Vitalina and reported the time of arrival and the number of the carriage. He also described Aisha again, to make sure his ex-wife would recognise her.

"What's wrong?" she asked, sounding worried.

"What do you mean?"

"Your voice is shaky . . . Are you crying?"

"Just tired." Sergeyich sighed. "Haven't slept much. And they gave me trouble at the border."

She said nothing. He listened to her silence, which reached him from afar, from Vinnytsia, which was seventeen hours away . . . And he, too, was silent, not knowing what else to say.

"Will you visit us too?" she asked all of a sudden. Her voice sounded gentle, as it had sounded in those early days, before and after their wedding.

"Oh, yes," he said, though he immediately took fright at his answer, hastening to add: "Probably. But first I need to go home. The Baptists are bringing us coal for the winter."

She did not respond.

"Give Angelica a kiss for me," Sergeyich requested, after a pause. "I've got to go . . . I'll call you later. Goodbye."

"Goodbye," Vitalina replied.

# 71

The road to Melitopol ran like a smooth ribbon between the fields. The sun kept hitting Sergeyich in the eyes, which were already tired from the wind blowing in his face. He wanted to close them, to give them a rest from the sun and the wind. Instead he squinted – squinted and yawned, sensing that his nearly sleepless night, his early morning, the nervous waiting at the Russian border, and all the running around between the buses and the train station in Novooleksiyivka had piled up on him, crushing him like ten tons of coal. He would have loved to get out from under this heaviness, to sleep for a while . . . His hands were tired of turning the wheel too, his fingers going numb . . .

Sergeyich flinched, then glanced back to see whether his slow driving was bothering anyone, and his gaze accidentally fell on the bag in the back seat.

My God, Sergeyich thought. She left without eating . . .

The beekeeper slowed down, pulled over and got out, swaying on his feet. First he checked on the trailer, and noticed that the board at the base of the damaged hive was loose again. He wanted to press it shut with his palm, but saw that a bee had crawled into the crack. He bent over, blew the bee back in, and pressed the board. But it came loose again right before his eyes.

The sun was baking hot, as if it didn't care one whit about the approach of autumn. Sergeyich wanted shade – and a meal. He got back behind the wheel, with the firm intention of finding a calm place to rest.

After about twenty minutes, fields of sunflowers began to sail past his car. Sergeyich saw an exit and gently rolled off onto a dirt road. He drove at a leisurely speed, with the lowered faces of the sunflowers looking right down into the Lada. The smell of burnt seeds reached his nose.

Sergeyich smiled wearily – he would have liked to drive all the way home through the sunflowers. A crossroads appeared up ahead: a good place to turn round. He stopped the car, got out his bedspread, and unfurled it over the blackened foliage stamped into the dry ground. Then he retrieved the bag of food, and found that it also held a bottle of *äyrän*. He ate everything Aisylu had prepared for two, and drank all the *äyrän* too. Then he stretched out on his back and fell asleep – and almost immediately heard a buzzing. It was loud, and not as soft and delicate as that made by a flying bee. In his dream, this buzzing came from the hive which the F.S.B. had confiscated and returned, and which now stood apart in the field, for some reason. Sergeyich wanted to approach the hive, to work out why the bees were buzzing so loudly. As soon as he took a step towards it, the roof rose up and an enormous grey bee, the size of a human being, crawled out of the hive. It looked round, didn't notice him, and cautiously set off, on two short legs, towards the sunflowers – only not the ones that were growing around his sleeping body, but youthful, rowdy ones, whose round faces were lifted up to the sun. Sergeyich followed the bee with his eyes until it disappeared into the sunflowers. He realised he hadn't paid attention to its wings: maybe they'd been responsible for that loud buzzing?

But the buzzing continued, and another bee crawled out of the hive, then another, and another. All of them followed the first into the sunflowers, hunching over like military scouts on a mission. And at some point Sergeyich realised that they looked grey because they were wearing camouflage overalls – or maybe not overalls, maybe something like raincoats, but definitely of a military type. They kept crawling out of the hive as if from an underground tunnel, and all moved in the same direction: towards his house in Little Starhorodivka.

Sergeyich was frightened. His forehead was covered with cold sweat.

What is this? he thought in his dream. They recruited my bees? Intimidated and recruited them? Now they're no longer my bees they

303

don't work for me, and they aren't searching for pollen . . . Just then another enormous bee crawled out of the hive, carefully lowered the roof, looked round, and trained its many-pupilled eyes on Sergeyich. It stood there motionless, as if trying to decide whether to approach him or to follow the others.

In the end it, too, disappeared into the sunflowers, leaving the dumbfounded beekeeper behind to tremble fearfully in his dream. Sergeyich woke up soaking wet, his T-shirt clinging to his body, his hair clinging to his temples.

It took him a while to regain his senses.

At long last he did, rose to his feet, and sought out the hive with his eyes. It was the last one on the trailer, and the damaged hive stood immediately next to it, wall against wall, in the middle.

Worry about the hive with the axe mark distracted Sergeyich from his dream. He retrieved his bag of tools from the Lada's boot. It turned out he had no hammer, but he did have a heavy spark plug wrench and a pair of pliers.

He used the pliers to pull out a nail, then positioned it closer to the edge of the plank and tried to hit it with the wrench – but missed. The tool struck the wood with a loud thud.

"Sorry," Sergeyich whispered to the bees. "I'll make it quick." He swung once more and the nail dug in. Then he swung again, trying to do it as lightly as possible so as not to scare the bees. At that point he heard a strange sound, just behind the hive's wall, as if something heavy had rolled down inside it.

The beekeeper left the wrench on the edge of the trailer and decided to look into the hive. He climbed up, removed the strap, and lifted the hive's roof. Brushing aside the bees crawling on top, he carefully drew out the comb closest to the entrance. A sunbeam dived into the narrow, newly freed space and fell on something round and green. Sergeyich drew out the neighbouring comb – and saw a grenade, a green grenade, the very one that Petro had given him last winter. Bees were crawling all over it.

He reached in, pulled out the grenade, and blew the bees off it. He was surprised by how warm it felt.

"So that's where you've been hiding," he whispered fearfully.

He placed the grenade in his trouser pocket and immediately felt its heaviness, its unpleasant size. After reinserting the combs and lowering the roof, he fastened the strap over it once more. Then he jumped down from the trailer and immediately touched the grenade with his palm; he could feel its heat through the fabric of his trousers.

Back in the car, he pulled it out of his pocket, placed it on the passenger seat, and thought of the soldier. What had happened to him? Was he dead? Injured?

He got his mobile from the glove compartment and called Petro. Long beeps sounded in his ear. He listened to them for a couple of minutes, then put the mobile back.

# 72

The evening caught up with Sergeyich out past Melitopol. A short convoy of military equipment came crawling his way: two armoured personnel carriers, one of them towing a tank on a trailer, followed by two Ural 6x6s and a green U.A.Z. jeep. Sergeyich could see on the drivers' faces that they were heading back from the war. He himself was not heading for the war; he was going back home. It wasn't his fault that his home was now in the middle of the war. In the middle, yes, but taking no part in it. No-one shot at the enemy from his yard, his windows, his fence, which meant his home had no enemies. Maybe that's why it was still standing, untouched by all the mines and shells that had fallen on Little Starhorodivka over the past three years.

I should stock up on necessities before I reach the checkpoints, he thought.

Ahead of him lay only the open road, bordered by apricot trees that came sweeping past the car. The fields behind these, on the right, were full of watermelons, and those on the left full of beans. Not to worry. Some village with a little shop will pop up soon, Sergeyich promised himself.

In his thoughts, he began to load bags of groats, noodles and biscuits onto his back seat, and cans of stewed meat and bottles of sunflower oil onto the floor behind the front seats.

Then he grinned, remembering that he could also put things on the passenger seat, and under it.

The beekeeper glanced at the neighbouring seat and his lips lost their grin. There was the grenade. He reached over and put it away in the glove compartment.

In the first roadside village, he bartered some of his honey for groceries. The exchange was quick and easy, just as he'd expected. The woman valued his honey at seventy hryvnias per kilo and he took more than a thousand hryvnias' worth of buckwheat, barley, millet and other goods. The heavy-laden Lada pulled away from the shop with an effort, but Sergeyich was happy, sensing his future satiety. Coming home with full hands was the right way to do it – the manly way, the way of the provider. He had also got a tray of eggs; the young but brisk woman in her lilac scarf had covered the eggs with corrugated cardboard and taped it closed. Now he didn't have to worry about food for a long time.

Battered by the wind, Sergeyich lowered his eyes to the speedometer. Thirty kilometres an hour wasn't very fast . . . But he had his trailer, so people were overtaking him without angry honks. They saw he was transporting fragile cargo: bees. This they saw, but they didn't know that he had other reasons for going so slowly. He wanted to get home, but he wasn't so eager as to fly at full speed. After all, there was no-one waiting for him there. The only person in the whole village was Pashka. True, Pashka was waiting for him – he was bored, having spent all summer alone. But his separatist buddies from Karuselino had probably paid him a few visits, and he had probably gone to see them – so why feel sorry for Pashka? The other reason that Sergeyich was in no hurry was the checkpoints, which would pop up unexpectedly, breaking his journey into segments; and there was no telling how long he would have to wait at each of them, how many cars would be queued up to present their documents and luggage to the soldiers in charge . . .

Sergeyich's mood grew grimmer. It occurred to him that this was a road from which he could still make a turn; there were turnings to the right and to the left, towards the war and towards peace and tranquillity.

Then Galya entered his mind. It's strange, he felt, that he had not thought of her back at the shop, when he was exchanging honey for goods with another woman. Like Galya, that young woman had been brisk and businesslike.

Evening was descending, and the cars coming towards Sergeyich were switching on their headlights. He flipped his on as well.

Another signpost flew by: Novobohdanivka and Vesele to the left, Troitske and Starobohdanivka to the right.

So that's why I thought of her, the beekeeper realised. I'm coming up to the turning to Vesele . . .

His foot pressed gently on the brake pedal, all by itself. He pulled over to the side of the road, turned off the engine, got out of the car and squared his shoulders, feeling a pain in his collarbone. His lower back ached too.

"God, I'm a wreck," Sergeyich said, pitying himself.

And again he thought of Galya thought of her borscht, her cosy home. Maybe he should pause there? Spend the night? He was in no shape to keep driving, and it was too dark anyway . . .

The beekeeper considered it. She was a good woman, no doubt about that. But the idea of stopping just to spend the night with her felt wrong, somehow. That's not what she had in mind either. When they last spoke on the telephone, she had invited him to stay with her, not just to stay over.

Sergeyich got out his mobile and found her number.

"Seryozha?" her pleasantly surprised voice came across the line. "Are you still down in Crimea?"

"No, already driving back."

"Back where?" she asked timidly.

"Well." He hesitated. "I put my friend's daughter on the train . . . and now I'm heading home."

"Will you visit us?"

"Ah, you know, listen – the Baptists are bringing coal for the winter, and they'll only give it to people who are there . . ."

"And what about later? I mean, after they bring it?"

"I don't know. Probably. I'll call."

Sergeyich sat down wearily. He propped himself up on his palms and felt the earth's warmth inviting him to sleep.

He sat there for about five minutes, resting, calming himself with the help of the evening's peaceful silence.

Then the mobile rang in his pocket.

Sergeyich was irritated, having decided that it was Galya calling. She must have felt that he was somewhere nearby, and would now try to persuade him to come and see her. Reluctantly, he took out the mobile, looked at the screen, and was stunned: it was Petro! He brought the device to his ear, and instead of "Hi!" or "Hello!" what flew from his mouth, with undisguised joy, was, "Alive! You're alive, brother!"

"Yes, I'm alive," the soldier confirmed. His voice, too, was unable to hide his joy. "I'm back home now. After the hospital. Limping around."

"Well, thank God you're limping – that means you're alive."

"How are you?" Petro said.

"Not bad, not bad – going home too," Sergeyich said, then turned to look at his Lada. Either its miserable appearance or the mention of home shifted his mental gears. It seemed to him that the car was radiating cold. "Tell me," he began again. "That guy who was killed, out on the field . . . Is he still there?"

"No, they took him away. Before the other side bombed us to bits. The guys from Cargo 200 got him, took him back to his family.[26] A volunteer from Dnipro, turns out."

"That's good." The beekeeper sighed. "Good that they got him. Listen, when you have time, come and pay me a visit."

"Are you kidding?" the young man laughed. "The war's still on!"

"Right, no, I mean when the war's over," Sergeyich amended his thought.

"When the war's over, for sure," Petro promised.

# 73

The Lada's headlights snatched the start of the dirt road out of the darkness and Sergeyich, braking, twisted the steering wheel to the right. He drove some two or three hundred metres, then stopped, stepped out and checked the trailer hitch. After making sure that everything was in order, he got back behind the wheel and the car set sail across the endless field, swaying over the road's rough spots. The headlights pierced the darkness, and their beams also touched the land on either side, but Sergeyich couldn't make out what was growing there – couldn't and didn't want to. His eyes, tired of the wind, were watering.

Finally he pulled over, got out, and unfurled his bedspread, laying his sleeping bag on top. It occurred to him that this night would be cooler than the last. He was going east, after all – northeast.

As soon as he lay down, his mind grew anxious. The car couldn't be locked, and there was a grenade in the glove compartment. Anyone might get in there at night – both into the car and into the glove compartment . . . They'd find the grenade, pick it up, and then he, the owner of the car, would hear the noise, wake up and rush over – only to find a thief with a grenade in his hands! And what would the thief do? Obviously lob the grenade right at Sergeyich! It couldn't be easier: just pull the pin, throw it and dive to the ground, just like in all the old war films.

Sergeyich rose up, went to the car, retrieved the grenade and returned to his sleeping bag. He slipped the thing under the edge of the bedspread, and only then lay back down. He lay on his stomach, and his right hand reached out towards the grenade of its own volition. That's how Sergeyich drifted off, with his right palm resting on top of the grenade. It was as if the object gave him comfort, assuring him a good dream.

Yet it turned out to be a strange dream all the same. Sergeyich found himself gathering mushrooms in the woods, which meant the action was taking place in autumn. He had two baskets, and there were already a lot of birch boletuses and porcini in each of them – so many, in fact, that he'd already stopped picking up slippery jacks and even took pleasure in crushing russulas underfoot. When both baskets were full and heavy, he turned for home – turned, that is, to where he had come from – and, at the same time, began to wonder what woods these were, exactly . . . After all, there were no woods near his village. But wherever there was a forwards there was always a back, and so he went back, and even began to recognise places he passed through. This meant that his legs were sure to lead him to the spot where he had entered the woods. He trusted his legs, especially since they walked with such confidence, never once asking his head for directions. Nor was he troubled by any doubts. On the contrary, he was seized with curiosity, wanting to reach the edge of the woods as quickly as possible in order to understand how one could forget the passage from a space of light into a space of darkness . . . It was always brighter, after all, where the woods ended – even at night, if the moon and stars weren't hidden by clouds.

And so he hurried on, anticipating that passage from one space to another, listening to the twigs and cones crackling beneath his feet. He walked so quickly that this crackling merged into an almost continuous music – a sad, tense music. And at some point it seemed to him that this music grew louder, much louder. He stopped, thinking that it, too, would break off; he was playing it with his feet, after all. But no, it continued, reaching him from behind, out of the depths of the woods.

Sergeyich's hands began to ache. He remembered that he was holding baskets full of mushrooms and lowered them to the ground, while the crackling of twigs, the noise of the wind and the rustling kept growing louder. Turning around, he saw movement in the wooded darkness, as if the tree trunks were stepping back and forth. And then a sound very familiar and dear to him was added to the music. He listened closely: it was the buzzing of bees. Only this buzzing wasn't clear, subtle and gentle – no, it was a dense, heavy droning.

He was frightened, but he stood still a few moments longer, until he saw a strange figure emerge from the deep, invisible darkness into the near, half-visible kind. This human-sized figure did not belong to a human being. The creature's torso was long, reaching almost to the ground, only down there, beneath it, short little legs were carrying it forwards with mincing steps.

Scared out of his wits, Sergeyich took off, leaving his baskets on the ground, and ran as quickly as possible towards the way out of the woods that his legs remembered.

He woke up in the middle of the night, his forehead wet with sweat. He rolled onto his back but couldn't fall asleep again. So he rolled onto his stomach once more, and his right hand reached out, covering the grenade with his palm.

# 74

The sun was already hanging rather high on the eastern horizon. As he climbed out of the sleeping bag, Sergeyich crushed a tomato with his palm. He looked round and saw tomatoes to the right and to the left of him, but the field looked neglected. The harvest must have been poor, and so was the fruit itself. Apparently, the farmer had said "to hell with it" – gathered the few good ones and left the rest to rot.

Sergeyich rolled up the sleeping bag and stowed it away in the Lada's boot. Then he picked up the bedspread, intending to fold it, and saw crushed tomatoes underneath – as well as the green grenade. He shook out the bedspread, ridding it of leaves and clumps of earth, and put it in the boot. Then he came back and stared at the grenade. He felt he couldn't tear his eyes away from it.

"No," he whispered, forcing himself to look up.

He turned towards the hives on the trailer and reflected with pity on the fate of the locked-up bees. He needed to get them home as quickly as possible, so that they might stretch their wings before the cold came.

Then his eyes returned to the grenade.

No way I'm taking you with me, Sergeyich thought. It's a wonder you didn't land me in hot water earlier . . . How many checkpoints have I taken you through? And Russian and Ukrainian customs too. What if they had found you? I'd be locked up for life . . .

He gave a heavy sigh.

He realised he couldn't take it with him, but he couldn't leave it behind either. What if someone should find it? Some kids, God forbid? Such a sin would be too great a burden . . .

The beekeeper shook his head in dismay.

Maybe he ought to bury it? No, a tractor might dig it up and blow itself to smithereens.

And just then, from somewhere far away, came the roar of just such a machine. Sergeyich raised his head and peered at the horizon. It seemed to him that he saw the moving dot of either a tractor or a combine harvester.

He turned towards the hives again, but this time his gaze stopped on the one that was home to the bees that looked grey to him. This was the hive that had come to him in his nightmare, the hive from which enormous, hunched-over warrior bees had emerged. They had crawled out as if from the turret of a tank or from an underground tunnel, and then sneaked off on their military mission.

Sergeyich recalled his latest dream, too, in which strange figures had loomed out of the dark woods.

That was them too, the beekeeper realised. No, these dreams were no accident . . . It's through our dreams that God tells us what to do.

Sergeyich climbed onto the trailer, loosened the strap that held the officially inspected hive and its neighbour to the bed, and pulled the grey bees in his direction. He was surprised by how easily the hive budged, as if his arms had regained their former strength.

"Look at that," Sergeyich said with a grin, taking a step back like a weightlifter before a big lift.

He approached the hive once more, only now with greater determination, wrapped his arms around it, and took it off the trailer.

Taking short breaks, he carried it about a hundred metres from the

Lada. Then he lifted its roof and peeked inside. There were a few bees on top of the combs, and, sure enough, they looked grey to him.

Maybe they infected them on purpose, so that I'd introduce the disease to Ukraine? the beekeeper wondered. He had heard about biological weapons. And he himself had done battle with the Colorado potato beetle, which the Americans had sent to undermine the Soviet Union.

He examined the inner walls of the hive, running his fingers over their smooth planks.

And maybe they installed some equipment? To spy on me and on our war?

Fear flashed in Sergeyich's eyes and his heart began to beat faster. He recalled a programme on Russian television, about the smallest possible gadgets, which you couldn't even see. They had some funny name for this stuff – was it "nano"? "Nanatechnology"? Leaving the roof off, the beekeeper backed away towards the car. He picked up the grenade, which still felt warm, as if it were alive. Hefting the weapon in his palm, he accustomed himself to its weight. Then he went back to the hive, stopping about twenty metres away from it, pulled the pin, tossed the grenade and immediately threw himself to the ground, just as they did in the movies.

And so he didn't even see how close to the grey bees the thing exploded.

The force of the explosion made him press his face into the dry, black earth. Both a whistle and a buzzing sounded above him. Something wet landed on the back of his head. Sergeyich didn't move an eyelash. He breathed as though through an earthen filter, never taking his mouth off the ground, sensing its crumbs scratch his lips. It was getting harder and harder to breathe; the earth wouldn't let him. And when the thunder died away in his ears, it was replaced by silence – a ringing silence. His head rang as if it had been hit with something heavy, like a bell or a frying pan.

He rose to his feet, and the earth swayed beneath him.

Where the third hive had stood, nothing remained. Only a crater. Chips of wood lay at his feet, a fragment of a comb. A bee flew past.

They've survived, Sergeyich thought. Not all of them, but some . . .

He began to walk, carefully carrying the ringing in his head towards the trailer.

Once again, he heard buzzing, looked round, and saw a bee flying from the direction of the explosion. It reached the trailer and landed by the entrance of the hive he had repaired on the road.

Sergeyich examined the bee closely. Was it grey? No . . . Or maybe it was . . . It was trying to poke its way into the hole, but the hole was closed; he'd shut it for the duration of the journey.

The beekeeper climbed onto the trailer, removed the strap from the second row of hives, lifted the roof, reached inside, and opened the entrance.

"Alright, get in," he said to the bee.

It seemed to hear him and crawled eagerly into the hive.

Sergeyich didn't even have time to blink before he saw the bee tumble back out of the entrance, followed by three or four others. These other bees began to push the newcomer away, and eventually shoved it off the landing.

So that's how it is. Sergeyich sighed, bending over the bee. He lifted it off the ground, planted it on his palm and closed his fist, as if making a little hive for it.

Then he looked back at the entrance.

"Why are you acting like people?" he asked the bees bitterly. But they had already returned to the hive, and so didn't catch his words.

He looked down at his loosely closed fist again.

What do I do with you now? You can't fly anywhere – you're alone.

His fist began to clench. Soon he felt the bee trembling with a sense of danger. And then it stung him.

He twisted his lips, unclenched his fist, and looked at the bee, which had left its stinger in the skin of his palm but had failed to pierce it properly. He scraped off the stinger with a fingernail and threw it away. Then he turned his palm and the bee fell down onto the grass.

"That's the end of that," he whispered.

After returning to the Lada, he spotted a fragment of the grenade on his seat. He picked it up and threw it away.

It's a good thing the windows are gone, he thought. They would have shattered for sure.

An hour later his mobile rang. Sergeyich slowed down, although he hadn't been driving very fast to begin with.

"Listen," Pashka's voice said. "You on your way back already?"

"Yeah, just passed Tokmak."

"Could you buy me some smokes – Primas, about thirty packs? They've run out in Karuselino. You won't forget?"

"Why should I forget?" Sergeyich asked calmly. "I'll get them."

"But make sure to hide 'em, OK? They might grab 'em at one of the checkpoints."

"I'll hide them," Sergeyich promised.

"But hide 'em good, OK? They're checking everyone's boots these days."

"I won't hide them in my boot," the beekeeper replied calmly. "I'll hide them where no-one ever looks."

"Where's that! Sometimes they even check petrol tanks . . ."

"I'll hide them with the bees," Sergeyich explained. "They won't stick their hands into my hives."

"Yeah, you're right about that," Pashka agreed, and his voice seemed almost happy. "OK, then – keep driving. I'll be waiting."

Well, at least someone's waiting for me, Sergeyich thought, pressing the accelerator.

# NOTES

1. Born into serfdom, Taras Shevchenko (1814–61), Ukraine's national poet, first won recognition as a painter and was able to secure his freedom with the help of his patrons. In 1847 he was arrested by the tsarist regime for his Ukrainian writings, and eventually sent into internal exile in Kazakhstan. Shevchenko was amnestied in 1857, and in 1859 he returned to St Petersburg, where he died two years later, the day after his forty-seventh birthday. Ivan Michurin (1855–1935) was a Russian horticulturalist who cultivated some three hundred varieties of fruit plants. The Bolshevik regime took great pride in his experiments, but later mischaracterised his legacy when Soviet science turned against genetics.

2. Viktor Yanukovych (born 1950), who served as the fourth president of Ukraine (2010–14) before being removed from power in the wake of the Euromaidan Revolution, had been the governor of his native Donetsk region from 1997 to 2002. Currently in self-imposed exile in Russia, he was convicted in *absentia* of high treason by a Ukrainian court.

3. Stepan Bandera (1909–59) was the leader of a militant Second World War-era Ukrainian nationalist organisation (O.U.N.-B.). He remains a controversial figure; many embrace him as a hero for his struggle against Soviet Russia, while others characterise him as a fascist and anti-Semite, pointing to atrocities perpetrated by members of the O.U.N.-B. particularly against Poles and Jews.

4. The Verkhovna Rada (Supreme Council) is Ukraine's unicameral parliament, which seats 450 People's Deputies. Olena

317

Bondarenko (born 1974) is a former People's Deputy (2006–14), who represented the pro-Russian Party of Regions. In 2014, during the Euromaidan Revolution, she was confronted by a group of journalists about the plight of their colleagues, several of whom had been beaten and killed; she responded by saying that journalists working in a war zone should know that they are taking a risk. The scene depicted in the novel is fictional, but several politicians in Russia and Ukraine were splashed with brilliant green dye (a common topical antiseptic) in the late 2010s.

5.    Defender of the Fatherland Day is celebrated in Russia and several other former Soviet republics, but not in Ukraine. The holiday, which was formerly known as Red Army Day and Soviet Army and Navy Day, dates back to the Russian Civil War; it was given its current name by Vladimir Putin, in 2002.

6.    Right Sector was founded in 2013 as an ultranationalist paramilitary coalition, and participated in many clashes with riot police during the Euromaidan Revolution. Russian state media have given the group an inordinate amount of coverage, labelling its members as fascists and neo-Nazis and accusing them of anti-Semitism and hate crimes. Right Sector became a political party in 2014; it currently boasts a membership of roughly 10,000 and holds no seats in the Verkhovna Rada.

7.    Iona Yakir (1896–1937) was a highly respected Red Army commander whose innovative military reforms received recognition both in the Soviet Union and abroad. Along with many other military leaders, Yakir fell victim to Stalin's paranoia; he was arrested, tortured and executed in 1937, at the height of the Great Purge.

8.    Nikolai Ostrovsky (1904–36) was a Ukrainian-born Soviet author whose novel *How the Steel Was Tempered* (also translated as *The Making of a Hero*, 1932–4) is one of the foundational texts of Socialist Realism.

9.    The Ukrainian government officially refers to the regions of Donetsk and Luhansk that lie outside its control as "The

Separate Regions of Donetsk and Luhansk", or by the Ukrainian abbreviation O.R.D.L.O.

10. Ukrainian officials characterised their military's actions in Eastern Ukraine as a counterterrorist operation.

11. The term "Banderite" – which is derived from the name of Stepan Bandera (see note 3 in Chapter 8) – has been applied by Russian propagandists to all modern-day supporters of Ukrainian independence. The cynical use of Bandera's name by Russian propagandists has led even some of his critics to embrace his legacy, if only ironically; for instance, Ukrainian Jews who support national independence have taken to calling themselves "Judeo Banderites".

12. *Samsa* is a savoury pastry, usually stuffed with meat, which is a staple of Central Asian and Tatar cuisines. *Hamsa* is the Russian and Ukrainian name for the European anchovy in the areas surrounding the Black Sea.

13. "Mother, who is it?" – "A friend of father's from Donbas." (Crimean Tatar).

14. In May 1944, hundreds of thousands of Crimean Tatars were forcibly deported to Uzbekistan by the Soviet state security service, the N.K.V.D., on Stalin's orders. Most of the deportees were women, children and the elderly. Some 8,000 died on the way, and thousands of others perished in exile.

15. Starting in 1922, all Soviet children between the ages of ten and fifteen were inducted into the Vladimir Lenin All-Union Pioneer Organisation, which was modelled on Scouting groups in the West. The centrepiece of the Young Pioneer uniform was the now iconic "red scarf" – a triangular neckerchief – and among the group's symbols was a bugle. The Young Pioneers were disbanded after the Soviet Union's collapse in 1991.

16. *Yantıq*, a traditional Crimean Tatar dish, is a stuffed pie-like pastry; *imam bayıldı*, a traditional Ottoman dish, consists of a whole aubergine stuffed with onion, garlic, tomato and parsley, and simmered in oil.

17. *Äyrän* is sour milk diluted with cold water.
18. Ivan Franko (1856–1916) was one of the most important cultural figures in Ukrainian history. As a poet, novelist, translator, critic, ethnographer, economist and activist, he was instrumental in the development of modern Ukrainian literature and political thought.
19. So-called "Crimean Self-Defence" units were formed after Russia first intervened in Crimea in 2014. These volunteer militias sought to secure Russia's interests on the peninsula.
20. Formed in 1992, the Berkut was a special Ukrainian police agency partly subordinate to the primary Ukrainian police force within the Ministry of Internal Affairs. In 2014, during the annexation of Crimea, Berkut units stationed on the peninsula defected to the Russian Ministry of Internal Affairs. Having kept their name, these units now function as the gendarmerie of Russian Crimea.
21. "Allah is almighty. My condolences." – "Thank you, my friend." (Crimean Tatar).
22. "May God rest his soul." (Crimean Tatar).
23. In the Eastern Orthodox tradition, the period of mourning lasts for forty days, with memorial services held on the third, ninth and fortieth days after death.
24. In the Russian Federation, one may not drive a vehicle registered to someone else – even if that someone is a close relative – without the owner's signed official permission.
25. "Dogs" (Crimean Tatar); pejorative slang for Russian police or secret service agents.
26. "Cargo 200" is a code word from the Soviet era, still in use today, for the transportation of military casualties.

Born near Leningrad in 1961, ANDREY KURKOV was a journalist, prison warder, cameraman and screenplay writer before he became well known as a novelist. He received "hundreds of rejections" and was a pioneer of self-publishing, selling more than 75,000 copies of his books in a single year. His novel *Death and the Penguin*, his first in English translation, became an international bestseller, translated into more than thirty languages. As well as writing fiction for adults and children, he has become known as a commentator and journalist on Ukraine for the international media. His work of reportage, *Ukraine Diaries: Dispatches from Kiev*, was published in 2014, followed by the novel *The Bickford Fuse* (MacLehose Press, 2016). He lives in Kiev with his British wife and their three children.

BORIS DRALYUK is an award-winning translator and the Executive Editor of the *Los Angeles Review of Books*. He taught Russian literature for a number of years at UCLA and at the University of St Andrews. He is a co-editor (with Robert Chandler and Irina Mashinski) of the *Penguin Book of Russian Poetry*, and has translated Isaac Babel's *Red Cavalry* and *Odessa Stories*, as well as Kurkov's *The Bickford Fuse*. In 2020 he received the inaugural Kukula Award for Excellence in Nonfiction Book Reviewing from the *Washington Monthly*.

Thank you all
for your support.
We do this for you,
and could not do
it without you.

 DEEP
VELLUM

# PARTNERS

# pixel ||| texel

EMBREY FAMILY
FOUNDATION

## ADDITIONAL DONORS, CONT'D

Mark Haber

Mary Cline

Maynard Thomson

Michael Reklis

Mike Soto

Mokhtar Ramadan

Nikki & Dennis Gibson

Patrick Kukucka

Patrick Kutcher

Rev. Elizabeth & Neil Moseley

Richard Meyer

Scott & Katy Nimmons

Sherry Perry

Sydneyann Binion

Stephen Harding

Stephen Williamson

Susan Carp

Susan Ernst

Theater Jones

Tim Perttula

Tony Thomson

## SUBSCRIBERS

Ned Russin

Michael Binkley

Michael Schneiderman

Aviya Kushner

Kenneth McClain

Eugenie Cha

Stephen Fuller

Joseph Rebella

Brian Matthew Kim

Anthony Brown

Michael Lighty

Erin Kubatzky

Shelby Vincent

Margaret Terwey

Ben Fountain

Caroline West

Ryan Todd

Gina Rios

Caitlin Jans

Ian Robinson

Elena Rush

Courtney Sheedy

Elif Ağanoğlu

Laura Gee

Valerie Boyd

Brian Bell

# AVAILABLE NOW FROM DEEP VELLUM

SHANE ANDERSON · *After the Oracle* · USA

MICHÈLE AUDIN · *One Hundred Twenty-One Days* · translated by Christiana Hills · FRANCE

BAE SUAH · *Recitation* · translated by Deborah Smith · SOUTH KOREA

MARIO BELLATIN · *Mrs. Murakami's Garden* · translated by Heather Cleary · *Beauty Salon* · translated by Shook · MEXICO

EDUARDO BERTI · *The Imagined Land* · translated by Charlotte Coombe · ARGENTINA

CARMEN BOULLOSA · *Texas: The Great Theft* · *Before* · *Heavens on Earth* · translated by Samantha Schnee · Peter Bush · Shelby Vincent · MEXICO

MAGDA CARNECI · *FEM* · translated by Sean Cotter · ROMANIA

LEILA S. CHUDORI · *Home* · translated by John H. McGlynn · INDONESIA

MATHILDE CLARK · *Lone Star* · translated by Martin Aitken · DENMARK

SARAH CLEAVE, ed. · *Banthology: Stories from Banned Nations* · IRAN, IRAQ, LIBYA, SOMALIA, SUDAN, SYRIA & YEMEN

LOGEN CURE · *Welcome to Midland: Poems* · USA

ANANDA DEVI · *Eve Out of Her Ruins* · translated by Jeffrey Zuckerman · MAURITIUS

PETER DIMOCK · *Daybook from Sheep Meadow* · USA

CLAUDIA ULLOA DONOSO · *Little Bird*, translated by Lily Meyer · PERU/NORWAY

RADNA FABIAS · *Habitus* · translated by David Colmer · CURAÇAO/NETHERLANDS

ROSS FARRAR · *Ross Sings Cheree & the Animated Dark: Poems* · USA

ALISA GANIEVA · *Bride and Groom* · *The Mountain and the Wall* · translated by Carol Apollonio · RUSSIA

FERNANDA GARCIA LAU · *Out of the Cage* · translated by Will Vanderhyden · ARGENTINA

ANNE GARRÉTA · *Sphinx* · *Not One Day* · *In/concrete* · translated by Emma Ramadan · FRANCE

JÓN GNARR · *The Indian* · *The Pirate* · *The Outlaw* · translated by Lytton Smith · ICELAND

GOETHE · *The Golden Goblet: Selected Poems* · *Faust, Part One* · translated by Zsuzsanna Ozsváth and Frederick Turner · GERMANY

SARA GOUDARZI · *The Almond in the Apricot* · USA

NOEMI JAFFE · *What are the Blind Men Dreaming?* · translated by Julia Sanches & Ellen Elias-Bursac · BRAZIL

CLAUDIA SALAZAR JIMÉNEZ · *Blood of the Dawn* · translated by Elizabeth Bryer · PERU

PERGENTINO JOSÉ · *Red Ants* · MEXICO

TAISIA KITAISKAIA · *The Nightgown & Other Poems* · USA

SONG LIN · *The Gleaner Song: Selected Poems* · translated by Dong Li · CHINA

JUNG YOUNG MOON · *Seven Samurai Swept Away in a River* · *Vaseline Buddha* · translated by Yewon Jung · SOUTH KOREA

KIM YIDEUM · *Blood Sisters* · translated by Ji yoon Lee · SOUTH KOREA

JOSEFINE KLOUGART · *Of Darkness* · translated by Martin Aitken · DENMARK

YANICK LAHENS · *Moonbath* · translated by Emily Gogolak · HAITI

FOUAD LAROUI · *The Curious Case of Dassoukine's Trousers* · translated by Emma Ramadan · MOROCCO

# FORTHCOMING FROM DEEP VELLUM

MARIO BELLATIN • *Etchapare* • translated by Shook • MEXICO

CAYLIN CARPA-THOMAS • *Iguana Iguana* • USA

MIRCEA CĂRTĂRESCU • *Solenoid* • translated by Sean Cotter • ROMANIA

TIM COURSEY • *Driving Lessons* • USA

ANANDA DEVI • *When the Night Agrees to Speak to Me* • translated by Kazim Ali •
MAURITIUS

DHUMKETU • *The Shehnai Virtuoso* • translated by Jenny Bhatt • INDIA

LEYLÂ ERBIL • *A Strange Woman* •
translated by Nermin Menemencioğlu & Amy Marie Spangler • TURKEY

ALLA GORBUNOVA • *It's the End of the World, My Love* •
translated by Elina Alter • RUSSIA

NIVEN GOVINDEN • *Diary of a Film* • GREAT BRITAIN

GYULA JENEI • *Always Different* • translated by Diana Senechal · HUNGARY

DIA JUBAILI • *No Windmills in Basra* • translated by Chip Rosetti • IRAQ

ELENI KEFALA • *Time Stitches* • translated by Peter Constantine • CYPRUS

UZMA ASLAM KHAN • *The Miraculous True History of Nomi Ali* • PAKISTAN

ANDREY KURKOV • *Grey Bees* • translated by Boris Dralyuk • UKRAINE

JORGE ENRIQUE LAGE • *Freeway La Movie* • translated by Lourdes Molina • CUBA

TEDI LÓPEZ MILLS • *The Book of Explanations* • translated by Robin Myers • MEXICO

ANTONIO MORESCO • *Clandestinity* • translated by Richard Dixon • ITALY

FISTON MWANZA MUJILA • *The Villain's Dance* • translated by Roland Glasser •
DEMOCRATIC REPUBLIC OF CONGO

N. PRABHAKARAN • *Diary of a Malayali Madman* •
translated by Jayasree Kalathil • INDIA

THOMAS ROSS • *Miss Abracadabra* • USA

IGNACIO RUIZ-PÉREZ • *Isles of Firm Ground* • translated by Mike Soto • MEXICO

LUDMILLA PETRUSHEVSKAYA • *Kidnapped: A Crime Story* •
translated by Marian Schwartz • RUSSIA

NOAH SIMBLIST, ed. • *Tania Bruguera: The Francis Effect* • CUBA

S. YARBERRY • *A Boy in the City* • USA